Warwickshire County Council

ATH 06/23			

DISCARDED

This item is to be returned or renewed before the latest date above. It may be borrowed for a further period if not in demand. **To renew your books:**

- **Phone the 24/7 Renewal Line 01926 499273 or**
- **Visit www.warwickshire.gov.uk/libraries**

Discover • Imagine• Learn • *with libraries*

 **Warwickshire County Council**

 *Working for Warwickshire*

Also by Delores Fossen

The Law in Lubbock County

Sheriff in the Saddle
Maverick Justice
Lawman to the Core
Spurred to Justice

Mercy Ridge Lawmen

Her Child to Protect
Safeguarding the Surrogate
Targeting the Deputy
Pursued by the Sheriff

Also by Debra Webb

A Winchester, Tennessee Thriller

In Self Defence
The Dark Woods
The Stranger Next Door
The Safest Lies
Witness Protection Widow
Before He Vanished
The Bone Room

Colby Agency: Sexi-ER

Finding the Edge
Sin and Bone
Body of Evidence

Discover more at millsandboon.co.uk

TARGETED IN SILVER CREEK

DELORES FOSSEN

DISAPPEARANCE IN DREAD HOLLOW

DEBRA WEBB

MILLS & BOON

First Published in Great Britain 2023
by Mills & Boon, an imprint of HarperCollins*Publishers* Ltd
1 London Bridge Street, London, SE1 9GF

www.harpercollins.co.uk

HarperCollins*Publishers*
Macken House, 39/40 Mayor Street Upper,
Dublin 1, D01 C9W8, Ireland

Targeted in Silver Creek © 2023 Delores Fossen
Disappearance in Dread Hollow © 2023 Debra Webb

ISBN: 978-0-263-30728-3

0623

This book is produced from independently certified FSC™ paper
to ensure responsible forest management.

For more information visit: www.harpercollins.co.uk/green

Printed and Bound in the UK using 100% Renewable Electricity at
CPI Group (UK) Ltd, Croydon, CR0 4YY

TARGETED IN SILVER CREEK

DELORES FOSSEN

Chapter One

Deputy Jesse Ryland slid his hand over the Smith & Wesson in his holster. Normally, that wasn't something he'd do when paying a visit to Hanna Kendrick, but there was nothing normal about this evening.

Not with a killer on the loose.

A killer who might at this very second be making his way to Hanna.

Jesse couldn't rein in the motherlode of flashbacks that the killer's escape from prison was giving him because he knew just how serious a situation this was. As serious as it got for both the job and his personal life.

He'd been a deputy for nearly eight years now in Hanna's and his hometown of Silver Creek, Texas. Eight years of the badge in a family of badges. Being a cop was in his blood, and in those eight years he'd honed some instincts. Ones that had saved his life. And sometimes they'd let him down.

But he couldn't allow his instincts to fail him now.

Jesse made his way up the steps of the porch that stretched across the entire front of the pale yellow one-story house. It was a familiar trek for him since he came here at least four times a week to see his six-month-old son, Evan. Those visits with his little boy were priceless, but Hanna hadn't exactly made him feel welcome here. She wouldn't now either, and it didn't take long for Jesse to get confirmation of just that.

Hanna had obviously seen or heard him pull up because she unlocked and opened the door before Jesse could even knock. Even though it was fairly early, she'd already called it a night since she was wearing comfy purple PJs and had her long blond hair loose on her shoulders instead of scooped back in her usual ponytail.

Jesse caught the scent of lemon tea. And Hanna. Nothing flowery or from a bottle. Just her.

As usual, there was wariness in her deep green eyes, and she automatically stepped back as if to make sure they didn't accidentally touch or breathe in the same air. Not because she hated him. At least, Jesse didn't think she did anyway. But it was more of her not trusting him. Or anybody else for that matter.

The thin scar on the left side of her forehead had plenty to do with that.

A scar that caused even more flashbacks and bad memories for Jesse than a killer's escape had. Because that scar was a reminder of just how close she'd come to dying. When she'd been nine months pregnant with their son, no less. Evan and she had survived, thank God, but Hanna had paid a heavy price.

They all had.

"Jesse," she murmured on a rise of breath.

He heard the wariness that was always there but, as usual, Jesse saw something else. The glimmer of the heat between them. The same heat that had brought about the one-night stand resulting in her getting pregnant with Evan.

Of course, Hanna immediately concealed that glimmer

by dodging his gaze. Again, that was the norm. She didn't want to feel heat for a man she didn't trust. A man she didn't even remember.

Hanna was holding her phone, and Jesse could see the app was still open for her security system. She would have had to disarm it before opening the door or it would have triggered the alarms, but he had no doubts that it had been armed when he'd arrived. There was no feeling of a safety net for her anymore, no carefree attitude. She structured her life around locks and security systems.

"Evan's already asleep," she added as that breath fell away. Hanna picked up the baby monitor from the foyer table where she'd likely set it when she had opened the door and showed him the image of the baby in his crib.

He nodded. Jesse knew his son's schedules and routines, and since it was going on eight thirty, Hanna would have already bathed Evan and put him down for the night.

"We need to talk," Jesse said.

She opened her mouth, closed it and then looked at him as if trying to suss out what this was all about. It definitely wasn't the norm for him to come to her place when he hadn't arranged a visit with Evan.

"If this is about my amnesia, it hasn't gone away," Hanna volunteered. She absently touched the scar, the evidence of the gunshot wound that had robbed her of the memories of the attack.

And of Jesse.

As far as Hanna was concerned, she didn't recall a thing about meeting him. Or having sex with him. Didn't remember even a second of the bond they'd built when she'd been pregnant. Of course, it wasn't a strong enough bond for Hanna to marry him. Or to fall in love with him. But there sure as heck hadn't been this distance and mistrust that was there now.

"Did something happen to my mom?" she asked with some fresh alarm straining the muscles in her face.

"No," he assured her. "As far as I know, your mother is fine. It's about Bull Freeman."

Hanna's eyes widened and, while dragging in a hard breath, she dropped back another step. She might not have any actual memories of Bullock "Bull" Freeman shooting her in what had been a botched attempt to evade arrest, but Hanna was well aware that the man was behind bars.

Or rather that's where he should be.

A place he should have stayed until his upcoming trial since Bull hadn't been let out on bail.

"They let him out of jail?" she murmured.

Jesse shook his head and glanced behind him and around the yard. "He escaped."

He gave her a couple of seconds to let that sink in. Of course, it would take a lot longer than that for her to deal with it, but this was a start. There were lots of steps that needed to happen now.

Because the sweltering summer sun had finally set, making it next to impossible for Jesse to see if Bull was anywhere near the house, he took hold of Hanna's arm. Keeping his touch light and brief, he eased her backward so he could step inside and shut the door. He locked it and then motioned toward her phone that she was now holding in a death grip.

"Use your app to turn the security system back on," Jesse instructed, knowing it was going to give her another mental jolt.

It did. Her fingers were trembling when she did as he'd said. But she didn't stop there.

"Evan," she breathed, and she turned and started running down the hall in the direction of the nursery. Her bare feet sounded out in quick, soft thuds on the hardwood floors.

Jesse followed her while he glanced around the living room, taking particular notice of the windows. As usual, they were all shut, and Hanna had all the blinds fully lowered. That was routine for her now, but before she'd been shot and had her life turned upside down, those blinds had usually been open. No doubt so she could see the amazing views on the five acres of her property.

The house and the land had been in Hanna's family for several generations. An old money kind of place that managed to look both important and welcoming at the same time. A hard thing to accomplish, which was probably why Hanna had chosen to live here after her late father had left her the property when she'd barely been twenty. This was her home in every sense of the word, which meant it was Evan's home as well.

The main area had an open floor plan, so it was easy for him to take in the living room, dining room and kitchen with only a couple of sweeping glances. After Jesse had finished checking to make sure all the windows in this part of the house were locked—they were—he went down the hall, tracing her steps, and he found Hanna standing over Evan's crib.

The room was dark except for a smattering of milky-colored stars on the ceiling from the machine pumping out the soothing sounds of a gentle rain. All very serene. The perfect place for a baby to sleep.

Jesse went closer, moving shoulder to shoulder with her while looking down at their son, and got the same slam of emotion he always did when he saw that precious little face. The love. The fierce need to make him happy and keep him safe.

Evan's hair was nearly identical in color to Jesse's own dark brown. So were his son's eyes, though Jesse couldn't see them now because Evan was sacked out. He certainly made a precious picture lying there.

When Jesse had been younger, he'd vowed he would never have children, but that had all changed with Evan. The love had been instant and solid. Of course, that love only reminded him of just how much was at stake right now. If Bull wanted to get back at him in the worst possible way, then going after Evan would be the way to do it.

And Jesse wasn't going to let that happen.

"When? How?" Hanna asked in a whisper.

There was no need for her to clarify her questions, and Jesse was ready with the answers. "Bull escaped this afternoon. I didn't get the call, though, until about twenty minutes ago."

That'd felt like a gut punch, and Jesse's first instincts had been to call Hanna to tell her to lock up. But since he'd known she would have already done that, he had decided this was news best delivered in person. Especially since he was going to do much more than just play messenger tonight.

"According to the prison official who called the sheriff's office," Jesse went on, keeping his voice at a whisper so he wouldn't wake up Evan, "Bull said he was having chest pains and was taken to the infirmary. He somehow knocked out the EMT on duty and escaped."

The details of that escape were definitely sketchy, but it wouldn't stay that way. Jesse would want to hear exactly what'd happened because he needed to know if Bull had

had any help getting out. The man had plenty of friends and even a sibling who might do his bidding to give him a second shot at getting revenge.

"Your family knows?" Hanna asked.

Jesse nodded again, and he tipped his head, motioning for her to follow him out of the nursery. Evan was asleep, but he didn't want the possibility of the baby picking up on anything he was saying. Of course, Evan was too young to understand the words or the danger. However, he might pick up on the vibes. Or Hanna's fear. Because Jesse knew that her fear was there and already skyrocketing.

"My family knows," Jesse assured her once they were out in the hall.

On the five-minute drive from the Silver Creek Sheriff's Office to Hanna's place on the edge of town, he'd called Boone Ryland, the man who'd adopted and raised him and his siblings after their widowed mother, Melissa, had married him when Jesse was ten. That adoption had given Jesse six more brothers and numerous cousins, many of whom carried a badge or were retired law enforcement. By now, Boone had no doubt informed the entire family, and they all had already started taking security measures.

Just as Jesse was about to do.

"Bull's never made a threat to come after you," Jesse reminded Hanna. "You were what he'd consider accidental collateral damage."

Bad collateral damage and a case of wrong place, wrong time.

Hanna had had the misfortune of coming to Jesse's house on the grounds of the Ryland family's Silver Creek Ranch to drop off photos of the latest ultrasound and some medical consent forms she had wanted him to sign. She'd been at the massive wrought-iron security gates that fronted the property at the exact moment Bull and his cohort, Arnie Ross, had arrived to confront Boone before they could be arrested.

To confront Jesse, too.

Boone had been the one to get the tip about Arnie and Bull being part of a dangerous gun-running militia. A tip that'd come from an old friend who was now a retired San Antonio cop. Boone had passed the info along to Jesse and the other lawmen in the Silver Creek Sheriff's Office, and that, in turn, had spurred a full-scale investigation.

Since there'd been a security camera mounted on the gate, Jesse had caught glimpses of how everything had gone to hell in a handbasket the night Bull and Arnie had come for that confrontation. The men had both exited Arnie's truck and had words with Hanna, who had arrived just seconds earlier. Exactly what words, Jesse didn't know since there'd been no audio on the camera and Hanna couldn't remember because of the brain trauma.

Whatever had been said had obviously caused Arnie to snap. Maybe because he'd been high. Maybe because he just had a very short fuse. Along with being a serious drug user and a member of that notorious militia group, Arnie had also been on the verge of being arrested, and he'd been the one to drag Hanna out of her car.

Something that Bull damn sure hadn't stopped.

Nor had Bull stopped Arnie from shooting out the camera. But that hadn't happened before Jesse had seen Hanna, and it was an image that was forever branded in his mind.

Jesse had witnessed the stark fear on Hanna's face while she'd tried to keep her hand protectively over her pregnant belly. Arnie had then started running with her. So had Bull.

They'd disappeared into a cluster of thick oaks about fifteen yards from the gate.

That's where Jesse had found them.

After the frantic race to get to Hanna. After he'd heard the two shots. After everything inside had pinnacled in a red haze of fury and sickening dread.

Jesse had found Hanna on the ground, shot and bleeding.

Arnie had been shot and bleeding, too, and he was no longer the one holding the gun. Bull was. Arnie had used his dying breath to say that Bull had shot both of them when Hanna had struggled to get away. The .38 jacketed bullet had hit her in the frontal lobe of her brain.

Immediate surgery had saved Evan's and Hanna's lives. But not her memories. There were times when Jesse thought that was more of a blessing than a curse.

Jesse expected her to blow off his reminder that Bull hadn't intentionally targeted her, to give in to the fear that had to be crawling its way through her right now. But she didn't. Standing across from him, Hanna released a long, slow sigh and leaned back against the wall, but she also seemed to be steadying herself. Her hands certainly weren't shaking any longer.

"But Bull has threatened you," she pointed out, putting some of that steel in her voice. "And your father."

Yeah, he had indeed. Bad blood sometimes turned ugly, and that's what had happened with Bull and Boone. Even before Boone had gotten the tip about Bull being in the militia, there had been a land dispute that had escalated into a lawsuit and more than a year of ill will.

Of course, Bull had denied being in the militia. The man had also claimed that shooting Hanna and Arnie had been purely an accident, that the gun had gone off when he'd tried to wrestle it from his buddy, Arnie, and that he'd never intended Hanna and the baby any real harm. The last part might have been true.

Back then anyway.

But with six months of prison under his belt, Bull might be willing to act on that bad blood by going after anyone and everyone in the Ryland clan. If so, that gave the man a hell of a lot of targets. Dozens, what with Boone's kids, grandkids, nieces and nephews. Friends, too, who might be on Bull's hit list. That meant anyone in Silver Creek could become another victim of Bull's so-called collateral damage.

"Have you had your security system on for the past couple of hours?" Jesse asked her just to verify.

"Yes, and I haven't gone outside." She paused. "It was a tough day because I couldn't stop thinking about tomorrow, when Bull's trial starts. Or rather, when he *was* due back in court."

Jesse certainly hadn't forgotten that, and he'd figured it would be hard on Hanna.

Bull had been put in jail, yes, but there was always the possibility that a jury would buy his insistence that it was an accidental shooting. Added to that, the trial meant going over all the details of what'd happened to her. Details she couldn't remember. Couldn't confirm. And that might sway a jury, too, in the wrong direction.

So, why had Bull escaped when there'd been the looming possibility that he could walk out of that courtroom as a free man? Well, free of the charges against Hanna and Arnie anyway. Eventually, he would have to stand trial for his participation in the militia.

"I looked out the window a couple of times but didn't see

anyone or anything," Hanna added a moment later. "You think he'll come here?"

No way could he try to lie to her or give her false hope. "I think that's a strong possibility," Jesse answered.

Hanna nodded, and she clamped her teeth over her trembling bottom lip. He would have added a whole lot more if his phone hadn't buzzed with an incoming call. When Jesse saw the name on the screen, he knew he had to answer it right away.

"It's Grayson," he relayed to Hanna.

Sheriff Grayson Ryland, who was Jesse's adopted brother and the oldest of the Ryland siblings. He was also the law in Silver Creek, for the next couple of months anyway until his well-earned retirement.

"Just making sure you're with Hanna and that everything's secured," Grayson said the moment Jesse answered.

"I am and it is," Jesse verified and, after giving it a couple seconds of thought, he put the call on speaker. It was possible Hanna would hear something in this conversation that would upset her even more than she already was, but Jesse didn't want to keep anything from her. "I'm with Hanna now, and she's listening. Has anyone reported seeing Bull?" He'd tacked the question on.

"Not yet, but they found the EMT's truck that Bull used to escape. It was abandoned on a side road about ten miles from the prison. An *isolated* side road," Grayson emphasized.

"Has anyone reported a stolen vehicle in the area?" Jesse immediately asked. Because a remote area meant Bull had needed some way to get out of there, and Jesse doubted the man planned to walk to whatever destination he had in mind, especially since he would have likely still been wearing an orange prison jumpsuit.

"No reported stolen vehicles," Grayson attested. "And Bull didn't have the EMT's phone."

Jesse cursed under his breath because it meant this escape had likely been set up so that Bull could flee the prison and meet up with someone at that specific location. Someone who'd aided and abetted the escape. Someone who at this very moment could be helping Bull get to Silver Creek to carry out whatever plan he had in mind.

"You need me to start the process to access Bull's visitors' log at the prison and question all of his cronies from the militia?" Jesse asked.

"All of that is already in the works. Most of the militia members went under and disappeared after his arrest, but I'm sure we can find a couple of them. I'll also pay a visit to his sister."

Good. Because even though Bull's sister, Marlene, didn't have a criminal record and hadn't showed any support for him after his arrest, it didn't mean Bull hadn't talked her into helping him. And even if she'd turn down any request for help, she might still know where he was.

"There are no indications that the EMT was involved in the escape," Grayson went on. "He has a clean record, and there are no suspicious funds in his bank account. Bull punched him, and when he hit the floor, it knocked him out. He's got a concussion."

Jesse heard the slight groan that Hanna tried to silence by pressing her fingers to her mouth. She'd seen Bull at the hearing where he'd pleaded not guilty to murder and attempted murder, and she knew the guy was plenty big and strong. His nickname definitely suited him.

"Dad and your mom are at my house," Grayson continued a moment later. "Everyone here is on alert."

Good. His folks could likely protect themselves, but it was better for them to be with family right now. Jesse intended to be on alert, as well, and it'd stay that way until Bull was back where he belonged.

"What's your status there?" Grayson asked.

"No sign of Bull, and Hanna's had her security system on all day. I'm about to work things out with her," Jesse assured him and added a "Keep me posted" before Grayson and he ended the call.

Slipping his phone back into his pocket, Jesse met Hanna's gaze head-on. "I either need to stay the night here with you or move Evan and you to my place on the ranch."

It wasn't an ordinary ranch either. The Rylands' sprawling Silver Creek Ranch had hundreds of acres, more than a dozen houses, and enough lawmen to staff an entire small-town police force.

But it was also the place where Hanna had been shot.

Even though Hanna didn't have memories of that, she'd unfortunately seen the photos of the aftermath. Partially as a result of the psychologist trying to help her regain her memories. Other times as a result of glimpses of them when she'd visited the sheriff's office to give statements or for pretrial briefings.

"I don't think I can be at the ranch," she muttered. "I haven't had a panic attack in weeks, but I think just being there might trigger one."

Yeah, he'd figured that. "Being here could trigger one, too."

She nodded so fast that he understood she'd already come to that particular conclusion. "I have to make sure Evan stays safe, and that means me being as mentally sharp as I can manage. It won't help him if I lose it and give in to the panic."

His own nod was equally fast. "If I stay here, I can have some of the ranch hands come over and patrol the grounds." Something he was certain was already going on at the ranch.

This was obviously a rock and a hard place for Hanna. She didn't want him to be this big of a part of her life. Maybe because he was a blank spot when it came to her memories, but he suspected it went deeper than that. After all, she knew from the police reports of her attack that he'd been there that fateful night.

And that he hadn't been able to stop Bull from shooting her.

There was a bottom line to this, and it was a bad one. She wouldn't have been in Bull's path that night at all if it hadn't been for him. Because he hadn't been able to stop Bull when he'd had the chance. Even though for Hanna it was something she couldn't remember, her mother no doubt reminded her of it often.

"All right," Hanna finally said, pushing herself away from the wall. "Call for the ranch hands to come over. You can stay in the guest room. If Bull isn't back in custody by morning, I'll come up with a long-range plan."

That tightened his jaw because she was no doubt talking about private security. Bodyguards, maybe extra monitoring equipment. And while he was on the same page with her about keeping Evan safe, Jesse intended to stay with his son until the danger had passed.

However, that was an argument he'd save for when it came up.

For now, he fired off the text to the head ranch hand,

asking for two armed men to keep watch. When he'd finished and gotten the "will do" response, he went looking
for Hanna.

He walked past her bedroom, where Jesse got a jolt of
memories. Ones not associated with being pissed off about
her *long range* plan. Nope, these particular memories were
sizzling hot and reminders that the one and only time he'd
ever had sex with Hanna, it'd been in that bedroom.

There were only two other rooms off this particular
hall. A bathroom and her guest room, which she was obviously doubling as an art studio. Hanna was in there, and
she sighed when she looked at the bed that she apparently
used for preparing her paintings for shipping. There were
five of them and another on the easel. A watercolor of the
Texas Hill Country, her specialty. And she was darn good
at it, too. Enough for her to earn a comfortable living even
though she no longer taught art classes.

"I've been using this room instead of the studio," Hanna
explained. "So I can be close to Evan when I'm painting.
The studio's small, and I didn't want to expose him to the
smells from the paint and the brush cleaners. Plus, there's
no security system out there."

That made sense. "Don't worry about moving the paintings," Jesse told her. "I won't be getting much sleep tonight.
If I get too tired, I'll just crash on the couch."

She made a sound of agreement, maybe because she figured she wouldn't be getting much sleep, either, and she took
a quilt and pillow from the closet. She handed them to him
and pulled out a second quilt.

"For me," she said. "I'll stay in the nursery with Evan."

No way would Jesse try to talk her out of that. It was
probably overkill but, at the moment, no precaution seemed

too much for them to take. In fact, he just might end up in the hall outside the nursery door. That way, they could both make sure Bull didn't get close to the baby.

Hanna opened her mouth again, maybe to voice the worries that he knew had to be eating away at her, but she must have changed her mind about that because she just shook her head.

"Let me know if you need anything," Hanna added, already turning toward the nursery.

Jesse watched her go in and was about to head to the living room when his phone buzzed again. It was a soft sound, but Hanna must have heard it because she hurried back to him.

"It's Grayson," he told her and, as he'd done before, Jesse put the call on speaker.

"Make sure everything's secure," Grayson immediately said. "Bull's just been sighted in Silver Creek."

Chapter Two

Breathe, Hanna reminded herself. She tried a trick that her doctor had recommended to help her with the panic attacks. She brought up the image of her son in her mind.

The image of Evan smiling and babbling.

As usual, it slowed her racing heart, but she knew she would no doubt need a lot more steeling up to listen to the rest of what Grayson had to say.

"Where was Bull spotted?" Jesse asked the sheriff while he walked to the front window to look out.

Hanna went with him, and she grabbed the baby monitor from the foyer table so she could keep an eye on Evan while she also looked to see if a killer was nearby. Yes, she would definitely need more steeling up.

"Out on Miller Road," Grayson answered. "Sheri Cartwright was driving home from work and said she saw Bull behind the wheel of a black truck. He was going in the opposite direction from her."

Hanna was familiar with the road since it was only about a mile from her house. Much too close. She was familiar with the name Sheri Cartwright, too, and was told that they'd been friends in high school.

"It's dark," Jesse pointed out. "You think Sheri could be mistaken about it being Bull?"

"No, I think she saw him. It hasn't hit the media yet about Bull's escape, so Sheri wasn't actually looking for the man. She said she passed him and when she caught a quick glimpse of his face, she did a sort of mental double take at seeing him out and about. She decided to call the sheriff's office."

Good thing that she had made that call because at least now they had a heads-up about Bull being so close. Of course, Hanna knew a heads-up wouldn't stop the man from trying to get onto her property and into the house.

So he could try to kill her.

But Bull had to know that Jesse would be there with her, that he would do whatever it took to protect Evan and her. Bull, though, might be in the "whatever it takes" mode as well. He could be willing to take all kinds of risks to get to Jesse and her.

"I don't suppose Sheri got a look at the license plate of the truck Bull was driving?" Jesse pressed.

"No, and she didn't have much of a description for the vehicle itself either. Older model, black or dark blue. That's it. We'll get out the word, ask if anyone's missing a truck like that or if one was recently sold in the area. We might get lucky."

Grayson didn't sound especially hopeful. Neither was Hanna. She'd done a lot of reading about Bull in the past couple of months and knew he was a smart man. He was not only former military, but he'd also run a successful real estate business before moving to Silver Creek three years earlier. If he'd arranged this escape, then he would likely have also arranged to trade out vehicles to throw the cops off his trail.

She had also done some reading about the militia group that Bull had been part of. The Brotherhood. According to the reports Hanna found, there had been at least a hundred members, and they'd been involved in all sorts of illegal activity including weapons, drugs and perhaps even human trafficking.

What was missing from those reports was why Bull had gotten involved with a group like that in the first place. He'd gone to school with Arnie Ross, the man who'd taken Hanna from her car, so maybe that was the link. Or maybe Bull had just gotten greedy and wanted a piece of the lucrative illegal deals being made. Added to that, his real estate business would have been a good place to launder any money from those ill-gotten gains.

"I sent two of the reserve deputies out to Miller Road," Grayson continued. "And I'll get out the word to make sure anyone who sees Bull reports it."

"It wasn't smart, though, for Bull to come to Silver Creek," she muttered.

Until she heard the words, Hanna hadn't even known she was going to say them, but it was the truth. He might not have lived in Silver Creek that long, but he would still be very recognizable since his name had been plastered all over the news.

"No, not smart," Jesse and Grayson agreed in unison.

"But this means he's taking unnecessary risks," Jesse continued a moment later. "And it'll make it easier for us to catch him."

True. But Hanna knew Bull might shoot someone else before the cops were able to stop him.

"Bull's sister lives close to Miller Road," Jesse pointed out.

"Yeah. I'm going over to check on her now," Grayson explained. "You'll be moving Hanna and Evan to the ranch?"

A muscle flickered in Jesse's jaw. "Not tonight."

Grayson's jaw had probably gone a little tight, too, and Hanna hoped she wasn't making a huge mistake by wanting to stay put. Still, if she was truly Bull's target, he would come after her no matter where she was. Ditto for Boone. And since he probably wanted Boone more than he did her, then that was even more reason to steer clear of the Ryland ranch.

That could also put her even closer to Jesse.

Of course, he was close now and would be staying the night. Hanna wanted that, for Evan's safety, but being around Jesse was never easy. Yes, the heat was there between them but, as her mother so often reminded her, Jesse and his family were the reason she'd been shot, the reason she had come so close to losing her precious baby before he'd even been born.

The logical part of her knew the Rylands hadn't intended for her to be shot, but it was hard for her to trust them. To trust anyone. Without the memories, there were just too many blank spots, which meant there were too many doubts. Plus, she'd proved that her instincts weren't that stellar since she had been told she was the one who'd decided to go to the ranch that night Bull had shot her.

"I'll let you know what I find out from Marlene," Grayson finally said before he ended the call.

Jesse slipped his phone back in his pocket and met her gaze for a couple of seconds before he turned his attention back to keeping watch out the window.

She didn't need memories to know what was going

through his head. He loved Evan. She had no doubts about that. And he wanted to keep their son safe. But he probably felt safety was better met at the ranch.

Where her life as she'd known it had ended.

For all intents and purposes, her life had begun six months ago, and her first memories had been waking up in the hospital. She had been in pain, *so much pain*, and terrified. She hadn't even known she'd had a child, one delivered by an emergency C-section, until several hours after she'd awakened.

Little by little, Jesse, her mother and the medical staff had filled her in, but other than Evan, it hadn't felt real. More like hearing a story about someone else's life. It was still like that.

Except for the heat between Jesse and her.

No way could she deny that they had once been attracted enough to one another to have sex. No. Because the attraction was still there. Of course, she figured most women would be attracted to Jesse.

He wasn't a Ryland by blood, but she'd seen others in that family and knew the men were undeniably hot. Jesse was no exception with his dark hair and sizzling brown eyes. This cowboy cop had it all. The toned and tanned body. The thick, rumpled hair that looked as if he'd just gotten out of bed. And the strong jaw, sporting just enough stubble to add even more character to that face.

As if it needed that.

Her first memory of Jesse was seeing him in the doorway of her hospital room shortly after she'd been moved out of recovery from her C-section. He'd been wearing jeans that day, too, and a blue shirt. It'd had blood on it.

Her blood, she later learned.

Hanna remembered the penetrating look in his eyes that had robbed her of her breath. She hadn't understood that intensity at the time. Hadn't known the guilt he'd no doubt been feeling. Hadn't known he was the father of a son she'd yet to see or hold. But even with her mind whirling and nothing making sense, she had understood that this man was somehow connected to her. And always would be.

She yanked herself out of her untimely trip down memory lane and snapped her eyes to the window when she heard the sound of an approaching engine. Her heart went into overdrive, causing the blood to rush to her head. She fought the instinct to run to the nursery and watched as the silver muscle truck pulled to a stop in front of her house. The logo on the side of the driver's door let her know these were the hands from the Silver Creek Ranch.

Two cowboys got out, both armed with rifles, and one greeted Jesse with a nod and then motioned toward the east side of her property, where he headed. The other one went to the west.

"They're good men," Jesse said, maybe because he'd glanced back at her and had seen the apprehension in her eyes.

The ranch hands were a necessary safeguard. She wanted them there. But they were still strangers to her, and that always brought on a fresh wave of alarm.

"Breathe," Jesse murmured to her.

Since he'd witnessed firsthand one of her panic attacks, he no doubt knew the signs and had recognized how things could quickly spin out of control for her. That's why she took his advice and tried to level her breathing while also going through one of her "anchoring" steps.

Hanna set down her phone and the baby monitor so she could apply pressure to the skin between her thumb and index finger on her left hand. She kept pressing, kept locking on to the image of a smiling Evan, until she had the anxiety better under control, until the sound of her throbbing heartbeat got quieter and slower in her ears.

Jesse continued to volley his attention between her and the front window, and he watched until she had steadied herself enough to pick up the monitor and her phone again.

"I'm okay," she assured him, which, of course, was a lie.

She was far from okay, but she couldn't let something like panic interfere with her helping Jesse. That meant she, too, needed to be keeping watch for Bull. That's why she went to the side window. It was only a few feet from where Jesse was standing, but it would give her a different view from his. A view that might allow her to spot Bull before he got into a position where he could do some more harm.

Her phone dinged with a call, the sound startling her, and she silently cursed when she saw her mother's name on the screen. Hanna knew she should have already contacted her mom and told her the same lie about being okay.

Drawing in another deep breath, Hanna answered while she continued to keep watch outside. Unlike Jesse, Hanna didn't put this call on speaker. No need for him to hear what was no doubt about to be said. Over the past six months, Hanna had learned just how much venom her mother had for Jesse and the rest of the Rylands.

"I had to learn about that horrible man's escape from one of the nurses who's got family in Silver Creek," her mother immediately greeted. "I'm coming over there right now to stay with Evan and you. I had my assistant bring me a car a couple of weeks ago, and I can be there in under an hour."

"No, please don't come." Hanna couldn't say that fast enough.

For one thing, her mother, Isabel, was recovering from a recent stroke and was still convalescing in an upscale nursing home in San Antonio. There was no way she should be behind the wheel of a car. Of course, her assistant shouldn't have brought her a vehicle, either, but that was a beef for Hanna to tackle some other time.

"But you shouldn't be alone," her mother protested.

"I'm not alone. Jesse's here and so are two armed ranch hands."

Hanna had already anticipated her mother's disapproving silence, so it didn't come as a surprise. Neither did the continued protest that immediately followed.

"I'll make some calls," Isabel insisted, going into the full "protective mom" mode. "I'll get some bodyguards out there ASAP. I can also call a friend in the Texas Rangers to take over the hunt for the man who nearly killed you."

"Please don't do any of that." Hanna kept her tone respectful, but it wasn't always easy to do that with her mom. Especially when Isabel rarely bothered to keep her own tone in check. "Jesse's staying the night, and Grayson already has someone out looking for Bull. It's possible the sheriff's office will soon have him back in custody."

"The Rylands." Isabel spat the name out like a profanity. "You shouldn't be putting your life and Evan's in their hands."

Again, this was no surprise because it was an opinion that Isabel often voiced. Hanna might have reservations about ever getting intimately involved with Jesse again, but she didn't doubt his commitment to Evan. Isabel probably didn't doubt it, either, not really, but since the woman had bad blood with the Rylands, she would likely never want to believe anything but the worst about any of them.

Hanna had only gotten Isabel's side of the story, but the bad blood had started when Hanna had been a toddler, and Grayson, who'd been a deputy at the time, had arrested Hanna's father for assaulting a young woman. Isabel had insisted the assault hadn't happened and had equally insisted that her husband hadn't been having an affair with the battered woman. Isabel had fought the charges even though they'd led to her husband's conviction and subsequent parole.

Since Hanna's father had died of a heart attack shortly thereafter, she wasn't sure she would ever know the full truth. She certainly didn't expect to ever get it from Isabel, but from everything she'd heard, her father had indeed been cheating, and he had a vicious temper that could have spurred the attack.

"Did you hear me?" Isabel snapped. "You can't trust the Rylands. You can't trust them with your life or Evan's."

"It'll be fine," Hanna said, knowing that wouldn't come close to soothing her mom. "I'll call you in the morning with an update." Hanna ended the call. No need to drag out what would only escalate into an argument.

Even though Hanna only had six months of memories when it came to her mother, she'd learned that Isabel could be stubborn and demanding. She wasn't in the mood to deal with that tonight. But she also didn't want the woman in harm's way, and that's exactly where she could be if she tried to drive to Silver Creek.

Hanna quickly texted her mother's doctor, Michael Warner, and told him about the possibility that Isabel might try to leave the facility. Dr. Warner would make sure that she stayed put. Hanna also asked him to check that everything was secure at the facility and gave him a brief explanation about Bull's escape from prison. The doctor would no doubt see to that, too, since it could put some of the other residents in danger if by some long shot Bull showed up there.

"Isabel didn't approve of me being here at your place," Jesse commented when Hanna finally set her phone aside. It wasn't a question.

"She didn't," Hanna verified. She sighed. "It's funny. Most people have given me plenty of space since I lost my memory. But not her. Part of me understands that, because I'm a mother, too. Still…" She trailed off, leaving it at that.

Best not to get into the frustrations. Or the fact that she wished Isabel would get on board with giving her that space.

"Your mother wants Evan and you safe," Jesse said, using that soothing drawl that was now so familiar. It spun through her like warm honey.

Hanna didn't doubt that about her mother's intentions, but Isabel could be overwhelming, and that was the main reason Hanna had resisted her mother's pressure to move into the family estate with her. The estate wasn't far, just on the other side of Silver Creek, but she didn't want to be under Isabel's thumb 24/7, especially since being there would make it next to impossible for Jesse to come and visit his son.

"It isn't always easy," Hanna murmured when she realized Jesse was giving her that look. Not the heated one that he sometimes wasn't able to shut down fast enough. This was essentially a raised eyebrow, without the actual gesture, that was asking her to explain her *still* comment about her mother.

He nodded in that same slow way as his drawl and rephrased. "I'd imagine it's rarely uncomplicated for you these days. I'm sorry about that." Jesse shook his head and said something under his breath she didn't catch. "Sorry you're having to go through this on top of everything else you've had to deal with."

She didn't have to remember him well to know it was guilt she was hearing in his voice. Hanna had heard it plenty of times before. Had seen it, too, and it was just as strong as her mother's insistence that the Rylands were to blame for what had happened to her.

Hanna shifted her attention to the baby monitor when she saw Evan squirm a little. He shouldn't be anywhere close to waking up yet, but there were still times when he didn't sleep through the night. She had her attention on the baby when Jesse's phone beeped again.

"It's Grayson," Jesse relayed.

That got her attention, and it only took a few seconds before Grayson's voice poured through the room. "Marlene's not at her house. There are signs of a struggle. And blood," he added.

Hanna's heart dropped to her knees. Oh, mercy. This had to be Bull's doing. The man had gone after someone else.

"There's an old black truck parked at the back of her house," Grayson went on. "It might be the one Bull was driving when Sheri saw him. Also, Marlene's car isn't in the garage."

So that probably meant Bull had taken his sister in her own vehicle. Had maybe even killed her. Or he could be planning on using her as a hostage if he got cornered by the cops.

"You need me to call and put out an APB on Marlene?" Jesse asked.

"No, I'll take care of it. I just wanted you to know in case you saw a silver Lexus near Hanna's place." Grayson rattled off the license plate of what was no doubt Marlene's vehicle. "Marlene also has a permit for a Beretta. It's my guess I won't find it here at her house."

Hanna was betting the same thing, which meant Bull was now armed. Perhaps had money, too, since Marlene would have almost certainly had some cash at her place.

"Keep watch and stay safe," Grayson said.

Even though the sheriff ended the call, Jesse stared at his phone still gripped in his hand. Shaking his head as if trying to clear his thoughts, he had just turned back to the window when he got another incoming call.

Hanna hadn't relaxed or let down her guard one bit, but she experienced another rush of adrenaline because she thought it was Grayson with yet more horrible news.

"It's Dispatch," Jesse muttered, putting the call on speakerphone.

She pulled in her breath. Held it. And waited.

She didn't have to wait long before she heard the familiar voice. Not Grayson or one of the other Silver Creek lawmen.

"It's me," the caller said.

Bull.

This time it was much more than an adrenaline crash. This was like an avalanche of emotions, yanking her right back to the pain of her injury. Right back to the nightmare she knew this man had put her through.

"Where are you?" Jesse growled, sounding exactly like the tough lawman that he was.

Bull obviously ignored the demand.

"We have to talk. There's a whole lot going on you don't know about, and it could get us all killed."

Chapter Three

Jesse heard every word that Bull had just said, but he didn't respond. Didn't believe him either.

Not for one second.

But the reason Jesse didn't reply was that he fired off a text to the dispatcher and asked for an immediate trace on the call just in case that hadn't already been set into motion. Bull was likely using a burner since he hadn't taken the EMTs phone, but if Bull was using a stolen phone, then a trace was still possible.

Jesse also continued to keep watch out the window because he wouldn't put it past Bull for this phone call to be some kind of ploy, a distraction so he could try to sneak up on them.

Jesse did a quick visual check on Hanna. Thankfully, she didn't look on the verge of a panic attack like the one he'd witnessed shortly after she'd gotten out of the hospital. She was clearly shaken by hearing from the man who'd come way too close to killing her, but she was holding it together. She was also looking out, no doubt scanning the grounds for Bull.

He moved to her, taking hold of her arm as he'd done earlier in the doorway, and Jesse eased her to the side of the window. Best not to give Bull an easy target in case he was close enough to the house to start shooting.

Stay back, Jesse mouthed to her, and the reminder of the possibility of her being shot had her attention flying back to the baby monitor.

Jesse had already considered the position of his son's crib. Away from the windows and tucked against a wall with the adjoining bath. There were no guarantees that a bullet couldn't make it through there, but there was no place in the house they could move the baby to ensure that didn't happen. However, if they or the ranch hands did spot Bull, Jesse would have Hanna take Evan into the bathtub. For now, though, he didn't want to wake his son unless it became necessary.

"Did you hear me?" Bull snarled. "I said this mess could get us all killed."

Jesse had no doubts about that, but he figured there was no "us" in this scenario. Bull would be the one doing the killing. He was puzzled, though, as to what the heck the man meant by "this mess." However questions about that would have to wait since there was something else at the top of the list of things Jesse needed to know.

"Where are you?" Jesse countered.

"Trying to get some place safe so I won't be gunned down. Just tell your cowboy cop friends that all isn't what it seems and not to shoot first without asking questions. The *right* questions," Bull emphasized.

"And what would the right questions be?" Jesse prodded, not only because he wanted to know where this was leading, but also because he wanted to give the dispatcher time to trace the call.

It was possible Bull was using a burner that couldn't be

traced, but he could also be using his sister's cell. If so, they might be able to ping a location. Unfortunately, from the background noise Jesse was picking up, it sounded as if the man was driving. That would make pinpointing his whereabouts a lot harder.

"Questions about what really went on that night Hanna was shot." Bull stopped, cursed. "None of this should have happened."

Yeah, Jesse could agree with that, too. "If you hadn't tried to evade arrest, no one would have been hurt or killed," Jesse pointed out. He didn't wait for Bull to react to that. Instead, Jesse went with some important questions. "Where's your sister? Is she still alive?"

"My sister?" Bull seemed genuinely surprised by the question. *Seemed.* "What about Marlene? Did something happen to her?"

"You tell me," Jesse responded, and he kept it at that.

"What the hell is wrong with my sister?" Bull demanded.

Jesse had plenty of bad feelings about this little chat, but he had to wonder if Bull had already killed Marlene and was trying to make it sound as if he'd had no part in that.

"Turn yourself in, and you'll find out what happened to Marlene," Jesse countered.

He figured that would cause Bull to keep up the innocent act, but the man cursed and Jesse heard the sound of brakes squealing. Not nearby, but from Bull's end of the phone connection.

What the heck was Bull doing? Was it possible he was changing directions so he could go to Marlene? If that was the case, Jesse sent another quick text to Grayson to alert him of that possibility.

"You need to ask yourself about what really took place

that night Hanna was shot." Bull threw it out there. "Then you'll find out the truth."

With that, the man ended the call, leaving Jesse with a whole lot of questions. That bad feeling he was already having went up a couple more notches.

"What did he mean?" Hanna immediately asked. "Are you keeping something from me about the shooting?"

"No." Jesse couldn't answer fast enough. "I haven't kept anything from you." It was important for her to hear that, to believe it, because he didn't need to have her distrusting him right now. Besides, it was the truth. "As for what Bull meant, I don't know. Could be he's just trying to muddy the waters."

If so, it had created some mud, all right, and Jesse had to at least consider the possibility that Bull hadn't had a part in Marlene's disappearance. Even though it would be one hell of a coincidence, there was a chance that what'd happened to the woman had had nothing to do with her brother. Marlene was a wealthy woman who lived alone; someone else could have broken in and kidnapped her. Still, Jesse's money was on Bull for this.

"'You need to ask yourself about what really took place that night Hanna was shot,'" she said, repeating Bull's words. "Are there any doubts or questions about what Bull did that night?"

Five minutes ago, Jesse would have said no, but he forced himself to go over it again. Not that it was ever too far from his thoughts. But it was possible to miss something when a case or investigation was personal. This one had been as personal as it could get.

"One of the ranch hands heard a commotion at the gate," he said, spelling it out for her. He hoped that by saying it aloud again, he'd notice any gray areas that might answer her concerns, and his, about what Bull had just told them. "It was already dark, but he used his phone app to look at the security camera. He saw the two vehicles—your car and Arnie's truck. There was no audio, but since the ranch hand thought there was some kind of argument going on, he called me and Noah."

No need for Jesse to explain that Noah was another cop and someone who'd been raised on the ranch. Or that the reason the hand had contacted both of them was that he'd known they were home and could make a quick response.

"When Noah and I approached the gate, Arnie had already pulled you out of your car," Jesse went on. "We think he did that to use you as a human shield so we couldn't arrest him."

"He knew for a fact you were going to arrest him?" Hanna asked.

This was yet something else Jesse had already answered, but he tried to see it with fresh eyes. "Bull and he both knew arrests were imminent. Grayson had them scheduled for questioning the following morning, and he'd advised them to bring their lawyers." Jesse paused. Because he had to do that. He needed a moment to try to rein in what guilt he could. "I should have expected they'd panic and would try to do something stupid."

"Is that because they'd done something stupid before?" she quickly challenged. "I mean, had they ever come to the ranch to confront Boone or you?"

"No," Jesse had to admit. But it was still something he should have anticipated. "Since Arnie and Bull knew they would be arrested, that obviously escalated their need to go through with the confrontation."

Hanna stayed quiet a moment. "But instead of confronting Boone and you, they tried to take me. Maybe because something I said provoked one of them?"

His gaze fired to hers. "There's nothing you could have said that should have provoked them to do what they did." Jesse wanted to make that crystal clear. She'd been the victim in this. Evan and her. He didn't want her shouldering any of the blame that should be her attackers'.

And his.

"Bull's been vague about what led up to the escalation," Jesse continued. "We do know from the security camera footage that Arnie first tried to get you into his truck, but he dropped his keys and apparently didn't see them on the ground. They didn't get in your car because Arnie's truck was behind it, blocking it. That's when Bull and Arnie seemed to have panicked and fled into the trees with you."

Jesse stopped, took in another much-needed deep breath. None of this was new to Hanna. She'd heard and read about it heaven knew how many times. But she also knew these next few minutes were blind spots for all of them.

Except Bull, that is.

"It's possible Bull just told us what he did to try to make up something to put himself in a better light," Jesse reminded her. *You need to ask yourself about what really took place that night Hanna was shot.* "He's desperate, and he probably wants us to believe he wasn't responsible for what happened to you."

He would have added to that, trying to soothe her while still spelling out the reality of the situation, but Jesse heard something that put him on full alert.

"I see somebody in the backyard," Miguel Navarro shouted. He was one of the ranch hands patrolling the grounds.

Jesse didn't waste a second. "Go to the nursery," he told Hanna. "Take Evan into the bathroom. Lock the door and get in the tub with him."

She didn't waste time arguing. Hanna started running toward the hall, but did look over her shoulder at Jesse. "Be careful," she uttered.

He would be, because he couldn't risk doing something stupid, like going outside to confront the wanted man. It could end up causing Hanna and Evan harm. If Bull shot him, that'd be one less barrier against Bull getting into the house.

Since Grayson already had his hands full, Jesse sent a text to the dispatcher and requested immediate backup. This could turn out to be nothing, but considering everything else going on, Jesse figured it was the real deal. Some kind of threat or attack from Bull.

He hurried to the kitchen, where he'd be able to see the backyard, and turned off the lights so he wouldn't be an easy target for Bull or anyone else who might wish to hurt them. Peering out into the darkness, he spotted Miguel, who'd taken cover on the side of a gardening shed. No sign of the other hand, Rex Corbin, but Jesse suspected he was moving in as well.

Jesse resisted the urge to text Miguel to find out exactly what he'd seen and where. The ranch hand didn't need that kind of a distraction and, like the light in the kitchen, it might allow Bull to pinpoint the man's location. Instead, Jesse tried to create his own distraction after he calculated that Hanna would have had time to get Evan into the tub. He also calculated the angle of any shots Bull might take. That particular bathroom wasn't anywhere near the kitchen.

"Bull?" Jesse called out, shouting loud enough so his

voice would carry into the backyard. "This is a good way to get yourself killed. Put down any weapons you have and surrender."

No response. Not that Jesse had expected to get one, but he kept watching, trying to pick through the night and see the man. He didn't see Bull, but he heard something else. A hissing sound, followed by a small pop. The kind of noise a firecracker would make.

"He's running away," Miguel yelled, moving out from the shed to take aim. He must not have had a clean shot because he didn't pull the trigger.

Jesse didn't have a shot, either, but that's because he didn't even get a glimpse of the intruder. However, he did get a glimpse of something else.

A fire.

Obviously ignited by some kind of accelerant, the flames shot up the side of Hanna's studio. Hell. The small building might be a good ten yards from the house, but it was still possible for the fire to spread. Or worse. Maybe Bull or whoever was responsible had already set fire to the house as well.

Jesse made a quick call to the dispatcher to send the fire department and alert backup to the danger before he contacted Miguel. He watched as the ranch hand moved back behind cover and took out his phone to answer.

"I've already made the 9-1-1 call," Jesse informed him. "Any sign of fire to the house?"

"None back here. Let me go to the side and I'll have Rex Corbin do the same on his side."

Jesse trusted both men, but he didn't want them hurt. "Don't leave cover if you think this SOB's armed. Could you tell if it was Bull and if he had a gun?"

"Couldn't tell on either count," Miguel answered.

Jesse sighed. "Then stay put and tell Rex to do the same. Everything is locked down inside, but if that fire starts to spread, let me know. I'll be with Hanna and the baby."

He ended the call and took one last look around the yard, hoping he'd spot Bull or someone else. But he saw nothing. So, Jesse headed to the nursery. Hanna was no doubt terrified for Evan, and he wanted to be close by in case the fire starter had decided not to run after all and instead tried to break into the house.

The nursery door wasn't locked but the one leading into the bathroom was, so Jesse tapped on it. "It's me," he said.

It only took her a couple of seconds to open the door. She wasn't holding Evan but instead had left the sleeping baby wrapped in his blankets in the tub. Good. That would keep him as safe as possible, and it was an added bonus that there were no windows in here. No way for Bull to get in without coming through the door, which Jesse would make sure didn't happen.

He stepped inside the small bathroom and motioned for her to get back in the tub. He would have launched into an explanation as to what was going on, but Hanna spoke first.

"I smell smoke," she whispered.

Jesse nodded. "Someone set fire to your studio."

He got the reaction that he'd expected. Her eyes widened. Her mouth dropped open. But then he saw something else. The anger.

"How dare he put my baby in danger again?"

Jesse was right there with her. Riled to the bone, he would make Bull pay—and pay hard for this.

"The fire department and backup are on the way," Jesse

told her. He could hear the wail of sirens in the distance. "And the ranch hands are still keeping watch."

She shook her head, as if trying to process everything and returned to the tub. "Why set a fire?"

Since Jesse had already had a couple of minutes to process things, he thought he might have an answer for that. "It could have been to draw me out."

So Bull could then gun him down. If that was the case, then this was about revenge, pure and simple. Maybe then Bull would have tried to get more revenge on Hanna by firing shots into the house.

But, if so, why hadn't Bull started with the shots?

Bull had no doubt seen the Silver Creek Ranch truck parked out front and would have guessed there were hands on the grounds or in the house. Why take the risk of coming to the studio instead of staying in the tree line and shooting? It was something he intended to ask Bull once he had him in custody.

Jesse's phone dinged and he relayed the text to Hanna. "Grayson will be here in a couple of minutes." He tipped his head to the front of the house. "From the sound of it, the fire engine just pulled up, so I want you to lock yourself back in here until I let you know it's safe."

She didn't argue with him. Not exactly. Hanna shook her head. "Bull might be waiting to shoot you."

Yeah, he might. Hell, he might try to do the same to Grayson even though the sheriff hadn't been the lead investigator on Bull's case. That's why Jesse would give Grayson a heads-up reminder even though he was certain he would be taking every precaution.

"Be careful," Hanna said as he went to the door. She got

out of the tub, no doubt to lock up behind him, but stopped when his phone buzzed again.

This time it was a call, not a text, and it wasn't from Grayson. Though it was a name he recognized: Ryan Shaw. He was the ATF agent Jesse had touched base with after Bull had been taken into custody; the ATF had wanted copies of any info that Jesse had gathered on the militia. Agent Shaw had likely heard about Bull's escape and wanted an update.

"We haven't found Bull yet," Jesse greeted the moment he answered. "But he's been sighted in Silver Creek."

"Yes," Agent Shaw said, and he followed that with a sigh. "Deputy Ryland, you and I need to talk."

Everything inside Jesse went still. It sounded similar to what Bull had said when he'd called. "I'm listening," Jesse assured him.

"I can't do this over the phone. I need to see you, to talk to you in person."

"Not a good time. Bull or one of his cronies just set fire to a building on Hanna Kendrick's property."

This time the ATF agent didn't sigh. He cursed. "I'm on my way out there. And FYI, whoever set that fire, it wasn't Bull."

"How the hell would you know that?" Jesse snapped.

"Because…" Shaw stopped, cursed again. "Deputy Ryland, Bull isn't behind what happened tonight. But there's trouble. Big trouble. Because somebody wants you dead."

Chapter Four

Hanna took one step into her kitchen. And she stopped cold. Not because of who and what she saw. She'd expected to see Jesse feeding Evan in his high chair. After all, Jesse had volunteered to do that while she'd grabbed a quick shower.

What she hadn't expected was the sudden jolt of memories.

At least, she was pretty sure that's what they were. Actual memories. She had a crystal-clear image of a shirtless Jesse standing in her kitchen with the morning sunlight spearing through the window onto him. Of Jesse with his sleep-tousled hair and dreamy bedroom eyes turning to look at her when she walked in. Of Jesse sipping coffee and smiling at her. The kind of smile a man gave a woman when he had just gotten out of her bed—and wanted to head back for a second round.

She felt the flood of heat, both then and now, and it was way too hot considering her son was babbling and having a messy time with the oatmeal. Her focus should have been on her little boy, on the fact that her house was basically on lockdown, with a deputy standing guard and armed ranch hands patrolling the grounds. She should be worrying about whether or not Bull Freeman would try to come after them again and if Agent Ryan Shaw would soon be cleared to pay them a visit. A visit that could maybe give them answers about Bull and the attacks.

She shouldn't be ogling Jesse and feeling this intense attraction.

"Are you okay?" she heard Jesse ask, and that yanked her back from her thoughts. And the heat.

Hanna nearly lied, nearly told him it was nothing, but even a flash of a memory might be the start of others returning. If so, that was something Jesse needed to know. That way, he could confirm it. Or not. If it was the "or not," then she might have to admit her imagination ran wild and hot whenever she was around him.

"You drank coffee from one of the blue mugs," she said, tipping her head to the open-faced cabinet where there was a row of the cobalt-colored cups. There were only four of them and eight of the sunflower-yellow ones. "That morning after you'd stayed the night," Hanna added after he gave her a puzzled look. "The blinds weren't shut then like they are now."

She watched the realization dawn in his eyes as Jesse slowly stood, Evan's oatmeal spoon still in his hand. He nodded. "I was drinking coffee, and you came into the kitchen after you'd gotten dressed. Like now," he muttered.

For just a moment, he got that smile again. But it vanished in a blink. Hanna didn't think that was because Evan's cheerful babbling had reminded him they weren't alone. No. It was probably because he remembered things hadn't gone well shortly after that. Hanna wasn't sure how much time had passed before she'd ended things with Jesse but, according to her mother's account, it hadn't been long before she'd "come to her senses."

"Ma, Ma," Evan chattered, which got Hanna moving toward him so she could give him a kiss. She got a smear of oatmeal on her cheek in the process, but it was worth it. She didn't have to force or rein in her happiness, or worry about trust, when she was around her son.

"I can finish feeding him," she said, sitting in the chair that Jesse had just vacated.

Jesse didn't complain though he would have likely wanted to continue since giving his son breakfast wasn't something he got to do very often. However, he stayed close, watching not just Evan and her but also making glances out the narrow side window of the kitchen door. A reminder that the danger was out there with Bull still at large.

"Agent Shaw will be here soon," Jesse said while he poured himself a cup of coffee—and he used one of the cobalt mugs. "FYI, he's riled that Grayson wouldn't let him on scene last night. He's still insisting its urgent that he talk to us."

"Not urgent enough though for him to tell you what it was about over the phone," Hanna concluded.

"Exactly. I suspect the agent wants to cut some kind of deal with Bull. Though why he'd want us in on that, I don't know. That would be between the ATF and the district attorney." He paused, sipped his coffee. "You want to talk about the memory you just had?"

She managed to smile when she got Evan to eat another spoonful of the oatmeal, but she was definitely giving that question some thought. It was a personal, kick-to-the-gut hot kind of memory, and she doubted that discussing it with Jesse would do anything but fire up more of the heat already there between them.

That, in turn, would stir up her frustration.

Even if her memory fully returned, it didn't mean she'd be giving in to that heat and getting back together with Jesse. After all, there was a reason they weren't together, and until she'd had a chance to go over that reason, and know what was true and what was being filtered through her mother's venom, the hot cowboy cop was off limits. Besides, with the danger caused by Bull's escape, she didn't have the mental energy to deal with the personal stuff.

"No, I don't want to talk about it. Not now anyway," she finally answered. She didn't get a chance to add more because Jesse's phone dinged with a text.

"My folks and Noah are here," Jesse said, reading the message. "You remember them."

She did. Again, no recollection of them prior to her being shot, but Boone Ryland and Jesse's mom, Melissa, had come with him several times to visit Evan. She'd met Jesse's cousin, Noah, while she'd still been in the hospital. Noah was a cop, too, at San Antonio PD. From all accounts, Jesse and he were as close as brothers.

"They're not here about Bull," Jesse explained. "They're just bringing me a change of clothes and want to see Evan for a couple of minutes."

That was a reminder of how stressful this had to be for the entire Ryland clan. There was probably added stress for Boone since he might be blaming himself for the shooting that had nearly killed Evan and her.

Hanna nodded. "Let them in."

Jesse nodded, too, and headed toward the front door while he typed something on his phone. Probably using the app to disengage the security system. Hanna had given him the log-in info and access code the night before since she'd figured he would be coming and going until they had this situation with Bull under control.

She heard the voices when Jesse opened the door and finished feeding Evan the last of the oatmeal. She'd just wiped the baby's face and had taken him from his high chair when the trio came in. Suddenly, the kitchen was filled with Rylands.

Melissa, Boone and Noah all greeted her with smiles that somehow managed to look both friendly and cautious at the same time. Hanna had no idea if they resented her because she'd ditched Jesse or if they considered that Jesse had dodged a bullet by being entangled with someone who couldn't even remember him. Well, not remember him much anyway.

While Melissa went straight to Evan, Boone kept his distance, and he set the overnight bag he'd brought in on the counter. Tall and lanky, with hair more silver than black, he had to be in his eighties, but he looked much younger. Fit. Of course, that probably had something to do with the active part he still took in running the family ranch.

Noah was fit, too, and sported those amazing Ryland genes. She suspected he was the spitting image of Grandfather Boone in his earlier days.

"Da, Da," Evan babbled, reaching out for Jesse to take him.

"He's growing fast," Melissa remarked, and she gave Evan's toes a jiggle that caused him to laugh. She was a good twenty years younger than Boone and had once been a Silver Creek deputy before she'd married him and he'd adopted her three children.

"I'm sorry all of this is happening," Boone murmured, aiming that directly at Hanna.

She tried to come up with the right answer to that, especially since she couldn't just dismiss Bull's escape as not being the serious threat that it was. Hanna ended up settling for a nod.

"Uncle Grayson will be here soon with Agent Shaw," Noah explained. He glanced at Melissa, who was chattering with Evan, and she picked up the rest of the explanation.

"I thought I could take Evan to the nursery while Hanna and you talk to the agent," Melissa told Jesse. "Noah and Boone have to get back, but I drove separately so I can stay as long as you need."

Again, Hanna had to think hard before she responded. She truly didn't want Evan to be part of a discussion about Bull, but with the danger, she also wasn't sure she wanted him out of her sight. Still, Melissa had been a deputy; she knew how to take precautions to make sure her grandchild was safe.

"Thank you," Hanna finally said.

That caused Melissa to beam. She muttered something about reading some books to Evan before she carried the baby into the adjacent living room where there was a basket filled with books.

"Grayson's been sending me updates," Jesse said, shifting his attention to Noah. "But is there anything new on Marlene?"

Noah shook his head. "Still no signs of her, but we know it was her blood that they found in her house. Not a large amount," he added and, considering he glanced at Hanna when he said that, it was likely meant for her benefit. Maybe to try to reassure her that the woman was still alive.

And perhaps she was. Bull could have plans to try to use

her as a bargaining tool, and he wouldn't be able to bargain with a dead woman.

"Grayson has the Texas Rangers looking for Marlene," Noah went on. "SAPD, too. Sooner or later, she'll surface."

Hanna hoped that wasn't wishful thinking. They needed to find Marlene because then they'd almost certainly find Bull. Added to that, Marlene could be hurt and terrified, so finding her was critical.

Her heart rate kicked up when she heard a vehicle come to a stop in front of the house. The sound came just as Jesse received another text.

"It's Mason," Jesse announced. His uncle and a reserve Silver Creek deputy. "Grayson's tied up with an interview, so he had Mason bring over Agent Shaw."

"We should be heading out," Noah explained as they made their way to the door with Jesse following right behind them. Boone and he said their goodbyes, Boone stopping to give both his wife and Evan a kiss before leaving.

Hanna heard murmurs of the brief conversation on the porch and, several seconds later, Mason walked in. Even though he spent most of his time running the family ranch, he was still a police officer, and he made one of those sweeping cop glances around the living room and kitchen.

Mason definitely had the tall, dark and hot Ryland looks, but those features were harder on his face, and even though she'd run into him more than a half dozen times, she'd yet to see him smile. He reminded her of one of those Old West cowboys who was always braced and ready for a gunfight. One that he would win hands down. All the Ryland lawmen looked formidable, but Mason topped the heap when it came to that particular trait.

"Agent Ryan Shaw," Mason said, hitching his thumb to

the blond-haired man who stepped in behind him. He was a good six inches shorter than Mason and had a stocky build.

"Evan and I can finish our reading in the nursery," Melissa commented, and she thankfully got the baby out of the room.

Jesse shut the front door, locked it and reengaged the security system.

This wasn't a social visit, but Hanna was still about to offer coffee. However, Agent Shaw spoke before she could say anything.

"It wasn't a good idea to delay this visit," Shaw snarled.

Mason's reaction was subtle. A slight lift of his gunmetal eyes to the ceiling. A barely audible huff.

"The agent thinks we should have broken protocol by bringing him to an active crime scene before we could even verify his credentials," Mason responded. He snarled, too, and it was a lot better than Shaw's. "They've been verified." He glanced back at the agent. "I suggest you stop whining and use your time to inform Deputy Ryland and Miss Kendrick why it was all so hell-fired important that you come here."

That caused the agent's jaw to tighten, and it tightened even more when Mason tapped his watch. Obviously, Jesse's uncle had made it clear to Agent Shaw not to waste their time.

"Like I told you on the phone last night," Shaw said, "we have to talk."

"You said a lot of things last night," Jesse countered. "Paraphrasing here, but you insisted Bull didn't set the fire and there was big trouble. You also mentioned someone wanted me dead, but you refused to tell me who or why."

That didn't ease the clamped muscles in Shaw's face. "Because it was something I needed to tell you in person."

"So you said." Jesse's tone was as iron-hard as Mason's glare. "Well, you're here, so tell me."

Shaw certainly didn't jump right in with an explanation. Instead, he slid a glance at Mason. "I need to divulge this info to as few people as possible."

Mason gave him a flat look. "If you think that'll get me to leave, think again. I'm a cop, and that's my nephew and the mother of my great-nephew. I'm staying put unless Jesse or Hanna want me to go."

"Stay," Jesse insisted, and there was plenty of impatience in his expression when he turned back to Shaw. "Are you here to tell me you're trying to work out a deal with Bull?"

Shaw dragged in a long, slow breath. "No, I'm here to tell you something that stays in this room. Bull is a deep cover ATF agent who infiltrated the militia three years ago in order to find its leader and suppliers."

Hanna shook her head and mentally repeated each word. "An ATF agent tried to murder me?" she snapped.

"No," Agent Shaw quickly answered. "Bull wasn't the one who shot you. Arnie did, and Bull shot and killed him before he could fire a second shot that would have almost certainly left you dead."

Again, she went through the mental repeat, but Hanna could already feel the slam of emotions crashing into her. Emotions that came with one huge question—was all of this true? Since she didn't have any real memories of the shooting, Hanna had had to rely on other people's accounts. She so wished she knew what had actually gone on in those trees because she believed with all her heart that it was now coming back to haunt them.

Or kill them.

"If Bull's really an agent, why'd he end up in jail?" Jesse demanded. Obviously, he was considering the truth of this, too.

Shaw sighed and scrubbed his hand over his face. "Since plenty of the militia members were in that same prison, Bull thought he'd be able to find out the name of the leader."

"So, why would Bull escape if he's in such a great position to get intel?" Jesse demanded.

"Because someone ordered a hit on him. I don't know who," Shaw immediately added. "But from the short phone conversation I've had with Bull, he believed his life was in grave danger. Yours, too. Bull heard talk that somebody was going after you because you haven't given up on investigating the militia."

Jesse cursed. "Hell no, I haven't given up. That militia was responsible for Hanna and my son nearly being killed. I won't give up until every last one of them is behind bars."

Shaw looked him straight in the eyes. "And that's why you're a target."

Oh, mercy. *A target.* So, Jesse was probably right about the fire in her studio being set to draw him out. The same person might use Evan or her to try to get him, too.

Jesse must have heard the soft gasp she made because he automatically ran his hand down the length of her arm. "It's okay," he murmured to her. "Just breathe."

He was soothing her. Or rather, trying to do that. Hanna did as he said and breathed, forcing herself to stay level. Focusing in an effort to rein in the panic. She wouldn't get any answers if she lost the battle with the panic right now.

"Who put the hit on Jesse?" she asked the agent, and she managed to add some steel to her voice.

"I don't know, and I haven't been able to have a face-to-face conversation with Bull."

"Why the hell not?" Jesse protested. "If he's really an agent, why wouldn't he go straight to you or somebody else in the ATF?"

This time Shaw wasn't quite so quick to answer and he glanced away when he spoke. "Bull says he's not sure who to trust. He thinks he'll be gunned down if he comes out in the open. We got a lot of the suppliers for both the guns and the drugs, a lot of the militia members, too. But we still don't know who's running the operation."

"Arnie?" Jesse suggested.

Shaw's headshake was fast and firm. "No. He didn't have the brains for it."

"Certainly, you have suspects then," Jesse said on a huff.

"We do, but so far none of them have panned out. That's why Bull insisted the way to learn the truth was from the other militia members who'd already been arrested. We know the operation has continued, so somebody sure as hell is still running it."

"*Somebody,*" Jesse repeated in a cop's tone. He put his hands on his hips and kept his hard stare pinned to the agent. "You're so certain that Bull is clean and has been telling you the truth about the militia?"

Hanna expected Shaw to issue a firm yes in response to Jesse's question. He didn't. Shaw stood there and muttered something she wasn't able to catch.

"No," Shaw finally said. "I can't be positive that he's clean."

Sweet heaven. So it was possible there was a rogue agent out to murder Jesse. Probably her, too, since he couldn't be sure how much she had, or would, remember.

"Here's what I know," Shaw finally went on. "The ATF didn't sanction Bull's escape, and he's refused to come in and talk to me or anyone else in the agency."

"Maybe because he doesn't trust you," Mason quickly pointed out. "Maybe because he knows you're the dirty agent he can't trust."

Shaw didn't jump to deny that, either, but the anger flared in his eyes. "I'm not dirty. But Bull might believe I am. He might think I'm looking for a scapegoat. I'm not," he assured him. "I'm looking for the truth."

"The truth," Jesse grumbled. "And what exactly would that be? Why would Bull suddenly not be trusting his own agency?"

Again, Shaw paused and, judging from the way his jaw muscles were flexing, he was having a battle with himself as to what to say. Or not say.

"I think Bull stopped cooperating with the ATF and me because I got word to him that we have a new suspect," Shaw finally explained. "A suspect he might believe is innocent."

"That scapegoat you mentioned—" Jesse spat out the words "—who is it? Give me a name."

Again, Shaw seemed to have another mental debate before he finally turned his gaze back to Jesse.

"Our prime suspect is Marlene, Bull's sister."

Chapter Five

Marlene.

Jesse had to admit he hadn't seen that particular accusation coming, and he reminded himself that it might be just that.

An accusation.

He didn't know Agent Shaw that well, and the agent might be handing him a load of lies to throw suspicion off himself. Jesse didn't think he had that much in common with Bull but, at the moment, it appeared they shared a mutual distrust of Shaw and the ATF.

"What evidence do you have that Marlene might be the militia leader?" Jesse demanded.

"Evidence that I'm not at liberty to share with you. I'm sorry," Shaw quickly tacked on, "but it involves intel from informants."

"Criminal informants?" Jesse questioned, and even though Shaw didn't confirm or deny that, his steely expression was enough of a confirmation as far as Jesse was concerned.

The info had likely come from one of the jailed militia members who might or might not be telling the truth. Jesse was going to go with the *might not* in this case because Marlene certainly hadn't been arrested for any crime in Silver Creek. That didn't mean Jesse wouldn't check to make sure she was clean, but for the moment, he would consider her a missing person. One who might be dead or in danger from her brother, a supposed dirty agent.

Yeah, he had plenty of questions.

"Since I'm not sure of Bull's intentions," Shaw continued while he turned to Hanna, "it'd be best for you and your son to be in protective custody. I can arrange for that."

A burst of air left Hanna's mouth. Part laugh, part huff, and with a whole lot of "no thanks" that made Jesse proud of her for standing up to the agent. This danger and fear had to be taking a serious toll on her, but she wasn't just going to run for cover in what could be the wrong place.

"We're already in protective custody," Hanna assured the man. "Jesse's. I think he'll do a much more thorough job of protecting his son than whatever agent you can assign to the task."

"Fine," Shaw grumbled. "Suit yourself. But you might want to remember that Jesse's the target here."

"The possible target," Hanna corrected before Jesse could. "It's also possible that someone planted the info about Jesse being a target to separate him from Evan and me so we'd be easier to take or kill." She tapped her head. "I'm the one who could confirm or dispute Bull's claims."

Shaw's eyes widened. "Your memory's coming back?"

"No." Jesse couldn't say that fast enough. He didn't want Bull or someone else going after Hanna even if it was true.

Or rather, true-ish.

Yeah, she had recalled at least bits and pieces about him being in her kitchen the morning after they'd had sex. Judging from the heat Jesse had also seen in her eyes, she'd maybe recalled the sex, too, but Bull or even Shaw might want to ensure she stayed silent.

"No," Hanna echoed when Shaw just kept that hard stare on her. "My memory isn't coming back. It might never come back, and from what you said, it seems as if your now-rogue agent is responsible for that. You as well."

"Me?" Shaw snarled.

"You," she verified. Her voice was not only stronger, but she also took a step toward Shaw. "Because I don't need to learn all the details of your investigation to know that you should have kept a better leash on Bull. You should have known he was accompanying a desperate, violent militia member to the Silver Creek Ranch and that bystanders, like me and my baby, could have been hurt or killed."

Shaw didn't deny any of that. Couldn't. Because Hanna was right. Even if Bull claimed he had no idea what Arnie was going to do that night, he should have requested some kind of backup from Shaw to deal with Arnie, who'd obviously gotten out of control.

"Mistakes were made," Shaw finally said, clearly not personally taking any blame. "But remember that Bull saved your life."

Hanna took another step closer to the agent, and even though Jesse could see her hand trembling, she was staying strong. "I don't have a memory of that because Arnie took it away from me. All I have is the word of a deep cover agent who might or might not be dirty. A deep cover agent who might or might not have told the truth. Excuse me if I don't jump on the *Bull did me a favor* bandwagon because, as far as I know, he could have been the one who shot me."

Jesse had to force himself not to smile. This was the

Hanna he'd known before the shooting, and it was good to see her fighting back.

Shaw didn't acknowledge what she'd just said, not verbally anyway, but he stayed quiet, obviously stewing for a couple of long moments. He was still in "glare" mode when he shifted back to Jesse.

"I read your report that Bull called you last night," Shaw said. "Has he contacted you again?"

Jesse wasn't surprised that Shaw had read the report. Grayson would have legally been forced to inform the ATF of the details of the investigation—especially since there was no proof that the ATF had any wrongdoing in this.

"No further contact," Jesse assured the agent. However, he wasn't about to forget what Bull had said.

You need to ask yourself about what really took place that night Hanna was shot.

Jesse had spent a good chunk of the night thinking about just that, and he still didn't know what Bull had wanted him to figure out. That's why he needed another conversation with Bull, but that wouldn't happen until the man called him back or resurfaced.

"You need to let me know ASAP if you hear from Bull," Shaw said, extracting a business card and handing it to Jesse. "You already have my cell number, but my office number is on there."

"You do the same and let me know if Bull contacts you," Jesse insisted. He didn't have a card on him so he took a notepad from the kitchen counter and jotted down his number.

Shaw took the piece of paper, shoving it into his pocket, and he looked at Hanna again. "I'd appreciate your cooperation in this investigation. If you remember anything, I need you to let me know."

She nodded after a long pause of her own, and that confirmation seemed to signal to Shaw that it was time to leave. He muttered a lukewarm thanks and turned toward the door.

"Don't trust him any further than you can throw a herd of longhorns," Mason muttered as he followed Shaw out of the house.

Good advice; Jesse was on the same page as his uncle. He locked up, reset the security system and looked at Hanna to see if she was about to lose it now that some of her annoyance had faded. Nope. She seemed all-business now.

"You believe anything Shaw said?" she came out and asked.

"Not sure." Hopefully, that would change, and he'd be able to get some confirmation on things and maybe disprove others. "Are you okay?" He had to know.

She nodded then muttered something under her breath. "I'm very angry that Bull or someone connected to this is putting our baby in danger again."

Jesse matched her nod with one of his own. Yeah, he was not happy about that at all.

"What about Marlene?" Hanna asked. "Is there anything in her background to suggest she could truly be head of the militia?"

"Nothing that jumps out at me, but I suppose it's possible."

Along with interviewing the woman multiple times, Jesse had also done a thorough background check on her. He'd known her for years, but now he tried to determine if everything he remembered added up to her running an illegal operation.

"Both Bull and she were born into money, and Marlene is nearly ten years older than he is," Jesse added. "Their father was a hard man who, from all accounts, browbeat his kids. Bull had a falling out with him and left right after high school. Marlene stayed and, when he died, he left his entire estate to her. It was worth millions, and Marlene has kept the business going though she did move the operation from San Antonio to Silver Creek." That move had happened years ago, right about the time Jesse's mom had married Boone.

"Marlene sells real estate, right?" Hanna asked.

"Yes, and she specializes in commercial property and ranches. I ran financials on her when Bull was arrested. Just routine stuff, and I didn't see any red flags. Still, a real estate business would be a good cover for money laundering and such that a militia might need."

Her forehead bunched up as she obviously tried to process that. "Maybe Bull moved back to Silver Creek to investigate the militia and then found out his sister was involved. That could have possibly caused him to go rogue. Rogue enough, though, to attack and kidnap her? I mean, what reason would Bull have for doing that rather than just turning her over to the ATF?"

He paused, considered it. "Bull might not have taken her. She could have possibly staged the attack in her home. *Possibly*," he emphasized. "It would have involved injuring herself or drawing her own blood."

Even though this was an important and serious conversation, it occurred to him that they hadn't talked like this in a long time. In fact, they hadn't talked much at all since the shooting. It felt good, but he got an instant reminder of just how high the stakes were when he heard Evan's and his mother's laughter coming from the nursery. That's where his focus had to be right now. Keeping Evan safe. Hanna and the rest of his family, too.

"Your shirt had blood on it," Hanna said when Jesse walked back to the kitchen counter where he'd left his laptop.

He stopped, turned and stared at her. "What?"

Hanna swallowed hard. "The first time I saw you. Remember seeing you," she corrected. She motioned toward his chest. "You had blood on your shirt."

He drew in a slow breath. "Yes." Another breath. "Noah had come running to restrain Bull, so I picked you up and took you to the hospital. I didn't want to wait for the ambulance to get all the way out to the ranch." He paused and blinked hard to try to erase some of what he was reliving in his head. "The baby kicked me."

"What?" she asked, her tone very similar to his just moments earlier.

"When I was running to get you into my truck, you were unconscious, but I could feel Evan kicking. That helped me get through those moments."

She nodded. "You were there with me when they did the C-section?"

He shook his head. "It was an emergency. Medical staff only. But they brought Evan out to me after they cleaned him up." He felt the corner of his mouth lift in an automatic smile. "He was still kicking and crying. He looked like a really-pissed-off hobbit. And in that moment, I knew my life would never be the same."

Hanna smiled, too, because she no doubt knew exactly what he meant. But the smile didn't last. "I heard your mom say something to Boone when I was in the hospital. They were in the room but thought I was asleep. Your mom said you'd had flashbacks of your father's death."

Jesse wanted to curse. He definitely hadn't wanted Hanna to hear something like that when she'd been dealing with her trauma, but yeah, he had had a flashback or two when he'd been trying to save Hanna's life.

"My dad died when I was eight," he said, choosing his words. No need to add more bad images to the ones she no doubt already had. "A car accident. I was with him when a tire blew out and caused him to crash into a tree. I tried to do CPR, but it didn't work."

"Eight," she murmured. Maybe to remind him that he'd been a kid and not responsible. Both of those things were true, but guilt was greedy and apparently had the power to last a lifetime.

"I'm guessing that was one of the things we had in common," Hanna continued. "Because I lost my father when I was young, too. He had a heart attack."

Jesse studied her face. "You remember any of that?"

"No, but my mother told me about it." Her sigh was long and heavy. "And that's the problem. Not specifically with the memories of my father, but the memories of everything. Especially those of when I was attacked."

"'You need to ask yourself about what really took place that night Hanna was shot,'" he said, repeating what Bull had said. Of course, Jesse had to keep considering the theory that Bull could be trying to create some kind of smoke screen, but they wouldn't know until they had a complete picture.

Hanna's memories were a big piece of that picture.

"You recalled me being in your kitchen," Jesse pointed out. "Maybe more will come."

"I could maybe help things along," she said in a murmur, and it seemed to Jesse that she was talking to herself. Trying to steel herself up, too. "I could do hypnosis sessions."

This wasn't the first Jesse was hearing about the particular therapy that one of Hanna's doctors had suggested. A therapy that she had flat-out rejected. She hadn't spelled out the reason she hadn't wanted to do it, but he suspected she hadn't wanted to deal with the flood of bad memories that would come if the therapy worked.

"I'll call and set up an appointment," Hanna insisted as she took out her phone. But before she could do that, there was the sound of a vehicle in the driveway.

Jesse went on instant alert because he knew if this was someone in his family or from the sheriff's office, he would have gotten a text to notify him.

"Stay back," Jesse warned her, and he went to the window where he saw someone he definitely didn't want to see.

Hanna's mother, Isabel.

The woman wasn't alone. There was a tall, dark-haired man with her, and Isabel was clearly arguing with the deputy, Theo Sheldon who had blocked her from coming closer to the house. Jesse's phone dinged with a text from Miguel Navarro, the ranch hand who was standing guard.

Should we let her in? the ranch hand asked.

"It's your mother," Jesse relayed to Hanna, and that caused her to groan. She groaned a second time when she heard Isabel shout for the deputy to get out of her way, that he couldn't stop her from seeing her daughter.

"She'll have another stroke," Hanna muttered. "Best to let her in."

"She's not alone," Jesse pointed out, causing Hanna to come closer to the window for a quick glance.

"That's Dr. Warner."

Since Jesse was also worried about the woman possibly having another stroke, he responded to Navarro's text. Let her in but search the doctor for any weapons.

That was probably overkill, but Jesse didn't know the man, and he didn't want to take the risk. After all, Bull had had plenty of time to put a plan into motion, a plan that could involve forcing the doctor to help Bull get to them.

Jesse watched as his cousin, Deputy Theo Sheldon, frisked the doctor and then gave Jesse a thumbs-up before he let the pair head for the house. Isabel was obviously spitting mad, but he was surprised at how healthy she looked. He'd seen other stroke victims with limited mobility and serious speech problems, but Isabel was moving just fine. And, judging from her shout at the deputy, she had no trouble talking.

As he'd done with Mason and Agent Shaw, Jesse temporarily disarmed the security system and opened the door. Isabel made it to the porch first and she greeted him with a glare.

"You Rylands can't keep me from my daughter," Isabel added in a snarl.

Dr. Warner didn't protest, but Jesse heard the man's heavy sigh as he followed his patient into the house. Isabel went straight to Hanna and dragged her into her arms.

"How are you holding up? Is the baby okay?" Isabel asked. Coming from her, it sounded like her usual demand.

"We're both fine." Hanna untangled herself from her mother's grip and took a step back. "I told you not to come," she added, aiming that at the doctor.

Dr. Warner lifted his shoulder in a gesture that managed to convey a whole lot of frustration. "Isabel insisted on coming and she was going to drive herself. I opted to bring her for a short visit. Short," he emphasized, aiming a long look at Isabel. "And if she becomes agitated, then I'm taking her right back."

Isabel was already agitated, but she seemed to make an effort to relax her stiff posture. "I just needed to see that my daughter and grandson were okay and to let Hanna know that I'm arranging for some bodyguards. They'll be here within the hour."

Hanna closed her eyes a moment as if fighting to keep her composure. Jesse knew the feeling. He always had to do that around Isabel.

"When the bodyguards arrive, I'll send them away," Hanna informed her mother. "I don't want anyone on the grounds who Jesse hasn't vetted."

Isabel's mouth dropped open and she made a sound of outrage before she whirled around to confront Jesse. "You're trying to control my daughter."

"I'm trying to keep control of the situation," Jesse clarified.

"A situation that wouldn't be happening if you cops had done your job and kept that killer behind bars."

"The cops didn't let Bull escape," Hanna pointed out just as the doctor cautioned her mother.

"Calm down. Now. Or we're leaving."

Dr. Warner took the woman by the arm and led her to the sofa where he had her sit. He got right in her face. "Remember what we talked about on the drive over," he warned her.

"Yes, you threatened to have me dragged back to the rehab facility," Isabel sputtered angrily.

"Not dragged, but taken back," the doctor corrected. "I told you I couldn't stand by and watch you work yourself up into a frenzy. Your meds will only do so much to keep your blood pressure down. You have to do the rest by staying calm. Hanna and your grandson haven't been harmed, and Deputy Ryland here has set up security."

"Security they wouldn't need if the cops had kept that monster where he belongs," Isabel grumbled, but at least she hadn't shouted, and she did seem to be leveling out just a little.

Hanna came into the living room and sat across from her mother. Jesse hoped she wouldn't mention anything about what Shaw had told them or the phone call from Bull. She didn't. Hanna just sat there, staring at her mother, waiting for her to continue. She didn't have to wait long.

"Your studio is gone," Isabel stated. She was definitely calmer now. "How will you work?"

"I've been using the guest room, and I'll keep using it until I can rebuild the studio."

"Or you could just move back to the estate with me where you and Evan would have plenty of room, and you wouldn't be out here all by yourself."

"I'm not moving," Hanna insisted. "I like it here, and the quiet makes it easier for me to paint."

Jesse knew Hanna had felt that way before she'd been shot, and he was always a little surprised to hear she still felt the same. Maybe she didn't need the memories for this place to feel like her home.

"You look different," Isabel volunteered, studying Hanna. "You sound different, too. Is that Jesse's doing—"

"I'm remembering some more things," Hanna interrupted, no doubt cutting off what would have been her mother taking another jab at him.

Isabel pulled back her shoulders, causing Jesse to tune

in to the changes in her expression. Not relief or joy. But rather, concern. Maybe because Isabel was worried about the traumatic memories of the shooting?

"More?" Isabel muttered.

"I told you last week that some memories were starting to return," Hanna said. "Bits and pieces."

This was the first Jesse was hearing about that, and he'd seen Hanna at least every other day. Hell. Why had she kept that from him? But he immediately thought of the answer to that. If she'd recalled having sex with him, that probably wasn't something she would feel comfortable spelling out.

"What did you remember?" Isabel asked her after a long pause.

Hanna paused, too. "Some things about Jesse."

So, maybe sex, but after studying Hanna, Jesse thought it might be more than that.

That concern in Isabel's eyes went up a significant notch. "What things about Jesse?" her mother demanded.

Hanna kept her attention nailed to her mother. "Did you tell me you'd make trouble for Jesse if I didn't end my relationship with him?"

What the hell? Jesse definitely hadn't been expecting her to say that. He'd thought Hanna would tell her mother a G-rated version of him in the kitchen the morning after they'd had sex.

Isabel shifted her position and looked away from her daughter. "You remember that?"

"No, I guessed," Hanna admitted. "I figured, with all the other things you'd said about Jesse and his family, that you'd tried to pressure me into not having a relationship with him."

Jesse stared down at Isabel. "What kind of trouble did you plan on causing?" he snapped.

Isabel dodged his gaze as well. "I know people. People like state senator Edgar Lawson."

Since the senator was also the father of one of Silver Creek's deputies, Ava Lawson, Jesse knew the man, too. And didn't think much of him. Many in law enforcement didn't, even though the senator had recently been cleared of having a part in an elaborate money-laundering scheme.

"What exactly did you think the senator would do?" Jesse pressed.

Isabel shrugged again. "Your family runs that huge ranch, and I thought all it would take was a word from Edgar and you wouldn't have buyers lined up for your livestock."

Fat chance of that since the ranch supplied to plenty of people who wouldn't give a rat what the senator thought. Still, it pissed him off that Isabel had threatened his family in any way.

But it had worked.

Well, maybe. Hanna wasn't a pushover, but she might have backed off from him if she'd thought her mother could truly do him or his family some harm.

That could be wishful thinking on his part though.

Jesse would have liked for it to have been something like that, but the truth was that Hanna had been resistant to having a real relationship with him before she'd lost her memory. He'd always thought that might be connected to her broken engagement to Darrin Madison, the son of one of Isabel's close friends, but that might not have played into it either. The bottom line was that Hanna hadn't loved him and hadn't wanted the marriage he'd offered for the sake of their baby.

Isabel groaned, causing Jesse's attention to snap back to her. He was both shocked and confused when he saw the tears in her eyes. "I asked Marlene to help. Hanna had already stopped seeing you, but I was worried she might change her mind and go back to you. I couldn't live with that, not after the way your family tried to ruin my life."

Jesse had to do a mental double take, and he cut through the bulk of the woman's confession to home in on one important point. "Marlene? Bull's sister?"

The woman nodded. "We travel in some of the same social circles, and we've been friendly for years. The last time I saw her, I mentioned that I wasn't happy about my daughter being involved with a Ryland. She must have seen how upset I was, and she said that maybe there was something she could do to help."

Everything inside Jesse went still. "When did this happen? When did Marlene tell you she could help?"

Isabel made a hoarse sob. "The day before Hanna was shot. Oh, God." She pressed her fingers to her mouth. "Do you think Marlene is the one who persuaded her brother into going to the ranch to confront you? Am I responsible for nearly getting Hanna and Evan killed?"

Chapter Six

Hanna set Evan's bottle aside and eased across the room to put him in his crib for his morning nap. Even though it was obvious he was already asleep and would likely stay that way for an hour or more, she stood there watching him. Just seeing her baby had a way of steadying her.

And scaring her, too.

Her precious little boy was in danger because of Jesse and her. Because someone might want to silence them, and she might have her mother to blame for the start of that.

Shortly after Isabel had dropped her bombshell that she might have spurred the shooting, Dr. Warner had convinced her that it was time to leave. Isabel had, crying her way out the door, and Hanna hadn't been able to force herself to offer any consolation. If Isabel had indeed had a part in what had happened, Hanna wasn't sure she could ever forgive her.

Hanna darn sure didn't expect Jesse or his family to forgive her either. Isabel had crossed one very big line, and it didn't matter that the woman hadn't known what the consequences would be. The bottom line was she'd put Evan and her at risk. Her actions could have cost Jesse and her their son.

Hanna went back into the kitchen where she found Jesse

exactly where she'd left him a half hour earlier, before she'd gone to the nursery to feed Evan and put him down for his nap. He was sitting at the kitchen counter, working on his laptop while he drank yet another cup of coffee.

"My mother already left," Jesse let her know. "One of the ranch hands came and picked her up."

That was good. While she truly appreciated Melissa's help with Evan while Jesse and she had been dealing with Shaw and then Isabel, Hanna had needed some quiet time with her son. Of course, Jesse was here, too, in the middle of that quietness, but it felt different with him.

Was different, she silently amended.

For the first time since the shooting, it seemed as if Jesse and she were on the same side. Then again, maybe that "same side" had been there before she'd lost her memory. That was the problem with this messy situation. What she didn't know, or remember, could be just as dangerous as her getting back her entire memory.

"I got a text from Dr. Warner while I was feeding Evan," Hanna told him, setting the baby monitor on the counter so she could keep an eye on Evan. "He has my mother back at the rehab facility. He said he'd given her a mild sedative because she was still upset."

Jesse turned, looked at her. "Are *you* still upset?"

There was no reason to hold back the truth on this. "Yes, and you should be as well."

Her mother's words just wouldn't stop repeating in her head. *Am I responsible for nearly getting Hanna and Evan killed?* It was definitely a question that needed answering.

"It was a good guess on your part that your mother would try to keep you away from me by threatening my family," Jesse remarked. "It was a guess, right?"

Hanna nodded, got a glass of water and leaned against the counter to face him. "But I don't remember if what my mom said had any impact on my decision not to accept your marriage proposal. Or to end things with you."

He opened his mouth, closed it, and seemed to have a debate with himself as to what to say. "You told me there was no relationship to end, that it was only a one-night deal between us."

She winced, hoping it hadn't been as hurtful as it sounded. But according to what Jesse had told her, it had indeed been just one night. One that'd left her pregnant. She'd never come out and asked Jesse why that had happened, but in one of their brief conversations after the shooting, she had brought up the pregnancy, and he'd mentioned that he had used a condom. So, they'd practiced safe sex. For all the good it'd done.

Except there was plenty of good when she considered she now had her son.

That was playing into this messy situation, too. Jesse was Evan's father. Always would be. And she didn't have to actually remember being with him to know what had drawn her to him. Then and now. The attraction, yes. But more. She knew in her gut that Jesse was a good man. One who her mother had tried to give a raw deal because of the bitterness she felt toward his family.

"You said you told your mother about a week ago that you were getting back bits and pieces of your memory." Jesse threw it out there.

"A lie," Hanna readily admitted. "I thought it would make her stop worrying. Or at least worry less about me. I didn't want her to lose hope that I'd make a full recovery, so I told her I was remembering some things."

In hindsight, that hadn't worked. Maybe nothing would. But that hadn't stopped her from trying to soothe Isabel and perhaps dole out some hope to herself, as well, that she wouldn't permanently stay in the dark when it came to all those missing years and memories of her life.

"A couple of days ago, I was going through all my old emails and texts, just to see if there was anything that would jog my memory," she told Jesse. "Did you or Grayson take a look at those?"

He shook his head. "You were a victim and not target-specific. At least, that's what we believed." His face tightened. "Were we wrong about that?"

"No," she tried to assure him. "I didn't find threats or anything like that. Definitely nothing from Bull, Marlene, Arnie, or anyone else with obvious connections to the militia or the attack." She paused. Had to. "I found some texts, though, from Darrin Madison."

Even though Darrin didn't live in Silver Creek, Jesse no doubt knew that was the name of her ex-fiancé. She was also betting the town's rumor mill had been plenty busy with gossip about their breakup. Darrin was an investment mogul who had the added bonus of being a Texas heartthrob.

Among other things.

She had ended their engagement a little less than two years ago and, five months later, she'd landed in bed with Jesse. Maybe for rebound sex. Perhaps because the attraction had simply been that strong between them. But even without her memories, those texts had given her some insight.

"He hit me," she heard herself say.

Jesse jerked back as if someone had punched him. He cursed under his breath, shook his head and then cursed some more. "I'm sorry. I hope he paid and paid hard for that."

Hanna couldn't be sure, but she doubted that he had. "I broke up with him, but he wasn't arrested because I didn't report it," she admitted. "I can read through the lines of the flurry of texts from him and my mother. Darrin went into the groveling 'but you caused me to do it' mode. He insisted I made him snap when I accused him of having an affair with his assistant. He was having an affair, by the way. He finally admitted that in one of the texts."

"And what the hell did Isabel say about it?" Jesse snapped.

Hanna managed a dry smile. "She thought I should forgive him and get counseling so I didn't trigger Darrin into another impulsive gesture. *Impulsive gesture*," she emphasized. "Those are the words Isabel used." She shook her head. "I'm betting there were a lot of phone calls and visits to try to pressure me into getting back with him."

"Did he pressure you too?" Jesse asked, the anger still biting in his voice.

"It seems that he did. According to the texts, he sent flowers, asked me to go on a romantic getaway so we could work things out, etcetera. I turned down all his offers, and then I stopped responding. He eventually stopped, too, and moved on. Isabel mentioned he recently got engaged again."

He studied her face, maybe looking for any signs that bothered her. It didn't. "I dodged a bullet with him." Then, she wanted to kick herself for phrasing it that way. "Sorry. Not an especially good reference, considering I didn't dodge the one Arnie fired. Or maybe it was Bull who pulled the trigger."

Her voice cracked a little on those last words and, for a second, she was right back in the hospital. In pain, terrified and with the panic swelling inside her because she couldn't remember what the heck had happened.

That crack in her voice and her troubled expression was probably why Jesse slid his hand over hers. For just a moment. Then he pulled back, which was normally something she would do. For just this one time, though, she wished he'd kept the contact there a little longer.

It was wrong to take comfort from him. Wrong to give him any kind of hope that she'd ever consider the marriage proposal he had told her would always be on the table.

"I still want to set up an appointment for hypnosis," she said. "But…"

"But even if you get your memory back, you might not want a relationship with me. Or with anyone. In fact, remembering might make things worse in that area. I get that." He stopped and looked her straight in the eyes. "FYI, I want to beat your ex to a pulp for hitting you."

She mentally compared that to her mother's reaction, and it touched her. So many emotions welled up inside her, and they collided with the fear and uncertainty. Maybe that's why she took those steps toward him. And why she went into his arms when he reached for her.

Her body landed on his and Hanna could feel herself melting against him. Now, this was what she needed. The close contact. Being in his arms with his scent right there for her to take in. He was strong, so strong, with the muscles corded in his chest and biceps. And while he would respect her no-marriage wish, she had a clear sense that he still cared for her.

So that's why she pulled back.

"Sorry," she muttered just as Jesse said, "Don't say you're sorry."

"You're shaken up," he continued a moment later. "You have a right to be shaken up."

She did, but playing with fire wouldn't help, and that's what she would be doing if she'd stayed in his arms. Scalding-hot fire that had led to sex once and could again if she wasn't careful. She was in no position whatsoever to allow that to happen.

"The investigation…" she said, forcing herself to change the subject. "Have you found anything that'll help?"

Jesse kept his eyes on her for a while longer. Perhaps because he was trying to decide whether to go with the new topic or linger on that hug that shouldn't have happened. Thankfully, he went with the first.

"I haven't been able to confirm that Bull is or isn't an agent," Jesse explained. "I don't know if I can trust Shaw, which means I don't know if he told us the truth. It's possible Bull is just his criminal informant. Possible, too, that Shaw's worked out some kind of deal with Bull to get him info on the militia so he can get the credit for taking it down."

Hanna imagined that would give Agent Shaw a stellar mark on his record, if he closed such a big case. The agent might go to any lengths to make that happen.

"A deal with Bull that Shaw's possibly kept off the books?" she asked.

Jesse nodded. "But it could be worse than that. A lot worse."

Hanna knew where he was going with this. "Shaw could be dirty and want to silence me before my memory returns."

Another nod. "And maybe he needs to silence Bull, too. Or anybody else who could prove he's dirty."

Yes, and that would include Jesse. With all the digging he was doing, Shaw had to know that something might be uncovered that he could want to stay hidden.

"Of course, there's the possibility that Shaw's clean and

that Bull actually is a deep cover agent," Jesse went on. "If so, that means Marlene could be the criminal in all of this."

"Are there any signs that's possible?" Hanna wanted to know.

"There are a few flags. Not bright red ones, but still flags." Jesse went back to his laptop and looked at the screen. Hanna took a glance at it, too, and realized Jesse had a financial report on the woman.

Hanna zoomed right into one particular bit of info. "Marlene has an offshore account."

"She does, and while that's not automatically illegal, it makes me wonder why she'd need something like that. Of course, it's possible someone else set up the account without her knowledge."

True. Because if Marlene had wanted to hide funds she'd gotten from the militia, then why use her own name? Then again, maybe the woman had thought the cops wouldn't look that deep into her background.

"Her local bank account and investments look normal enough," Jesse went on, "but since she buys and sells real estate, there's always ways to conceal things like money laundering or the purchase of weapons and such." He looked up from the screen and met her gaze. "She did business with your mother, sold her some land and worked with her to get tax breaks on some of the property she already owned."

"Isabel never mentioned that," Hanna muttered, "and she would have had the perfect opening to do that when you asked her about Marlene."

Her mother had said they were in the same *social circle* and were *friendly.* Nothing about doing business with the woman who might be a criminal.

Jesse made a sound of agreement, but his attention

whipped to his phone when he got a text. "It's Theo," he told her, and he started toward the door.

Theo Sheldon. Another deputy in the Silver Creek sheriff's office and a Ryland relative. Well, sort of. From what Hanna had gathered from the bits and pieces of talk she'd heard from Isabel and others, Theo's parents had been murdered when he was a kid, and he'd been raised by Grayson and his wife. If the other talk she'd heard was true, then Theo was the top candidate to replace Grayson as sheriff when he retired in a couple of months.

She stayed back, away from the door and windows, something Jesse had drilled into her, and watched as Jesse ushered in his fellow deputy. Unlike the dark-haired Rylands, Theo was blond, but he still had the cop's eyes.

"Hanna," Theo greeted while Jesse locked up. "We haven't found Bull or Marlene yet," he volunteered, probably because he knew that Hanna was about to ask that particular question. "No sightings of either of them."

Part of her hoped they were long gone and were now out of the state. Especially Bull. But that would be just a different kind of nightmare since she would always be looking over her shoulder to see if he had returned to finish the job he'd started. No. It was best for the cops to find him and figure out what the heck had actually happened when she'd been shot.

"I've been going through Marlene's financials," Jesse explained. "I highlighted some areas that need more digging. Any luck with her phone records?"

"Possibly," Theo answered. "She had no calls to or from the prison, but she did get two from an unknown caller shortly after Bull's escape. They were both very short, only lasting a couple of seconds, which means she could have realized they were spam and ended them."

Jesse nodded. "True. Is there a pattern of her getting calls from anyone who might be connected to Bull or the militia?"

"No, but I figure she'd use burners for that so they couldn't be traced." Theo paused, shifted his attention to Hanna. "Marlene did get calls from your mother. One the day before you were shot and two more the day after."

That tightened her stomach into a hard knot. "They were long conversations?"

"Long," Theo verified. "The one before the shooting lasted nearly a half hour. I'll need to go to the rehab facility in San Antonio to talk to your mother about exactly what was said during those calls."

He wasn't asking permission, and Hanna hadn't expected him to do that. The interview needed to be done, and Isabel had to come clean with what she knew. Hanna also thought of something else that should happen, something that might give them a few answers.

"My phone kept a record of my texts for the past year, but there are only two months of calls," she explained. "I'm wondering if someone can access those earlier calls, the ones I received prior to the shooting, to see if any of them... well, are unusual. If there are any flags."

That obviously got both Theo's and Jesse's attention. "You mean something like Marlene contacting you? Or Bull?" Jesse prompted.

She nodded then shrugged. Then sighed. "Maybe it's nothing. I mean, we know why I came to the ranch that night. I had ultrasound pictures and forms from the hospital in the car with me, and I'd told the nurse that I would take them out to you right away to get them signed, but maybe there was another reason I was there—"

"I'll have your calls checked," Jesse assured her, and he took out his phone to fire off a text that would get that started.

"Just how fragile is your mom's health?" Theo asked her while Jesse finished his text. "Because I need to know how much I can push to get answers."

"She seemed physically fine when she was here earlier, but go through Dr. Warner," she suggested. "Maybe even have him present during the questioning. He can perhaps keep her calm."

Of course, he could also put a stop to the interview if Isabel became too agitated, but they couldn't risk bringing on another stroke. Even if her mother had done something to instigate the shooting, she had indeed had a stroke, and a second one might be a lot more serious. It could kill her. Hanna didn't want that. However, if Isabel had played even a small part in what had happened, she expected her to have to pay for that in some way.

And maybe she had.

Hanna didn't doubt that Isabel loved Evan, and it was probably eating away at her to know that she'd inadvertently put her grandson and daughter in harm's way. She had possibly done that anyway, but it was just as likely that Marlene had been blowing smoke with her *something she could do to help.*

"Grayson got the crime lab to go through another enhancement of the footage from the security camera the night of the shooting," Theo went on. "It's ready if you want to take a look at it."

It took Hanna a moment to realize Theo had meant that

offer for both Jesse and her. She had to swallow hard and tamp down the blasted panic. Not now. This could be important, critical to getting to the truth, and that's why she nodded.

"Yes, I'd like to see it," she attested.

But Jesse didn't budge. "You've looked at the enhanced footage?" he asked his cousin.

Theo shook his head. "It just came in a half hour ago. You can access it through the online case file."

His gaze stayed on Jesse and something unspoken passed between them. Hanna was betting it had to do with her. Theo probably thought it a good idea for Jesse to review the footage to make sure it was something she could handle.

"I'll take a look at it then," Jesse muttered.

She heard what he wasn't saying. That he would look at it and decide if it was something she should see. But Hanna didn't want him making a decision like that for her. She couldn't risk Jesse trying to shield her from something that could help them uncover the truth.

Theo nodded, sliding glances at both Jesse and her before he continued. "Agent Shaw came by the sheriff's office after he left here." He was obviously moving on to the rest of the updates he'd planned on giving Jesse. "He's still pushing to get Hanna put in protective custody."

"Push back," Jesse advised.

"Oh, we are. The ATF has no jurisdiction when it comes to Hanna or Evan. Shaw can squawk all he wants, but he can't change that."

"Any indications that Shaw's dirty?" Hanna came out and asked.

Theo shrugged. "Not dirty, but he toes the line a lot. He's had two complaints filed against him for excessive force, and there's talk that he's bent the law a couple of times. Nothing to do with Bull or the militia, but it's possible Shaw's done unauthorized wire taps to get info on an investigation."

That didn't help the knot in her stomach, and Hanna frantically tried to recall if Agent Shaw had had the chance to plant a bug in her house.

"Shaw was never out of my sight when he was here," Jesse assured her. Obviously, he knew where her thoughts had gone. "And he was only in this room, nowhere else in the house. But I can have the place swept just in case."

Hanna nodded. She didn't want to risk the chance that a dirty ATF agent could be listening in on their conversations—both the ones that dealt with the investigation and those that were personal.

"I'm heading to San Antonio now to talk with Isabel, but I can schedule the sweep on the drive there," Theo offered, checking the time. "We're having the sheriff's office swept, too, just in case Shaw's trying to get an inside line on what we're doing." He glanced around. "In the meantime, if there is a bug, you two might not want to have any conversations in here."

"Good idea," Jesse muttered, and he walked with Theo to the door.

Once he'd locked back up, he grabbed his laptop and said, "Why don't we move to the guest room to finish looking at Marlene's financials?"

She nodded, nabbing her water and the baby monitor so she could follow him. This was the right thing to do, but Hanna knew it would be a little unnerving to be in a bedroom with Jesse. That hug sure hadn't helped in that department. Then again, she hadn't needed that hug to recall just how attracted she was to him.

"And the enhanced footage from the surveillance camera?" she asked.

He sighed in such a way that let her know he hadn't just expected her to drop that. "It could help if I view it first because there might be nothing new to see." The moment he finished saying that, though, he waved it off. "But there might be something new for you to see."

"Yes," she agreed, and she left it at that.

She watched Jesse try to deal with the dilemma, torn between sheltering her and using her. "Yes," he finally repeated. "We'll do that after we finish with Marlene's financials. I don't want to skip any steps here."

Neither did she, and that's why Hanna wanted to study those financial records, too. She didn't need memories to maybe clue in to something that just didn't seem right.

Jesse carried his laptop into the guest room and he'd just set it up when his phone rang. The sound shot through the room and frayed her nerves even more than they already were.

"Unknown caller," he told her after he glanced at the screen. "I'm going to put it on speaker." He also hit the record function on his phone.

"It's me," the caller said. Bull Freeman.

"Where the hell are you?" Jesse asked.

"Nearby. We need to meet."

"Why?" Jesse snarled. "So you can try to kill me?"

"No, so I can turn myself in. Meet me at the fence of that old, abandoned farm out on Franklin Road."

Hanna had no idea where that was, but she was betting

it was a remote location. The perfect place for Bull to lie in wait and try to gun Jesse down.

"I suppose you expect me to be alone and unarmed?" The sarcasm was heavy in Jesse's voice.

"No," Bull repeated. "You can bring your fellow lawmen and an entire arsenal with you. Just be there in two hours."

"If you're nearby, like you say, why do you need so much time?" Jesse argued.

"Because I've got some things to do." Bull paused, cursed. "I'm putting my life in your hands, Jesse. Don't do something that'll get us both killed."

Chapter Seven

Jesse listened to the chatter of the conference call with Grayson, Deputy Ava Lawson and Texas Ranger Harley Ryland. They were going over the same map that Jesse had pulled up on his laptop.

The map of the area where Bull had insisted he would surrender himself.

Jesse had serious doubts about Bull's intentions, but that wouldn't stop him from going to the abandoned farm. However, he would do that with plenty of backup and security measures.

One of the best measures was Harley himself because he was an expert sniper. And Grayson was placing Harley in the loft of the barn on the farm. During the past hour since Bull had called, Grayson had already had a team check out the barn and surrounding area for booby traps and such.

Grayson had also made other arrangements in that same hour. There'd be deputies in the wooded area across from the farm. The road to and from there would be monitored as well. Everyone would wear Kevlar, and Jesse wouldn't be exiting the bullet-resistant cruiser until Bull had assumed a position of surrender.

"It's still not foolproof," Jesse heard Hanna murmur.

She was watching the baby monitor since it was nearing the time for Evan to wake from his nap, but she was obviously listening to the conversation as well. Hard for her not to hear it, though, considering the small size of the guest room.

"It'll be as safe as we can possibly make it," Jesse assured her in a whisper.

That, of course, wasn't foolproof at all.

Bull could have assembled his own team who would try to kill every lawman on scene. He wouldn't be able to have that team in the immediate area since Grayson already had deputies posted there, but Bull's cronies could come storming in by using the trails.

But Bull could have something else in mind.

Something that was twisting Jesse up inside.

Because Bull could be planning a different kind of attack. One where he would use this so-called surrender as a diversion so he could come after Hanna. Jesse had tried to cover all the angles there, too, by arranging for more than a dozen armed ranch hands to be on the grounds. That was in addition to having his uncle Mason and cousin Noah and two more reserve deputies there as well.

Jesse's mother would be inside the house with Hanna and Evan, and because Melissa was a former cop, she would be armed with a gun that she most definitely knew how to use. His mother would lay down her life to protect Hanna and Evan, and yeah, that was twisting him up, too. He didn't want it to come down to his mom having to step in to assist because it would mean Bull and whoever he'd brought with him had managed to get past multiple lines of defense.

"Any questions?" Grayson asked when he finished the briefing.

No one said anything. Grayson had made clear everyone's

positions. Had made it equally clear that they wouldn't be giving Bull any chance to fire at any of them. They also wouldn't be letting Agent Shaw in on it. Too risky, since the man could be dirty.

Jesse ended the call and checked the time. "I'll have to leave in about an hour," he told her.

He also checked Hanna to see how she was handling this. She didn't seem to be on the verge of a panic attack, nowhere close to that, but her nerves were definitely showing. Even though he wasn't even sure it would help, he went to her and pulled her into his arms again.

"It'll be okay," he tried to assure her. Of course, they knew it wasn't something he could guarantee, but he would do whatever it took to keep them all safe. Bull was the expendable one here.

Hanna didn't move away from him, and she didn't go stiff from the close contact. The sigh that left her mouth was long and laced with fear and worry.

"You think Bull will actually surrender?" she asked.

"I don't know," he answered honestly.

It could go either way. If the man was truly an ATF agent, a clean one, then the chances were high that he'd give himself up. He would want to clear his name. But if he was truly a killer or a dirty agent, then all bets were off.

She nodded, her hair brushing against the side of his face. That gave him a kick of memories he didn't want at the moment. Memories not of the damage that Bull could do but of Hanna and him together. Oh, man. Even with everything that'd happened, she could still fire up his body and make him remember things best put on hold.

Obviously, they were on the same page about that "on hold" part because she cleared her throat and stepped back.

Her gaze automatically went to the monitor where she could see that Evan was still sleeping.

"I'm not sure how soon he'll be waking up," she said, her voice a low murmur, "but I can go ahead and start looking at that enhanced feed from the security camera that Theo mentioned."

That yanked him out of the haze from the heat, and Jesse couldn't shake his head fast enough. "I don't want you to have to deal with that now. Like I said, I have to leave in about an hour. If you see something that upsets you or triggers a panic attack, I want to be here." And it might take more than the hour to get her steady.

"I want to get started on this." She paused, and he could see her mentally regroup. "I *need* to get started on it. I need to do something to help so I don't just feel like a victim who needs protection. If we can put an end to the danger, then Evan will be safe."

Jesse couldn't dispute any of that, but the timing sucked. He'd seen that footage. Not the enhanced, but the original one. Hell, he'd studied it frame by frame, and he knew it was going to bring all that terror back for her. For him, too.

"I won't fall apart," she assured him. "I can't because I need to take care of Evan when he wakes up."

She would definitely need to do that, and their little boy could be the ultimate, good distraction. Still, he debated it for another moment before he finally went to his laptop and located the file in his inbox. He had Hanna sit in the chair, and he pressed the keys to get the footage started.

At first glance, Jesse couldn't see much of a difference in the enhanced footage in the first few frames. He watched as Hanna pulled to a stop in front of the gate and then opened her window to punch in the security code Jesse had given her. However, before she could do that, Arnie's truck came to a fast stop behind her, and both Arnie and Bull barreled out, heading straight for the gate.

Or maybe Hanna's car.

Because of the angle of the camera, Jesse couldn't see Hanna's expression, but at that moment, she wouldn't have necessarily been scared. The men didn't have weapons drawn. Not yet. But Jesse was betting the terror came and skyrocketed for her once she saw the rage on Arnie's face.

Jesse adjusted his own position so he could see both the laptop screen and the side of Hanna's face. That way, he could stop this if things got too intense. Better yet, maybe Evan would go ahead and wake up so it'd put an end to this. A temporary end anyway. Jesse knew that eventually Hanna would see every second of what the camera had captured.

"This appears to be when things escalated," Hanna muttered as she continued to watch.

Yeah, it was, and she was referring to the fact that she'd reached out of her window to punch in the code to open the gate. Arnie had stopped her from doing that by throwing open the passenger's-side door of her car, and then the man had taken hold of her.

The lab had indeed enhanced these frames. They'd managed to lighten the footage and make it clearer. Too clear. Jesse felt a wave of rage all over again when Arnie freed Hanna of her seat belt and dragged her out from the passenger's side. He'd had to do that because the metal post with the security pad would have prevented him from getting her out on the driver's side since she'd parked right next to it so she could reach it.

"We had no luck getting lip readers to interpret what's

being said," Jesse explained. But Arnie was clearly agitated, and it appeared he was yelling at both Hanna and Bull.

"I'm not going to focus on my own face," she told him in a ragged whisper. "That probably won't help."

Probably not. Though he wasn't sure it would help for her to look at Arnie's and Bull's faces, either, but that's what she did. She leaned closer to the screen, watching and focusing.

They watched Arnie hook his arm around her throat once he had Hanna out of her car. He still had his truck keys in that same hand, and they dangled from his fingers, hitting against Hanna's neck. Arnie took a few steps back before he whipped out a gun and started dragging Hanna toward his truck. Bull sure as hell hadn't tried to stop him. Not physically, anyway, but the men continued to talk.

Maybe even argue.

Jesse saw Arnie drop the truck keys. Hanna had been the reason for that because she'd been struggling to get away from him. Arnie had lost his grip on the keys and they'd fallen into the grass and shrubs lining the road. That obviously hadn't pleased the man, and his face had tightened with even more rage.

"There were drugs in his system," Jesse told her even though that was something she had no doubt already heard. Arnie had been stoned on a cocktail of alcohol and cocaine.

She shook her head. "I wish I could remember what he was saying. That's key. I have to remember."

Key was the right word, but it was possible she might never recover those memories. Hell, if seeing this didn't trigger the recovery, then maybe nothing would. Maybe not even the hypnosis. If that turned out to be the case, then that meant they'd have to pick through Bull's version of events to figure out what the heck had actually happened.

Jesse braced himself for the final frames, and he watched Arnie's wild eyes home in on the security camera. The drugs and booze obviously hadn't affected his aim because he lifted his gun and fired the shot to blast the camera to smithereens.

Hanna released a long breath and sat back in the chair. "I can keep watching it to see if I notice anything that'll help."

Jesse was about to nix that, but his phone rang and he saw Noah's name on the screen. An uneasy feeling slammed through him. Maybe something had gone wrong with the plan to meet Bull.

"What happened?" Jesse immediately asked.

"I'm here with your mother, but another car just pulled up," Noah explained. "It's Marlene."

Of all the things Jesse had expected his cousin to say, that wasn't one of them. "Marlene," he repeated. He saw the surprise that was on Hanna's face as well. "She's alive then. Is she hurt?"

"She appears to have a head injury, but she won't let me come near the car. She says she'll drive off if I get closer. She wants to talk to Hanna."

Jesse groaned then cursed. "That's not going to happen. Go ahead and bring my mother inside the house. I'll call for backup and then try to talk to Marlene myself."

Hanna quickly shook her head. "You can't go out there. It could be a trap."

Possibly, but he was a cop and he had to do his job. Marlene could be either a suspect or a key witness, and he needed to find out which.

Jesse headed to the front door and Hanna was right behind him after she grabbed the baby monitor. He got his mom and Noah inside and then looked out the window. It was Marlene all right. She was behind the wheel of a beat-up white car, and Jesse could see the blood on the side of her head.

"Is Evan okay?" his mom immediately asked.

Hanna nodded. "But he'll be up from his nap any minute now."

"I'll go to the nursery then, so I can be there when he wakes up." His mom gave both their arms a reassuring pat before she started down the hall.

While Jesse continued to keep his eyes on Marlene, he called for an ambulance. He knew Noah wouldn't have any trouble being his backup, and with so many of the deputies tied up, Jesse didn't want to call Grayson for help.

Once he was done with his call, he motioned for Hanna to stay back. When he was certain she was as safe as he could manage, he opened the door a fraction. He also drew his gun, but he kept it down by the side of his leg. Out of sight but ready in case things turned ugly.

"Marlene," Jesse called out. "How badly are you hurt?"

"I need to talk to Hanna," the woman answered, obviously dodging his question. She started and ended her response with loud sobs.

Sobs that could be fake, Jesse reminded himself, and injuries that could be staged. With the flags in her financials, Jesse couldn't just blindly trust her. However, he did have to secure the situation before the ambulance arrived.

"I need you to get out of the car," Jesse instructed. "And keep your hands where I can see them."

That brought on more sobs and what he thought was a yell filled with outrage. "I need to see Hanna. I have to tell her what happened."

"You can tell me." In contrast, Jesse kept his voice calm. "Just get out of the car, so I can help you."

The woman didn't budge, but he did see her pick up something. His hand tensed on his gun, but he didn't aim. Not yet. He watched and saw that it was a phone. It was some long snail-crawling moments before his own phone rang. From Dispatch. When Marlene motioned for him to answer it, he realized she wouldn't have had his number, but the call could have been routed to him through the emergency operator.

Without taking his attention off Marlene, Jesse hit the answer function with his left thumb and put the call on speaker.

"Please," Marlene begged. "Let me speak to Hanna."

Jesse wasn't ready to do that just yet. Besides, Hanna would no doubt be able to hear what was said.

"Did Bull hurt you?" Jesse asked the woman.

"Hanna?" Marlene shouted. "Please. I need to tell you something."

Jesse considered pressing Marlene for more info, but her crying had gotten even louder, and he could see the blood on the side of her head had started to trickle down her cheek.

"Hanna won't be going outside," Jesse told her so he could set the ground rules. "Tell her what you have to say and then let the EMTs help you. The ambulance will be here in a couple of minutes."

"No," Marlene shouted. "She'll have them kill me if she gets the chance."

Jesse had to mentally replay that. Marlene sure as hell had better not be talking about Hanna. "She?" he challenged.

But again, Marlene didn't answer his question. "I can't go to the hospital," she insisted. "She'll have her goons get to me. She'll try to silence me."

"No one will try to silence you. Detective Noah Ryland is here, and he can go in the ambulance with you to the hospital." He paused a moment to see if Marlene would have any objections to that. She didn't voice them if she did. "Now, tell me who this *she* is that you're so scared of."

This time the sound was more than a sob, and Marlene wailed out her answer. "Isabel. It's Hanna's mother who tried to kill me."

Chapter Eight

Hanna stood back from the window, but she was still able to see the EMTs loading Marlene into the ambulance. Noah was right there beside the woman and, judging from his body language, he was trying to keep her calm.

Trying and failing.

Marlene was crying and still going on about Isabel trying to kill her. Hanna didn't believe her. *Couldn't* believe her. Isabel wasn't exactly in a position to kidnap or hurt someone, but that hadn't stopped Hanna from calling her mother to try and get to the bottom of Marlene's accusation.

A call that'd gone straight to voice mail.

It was the same for the one she'd then made to Dr. Warner. It was only after multiple attempts to reach both of them that Hanna remembered they might still be in the interview with Theo. If so, they'd hopefully see that she had tried to contact them and would get back to her right away.

Jesse finished his call with Grayson, but before she could ask if Theo knew about Marlene showing up at her place, his phone rang again. "It's one of the EMTs," Jesse informed her.

He'd yet to shut and lock the door and was keeping watch, no doubt to make sure Marlene and his cousin weren't attacked. Even with the ten feet or so distance between Jesse and her, she had no trouble hearing the EMT when he spoke.

"I think she's been drugged," he told Jesse. "Can't confirm it, of course, but they'll run tests at the hospital."

Drugged. That might account for Marlene's confusion about who'd kidnapped her.

"What are her injuries?" Jesse asked.

"The most obvious one is the head wound," the EMT immediately answered. "It looks as if someone bashed her pretty hard, and she might have a concussion. Other than that, she has bruises and abrasions on her wrists and ankles, and some of those abrasions are fairly deep."

So, she had likely been tied up and held somewhere, if the woman's story was to be believed. The injuries could also be self-inflicted, but that seemed extreme for a fake kidnapping. A head wound could be serious—as Hanna well knew.

"Noah is to stay with Marlene at all times," Jesse reminded the EMT. "Once she's at the hospital, a deputy will come over and stand guard. I want her clothes bagged and her fingernails checked for any traces of DNA. I also don't want anyone other than medical personnel and law enforcement to talk to her, understand? If someone tries, have the deputy intervene."

"Got it," the EMT assured him before they ended the call.

Jesse checked his watch, something he'd been doing a lot in the past hour, and it was a reminder that even with all of this happening, he needed to leave soon for his meeting with Bull. He obviously had way too much on his mind, but that didn't stop him from going to her after he locked the door and reset the security.

He ran his hand down the length of her arm and took hold of her hand, intertwining his fingers with hers. "Since

Noah might be tied up with Marlene for a while, Grayson is having Deputy Ava Lawson come here to help keep watch."

Hanna shook her head. "But she's supposed to be at the abandoned farm with you and the others."

"A reserve deputy will take her place," he explained.

Obviously, Jesse figured an actual deputy would do a better job than a reserve one, which meant he was at greater risk for his meeting with Bull. A risk because he wanted the actual deputy here. Hanna wanted to argue with that, wanted Jesse to have that extra level of security, but she also knew their top priority was to keep Evan safe. Even if that put Jesse, or her, at greater risk.

"Thank you," she muttered. "Thank you for everything."

She tried not to show the worry since he was in that "full-plate worry" mode already, but he was well aware of what was on her mind.

"The person who kidnapped Marlene might have tricked her into thinking Isabel was behind this," Jesse suggested.

Since it was something Hanna had considered just moments earlier, she nodded. But the possibility of her mother's involvement was still weighing her down like heavy stones. "When do you have to leave?"

"I've got a few minutes. I figured I'd pop into the nursery and see Evan. Is he awake?"

"Yes." She showed him the monitor she still had so he could see his mother holding Evan in the rocking chair while she read to him. Soon, very soon, she'd need to fix him lunch, but since he wasn't fussing, it could wait until after Jesse had had those few minutes with him.

They started for the nursery but this time it was Hanna's phone that rang. She let out a breath of relief when she saw it was Dr. Warner.

"I just want you to know that we're doing everything possible to find your mother," the doctor said the moment she answered.

Hanna had put the call on speaker so, obviously, Jesse had heard that loud and clear. "What do you mean find her?" he asked just as his own phone rang. He cursed when Theo's name popped up, and he stepped aside to take the call.

"Dr. Warner, what happened to my mother?" Hanna demanded. She had to speak through the tight grip her muscles now had on her throat.

"She left the facility. She didn't tell anyone," he quickly added. "She just left."

Hanna resisted the urge to curse and forced herself to stay calm. "When did this happen and why? Was she upset with Deputy Sheldon's interview?"

"The deputy didn't even see her. When he got here, the nurse called Isabel's room, and Isabel said she was just getting dressed, to give her a few minutes. After those minutes dragged on, I went to check on her, and she wasn't there. We went through the footage on the security cameras and we spotted her leaving. She went to the parking lot, got in her car and drove away."

"Drove away in the car that shouldn't have been there," Hanna snarled under her breath. Again, she had to fight to hang on to her composure, and judging from the snippets she was hearing of Jesse's conversation with Theo, he wasn't hearing happy news either.

"Is my mother actually capable of driving?" Hanna asked.

"She's done very well with her exercises and has regained nearly all of the mobility she had before the stroke. Her response times might not be as quick, though, since she hasn't driven in a while."

And that was a huge reason for concern. "Has Deputy Sheldon alerted the San Antonio PD?"

"He has, and I'm sure they'll find her. He's also sending someone to her house in Silver Creek in case she goes there."

Good, so Theo was covering all the bases. Still, it was beyond frustrating, especially considering the accusation Marlene had made.

"Has a woman named Marlene Freeman ever visited my mother there at the facility?" Hanna asked.

"The name's not familiar, but I can check the visitors' log," the doctor offered. "You think this woman had something to do with your mother leaving?"

Hanna settled for making a noncommittal sound. She didn't know how her mother could have found out what Marlene was claiming, but it was possible she had. More likely, though, Isabel had panicked over having an interview with Theo. Now, Hanna needed to find out why her mother would have gone to such lengths to avoid answering a cop's questions. Because that could mean Isabel had something to hide.

"We've had no visitor by that name," Dr. Warner said after she heard some computer clicks. "You think your mother might go to this woman?"

Hanna repeated her noncommittal sound. "Would it be possible for me to get a copy of my mother's visitors' log? She did give permission for you to discuss her medical records with me." At the time, Hanna hadn't wanted such access. It might come in handy now though. "I think my mother might have gotten a visitor who upset her. I'd like to know who."

She hoped lightning didn't strike her for that lie. Well, maybe it wasn't a lie. Such a visitor might exist, but Hanna wanted to look at the list to see if it was possible that Marlene had indeed paid a visit to Isabel and that she'd used an alias when she'd done that. Of course, Hanna might not recognize an alias. Might not recognize the names of any of her mother's visitors, but this was a start, and if she saw something suspicious, Jesse could no doubt run background checks to figure out if there was any connection to everything else that was going on.

"I'll email the visitors' list to you," the doctor confirmed. "And please let me know the moment you hear from your mother."

Hanna assured him that she would do just that, and then she tried to call Isabel. It didn't surprise her when it went straight to voice mail, but it added another layer of worry. Worry that Isabel wasn't just dodging everyone but had maybe been in an accident. Hanna left a message for Isabel to call her back right away.

She waited for Jesse to finish his conversation with Theo, and he looked as frustrated with this turn of events as she was. "This could be my fault," Hanna blurted out.

Jesse's forehead bunched up, but he looked skeptical about that. "How?" That sounded skeptical, too.

"I explained to you that I lied to my mother and told her that my memory was coming back. A couple of days later, Bull escaped from prison and someone kidnapped Marlene."

"Or Marlene faked her kidnapping," Jesse reminded her after he took a moment to process what she was trying to tell him. He huffed and put his hands on his hips while he stared at her. "You can't believe that, when Isabel told Marlene you might be getting your memory back, it prompted Marlene to convince her brother to escape so he could eliminate you before you remembered anything about your attack."

She shook her head. Hanna wasn't so sure she could believe that at all. "But maybe what happened was my mother was worried about Bull coming after me again if he got out of jail. Isabel maybe said or did something that led Bull to believe someone had ordered a hit on him. That could have been the reason he escaped."

After she heard her own words, she realized that sounded just as far-fetched as what Jesse had just tossed out there. The bottom line was she simply couldn't see her mother doing any of that.

But maybe that was because she didn't *want* to see it.

It could be she had on blinders when it came to Isabel. Her mother and she didn't have a stellar relationship and Hanna didn't have memories of Isabel raising her, but the woman was still her mother. It was hard to believe the worst about her, and this could most definitely fall into the worst category if it turned out Isabel was behind everything that had happened.

"Theo's going to get a warrant to take a look at Isabel's financials," Jesse told her. "It's routine for something like this since we'll have to investigate Marlene's accusation. Of course, after Grayson talks to Marlene, he'll also want to interview Isabel right away to get her side of the story."

Yes, interview her to either rule her out as a suspect. Or arrest her. But for that to happen, they had to find her first.

"It's time for me to go," Jesse said on a huff, and he went ahead into the nursery to see Evan.

As usual, the baby gave Jesse a big gummy grin and went right to him for a cuddle and kiss. But then Evan reached back for his grandmother who had now pulled out a stash of toys to go along with the books.

"I can watch him as long as you like," Melissa offered, obviously noting their troubled expressions.

"Thanks," Hanna told her. She just might need a little time to herself to tamp down the worry enough so that Evan didn't pick up on it. If the tamping down was even possible, that is. "Jesse's about to leave, and I'll be in the kitchen fixing Evan some lunch."

Hanna followed Jesse out of the nursery and, after she closed the door, he turned to her, their gazes locking. "I'll be okay," he said.

For a moment, she thought he was about to kiss her. For a moment, she thought she might *want* him to kiss her, too. But then his phone rang.

He muttered some profanity when Unknown Caller was on the screen. "Bull," he grumbled, and he put the call on speaker.

"You found my sister," Bull snarled like an accusation. "Where has she been? Who took her? Is she all right?"

"How'd you know Marlene had been found?" Jesse countered.

Bull wasn't so quick to jump with a response this time. "Police scanner," he finally said. "Is she all right?" he repeated, and this time his voice was much lower. Not calmer though. Either Bull was genuinely concerned about his sister or he was putting on a good act.

"She was conscious when she arrived here, but she does have a head injury," Jesse told him. "I'll give you more details about her at the meeting when you turn yourself in."

Bull stayed quiet for a moment. "Have you arrested my sister?"

Jesse paused, too. "Why would you ask that? Has Marlene done something to warrant an arrest?"

Bull cursed a spate of raw profanity. "Don't play games with me. Tell me if she has been or will be arrested."

"We can talk about that after you surrender," Jesse countered.

"No," Bull snapped after another long pause. "I'm not turning myself in. The meeting is off."

Jesse didn't get a chance to bargain with the man because Bull ended the call.

"Hell," Jesse snarled and immediately texted Grayson to let him know what Bull had said.

Hanna figured there were a lot of angry lawmen right now since they'd spent so much time and manpower to set this all up. But it was puzzling why Bull had pulled the plug on this when he hadn't gotten the answers he'd seemingly wanted about his sister. Of course, maybe that was an act and he had never intended to go through with turning himself in.

"I need to talk to Noah," Jesse muttered after he finished talking with Grayson and made the call to his cousin. "Bull backed out of the meeting," he told Noah, "but he knows his sister has resurfaced. He might try to come to the hospital."

"I'll be on the lookout for him," Noah assured him. "The hospital security guard is here with me, too."

"Good. Grayson will be there in about a half hour. How's Marlene?"

"Agitated and still demanding to speak to Hanna." Noah sighed, and in the background, Hanna could indeed hear the woman insisting on talking to her. "They've run some initial tests on her, and the nurse is cleaning and stitching up the head wound."

"Hanna," Marlene yelled again.

"Could you put her on the phone?" Hanna suggested. "Or should that wait until after she's interviewed?"

"Put Marlene on the phone," Jesse said after he gave it some thought.

Hanna heard some shuffling around and a few seconds later, Marlene spoke. "Hanna?"

"It's me," she verified. "What do you need to tell me?"

Marlene's breath hitched, and Hanna was pretty sure the woman was crying. "I can't tell you over the phone. I have to see you, please," she begged. "Because I know the reason you were shot."

Chapter Nine

"This is the right thing to do," Jesse heard Hanna murmur. Not for the first time either. She'd already said a variation of that while Jesse had been making the security arrangements for Marlene to be brought to Hanna's.

Arrangements he sure as hell hadn't wanted to make.

He'd much rather keep Marlene as far away as possible so that Hanna and Evan would be safe. Well, as safe as he could make them anyway. With Bull still at large, Isabel missing, and perhaps a rogue ATF agent on their hands, maybe no place was truly free from danger. But as Hanna had pointed out, they were the likely targets. Perhaps Marlene, too. So, for that reason, it was best to go ahead and meet with the woman and hear what she had to say.

Of course, while Marlene had still been on the phone, Jesse had pressed the woman to clarify the reason she'd said what she had.

Because I know the reason you were shot.

But Marlene had continued to insist that she would only tell Hanna face-to-face. Part of Jesse wanted to dig in his heels and flat-out refuse. The other part of him wanted to hear what she had to say. Since Hanna was in the camp of wanting to hear out Marlene, too, he'd finally given in and made arrangements for an EMT to bring Marlene to Hanna's. That wasn't ideal, but it was much better than having Hanna leave the house and make the drive to the hospital. A trip like that would have meant traveling on a road where a shooter could easily be lying in wait for them. Especially if that shooter was working with Marlene and knew when to expect them to come driving along.

Even with having the meeting at Hanna's house, it had still taken time and coordination to put all the pieces in place for the visit. First, Marlene had had to get her doctor on board with the idea. According to the doctor, her injuries weren't that serious, but he'd wanted to keep her in the hospital for observation for at least twenty-four hours because of her concussion. Marlene had likely pressured him to agree to the plan by promising to return to the hospital as soon as she'd had her chat with Hanna.

Jesse had arranged for two deputies to accompany the EMTs and Marlene just in case Marlene turned out to be a target. Then he'd beefed up security at Hanna's by asking Deputy Ava Lawson to stay with Melissa and Evan in the nursery while the ranch hands and a reserve deputy kept watch of the grounds. They could still be attacked, but Jesse had made it as secure as he possibly could.

Now, Marlene had better come through on the promise of this revelation as to the reason Hanna had been shot. If not, Jesse intended to charge the woman with obstruction of justice and withholding evidence. He had zero tolerance for someone who could put Hanna and Evan at risk.

Hanna was pacing her living room while she kept her attention nailed to the baby monitor. Jesse had taken a look at it, too, and knew that Evan was having a blast with his grandmother and the deputy entertaining him. The plan, though, was for that entertainment to not have to go on too long. He knew that Hanna would breathe easier once they had Marlene in and out of the house and she could then be with their son.

Jesse silently groaned when his phone rang and, for a moment, he thought it might be Marlene canceling. But no. It was Agent Shaw. Since he didn't want the distraction, Jesse considered not answering it, but then he remembered that Bull had known about Marlene surfacing, and it was possible he'd gotten that info from the agent. If Shaw was in contact with Bull, then it was something Jesse needed to know.

"Make it quick," Jesse snarled when he answered.

"I want to be there when Marlene is questioned," Shaw immediately insisted.

Shaw would have obviously known they would interview the woman. Had to, since she was either the victim of a serious crime or she wanted law enforcement to believe that she was.

"This is my investigation too," Shaw went on, obviously taking Jesse's silence as a no. "I should at least be allowed to observe in case she describes or mentions someone in the militia. I've studied the files of every known member, and I might be able to help ID the person who either kidnapped her or assisted her in this plan."

"If Marlene's behind her own kidnapping, she isn't likely to give us an accurate description of anyone who helped her," Jesse pointed out, his voice a growl. "But you can request to see a recording of the interview whenever it happens."

"What do you mean *whenever*?" Shaw snapped back. "Marlene was taken from the hospital, and it's obvious she's on the way to speak to Hanna and you."

Jesse didn't bother to groan. Nor did it surprise him that the agent had the hospital under surveillance.

"I'm not interviewing Marlene," Jesse told him. "Not officially." Though he would Mirandize her in case she spilled something that incriminated her or someone else.

"It doesn't have to be official for me to need to know what she says," Shaw argued. "I need to be there."

This time Jesse voiced that no. "That's not going to happen." He couldn't risk having two of his suspects in the house, especially since they could be working together. "Like I said, contact the sheriff and work out your part, or lack thereof, in the official interview. I have to go."

He ended the call before Shaw could continue to press, but Jesse knew that wasn't the last he'd hear from the man. Nope. Shaw would likely just show up here, and that's why Jesse sent a text to the deputy patrolling the grounds to tell him not to let Shaw near the house. The ATF might give him and the sheriff's office some flak about that, but Jesse was in the "better safe than sorry" mode.

"Agent Shaw's coming here?" Hanna asked, the concern coming through loud and clear in her voice and expression.

"No," Jesse assured her, and even though it was probably a bad idea and a distraction, he went to her and pulled her into his arms.

She didn't resist. In fact, Hanna was the one who moved closer. "I just need this to be over," she muttered.

Yeah, he was on that very same page, and the stress and worry were eating away at both of them. Jesse brushed what he hoped would be a kiss of comfort on her forehead, but as he did that, Hanna looked up. Their eyes met. Held.

And, man, did he feel that gut punch of heat.

It was the kind of heat that made him remember just how

strong this attraction had been and still was between them. It also made him forget that the timing for it sucked. So did the timing for the kiss. But that didn't stop Jesse from lowering his head and touching his mouth to hers.

He got an even hotter jolt of heat. A jolt that shot through every inch of him when Hanna moved right into the kiss. When she turned it from something comforting to scorching.

The chain he'd kept on this heat snapped and Jesse dragged her closer to him. Until they were mouth to mouth. Body to body. Hanna certainly wasn't resisting, and he could feel the hunger. The need. Things that had always been there between them. Her mouth moved over his as if there'd been no breakup, no shooting. As if it were just the two of them ready to haul each other off to bed.

That couldn't happen, of course.

Jesse mentally repeated that to himself and kept repeating it until he got this fierce need back on the leash. Until he could finally end the sweet torture of her mouth and taste.

"I'm sorry," she immediately breathed.

He didn't bother telling her that an apology wasn't necessary. Or wanted. Jesse just pushed the limits of his willpower a little bit longer by brushing a kiss on her mouth. A kiss to remind her that an apology wasn't going to cool the fire. And that he fully intended to do this again, and more, the first chance they got.

She nodded as if she understood his point, and she continued to look up at him. Her eyes were wide, her face was flushed, and she was breathing through her mouth. All signs that made him wish taking her to bed was an actual option. Right now, no waiting.

But he quickly got a reminder of why that couldn't happen.

At the sound of the approaching vehicles, Hanna practically jerked away from him, and she pulled back her shoulders. Bracing herself. Jesse steeled himself up in a different kind of way. He put his hand over his weapon while he checked the window and spotted the Silver Creek cruiser. He continued to keep his hand on his gun after he opened the door. Even though Marlene was under heavy guard, it would be the ideal time for someone to launch an attack.

The EMT who accompanied Marlene stayed in the cruiser, but with Grayson on one side of her and Theo on the other, they led Marlene toward the house. There was now a bandage on the woman's head, and she was wearing a pair of green scrubs. Probably because her own clothes had already been bagged and sent to the lab for processing.

Grayson and Theo moved fast to get Marlene inside, Grayson scowling when a car came to a quick stop behind the cruiser. "Agent Shaw," he grumbled. "I'll handle this."

Jesse was glad Grayson had offered to do that since he didn't want to take his attention off Marlene. Added to that, Shaw could be there to launch that attack they were all worried about, so he had to be questioned. Had to be contained if he tried to get into the house.

Theo led Marlene inside, and Grayson went off to confront the agent. Jesse was thankful for it, too, since he wanted to focus on Marlene.

Marlene, however, obviously had her focus on Hanna. "Thank you for seeing me," Marlene said. She was trembling a little, and her voice was shaky.

Hanna nodded, but she didn't press the woman to jump right into an explanation of why she'd said what she had. *I know the reason you were shot.* But Marlene thankfully didn't waste any time. The fewer minutes she was in the house, the better.

"You'll want to know what happened to me," Marlene volunteered, looking at Jesse now. "I've already told Grayson and Theo, but you'll need to hear it, too."

Despite Jesse wanting to hear what she had to say, he held up his hand to put the pause button on this. "Have you been read your rights?" he asked.

Marlene nodded. "Grayson did that. He said it was routine."

Jesse got a confirming nod from Theo before he motioned for Marlene to continue.

"You'll need to help Grayson and Theo to make sure I'm not taken again." She stopped, blinked back tears. "Oh, God. They want me dead."

"*They?*" Jesse questioned, not reacting to the woman's crying. And he wouldn't. Not until he was convinced he could trust her, and they were a long way from that happening.

"The militia. My brother," Marlene revealed. Since her trembling got worse, Theo helped her to the sofa and had her sit.

"You think Bull had you kidnapped?" Jesse pressed. Neither Hanna nor he sat. They stood side by side, looking down at the woman. "And what does your kidnapping have to do with what you insist you have to tell Hanna?"

"It might have everything to do with it," Marlene muttered, and she swiped away a tear that slid down her cheek. "Let me start from the beginning. Well, one beginning anyway. Years ago, I had a relationship with Arnie Ross."

Jesse was sure he blinked. Of all the possibilities he'd

considered of what the woman might say, that one hadn't been on his radar.

"I know, Arnie doesn't look like my type." Marlene shook her head. "But this was before he started using drugs. Your mother can tell you just how handsome and charming Arnie used to be," she added.

It took Jesse a moment to realize that Marlene had aimed that comment at Hanna. "Isabel knew Arnie?" Jesse asked.

"Yes," Marlene confirmed. "She dated him when they were in college. I figured she'd told you."

"Maybe," Hanna admitted in a whisper, and her forehead creased with fresh worry.

Perhaps Isabel had told her before Hanna had lost her memory, but if so, that made Jesse wonder why the heck Isabel hadn't mentioned it after the shooting. He hoped Isabel had a good explanation. Of course, first they'd have to find the woman to get any answers.

"Charming and handsome," Marlene repeated. "But that was all before he got involved with the militia. An involvement I figure he used to feed his addiction since he'd already blown through his inheritance and trust fund by then."

"Any reason you didn't tell us about all of this when we were investigating Hanna's and Arnie's shootings?" Jesse didn't bother to take the anger out of his voice. Marlene shouldn't have withheld any info whether or not she thought it was pertinent.

"Because I didn't want anyone to know I'd had a relationship with a man like that. My business associates wouldn't understand." Marlene locked gazes with him. "And I swear I didn't have anything to do with the militia. I didn't even know Arnie was involved in that until hours before he was killed."

That got Jesse's full attention. "How did you find out?"

Marlene swallowed hard. "I'd dropped by to see Bull. He wasn't in his house, he was on his back porch. I overheard him talking to Arnie on the phone about a shipment of guns coming in. I can't recall Bull's exact words, but I could tell it was something illegal, and he mentioned the Brotherhood. I knew that's what the militia members called it."

Jesse had plenty of questions for Marlene, including how all of this connected to Hanna, but he went with a simple one. "You're sure your brother was talking to Arnie?"

"Yes," she quickly confirmed. "He said Arnie's name a couple of times, and it sounded as if Bull was angry with him. Lecturing him, you know, like demanding that Arnie stay sober until the shipment was done."

Hanna and Jesse exchanged a glance, and he saw some of the same skepticism in her eyes that he was also feeling. If Bull truly was a deep cover ATF agent, then why the heck would he have had that level of trust with a known drug user? Shaw might have some insight on that, but even if Shaw was clean, he would only know the info Bull had given him. Info that might be a bunch of lies.

"If I hadn't overheard that conversation," Marlene went on, shifting her attention to Hanna, "you might have never been shot."

Hanna didn't make a sound, but Jesse could practically feel the muscles in her body turn to steel. "What do you mean?" Hanna asked.

More tears welled in Marlene's eyes and she gathered her breath. "I confronted Bull. I demanded to know what he was involved with. He blew me off, saying I misheard him, that he wasn't involved with the militia. I played along because I didn't want him to know I was suspicious, and on the way back home, I stopped by Arnie's."

Jesse's skepticism went up a notch. "You went alone to visit a drug user you suspected was a member of a dangerous militia group?"

"I know it was a stupid thing to do," Marlene blurted out, "but I was worried about my brother. I just wanted to talk with Arnie and try to get him to admit if Bull was involved in something that would get him hurt. Or killed." She drew in another long breath. "I tried to keep the conversation casual, and I didn't specifically ask anything about the call I overheard or the militia, but Arnie figured out why I was really there."

"What did he do?" Jesse prompted when the woman didn't continue.

Marlene cleared her throat. "He was angry. Furious. And he said I should keep my mouth shut if I didn't want to have to visit my brother behind bars. I managed to get him calmed down. At least, I thought I had. I swore I wouldn't tell anyone, and I left." Her voice hitched and she pressed her trembling fingers to her mouth for a moment. "But he must not have been calm at all because that night he went to the ranch to confront you. That night, he shot Hanna."

Jesse thought about that for a couple of seconds and couldn't totally dismiss that the conversation with Marlene had played a small part in spurring Arnie to come to the ranch. But Jesse was betting it was the news of the man's imminent arrest that had sent Arnie on the fateful trip.

And that was right back on Jesse.

Jesse would have liked to put some of the blame for the shooting onto Marlene, but he couldn't. Arnie and Bull had come to the ranch because Jesse hadn't been fast enough in making that arrest. It didn't matter that he'd still been trying to build a case against the men. He should have moved sooner, should have had them behind bars so they couldn't hurt Hanna or anyone else.

"Are you convinced that Bull was trying to stop Arnie from shooting Hanna, or do you believe he was responsible for it happening?" Jesse asked bluntly.

Marlene certainly didn't voice a quick answer this time. "I don't think my brother is innocent," she finally said. "In fact, I think he's the one who arranged to have me kidnapped."

All right then. Maybe they were getting somewhere. Then again, the only place they might be getting with this was where Marlene was trying to lead them.

"Why would you say that?" Jesse asked, hopeful that the woman had some actual proof and not just suspicions. "Did you actually see Bull when you were taken? Because earlier, you thought Isabel was the one who'd arranged your kidnapping."

"No, I didn't see him or Isabel," she said on a heavy sigh. "And Isabel might have had a part in it. I can't be sure."

Jesse huffed. "What are you sure of then?"

"Like I told Grayson and Theo, I heard someone on the back porch of my house. I thought it was a stray dog who'd been coming to the door, but when I opened it, a man wearing a ski mask hit me on the head." She lightly touched the bandage. "He knocked me out and apparently drugged me, too. The next thing I remember, I woke up blindfolded and tied to a chair."

"Where?" Jesse immediately asked.

"A cabin."

Jesse looked at Theo to get his take on that. "She was able

to give us a description of the place where she was held, and the CSIs are heading out there to take a look. We believe it could be one of the old fishing cabins on the north fork of Silver Creek."

Good. Maybe the CSIs would find something to shed some light on all of this.

"Did your kidnapper speak or tell you why you'd been taken?" Jesse continued.

"Oh, he spoke, all right," Marlene verified with some anger in her tone now. "It wasn't Bull, but the man threatened to kill me if I didn't give him my ATM card and pin and the location and combination of the safe at my house."

So, the motive was money. Well, maybe. Jesse was still deciding whether or not Marlene was giving them the full story.

"The safe had been emptied," Theo confirmed. "But the ATM card wasn't used."

"I had ten thousand in cash in the safe," Marlene explained. "And some family jewelry. Theo said my attacker took that, too."

"Did he bring the money and jewelry to the cabin?" Jesse wanted to know.

"No. After I told him about the safe and gave him my ATM card, he left and didn't come back. Other than that glimpse of him before he hit me, I didn't see him, but Bull must have sent him to get the money from me. He must have been part of the militia."

That would certainly fit, but Jesse recalled how upset Bull had seemed when he'd learned his sister had been taken. Of course, Bull could have faked that. Or maybe it was Bull's plan and he hadn't intended for Marlene to be hurt.

"How'd you escape?" Jesse prodded.

Marlene held up her wrist for him to see the bandages there. There were also abrasions around her ankles. "I just kept tugging and pulling until I got free. Then I got out of the cabin and started running."

"Marlene said she ran to the nearest cabin, but no one was there." Theo filled him in when the woman stopped. "But there was the old car, and the key was under the mat. She used the car to come here to Hanna's."

"Why not go to the sheriff's office?" Jesse queried.

Marlene shook her head. "I wasn't thinking straight, and Hanna's house was on the way."

Depending on which road Marlene had taken, Hanna's could have indeed been on the way, but the most common instinct should have been for Marlene to go straight to the cops. Still, it was possible she had been drugged, so that could have played into her decision.

"We still haven't found Marlene's car," Theo disclosed, "and we're processing the truck left at her house."

"The truck the kidnapper must have used," Marlene provided. "He put me in my car and drove to the cabin."

"We told her that Bull had been spotted earlier in a truck that matches that description," Theo told Jesse.

"And that's another reason why I believe my brother has to be involved. First, the militia connection and now the truck," Marlene muttered, and she got to her feet. "I don't want to think he would do something like this, but I can't just bury my head in the sand. I've told Grayson and Theo this, and I'm telling you now. If Bull contacts me, I'll let you know ASAP. He has to be stopped."

If he was behind all of this, then yes, he would be stopped, and if Marlene could help with that, then something good had come out of this chat.

"Have you remembered anything about the shooting?" Marlene asked, turning to face Hanna. "Did Arnie say anything about me being the reason he hurried to the ranch to confront Jesse?" She made a hoarse sob. "I hope and pray I wasn't the reason."

Hanna stared at her a couple of seconds and shook her head. "I'm sorry, but I still don't have any memories of that night."

Marlene nodded, wiped away some tears and headed for the door.

"Grayson will be doing the official interview as soon as we get her back to the hospital," Theo murmured to him. "I'll let you know if we get anything new from that."

Jesse followed them to the door and saw Grayson on the phone while he waited by the cruiser. There was no sign of Shaw. Good. Jesse hadn't wanted him hanging around. However, he knew they hadn't seen the last of the agent.

The moment Theo and Grayson had Marlene back in the cruiser, Jesse went ahead and shut the door and locked up. He was thankful they had the room to themselves, not because he had plans to kiss her again, but because he wanted her take on everything Marlene had just told them.

"First chance I get, I'll be asking my mother about Arnie," she insisted. "I was telling Marlene the truth when I said my mother hasn't mentioned that since the shooting." She paused. "But, of course, I am getting back some of my memory."

Jesse studied her eyes. "Memories about the shooting?"

She shook her head. "About us." Hanna made a vague motion toward the hall and the bedrooms. "When you kissed me, I got flashes of when we were together."

Together as in when they'd had sex. "I hope they were good flashes," he said, trying to keep it light.

Her mouth quivered a little. Not in a bad way. But it was as if she was fighting a smile. "Good ones," she verified.

That might have sent him right to her for another of those ill-advised kisses, but the sound of his phone ringing shot through the room. Jesse frowned when he saw the call was from the ranch hand, Miguel Navarro. Hell. He hoped Agent Shaw hadn't returned.

"A problem?" Jesse immediately asked when he answered.

"Yeah, a big one," Miguel confirmed. "I spotted an armed man in a ski mask. He ducked into some trees, but I think he was heading straight for the house."

Chapter Ten

Even though Jesse hadn't put the call on speaker, Hanna had no trouble hearing what the ranch hand had just told him.

There was a gunman coming to the house.

Oh, mercy. If that person shot at them, Evan could be hit.

"Go to the nursery," Jesse insisted. "Lock the door and tell Deputy Lawson to stand guard."

Hanna desperately wanted to get to her son, but she was also concerned about Jesse. "What will you do?"

"I'll stop whoever it is from getting to Evan or you."

He was all cop now, and Hanna knew he was good at his job, but that wouldn't stop her from worrying that he could be hurt. Or worse.

"Be careful," she cautioned. Hanna held his gaze a moment longer before he went to the window and she hurried to the nursery.

"One of the hands spotted a gunman," Hanna explained to the deputy and Jesse's mom when she rushed in.

The alarm fired through Melissa's eyes. She was in the rocking chair, holding Evan, who was obviously getting a head start on his afternoon nap. The tray with the baby's lunch was on the table, his empty bottle sitting next to it.

Whipping out her phone, Ava locked the door. "Best if

the three of you get into the bathroom," the deputy advised, making a call while she raced to the window.

Hanna yanked out a quilt that she kept folded by the crib, and she went into the bathroom to put it in the tub. She forced herself not to give in to the fear. Not to be terrified for Jesse, for all of them. That wouldn't help, and right now she had to take some steps to make sure Evan was as safe as he could be.

Even though Melissa's heart had to be beating hard and fast, she managed to get into the tub with Evan without waking him up. Hopefully, he'd stay asleep, and while she was hoping, Hanna added that maybe one of the people guarding the house would catch the gunman before he could do any damage.

"Stay down," Ava called out to them. "An armed man was just spotted in the backyard."

Hanna couldn't hold back the slam of fear this time. Was this a second attacker? Or had the other one gone back there? Since they were likely dealing with a militia, it was possible they had sent several men.

But why?

That was the question that continued to race through her head. Was she the target? If so, was it because of something she might remember?

Groaning, she sank down into the tub across from Melissa and the baby, and she tried to will the memories to come. It didn't work. It was as if her brain had gone on lockdown and a wave of pure frustration coated the fear and worry.

The sound of a shot cracked through the air. Along with causing her heart to pound against her chest, it caused Hanna to latch onto Melissa so she could pull her lower in the tub. The woman ended up on her back with Evan nestled in her arm. There wasn't enough room for Hanna to lie down next to them, but she stayed as low as she could and prayed that bullet hadn't hit anyone but the intruder.

There was another gunshot blast. Then another. The sound whipped up Hanna's adrenaline and vised her lungs so that it was hard for her to breathe. Unfortunately, it didn't shut down the horrible thoughts she was having about Jesse. He was probably out there. Probably right in the line of fire, and he was doing that not only because it was his job but because he would protect them.

"It'll be okay," Melissa whispered, and Hanna heard the woman mutter a prayer. This had to be terrifying for her, too, since that was her son out there.

Hanna's phone dinged with a text. Her hands were shaking when she pulled it from her pocket and saw Jesse's name on the screen. Thank God, he was alive.

Isabel just pulled into the driveway. We're getting someone to her now.

Sweet heaven. Now her mother was out there in harm's way. But Hanna had to immediately rethink that. Was it actually harm's way or was this part of some plan to silence her before her memory could return? She didn't want to think the worst about her mother, but someone was behind this, and Isabel hadn't exactly been forthcoming about knowing Arnie.

She showed Melissa the text so that she'd know Jesse hadn't been hurt, and the woman's face relaxed just a little. "You know, I was a deputy when Grayson arrested your father."

Hanna shook her head. She hadn't known that, but of course, the timing worked since that arrest would have happened about thirty years ago.

"Your mother was so angry, and she attacked Grayson," Melissa went on. "She scratched his face and tried to stab him with a letter opener."

Even with everything else going on outside, that shocked Hanna. "Did Grayson arrest her?"

"No, he said it was just a fit of anger and that she had enough to deal with. He didn't want both your parents in jail, I guess."

Again, the timing for this wasn't stellar, but Hanna asked the question anyway. "Was my father guilty? Did he assault the young woman?"

"He never confessed, but all the evidence pointed to him, and there was an eyewitness. Mason," she supplied.

Hanna groaned. Isabel wouldn't have cared much for that, and it added another layer of her hatred for the Rylands.

"You should just be careful around Isabel," Melissa suggested. "I don't like to stir up trouble, but she wants to put a wedge between Jesse and you." She paused. "After Evan was born and you were still in the hospital, Isabel even threatened to try to get custody of Evan."

Another blow. Good grief. Just what lengths would Isabel go because of this old feud between the Rylands and her?

"Was I wrong to tell you all of that?" Melissa asked. She winced, shook her head. "Of course, I was wrong. Let's just say I no longer have nerves of steel the way I did when I wore a badge."

"You weren't wrong to tell me," Hanna assured her, and the woman's nerves seemed just fine to her.

"Stay put, but they've got the two men," Ava called out to them.

The relief came, but it was just as much of a punch as the adrenaline. And the worry was still there. "Is everyone okay?" Hanna asked the deputy, and she could have sworn her heart skipped a couple of beats when Ava didn't immediately answer.

"One of the gunmen is dead," Ava relayed, coming to the bathroom door. She still had her gun gripped in her hand. "No one else was hurt. Jesse and Grayson have the second man."

More relief came because Jesse and the others were okay. Better yet, they had someone in custody. "Who is it?" Hanna wanted to know.

"Not sure yet, but it wasn't any of our persons of interest."

So, not Shaw, and Hanna had known it wasn't Marlene or her mother because it was a man. However, that didn't mean one of the two women hadn't hired someone to do this.

The seconds crawled by while they waited, and Hanna tried to keep herself steady by watching the peaceful, rhythmic rise and fall of Evan's breathing. Unfortunately, it didn't cause much peace inside her because she couldn't stop thinking about those two men, and the person who'd hired them, putting her precious little boy in jeopardy.

"It's Jesse," Ava announced when she got a text. She went to the nursery door where Hanna heard her unlock it.

A moment later, Jesse walked in, and Hanna couldn't stop herself. She got out of the tub, hurried to him and clamped her arms around him. All the steeling up she'd done nearly vanished thanks to the relief at seeing he truly was unharmed.

"You're okay," Hanna murmured.

He nodded, ran his hand down the length of her hair and shifted his attention to his mom and Evan. "You can come back into the nursery now," he assured them, and they both helped Melissa out of the tub. "I locked up the house and reset the security. Ava will be staying inside with us until Grayson is sure the scene is secure."

That didn't help with the nerves. Someone else could be out there. But by now, Grayson probably had every available deputy either on scene or on the way.

When they were back in the nursery, Melissa immediately returned to the rocking chair. Maybe because, like Hanna, her legs were a little shaky. The rocking would also help to keep Evan asleep.

"Who are the gunmen?" Hanna asked him in a whisper so they wouldn't wake the baby.

Jesse shook his head. "I don't know either of them, and neither had any ID. Grayson will be taking the live one in for questioning, so we might know something soon."

"Maybe he'll want a deal and will give up the name of the person who sent him." She paused. "Someone did send them, right?"

"It looks that way. If they'd been local with a grudge against me, or you, I would have recognized them. Grayson can compare their photos to those of yet-to-be-identified militia members. We might get a match. Might get a match, too, when we run their prints."

Yes, because men like that probably had criminal records.

"I heard gunshots," Hanna said. "You're sure no one other than the gunman was hit?"

"Positive. The dead gunman fired two of the shots." He stopped, muttered some profanity, and she saw that was eating away at him as much as it was her. Those shots could have gone through the walls. "Grayson fired the third shot and killed him. The second man surrendered. Well, he surrendered after Grayson, me and the ranch hands all had our weapons pointed at him."

Jesse kept staring at her. "Did the sound of the shots trigger…anything for you?"

He was asking if she was on the verge of a panic attack. She wasn't, so Hanna shook her head. But she was well past the stage of being riled to the core.

"Where's my mother?" she asked.

"In her car with a ranch hand standing guard to make sure she stays put. She wants to see you, of course."

"Of course," Hanna mumbled. "I'll want to see her, too, and demand to know if she had any part in this."

Jesse did another of those soothing hand strokes, this time down her arm. "Trust me, I want to know the same thing." He hesitated a heartbeat. "Agent Shaw is out there, too."

Hanna groaned. "Why is he here? Did he have something to do with the gunmen?"

"He claims he just wanted to ask about what Marlene had told us," Jesse answered.

"You believe him?" she asked.

"Right now, I'm not inclined to believe him, Marlene, or your mother."

"I agree," Hanna couldn't say fast enough.

Jesse's phone dinged with a text, and he frowned when he read the message. "Grayson said your mother's been searched. She's not armed, and he wants to know if you want her to come inside for that chat?"

Hanna didn't have to debate that answer either. "Yes. Let's go ahead and get this over with."

She wanted to do this while the adrenaline was still high,

while she still had very vivid feelings of how close her son and Jesse could have come to being hurt today. Two shots. That's how many bullets Jesse said the gunman had fired.

Two shots that could have been deadly to anyone in the vicinity.

"If you don't mind, I'll just keep holding Evan instead of putting him in his crib," Melissa told them.

"Please do," Hanna agreed. "I'll come and get him when I finish talking to my mother."

"Good luck," Melissa whispered to her and, considering the conversation they'd just had, Jesse's mom no doubt knew this was not going to be a pleasant mother-daughter kind of chat.

Ava stayed put with Melissa while Jesse and she went to the front of the house. Jesse disengaged the security, unlocked the door and motioned to someone. Grayson, probably, because several moments later Isabel and he stepped onto the porch. Isabel actually froze, probably because she noted the expression on Hanna's face, but then she broke into a run and pulled Hanna into her arms.

"You're okay. Thank God, you're okay," Isabel said, her words rushing out. "I need to see Evan just to make sure he's all right, too."

"He's sleeping, and I don't want him disturbed." Hanna could hear the cold edge in her voice and didn't have plans to warm it up any time soon.

Isabel must have sensed the iciness, as well, because she let go of Hanna and backed up a few steps while she studied her face. Behind Isabel, Jesse went through the routine of locking up again—something Hanna was thankful for since she didn't want any other hired guns using this visit as a ploy to launch another attack.

"What's wrong?" Isabel asked.

Hanna nearly laughed. "You mean other than the obvious? Two gunmen came to my home, probably to try to kill Jesse or me, and one of them fired shots that could have hit Evan." Her voice had gotten louder with each word until Hanna nearly shouted the last part.

Isabel frantically shook her head. "You're acting as if I had something to do with that. I didn't." And she aimed a scalding glare at Jesse when he went to Hanna's side. "You're responsible for this—"

"Hush and answer some questions," Hanna said. She didn't shout this time, but she returned the glare that her mother had aimed at Jesse.

That caused Isabel's shoulders to snap back. "What is it you think I've done?"

"Oh, where to start," Hanna grumbled. "How about you explain why you just left the rehab facility without telling anyone? And why you haven't answered your phone. And while you're at it, explain why you did that when you should have been giving a Silver Creek deputy a statement about the investigation that could have prevented the shooting here today."

All right, so she hadn't totally gotten her voice under control; Hanna could hear the hard snarl in her tone. But it must have worked because Isabel didn't launch into more glaring and didn't aim any accusations at Jesse.

"I panicked," Isabel finally said, and she looked both disgusted with herself and ashamed. "I thought Deputy Ryland was there at the facility because I was a suspect in your attack. I had nothing to do with that," she stressed.

Hanna would put that last part on hold and stated the obvious. "If you're innocent, why run? Why not stay put, answer the deputy's questions, and clear your name?"

"Because he's a Ryland," Isabel railed. The venom had returned. "Maybe not in name, but he was raised by them. He's loyal to them. They've always had it in for me, and I wasn't going to sit there while Deputy Sheldon made false accusations."

Jesse lifted his hand as Hanna started to fire off another question, stunning Isabel by reciting the Miranda warning. That certainly didn't improve Isabel's mood, and she was spitting mad by the time he'd finished. But Hanna was glad he'd done it. If her mother did say something incriminating, she definitely wanted it used against her, to make sure she was punished for any wrongdoing.

"One of the things Deputy Sheldon intended to ask you about were some phone calls you got from Marlene. And before you say you didn't get them," Jesse added when Isabel opened her mouth, "you should know that we've seen the phone records and we know the calls were made."

Isabel closed her mouth and her jaw tightened. Hanna was pretty sure she'd been about to lie. "So what if Marlene and I talked? I told you we're in the same social circles, and every now and then we talk about parties, events and such."

Jesse kept his lethal cop's stare on her.

"All right," Isabel admitted grudgingly. "And sometimes I vented to her about Hanna and you, about how I didn't want the two of you together."

"Why Marlene?" Jesse persisted. "Did you believe she could do something to make sure Hanna stayed away from me?"

"No," her mother blurted. "Of course not. Like I said, I was just venting."

"The timing of that venting is suspicious," Jesse pointed out, not easing up on his stare. "One long phone call the day before Hanna was shot and two more the day after. It seems odd to me that you'd be *venting* about Hanna and me being together when your daughter was in the hospital fighting for her life."

Isabel's breath was gusting now and on a loud groan, she turned and sank down onto the sofa. "I felt guilty because I'd told Marlene those things. I was scared I was going to lose my daughter and my grandson, and I needed someone to talk to."

"And you chose to call someone in your social circle rather than a friend," Jesse reminded her.

"I don't have many friends," Isabel admitted on a heavy sigh. "And Marlene lives in Silver Creek, so she knows my history with your family. Some of my acquaintances don't."

The woman stopped, stayed quiet a moment. When she lifted her gaze to meet Jesse's, it was obvious she had calmed down some. Not Hanna though. Nothing her mother had said cleared her of suspicion.

"Look, I didn't have anything to do with the shooting and I've got nothing to do with the militia," Isabel insisted. "And I don't know why you think I'm connected to any of this. Those phone calls have nothing to do with what's going on. This is just you trying to poison my daughter's mind so she'll go back to you. Well, that's not going to work—"

"Stop," Hanna said when the images and sounds started to fly through her head. Memories, maybe. Of her mother's face when she'd been angry like this. Maybe when Hanna had told her she was pregnant with Jesse's child?

No.

Not then. In the flash that Hanna got, she was already

mega pregnant, so that was an argument they'd have had months earlier. This was something else. But it wasn't anything she could put her finger on.

"What is it?" Isabel slowly got to her feet. "Are you in pain? Did you—"

"Arnie and you used to be lovers," Hanna blurted out to stop her mother from asking more questions. "And you said something to him about Jesse and me."

The first part was true. Well, according to Marlene anyway. But the last part was a bluff, yet Hanna immediately saw that she'd hit the mark. The color blanched from Isabel's face and that's when Hanna realized it hadn't actually been a bluff after all. During that argument flashing through her head, she recalled her mother mentioning Arnie's name.

"Are you remembering…something?" Isabel asked. Still no color in her face and her voice was trembling.

"What did you say to Arnie about Jesse and me? And don't deny it," Hanna warned her. "I'm remembering enough to know if you're lying or not."

Isabel's throat worked when she swallowed. "I just thought Arnie could cause some trouble for Jesse, that's all."

That's all. Well, it didn't sound so innocent to Hanna, considering Arnie was a drug user and in the militia. And the flashes of memories weren't innocent either. She and her mother had had a full-fledged argument.

"What kind of trouble?" Hanna demanded, not taking her gaze off her mother.

"Nothing violent," Isabel rushed to say. She volleyed her attention between Jesse and her. "I swear, I didn't tell him to do anything violent. I sure as heck didn't tell him to drag my pregnant daughter out of her car and try to kill her."

Everything inside Hanna went still. And cold. An icy cold that went all the way to the bone.

"What did you tell him to do?" Hanna restated, enunciating each word through her now-clenched teeth.

Several moments crawled by before the woman spoke again. "I just warned him that if he didn't do something about Jesse that he was going to find himself in jail."

"When did you do that?" Jesse demanded. "When?" he snapped when Isabel turned away and started to cry.

"I told him that right before he went to the ranch and shot my daughter," Isabel muttered.

And with that confession, Isabel broke into a full sob.

Chapter Eleven

The adrenaline from the attack had come and gone, leaving Jesse with a fatigue that felt like he'd been drained dry. He was pretty sure Hanna was experiencing the same thing, but they were still doing what was necessary to take care of Evan while they waited for updates on the investigation.

Fortunately, the fatigue and stress didn't seem to be affecting Evan one bit. He was babbling and smiling while he ate his dinner in his high chair.

After Grayson had cleared the scene, Melissa and Ava had left, but the ranch hands and a reserve deputy stayed on the grounds to keep watch. Jesse hoped they wouldn't be necessary, that whoever was behind the attack wouldn't send someone else to try to finish the job, but he would keep the backup in place until he was sure it was safe.

Whenever the heck that would be.

At least they didn't have to deal with Isabel. After her tear-filled confession, she'd finally left with Grayson to give a statement on the info she'd withheld after Hanna's shooting. Info that Isabel kept insisting wasn't relevant, that it wasn't the reason Arnie had dragged Hanna out of her car.

But Jesse had heard the doubt in the woman's voice.

Had seen it on her face.

Despite what she was saying, Isabel did indeed blame herself. Of course, that particular layer of guilt might be just the tip of the iceberg because they still hadn't been able to rule her out as a suspect. He couldn't necessarily see her running a militia, but it was possible she was somehow involved with it. The fact that she'd had contact with Arnie at the time of Hanna's shooting proved that Isabel had stayed in touch with him. She might have been connected to other members as well.

At least nothing the woman had told them would have been eavesdropped on because of a listening device. Grayson had called in a favor and managed to get a CSI over to Hanna's to do a search for a bug that Agent Shaw might have planted. Nothing had turned up.

In the grand scheme of things, that didn't seem like a solid victory, but Hanna had been through enough. Jesse hadn't wanted her to feel even more violated because Shaw or someone else had been listening in on their private conversations.

Evan giggled when Hanna repeated some baby babble back to him, and it yanked Jesse from his worries. He hadn't had many moments like this with Hanna and Evan, and he wanted to hold on to them. Wanted to hold on to Hanna, too. That kiss had been a good start in that happening, but he knew he was a long way from this time together being the norm. First, he had to make things safe for them, and then he could start dealing with the more personal aspects of his life.

Hanna's phone dinged, so Jesse took over feeding the baby while she read the message. "It's from my doctor," she told him. "He set me up for a hypnosis appointment day after tomorrow in San Antonio." She shook her head. "I can't go. Not with things so uncertain here."

Jesse had been about to suggest the same thing, but Hanna had already started to reply to the text. Yes, it was important for her to get her memory back, but they could be attacked en route to and from the appointment.

"Going to my house on the ranch is still an option," Jesse ventured.

He didn't need to spell out why he knew she was hesitant to go there, but she didn't immediately dismiss it as she'd done the other time he'd brought it up. "Maybe in the morning," she agreed, though he could see her trying to steady herself for having to face the security gate where Arnie had taken her at gunpoint.

Jesse was about to try to assure her that it would be okay, but his phone rang. Not Unknown Caller, thank God, because he was too tired to deal with a chat with Bull tonight.

"It's Grayson." Jesse let her know. "Should I put it on speaker?" he added, tipping his head to Evan. Of course, their son wouldn't understand what was being said, but Jesse wanted to make sure Hanna was okay with it.

"Speaker," Hanna verified with a nod.

"Please tell me you have good news," Jesse told Grayson when he answered, adding that Hanna was listening.

"Some. We got IDs on the two attackers. The dead guy is Vince Lutz, and the one we have in custody is Jeremy Cowen. Both have records. Both belong to a militia in Oklahoma. Their group apparently did business with the one here."

That explained why the men hadn't looked familiar to Jesse. "Who hired them?"

"Don't know. Not yet. Cowen says he doesn't know, that he was doing Lutz a favor by going to Hanna's."

Jesse bit on the profanity that came with the jolt of anger. "*A favor?*" he snarled. "One that endangered a baby."

Grayson made a sound to indicate he was in perfect agreement with Jesse's anger. "Cowen claims he had no idea that a baby was in the house, that Lutz told him they were just going there to scare somebody who was ratting out members of the militia. He also said it was Lutz who fired the shots, but we're having both men's guns tested."

That was standard procedure, though Jesse didn't care which of them had pulled the trigger. He wanted Cowen to be charged with attempted murder, child endangerment, trespassing and any other charges Grayson could tack onto those.

"Cowen put a stop to the interview when I pressed him for details about how Lutz and he had gotten those orders," Grayson explained. "He then asked for a lawyer."

It surprised Jesse that the man hadn't lawyered up right away since he'd been caught at the scene, and he'd been armed. With his record, he had to know he was going to land in jail.

"Theo requested Hanna's phone records," Grayson continued a moment later, "and they arrived about a half hour ago. I've been going through them while I'm waiting for Cowen's lawyer to show. Hanna, do you have any recollection of Agent Shaw calling you the day you were shot?"

Jesse could tell from the way her breath stalled that the answer to that was no. "He didn't mention it either."

"Was it a long call?" Hanna asked.

"Twelve minutes, so long enough. I can contact him and ask what you two talked about," Grayson offered.

"Let me do that after we get Evan down for the night," Jesse said. "That way, Hanna will be able to hear what he has to say. I'll let you know, too."

"Thanks. Oh, and just a heads-up, Dad might be coming over there tonight. Melissa ordered Evan a bunch of books and toys, and he might drop them off. He said if it was late, he'd just leave the stuff on the porch."

Well, it wasn't late, not really, but Boone might go the porch route since he'd know that it was already past Evan's bedtime. Still, the hands would alert Jesse that his father had arrived, so he'd go out and have a quick chat with him to try to assure him that he had things under control.

That might or might not be the truth.

Boone had to be feeling the motherlode of guilt right now because he would be blaming himself for what had happened to Hanna. And for what was still happening to her. It wasn't his fault that Arnie had snapped but, like Jesse, he hadn't been able to stop Hanna from getting hurt. That kind of guilt stayed with you.

As Jesse well knew.

Grayson and he ended the call while Hanna took Evan from the high chair and started the nightly routine of getting the baby ready for bed. First, there was a very messy bath with lots of laughter and splashing, and once he was dry and in his footed PJs, Hanna fed him a bottle while Jesse sat in the kitchen and read through Grayson's initial report on the two gunmen.

Even though the background on both men was thorough, Jesse just couldn't see how they'd crossed paths with any of their suspects. Then again, there probably wouldn't be anything obvious that could give the cops that particular link, but there might be something in the financials to show an unusual transfer of funds. After all, hired guns weren't cheap.

He looked up when Hanna came back in, and Jesse saw that she was still looking exhausted. Still looking amazing, too, as she usually did, but he pushed that aside and held up his phone.

"Are you ready for me to call Agent Shaw, or do you need to try to settle first?" he asked.

"Make the call." On a heavy sigh, she sat next to him at the counter. "The problem is I won't know if he's lying about why he contacted me."

"Maybe not, but just hearing what he has to say might trigger something. The way it did when you were talking to your mother."

In hindsight, he wished he'd held back on that reminder because it seemed to add to her weariness. Still, she motioned for him to make the call, so that's what Jesse did. The agent answered on the first ring.

"The sheriff is stonewalling me about talking to the man he has in custody," Shaw immediately groused.

"That's between the sheriff and you," Jesse responded, and he didn't pause even a heartbeat before he continued. "Why did you call Hanna the day she was shot?"

There was a long pause, followed by some muffled profanity. "Well, it wasn't to tell her that I was dirty or that I had ordered a hit on her. Judging from your tone, though, that's what you think."

"I'm not sure what I think yet," Jesse countered. "I just want to know about that call. And FYI, Hanna has remembered some details about it, so don't bother to lie."

Shaw's next pause was significantly longer and Jesse wished he could see the man's face to try to figure out how he was handling the threat. A bogus threat since Hanna didn't actually have memories of that particular conversation.

"I called Hanna because of her mother's connection to Arnie," Shaw finally said. "I thought maybe Hanna had overheard something I could use to start closing down the militia. Bull had been undercover there too long, and he wasn't reporting as regularly as he should have been. I was worried about him."

"And what did I tell you about Arnie and my mother?" Hanna challenged. Despite the fatigue, she'd managed to add a threatening tone to her voice.

"Nothing. That's the truth," Shaw said when Jesse huffed. "Hanna claimed she didn't know her mother had ever been involved with Arnie."

"But you knew," Jesse said. "How'd you find out?"

"Marlene. She mentioned it in an interview I did with her when I was trying to learn if she was aware of any illegal militia activity in the area."

It seemed an odd thing for Marlene to bring up when talking with a federal agent, but maybe Shaw had said something that'd prompted her to include it.

"Funny that you'd talk to Marlene about that and not the Silver Creek sheriff's office," Jesse pointed out.

This time it was Shaw who huffed. "I've already said I was worried about Bull, and I thought I could subtly question Marlene to find out if she thought there'd been a change in her brother's behavior."

"And?" Jesse pressed when Shaw didn't add anything to that.

"She said she had seen some changes in him and thought he wasn't paying as much attention to his business as he should. Plus, she didn't like that he was keeping company with Arnie."

Considering Arnie's known drug use, that last part made sense. "Did she have any suspicions that he was a deep cover agent?"

"None," Shaw insisted. Then he paused. "Well, none that she shared with me anyway. Bull kept it secret that he was ATF because he always wanted deep cover. He especially wanted to infiltrate this particular militia and put a stop to it. He didn't think an outsider would be trusted as much as someone like him who was from the area."

Or maybe Bull chose it so he could play both sides. The militia had been around for years, maybe even decades, so it was likely that Bull knew more members than just Arnie. He could fake doing his deep cover assignment while profiting big-time from the sale of guns and such. That way, Bull could also make sure the group wasn't about to be brought down.

"When can I interview the man the sheriff has in custody?" Shaw finally asked.

"Again, that's between the sheriff and you," Jesse clarified.

Shaw grumbled something he didn't catch and ended the call. Probably to contact Grayson.

"If Shaw is the one who sent those gunmen here," Hanna said, "he could want to talk to the surviving one to make sure he doesn't rat him out."

Jesse gave a quick nod because that thought had already occurred to him. Shaw wouldn't even have to threaten the guy. Just by showing up, the gunman would know that Shaw could kill him before he talked to the cops.

Hanna leaned closer to him. "You really believe Marlene didn't know her brother was ATF?"

"Hard to say. I'm not sure how close they were, or still are."

But Jesse doubted Bull had traveled in those same *social circles* that Isabel and Marlene did. Even before Bull left Silver Creek, Jesse had always thought of him as a loner, and that impression of him had remained when Bull moved back three years ago.

Hanna's sigh was loaded with fatigue and frustration, but she must have seen he was feeling the same way because she brushed her hand down his arm. A gesture he'd done earlier to try and soothe *her*.

"I hate what's happening," she said, "but I'm glad you're here. I don't think I could get through this without you."

Oh, man. That gave him a punch of emotion. Not of their usual heat. But of the feelings that he'd failed to protect her six months ago, and he couldn't fail Evan and her again.

He stood, pulling her into his arms and brushing one of those chaste, and hopefully comforting, kisses on the top of her head. She didn't melt against him this time though. She stayed a little stiff when she looked up at him. It seemed to Jesse that she had something to say. What, exactly, he didn't know, but she didn't speak.

She kissed him instead.

Her mouth came to his, not some tentative, testing-the-waters gesture. Hanna kissed him the way she had the night they'd had sex. Holding back nothing. Diving right into the fiery-hot attraction.

It didn't take Jesse long to shift from the "guilt/comfort" mode to this and, despite the bad timing, he welcomed it. He needed this from her. The heat, the need. Because it felt like forgiveness, too. As if Hanna might be able to get past what had happened to her. Of course, that could be all wishful thinking on his part.

Soon, he wasn't able to think at all because she deepened the kiss and dragged him closer, tightening her grip around him. Jesse took things from there. He did some dragging of his own so he could feel her body against his. So he could take in her scent. Her taste. So he could deepen the kiss and cause the heat to skyrocket.

Even though Hanna likely couldn't remember this, Jesse experienced some déjà vu. The instant, soaring need. This fire that blazed between them. Suddenly, they couldn't get close enough to each other, and the deep kisses were fueling the flames higher and higher until he had to have more than just her mouth. Jesse slid his hand between them, cupped her breast and swiped his thumb over her nipple.

Hanna made a familiar sound. A low, throaty moan that revved up his body even more. Of course, he hadn't needed that, not with this primal ache spreading through him. An ache demanding that he take her now, now, now. But thankfully he managed to hold on to a shred of common sense.

And that's why he broke the kiss, why he quit touching her, and he pulled back.

"I can take you to bed," he said, looking her straight in the eyes, "but I have to make sure it's what you want. Not what your body wants," he amended when she gave a dry laugh. "I just don't want you to have any regrets."

Oh, it'd cost him to say all of that, and a certain part of his body thought he was pretty damn stupid to even bring it up. But this was Hanna, the mother of his son. The woman he was certain he loved. A round of sex would no doubt be amazing and burn off some of this fatigue, but he couldn't have it putting up more barriers between them if Hanna regretted it. There'd been enough barriers, and this dangerous situation had helped lower them. Jesse wanted to keep them down, and maybe, just maybe, they could have a future together.

He could see the debate she was having with her own body, but she didn't get a chance to voice her decision because his phone rang. The sound was a jolt that broke the tension, and the moment was lost. Since it could be Grayson with an update, or one of the hands reporting a problem, Jesse had no choice but to drag his phone from his pocket. But it wasn't them. Unknown Caller was on the screen.

"Bull," he grumbled. Jesse so wasn't in the mood to deal with him tonight, but he set up the record function and answered the call.

"I had no part in this," Bull immediately said. "I want you to know that."

"No part in what?" Jesse demanded.

"Your father. Boone," Bull blurted. "He's on his way to Hanna's place, and somebody's going to try to kidnap him."

Jesse threw off the slam of worry and anger. "Who's going to try to do that?" he roared.

"Not sure, but you need to get him some help fast." That was it; the only info Bull gave him before he ended the call.

Jesse quickly pressed his father's number, and his stomach muscles hardened when Boone didn't answer. "Call Grayson and let him know what Bull just said," he instructed Hanna, and he kept listening to the rings, kept praying, until Boone finally answered.

The relief came.

But it was short-lived when Jesse heard Boone's voice.

"I was driving to Hanna's when somebody plowed into

the side of my truck," Boone said, his words rushing together. "It was one of those big SUVs, and it flew out from one of the ranch trails. He tried to run me off the road."

Hell. It was true. Someone was after his father. "Are you all right? Were you hurt?"

"I'm okay. I didn't stop or end up in the ditch, but neither did the SUV. It's following me, and I don't want to take this to Hanna's doorstep."

Jesse didn't especially want that either, but it was their best option. "There's a deputy and ranch hands here. I'll alert them that you'll be driving in. I don't think the SUV will come onto the grounds once they see the armed men."

At least, he hoped they wouldn't, and he put his father on hold while he texted Miguel Navarro to let him know that trouble might be arriving soon.

"Grayson's on the way," Hanna relayed once Jesse was back on the line with his father.

Good, because that meant they could maybe sandwich in the SUV and find out who the hell was behind this. But just in case the person or persons behind the kidnapping scheme started shooting, Jesse had to tell Hanna something that was going to put the fear right back in her eyes.

"You'll need to take Evan into the bathroom again," he said.

She nodded, sucked in a hard breath and hurried in that direction. Since she knew the drill, she'd secure and stay down, but Jesse hated to have to put Hanna and the baby through this again.

Jesse whipped his attention back to the phone when he heard the loud crash. "The SUV rammed into my truck again," Boone reported.

That tightened every muscle in Jesse's body, and he had a

too vivid image of his father fighting the steering wheel just to stay on the road. It twisted away at Jesse that he couldn't storm out to help him, but that could be a fatal mistake for Hanna and Evan. Because whoever was doing this could want to use this to get to them.

"How far out are you?" Jesse asked, trying to keep his voice level. He hurried to the window to keep watch.

"A half mile," Boone answered just as Jesse heard another loud bang. The sound of metal crunching into metal. The SUV had plowed into him again.

Boone was no doubt going as fast as he could on the rural road, and that meant he would be here in only a couple of minutes. Minutes that would no doubt feel like an eternity.

"Can you describe the SUV?" Jesse asked. It was info he needed, but he also wanted to hear his father's voice, to make sure he wasn't hurt and was still capable of talking.

"A black Chevy Suburban, late model, with a reinforced bumper. I tried to get a look at the license plate, but it's been smeared with mud or something."

It didn't surprise him that his father had noticed all of that—even while he was under attack. Boone was in a family of lawmen, and he wasn't the sort to panic. Good thing, because it was obvious he was in grave danger.

"I'm guessing they obscured the license plate since it can be traced back to somebody who doesn't want to be traced. Or else it's stolen, and they don't want the cops seeing it and trying to pull them over," Boone added, and he was spot-on with that theory.

There was another loud crash, and Jesse heard his father ground out some profanity. He also heard the squeal of tires. He couldn't see the end of Hanna's driveway because of the trees, but this had to be his father. Well, unless the would-be kidnappers had sent another team to try to get to Hanna and him. Either way, Jesse drew his gun and went to the door. He disarmed the security system so he could open it and take aim.

That's when Jesse heard something else he darn sure didn't want to hear.

Gunfire.

Two shots had come from the vicinity of the end of the driveway, and he prayed the bullets hadn't hit his father. Seconds later, Boone's familiar red truck came into sight. He didn't stop in front of the house though. His father continued past to the far side of the property, to a cluster of trees. A position he'd no doubt chosen because it would keep the gunfire away from the house.

And on him.

Boone could be gunned down.

Jesse stepped out from cover, his gaze firing toward the other end of the driveway where the SUV could be approaching. But it wasn't. Just the opposite. There was a slash of headlights cutting through the darkness, and that's when he knew the vehicle was turning around. Trying to escape.

Again, Jesse had to fight the overwhelming urge to go after them and make them pay for what they'd just tried to do. But he couldn't take that risk. Besides, these could be more henchmen, like the one Grayson already had in custody, and there was too much at stake with Hanna and Evan for him to go after a long shot.

"I'm okay," his father assured him when he got out of his truck. Boone had a gun, and he was already taking aim down the driveway. So were two of the ranch hands and the reserve deputy. "They're running away like the cowards they are," Boone grumbled.

Cowards who didn't mind killing or endangering the life of a baby.

Yeah, they were going to pay. Jesse wasn't sure how to make that happen, not yet, but he'd figure out a way.

"I'm real sorry about this," Boone said, limping his way toward Jesse.

The apology riled Jesse because it wasn't necessary. This wasn't his father's fault. He'd simply gotten caught up in the crosshairs of this mess. But the limp cooled Jesse's anger.

"You said you weren't hurt," Jesse pointed out.

"I'm not. I just banged my knee when the cowards rammed into me. Are Hanna and Evan all right?"

Jesse nodded. Well, they were as all right as they could be. Hanna was probably terrified and huddled in the bathtub with Evan.

"Let Grayson know what happened once he gets here," Jesse shouted out to the deputy and the hands. Grayson would likely want to go in pursuit of the SUV or at least make some calls for a BOLO on the vehicle. He rattled off the specs Boone had given him so Grayson would know what he was looking for.

"And tell Grayson I'm not hurt," Boone added so that his son wouldn't worry. But Jesse intended to verify that Boone was indeed unharmed.

Jesse got Boone inside the house as fast as he could and shut the door so he could reset the security system. He didn't want a hired thug trying to sneak through one of the windows while the alarm was off.

"So, what the heck just happened?" Boone immediately asked. "Who tried to run me off the road?"

"I don't know, but it's possible we can get something from

the man Grayson has in custody. I'm pretty sure somebody in the militia is behind this."

Boone shook his head in disgust, but he obviously wasn't surprised. Everything that had gone on seemed to lead right back to the militia and their illegal activities.

"Let me tell Hanna what's going on," Jesse said, but he'd barely made it a step when he glanced out the window and saw the bobbing of headlights coming up the driveway.

Jesse drew the gun he'd just holstered. Beside him, Boone did the same.

"It's probably just Grayson," Boone muttered.

But one look at the vehicle and Jesse knew that it wasn't. This was an old blue truck, and when it came to a stop, the hands and the deputy all took aim.

"It's me," someone shouted. "Don't shoot."

Jesse watched as Bull stepped out. He put his hands on his head and stayed in place.

"Don't shoot," Bull called out again. "I'm here to surrender."

Chapter Twelve

Hanna eased Evan back into his crib and stood there to make sure he was truly asleep. He was. In fact, he'd hardly stirred when she'd made the mad rush earlier to get him into the bathroom when Boone was being attacked. Evan had stayed asleep through the entire ordeal and maybe that would continue while they got through the next couple of hours.

When Jesse had come into the bathroom to tell her it was safe to leave and that his father was okay, he'd given her the shocking news that Bull had come to her house to surrender. Hanna had no idea if that was true or if this was some kind of ploy on his part. If it was a ruse, though, she figured that Jesse would keep things under control.

She could hear the murmur of voices at the front of the house. Jesse's, Boone's. And Bull's. Yes, he was actually in her house. The man who'd been part of her nearly being killed was here.

Just yards away.

Jesse had explained that was necessary since he didn't want to be standing out in the open with Bull while waiting for Grayson and backup to arrive, and that none of the vehicles on scene were bullet resistant since the reserve deputy had come in his own truck. Hanna hadn't wanted Jesse or Boone at risk like that, either, but she was certain she had surprised Jesse when she'd told him she had wanted to speak to Bull. This wasn't just about confronting her fears or facing her nightmares. She wanted some answers, and she hoped that Bull would give them to her.

Hanna started out of the nursery, but her phone vibrated with an incoming call. She glanced at the screen, saw that it was her mother and considered letting it go to voice mail. But then she sighed and answered it because it was possible Isabel had heard about the attempted kidnapping and wanted to make sure Evan and she hadn't been hurt.

"We're okay," Hanna said the moment she answered.

"Why wouldn't you be?" Isabel asked just as quickly. "Did something else happen?"

Hanna groaned and mentally kicked herself. She decided not to hold back the truth since Isabel would hear about it anyway. Or maybe she already knew and this call was about playing the "I'm innocent" routine.

"Someone tried to kidnap Boone," Hanna explained. "He got away."

She didn't add the rest about Bull showing up and surrendering to Jesse. Best to keep that under wraps until Bull was actually away from the house and behind bars. Hanna didn't want to give hired guns, or anyone else, a reason to come here looking for the man.

"See, the Rylands are magnets for trouble," Isabel grumbled. "I know things aren't good between us right now, but I wish you'd bring Evan here where you'll both be safe."

Hanna so didn't have time for this. And she wasn't putting on the kid gloves to give Isabel a kind response. "You're right. Things aren't good between us right now, and it's because you didn't tell me the truth."

"I didn't tell you because I thought it would upset you," Isabel argued. "And it did. Listen, if you want me to feel bad because I was involved with Arnie, then know that I feel bad. I'm sorry I ever met the man, sorry that I talked to him, and I'm especially sorry that he almost killed you."

Hanna wanted to say "Good" and end the call, but she reminded herself that her mother might not be a devious criminal. She might only be guilty of bad judgment with a bad man. So that's why she eased back on her tone.

"I have to go," Hanna said. "We'll talk soon."

Isabel didn't try to change her mind or stay on the line. She simply muttered a goodbye and ended the call.

Hanna tucked the baby monitor in her pocket and, after a few deep breaths, made her way from the nursery to the living room. She immediately spotted Bull. He was kneeling on the floor with his hands tucked behind his head while Jesse and Boone kept guns trained on him.

Jesse looked over at her when he heard her footsteps, and she saw the instant disapproval on his face. He hadn't wanted her to go through this. Hadn't thought it was necessary. And he might be right. This could all be for nothing.

Bull's gaze met hers, too, and he didn't sneer or snarl, as she'd expected. In fact, there was nothing defiant about his expression or body language.

"I'm sorry," Bull immediately said.

She didn't ask if he was apologizing for the shooting or because of all the other havoc. Instead, she looked at Jesse. "How did Bull know someone would try to kidnap Boone?" she asked.

"He claims he got the info through a militia member he's still in contact with. A guy named Hector Ames."

"It's true," Bull insisted, but neither Boone nor Jesse

spared him a glance. "Hector's not happy with some of the things the militia has done, so I've stayed in touch with him."

"Grayson will be pulling Hector in for a chat about that very soon," Jesse added.

"Where's Grayson?" Hanna wanted to know.

"He went in pursuit of the SUV, and he followed it out to the interstate where he lost it. He's making his way back here so he can transport Bull to jail."

"The Silver Creek jail," Bull insisted. "You can't turn me over to federal custody because I'm not sure who I can trust."

"Welcome to the club," Hanna mumbled, but that wasn't exactly true. She knew she could trust Jesse, Boone and the other Rylands. She just wasn't so sure about everyone else.

Especially Bull.

Leveling her breathing as much as she could, Hanna walked closer to stand shoulder to shoulder with Jesse so she could stare down at Bull. Facing her own personal bogeyman.

"Tell me what happened the night I was shot," she said, and it wasn't a request. It was a demand.

Bull ground out a single word of raw profanity. "I was hoping you could tell me. I was hoping you'd gotten your memory back."

"I regained some of it," she told him and went with the threat she'd already used. "Enough of it that I'll know if you're lying."

Bull groaned. "You need to remember all of it. Because I'm damn sure you saw or heard something I didn't."

Maybe she had. That's what her gut was telling her anyway. But nothing she'd done so far had caused those particular memories to return. Perhaps talking with Bull would help with that.

"Go over everything that happened," Hanna insisted.

"I didn't lie when I was taken into custody," Bull argued. "I just didn't include certain things. Like the fact that I was ATF, because someone would have killed me right off. Somebody in the militia would have gotten to me, and since I didn't know who was pulling the strings there, I wouldn't have been able to watch my back."

"Everything that happened that night," she repeated. "I want to hear it."

Obviously, Bull had wanted her to be the one to provide the answers. Exactly what answers, she didn't know, but he was going to have to wait on that. Maybe forever if her memory never fully returned.

"Like I told Jesse, the sheriff, and every ATF agent and deputy who asked me after I was arrested, Arnie called me that night to say he was going to the ranch to have it out with Boone and Jesse. He was certain he was about to be arrested."

"He was," Jesse verified. "So were you and any other militia members we could round up."

"Yeah, well, Arnie had gotten wind of that, and he was spitting mad. And high. Not a good combination, so I told him to pick me up and we'd go together. I thought I could talk him out of doing something stupid." Bull paused, cursed again. "Needless to say, I failed."

"Yes, you did," Hanna agreed. "Keep going."

Bull didn't dodge her gaze, but his jaw muscles were tight and flexing. "I tried to calm Arnie down by saying we should go get a beer or something and work out a plan. That if we just showed up at the security gate, the hands probably wouldn't let us onto the ranch. But Arnie said we'd just break down the gate or go over the fence. He was determined to get to Boone and you."

Jesse huffed. "And at this point you didn't think to call me? Or Grayson? Or your handler in the ATF to warn us of Arnie's intentions?"

"I didn't know if I could trust you to keep it quiet that I was deep cover."

"You could have," Jesse assured him. "We aren't dirty cops."

"No, but I didn't know that, did I? And, as for my handler…well, that was Shaw." Bull snarled. "No way was I going to trust him."

"Why not?" Jesse pressed, but he held up his hand to put the pause on Bull's answer when they all heard a vehicle stop in front of the house. "Grayson's here."

Boone kept his gun trained on Bull while Jesse went to the door to let in the sheriff. Grayson stepped in, and he made a sweeping glance around the room.

"Are Evan and you all right?" Grayson asked her.

Hanna nodded, and Grayson did a repeat of the question to his dad. Boone nodded, too, but when Grayson glanced down at Boone's leg, Hanna knew that someone, probably Jesse, had told him of their father's possible injury. She was betting Boone would soon be making a trip to the ER to be examined.

"Bull here was just telling us how he already knew he couldn't trust Shaw the night Hanna was shot. Oh, and FYI, I read him the Miranda again in case he forgot his rights."

That earned Jesse a brief scowl from Bull, but obviously the man wanted to get on with his account. "I couldn't confide in Shaw because I thought maybe he'd made some side deals with the militia. There was talk that an insider was looking out for them. Things like making sure they were warned of a raid before it happened. That sort of warning could have come from someone in the ATF."

"It could have come from other people, too," Jesse pointed out. "But you zoomed in on Shaw. Any proof of one of those side deals?"

"None. I was trying to get the truth when Arnie went off the deep end and stormed out to your family's ranch."

"A ranch where I just happened to be," Hanna remarked. "What made Arnie go after me and pull me out of my car?"

Bull hesitated again, but he didn't seem to be trying to come up with a story she'd buy. Then again, he was a trained federal agent, a deep cover one, so he had been trained to lie.

"Did it have anything to do with my mother?" she straightforwardly asked.

She carefully watched Bull for his reaction, and what she didn't see was surprise. "Arnie mentioned that he'd talked to your mother," Bull finally said. "He didn't say about what." He stopped again, stared at her. "You think your mother had something to do with Arnie shooting you?"

"Do you?" she countered just as fast.

"No." But there was doubt in his voice. "Did Isabel have anything to do with what happened?"

"I'm not sure," she admitted. "What did Arnie say about the talk he'd had with her?"

Bull shook his head in a gesture to indicate he was thinking about that. "Nothing specific. He said something about Isabel having called him and he went over to see her. They had drinks. Gin and tonics," he added. "He said they were strong, and he was woozy when he left."

Hanna glanced at Jesse and saw that he had the same

question she did. Had Isabel drugged Arnie? Of course, she wouldn't have actually had to hide the drugs since Arnie was a user, but maybe Isabel had given him enough booze, drugs, or a combination of them, in the hope that he'd go after Jesse.

And that was what he did.

The theory fit. Well, it did if she could actually wrap her mind around the image of the prim and snobby Isabel setting up something so sinister. Hanna wasn't quite able to do that, but it didn't mean she believed Isabel was innocent. At a minimum, she'd provoked Arnie. It was possible she'd incited him so that he'd no longer known what he was doing.

"Other than Arnie, I never heard any of the other militia members talk about Isabel," Bull volunteered. He was still staring at her. "But if you think she was connected, then I need to know."

"Who did the militia members talk about?" Jesse asked Bull before Hanna had to answer. Good thing, too, since she hadn't been sure what to say.

Bull huffed and adjusted his position on the floor. He continued to keep his hands tucked behind his head. "You've arrested the big guns of the operation, and I've already given you Hector's name."

"But you haven't given us the biggest name," Grayson interjected. "You haven't told us who's actually running it."

"Because I don't know," Bull snapped. He repeated it, but this time there wasn't anger in his voice but rather frustration.

Hanna didn't want to empathize with the man she'd feared and hated all these months, but she did on that one point. Until they knew the identity of the person running this deadly show, none of them would be safe. Bull included. Because she believed him when he'd said that someone would try to kill him. The head of the militia would want him dead for sure. Maybe a dirty agent like Shaw would as well.

"Go over the rest of what happened that night," Jesse prompted when the room fell silent. "You and Arnie arrived at the gate to the ranch, and you saw Hanna. Why'd Arnie take her from her car?"

"Did I say something to provoke him?" Hanna added, and that caused Jesse to look at her. He was silently assuring her that she hadn't been responsible in any way, but Bull's expression said differently.

"I don't know for sure," Bull admitted. "You said something to him when he threw open the passenger's-side door, but I suspect you just asked him what the heck he was doing. Or something along those lines. Before that, he was ranting and carrying on, and then the next thing I knew, he bolted out of his truck and ran to your car. He pulled the gun and had you in a chokehold before I could stop him."

Since those were the images on the security camera, Hanna had no problem reliving those moments, and even though her mind had blocked out the actual memories, she could sense down to the bone the fear she'd felt. She had been terrified for her baby.

"Then what?" Jesse insisted. There was fresh anger in his voice now, no doubt because he was reliving all of this right along with her. He'd been terrified for Evan, too. And her. She didn't need memories to know that.

Bull took a long breath before he answered. "Arnie tried to take Hanna back to his truck, but he dropped his keys. He was mumbling and cursing, and when we heard someone from the ranch coming to the gate, he said we had to get the hell out of there. I didn't think he meant to drag Hanna along. I figured he'd just start running for the woods, but he took her."

"And you didn't stop him," Jesse snapped.

"It happened fast, and I didn't want to get into a struggle with him because I was afraid the gun would go off. Hell, by then Arnie had it aimed at her head."

"The gun did go off," Hanna noted pointedly.

Bull nodded, sighed. "Within seconds after we got into that thick cluster of trees. It was dark, so I don't know if the shooting was an accident. I think it was," he added, not sounding convinced of that either. "You fell, and Arnie went into a full panic. He was going to pull the trigger again, he said so you wouldn't be able to tell anyone he'd been the one to shoot you. That's when I shot and killed him."

Hanna studied his face and went through all of that word by word. She so wished she had a lie detector to know if Bull was telling the truth or if something else had gone on. She knew from reading the reports that the lab had matched the bullets. The one in her head to Arnie's weapon. The one in Arnie to Bull's gun. So that meshed with the story Bull had told, but again her gut said Bull was leaving something out.

"I know something else happened," Hanna insisted, and it wasn't a bluff this time. "Tell me."

Bull certainly didn't jump to deny that. "I'm pretty sure somebody else was there in those trees. Somebody other than you, me and Arnie."

Both Grayson and Boone muttered some profanity. They were obviously angry and disgusted that Bull hadn't told them this earlier.

"Who?" Jesse challenged.

"I didn't see the person," Bull insisted, "but I got a glimpse of a gun. Aimed at me. I dropped to the ground, trying to get into a position to defend myself, when you and your cousin arrived on scene. The person must have run off."

"And what reason do you have for not telling us this before now?" Jesse asked, his question filled with sarcasm and anger.

"Because I thought it was Shaw," Bull admitted. "Because if I'd told you I believed it was him, then I'd have to explain how I knew an ATF agent. I didn't want my cover blown. I figured it was best if I kept on letting everyone believe I was in the militia so I could keep gathering info about the leader."

"You thought it was Shaw," Jesse muttered. "Was it him?"

"I had my lawyer ask him. I couldn't talk to Shaw myself because I didn't want anyone making the connection between him and me. Anyway, Shaw said no, that he wasn't there that night."

"You believe him?" Hanna asked.

Bull stayed quiet a long time. "Yeah. About that anyway. I still think he could be dirty and playing both sides of this, but to the best of my knowledge, Shaw didn't know that Arnie would be going to the Silver Creek Ranch. There's only one person who for sure knew that Arnie would be going to the ranch to confront Boone and Jesse."

Everything inside Hanna tightened. "My mother?"

Bull shook his head. "I don't think she knew the timing of when Arnie would be there. Could be wrong and Arnie might have told her he was heading straight for the ranch when they were drinking. But someone else knew." He paused again. "My sister, Marlene."

Chapter Thirteen

Marlene.

Jesse didn't like that the woman's name kept coming up in connection with the shooting and the militia. But Bull obviously thought the connection was there.

"How would Marlene have known that you and Arnie would be at the ranch at that specific time?" Jesse demanded.

"Because I told her," Bull admitted. "She was at my place when Arnie called, and she would have heard me trying to calm him down. I specifically told him not to go to the ranch, and we argued about it. It wouldn't have taken much for her to piece together where we were going when Arnie got to my house."

No, it wouldn't have taken much, but Jesse still wasn't convinced. "If you're saying your sister followed Arnie and you, and that she aimed a gun at you, then you must believe she's part of the militia."

Bull's jaw went to iron. "She very well could be. I just don't know." He groaned, cursed. "I don't want to believe she'd kill me, or anyone for that matter, but she might have considered it if she found out I was an agent. Or if she thought I was going to rat out the militia."

Again, Jesse wasn't convinced, but he had no intention

of dismissing Bull's theory. If Marlene was involved in the militia, she might indeed have wanted to silence anyone who could have spilled secrets about the illegal operations in the group. In her mind, both Bull and Arnie could have done just that if they'd been arrested and interrogated.

"Anything else you want to ask him?" Grayson offered, glancing first at Hanna, then at Jesse and finally at Boone. When the three of them shook their heads, Grayson took out his handcuffs. "All right, then I'll go ahead and get Bull to jail." He put the cuffs on Bull's wrists.

"You won't be doing that alone," Jesse insisted.

Grayson tipped his head to the driveway. "Ava and Theo are already waiting out there, and they'll be my backup. I'm leaving the ranch hands and a reserve deputy here in case there's another round of trouble. If you need more ranch hands, just let me know," he added to Jesse.

"Wait," Bull said when Grayson hauled him to his feet. "I've got a plan. It's risky, but hell, just about everything we do at this point will be."

"What plan?" Again, Jesse didn't bother to tone down the skepticism.

Bull glanced at Grayson. "Are you sure you can stop someone from trying to kill me when I'm behind bars?"

Grayson gave him a flat look. "You'll be protected. Neither I nor any of my deputies has ties to the militia."

He said that with complete confidence because Jesse knew it was true. Like Grayson, he trusted every one of his fellow lawmen with his life. They'd die if it came to protecting a prisoner. Even someone like Bull.

"Then, let's go with that," Bull continued. "You'll guarantee protection, and I'll lay the groundwork to draw this snake out. Even if that snake happens to be my sister." He tacked that last bit on in a mumble. His gaze connected with Grayson's again. "You'll get the word out that I'm in custody and am cooperating. *Fully cooperating*," Bull emphasized. "And that I intend to spill previously undisclosed info about the militia."

Grayson stood there, obviously considering that from all angles. Jesse did the same, and he could see a huge potential problem. If someone sent an army of thugs to the sheriff's office, there could be a gunfight. And a bloodbath. Obviously though, that was something Grayson would consider.

"Can you lock down the entire building where you'll have me jailed?" Bull wanted to know.

"I can," Grayson confirmed. "The windows are all bulletproof, and the doors are metal and can be fully secured. Along with the cops inside, my stepbrother and cousin are Texas Rangers. I could have them positioned on top of the nearby buildings. They could spot anyone approaching."

"Good. Do that," Bull insisted. "Get everything in place and then let it leak that I'm ready to give you everything, including names, and that I'll do that as soon as my lawyer shows up."

In theory, that would give the militia leader time to launch an attack to silence Bull before he could rat them out, but Jesse saw another flaw in the plan. "The leader might not show. Not if he or she has henchmen to send."

Bull nodded. "Yeah, but then the sheriff here will have at least some of those henchmen in custody, and he could pressure one of them to cough up the name of their boss."

Grayson looked at Jesse, no doubt to get his take on whether or not doing this was worth the risk. It was. Because if it worked, Hanna and Evan might finally be safe.

As long as the leader was out there pulling the strings, then none of them could ever get on with their lives.

"It's a solid plan," Bull argued. "And if I'm going to put my life at risk, I'd rather do it while I'm in the custody of someone I can trust."

"How do you know you can trust us?" Jesse quickly countered.

Bull looked him straight in the eyes. "Because if you'd wanted me dead, I already would be."

That brought on a fresh round of anger for Jesse. "Oh, I still want you dead for the part you played in Hanna and my son nearly being killed, but I'm not a killer. Besides, I think you're right about using a fake confession to draw out the ring leader in all of this."

Jesse gave Grayson a confirming nod, and that was all it took to get him moving Bull toward the door. "I'll text you when I have everything in place and we're ready to do this leak. It'll probably be at least a couple of hours. I don't think this will cause any henchmen to come here for Hanna and you, but better safe than sorry. Be on the lookout for any and everything once I put it out there that Bull is selling out the group."

"I will. Good luck," Jesse added under his breath.

He hated that Hanna's and Evan's safety came down to such a thing like luck, but it was definitely going to play into this. Of course, there were no guarantees that the militia leader would take the bait. He or she might see this for what it was.

A ploy.

But so far, the leader had made some reckless moves by sending thugs to Hanna's and by trying to kidnap Boone. Maybe the recklessness would continue and by morning,

Grayson would have enough people in custody that they could finally get to the truth.

"You're riding with Ava and Theo," Grayson told Boone. "And you'll be taking a trip to the ER to have that leg checked out. Please," he added, no doubt when he saw an argument about that spark in Boone's eyes.

Boone finally nodded, and he turned his attention to Jesse. "If you need anything, just let me know." He extended that offer to Hanna by glancing at her as well. "FYI, I got the books and toys for Evan in my truck. I didn't forget, but since it's not a good idea to get them out, they'll have to wait. Stay safe," he added to both of them.

"We will," Jesse assured him, and he went with Grayson, Bull and Boone to the door.

Jesse didn't close it right away. He stood by, keeping watch with his hand over his gun in case goons were out there waiting for Bull to make an appearance. But all was quiet as Grayson secured Bull in the cruiser and Boone got in with Ava and Theo. As soon as they'd driven away, Jesse did the lockup and armed the security system.

Since he'd already checked, he knew there was an armed ranch hand on every side of the house. The reserve deputy was keeping watch in the driveway. Added to that, they could have extra men out here in less than ten minutes. So, all the bases were covered.

And that left Hanna.

One look at her and he could tell that she was beyond exhausted. So was he, and since Grayson had said it would be a couple of hours before he'd be ready to leak Bull's fake confession, then it was Hanna's best shot at getting in a nap. Especially since Evan was already asleep. Jesse confirmed that by glancing at the monitor she still had clasped in her hand.

He put his palm on the small of her back to lead her to the nursery, he knew there was no way she'd be using her own bedroom. "I promise I'll wake you when I get word from Grayson."

Then, as a precaution, he might go ahead and have her move back into the bathroom with Evan. Jesse didn't want to tell her that now, though, since he doubted she'd be able to sleep with that weighing on her. Of course, sleep might not happen anyway, but he wanted her to give it a try.

She stopped in the doorway of the nursery, gave Evan a glance no doubt to assure herself that he was still okay. He was. And then she turned back to Jesse. "You'll get some rest, too?"

"Absolutely," he lied.

Clearly, he didn't convince her that was anywhere near the truth because the corner of her mouth lifted in a dry smile. "Then, since we'll both likely be awake, why don't you stay in the nursery with Evan and me? The lounge chair in there pulls out into a twin bed. Please," she added in a pleading tone that was similar to the one Grayson had used on Boone.

Jesse didn't hesitate with his nod. No way would he turn her down, not when his being there might give her even a shred of comfort. Still, this was Hanna, and the idea of sleeping next to her, in a small bed, no less, had his exhausted body coming up with a whole different idea to help them relax.

A really bad idea.

Of course, bad ideas just always seemed to come to mind whenever he was this close to Hanna, and it didn't help that he hadn't fully cooled down from their earlier kissing session. Being next to her would be torture. The good, cheap thrills kind, but he'd just have to keep himself in check.

Or not.

Jesse immediately rethought that notion the moment they stepped inside the nursery. When Hanna slipped her hand around the back of his neck, pulled him down to her.

And kissed him.

HANNA HAD DECIDED on the kiss the moment Jesse had given her the nod about staying in the nursery with her. Of course, it hadn't been a nod of approval for them to launch into another make-out session, but she knew he'd be willing. Willing to give her a lot more than just kisses and comforting hugs.

Jesse wanted her.

She could see that want, that heat, in his eyes every time he looked at her, and each time it was somewhat of a surprise. After she'd basically rejected him and had likely crushed his heart, he still hadn't given up on her. She didn't deserve that kind of blind loyalty, but that didn't stop her from accepting it.

Because she wanted Jesse, too.

For months, she had tried to deny this fire between them. In part because of her mother's harping and also because she hadn't remembered exactly how it'd been between them. But now it no longer mattered if she recalled the memories that she'd made with Jesse when they'd had sex. What mattered were the memories they made right now.

Of course, this could turn out to be a huge mistake. One they'd both end up regretting. It would certainly complicate a situation that was always riddled with complications, but she was past the point of no return. Past the point of worrying about the consequences. She needed Jesse. He needed her. And she was going to take everything from him that he was willing to give her.

The heat from the kiss helped her confirm she was making the right decision to be with him. Even if it was just for this night. This moment. Even if it became their second "one and only."

Jesse didn't seem to question her decision. Maybe because the scalding attraction and need didn't give him a choice about that either. He just sank into the kiss, deepening it while he pulled her closer to him.

She felt the hard muscles of his chest against her breasts and her nipples tightened in response to the contact. Jesse upped that contact to the next level. Without breaking the kiss, he slid his hand under her shirt, pushed down the cups of her bra and touched her.

Hanna tried and failed to silence the moan that came from deep within her throat. The moan that no doubt told Jesse just how much that fueled the heat. He seemed to know her body and he definitely knew how to use his fingers to draw out every ounce of pleasure.

Then he drew out even more.

He lowered his head, took one of her nipples into his mouth. This time she didn't moan. She gasped, and Hanna took hold of his hair to anchor him in place. Not that he seemed to have intentions of going anywhere, but she didn't want to lose these wild sensations that were firing through every inch of her body.

Jesse kept up the kissing while he backed her toward the chair. He broke the contact only long enough to pull her shirt over her head. Her bra went, too, and this time when he returned to her nipple, he used his tongue.

The pleasure just kept flooding her. Until a thought flashed into her head, that is.

"Do you have a condom?" she asked, remembering full well that it hadn't stopped her from getting pregnant with Evan. "Please tell me you have one."

"I do, in my wallet." Jesse stopped, though, and met her gaze and waited. No doubt to make sure that a condom was enough for her to go through with what was about to happen.

It was.

And she didn't think that decision was because her body was on fire. All right, that played into it, but she reasoned that the odds were in their favor. Since they'd had one failed condom before meant they likely weren't going to have another. She could hope so anyway.

Hanna set the baby monitor on the table next to them, pulled Jesse back to her, and this time she was the one who went deep with the kiss.

He responded, all right.

It was as if a leash on his willpower loosened inside him and he eased her back in the lounger while he lowered the kisses to her stomach. Again, he hit all the right spots, and his breath was now so close to the front of her jeans that she felt herself soften. Her body, preparing for what it was insisting Jesse give her.

Jesse's body was all-in on this, too, and she had no trouble feeling his erection pressing behind the zipper of his jeans when he made his way back up her body to reclaim her mouth. She welcomed the kiss, the heat, but it revved up the need, and she knew she wanted more.

She started with his shirt.

Fumbling, she somehow managed to get it unbuttoned, and she shoved it off him. She immediately pulled him to her so she could feel his warm bare skin against hers. Yes, this was what she wanted, but like the kisses, it only upped the urgency.

Jesse must have felt that urgency because he went after her jeans. Obviously, his hands were steadier than hers because he got her unsnapped and unzipped, and he shimmied off her shoes and the jeans. Her panties went next.

And Jesse started a different round of kisses.

Right in the center of her body.

Hanna nearly climaxed then and there at the touch of his mouth on such a sensitive spot. She couldn't remember ever having sensations this intense. And maybe she never had. But she suspected it'd happened with Jesse a year and a half ago when they'd landed in bed.

"More," she heard herself murmur. "I want you naked now."

Jesse obliged her. Well, he did after giving her a few more of those well-placed, mind-blowing kisses. He stood and retrieved the condom from his wallet before he shoved his jeans and boxers down over his hips.

Hanna silently cursed the nearly dark room, and she wished she had more than the night-light so she could take a better look at him. But what she could see confirmed that Jesse was indeed a hot cowboy, both clothed and naked.

He settled back on the lounger and robbed Hanna of her breath while he got the condom on. The lounger wasn't wide or especially suited for having sex, but they were past the point of needing comfort. They only needed each other.

And Jesse gave her exactly that.

He was gentle when he pushed inside her. Obviously holding back so he didn't hurt her. But Hanna tried to rid him of any doubts about that when she hooked her legs around his back and lifted her hips. The leash inside snapped again and he started the hard thrusts that would eventually give her the pleasure and relief from the pressure-cooker heat building inside her.

She heard him whisper her name, felt his warm breath on her neck when he repeated it. And that was the final piece she needed to feel herself go over the edge. She buried her face against him and let go.

Moments later, Jesse followed her.

Chapter Fourteen

Jesse held Hanna while she thankfully got some sleep. Apparently, good sex was a cure for frayed nerves. A temporary cure anyway. The calm certainly wouldn't last, but he'd hang on to it as long as he could. Every peaceful moment he could give her was a gift. Unfortunately, it was probably also the calm before the storm.

Once Grayson had the plan set in motion, there was no telling what would happen, and it might be a long time before they had any kind of peace and quiet again. A long time, too, before he could be sure that Hanna and Evan were safe.

Across the room, he could hear the soft sounds of Evan's breathing, and it occurred to him that many parents probably had this. Great sex and the comfort of being with their child. Of course, most probably didn't go for that great sex in the nursery, but his son was none the wiser, and it almost certainly lessened the tension for them to be so close to him.

Hanna would no doubt have second thoughts about what they'd just done. Might even worry about another unplanned pregnancy. But for now she would have these moments, and it appeared she had fallen into a deep, restful sleep. She wasn't shifting or muttering from nightmares despite the cramped space on the lounger, so Jesse stayed still, too, despite the urgency building inside him to keep digging into the investigation. He could be only one piece of evidence away from finding out who'd been responsible for all this misery and havoc.

His phone dinged with a text, and even though it was a soft sound, it blared out like a security alarm in the otherwise quiet room. Hanna woke with a jolt, jackknifing in the lounger, and she seemed ready to jump into the middle of a fierce battle. She settled down, though, when her eyes met his and leveled out even more when she glanced at Evan and saw that he was okay.

"It's Grayson," Jesse told her, and he showed Hanna the message that had just arrived.

Everything's set up. But it's possible word is already out that we have Bull here. Nelda Baker was apparently looking out her window when we drove by her place, and she saw Bull in the cruiser. I didn't spot her at the time or I would have told her to keep quiet. Too late now. The cat's out of the bag because a couple of minutes ago, I got a phone call from Nelda's son asking if it was true, if we had actually arrested Bull.

Hell. Nelda was a notorious gossip and had likely let plenty of people know. Of course, even once the word got back to the militia and their leader, they would still have to come up with their own plan of attack. It was even possible that such an assault wouldn't involve thugs trying to storm the building. They could try to get to Bull by some other means, maybe by finding something or someone they could use to silence him.

Or maybe they'd already gone on the run, believing they were all about to be arrested.

That wasn't a best case scenario as far as Jesse was concerned. If this snake pit went underground, then heaven knew how long it would take to round them all up again. And Jesse doubted they wouldn't take the "go and sin no more" route. Not a chance. They would just set up their illegal operation somewhere else, bide their time and then come after them once they let down their guards. That meant Hanna, Evan, and no one in Jesse's family would be safe.

As much as the idea of a showdown sickened him, he was afraid it was going to come to that. Either now or later. Jesse preferred to save his "later" for getting on with life, and the only way that could happen was for them to neutralize this very large, very dangerous, threat.

"So, the militia's had…what?" Hanna stopped and checked the time. "Over an hour to prepare?"

"Probably," he verified because it had been nearly two hours since Grayson had left.

Even if Nelda had inadvertently informed a militia member with her gossip, it still would have taken some time to get back to the leader. Jesse didn't get the feeling that most members actually knew who the leader was. If so, that would have likely come out with all the arrests that had been made shortly after Hanna's shooting. That would have been powerful bargaining info for anyone looking for a plea deal.

It was a smart move for the leader to act more as a silent partner. A partner who no doubt had raked in big profits from all the illegal activities while keeping his or her identity under wraps.

Jesse sent back a quick Thanks for the update reply to Grayson and looked at Hanna to give her a quick kiss before he got up and started putting his clothes back on. His body was suggesting a whole lot more than a mere kiss though. It was pushing for another round of sex, but he didn't have a second condom. Plus, with the plan to lure out the militia leader now in motion, he needed to be focusing on that.

Hanna groaned softly when she glanced down at her naked body partly covered by a throw Jesse had gotten from a basket on the floor. The groan was likely because her right breast was exposed, giving him more of those "another round" thoughts.

She pulled the cover over it but gave him the quick kiss that he'd been fantasizing about. He wasn't stupid. He knew a kiss wasn't an announcement from her that all was right between them, but it was a good start.

So was the view when she stood to dress.

Her body was still just as amazing as it had been before she'd had Evan, but she frowned when she caught him looking at her. "The C-section scar is still there," she said, tracing the line across her lower abdomen.

Since she seemed to think that would make him remember the terrifying scramble to save Evan's life, Jesse went to her and dropped down low enough to kiss the scar. He didn't even mind the dirty thought he had about giving her some more kisses. He'd just wanted her to know that the scar was all part of who she was. Of what she'd survived.

"You're perfect," he heard himself say, and he winced a little because she could take it as too much, too soon.

She made a sound of disagreement, but it had a light tone to it. "Perfect with stretch marks and a stomach paunch."

Heck, he liked the little paunch, too. Then again, with his body starting to rev, he doubted there was anything about her that would cool him down. But since cooling down was exactly what he had to do, Jesse forced himself to move away from her. *Forced* being the operative word.

He'd already put back on his boxers, jeans and boots just in case he'd had to move in a hurry, but he'd kept the shirt off so he could enjoy the feel of Hanna naked and sleeping against him. He put on his shirt now and watched as she started to do the same with her own clothes.

"Do you think we can trust Bull?" she asked. "I mean do you believe he really intends to help bring down the militia leader?"

That was the million-dollar question, and even with the amazing sex, it hadn't been that far from his mind. "I think we can trust him to a point. If he's a dirty agent, it seems he's willing to throw the militia under a bus by drawing them out. But then, he had nothing to lose by doing that. Bull's in as much danger, if not more, than the rest of us."

"Yes," she murmured, and she ended the peep show by pulling on her panties and jeans. "The militia leader would want a federal agent dead." She looked at him. "Would they want Shaw dead, too? I mean if he's not the leader, that is."

"They would." Jesse didn't have to give that any thought. "The militia would be looking for payback for anyone who's been involved in tearing the group apart. But I haven't ruled Shaw out yet as a suspect. He could have orchestrated this, and he'd stand a better chance of getting to Bull than some thugs."

She stayed quiet a moment, obviously giving that some thought. "Because Shaw would be able to get into the sheriff's office."

Jesse nodded. "Grayson would keep an eye on him to make sure Shaw doesn't try to execute Bull. Or poison him. But Shaw wouldn't have to do the dirty work himself. Eventually, Bull will have to be transferred to another jail. Or into the custody of the ATF. Shaw could have friends or co-horts who could easily get to Bull and silence him before anything goes to trial."

"And it would be Bull's word against Shaw's if this turns into a federal investigation," she added.

He had to nod again. "I'm betting if Shaw's the culprit, then he's already hidden or destroyed any proof that Bull could use to point a finger at him."

Of course, it was just as possible there was no evidence to find because Shaw could be innocent. If so, Jesse would owe him an apology, but he had no intention of giving the agent any leeway, or access to Hanna, before he knew one way or another about the agent's involvement or innocence.

Hanna nodded as well. "That leaves Marlene and—" She'd obviously been about to bring up their other suspects, but she stopped when his phone dinged again with a text.

One look at it and Jesse's heart dropped. Because it wasn't Grayson this time. It was Miguel Navarro, the ranch hand who was standing guard.

"'Somebody's here,'" Jesse read aloud from Miguel's text. "'It's one person, on foot, walking up the road toward the house.'"

Hanna made a slight gasp, but he saw her quickly rein in the slam of panic. It could be nothing, but with every-thing else going on, Jesse was dead certain they wouldn't be that lucky.

Is the person armed? Jesse texted back to Miguel, and he added to Hanna, "Wait here. I'm going to have a look out the front window."

"Be careful," she murmured.

Because she looked many steps beyond the mere worried stage, he took the time to brush a kiss on her mouth before he went to the living room. Jesse had just made it to the window when Miguel responded.

Can't tell, the hand messaged. But it looks like a woman.

Well, that sure as hell didn't put Jesse at ease since two of their suspects were women. Added to that, there could be female members in the militia.

She doesn't look too steady on her feet, Miguel added several moments later. She's staggering like she's drunk. Or hurt.

There was a third option. She could be pretending to be drunk or hurt. A ruse to try to get closer.

Wishing he had binoculars, Jesse peered through the darkness to get a glimpse of their visitor. Of course, the ranch hands and deputy wouldn't let the woman actually approach the house without stopping her to find out what she wanted, but if she was armed, she could start shooting before they even got to her.

Jesse watched as Miguel hurried across the yard to duck behind a tree. He was obviously trying to get in position so he'd have a better angle to keep an eye on their visitor. The moon wasn't cooperating with that though. There was just enough cloud cover to give them very little illumination.

As a cop, Jesse wanted to be out there, to put an end to this himself. But he couldn't risk leaving Hanna and Evan alone.

Jesse's phone dinged again, and this time the text was from the reserve deputy, Roger Norris. It's definitely a woman, he said, adding the ranch hands onto the text. And she looks familiar.

Just as he read that, some of the clouds finally drifted

away, giving Jesse just enough light for him to make out the woman's face.

Hell. She was familiar all right.

Because it was Hanna's mother.

HANNA STAYED IN the doorway of the nursery, trying to hear any bits of info that Jesse was getting about this possible intruder, but she kept her gaze pinned to the baby monitor that she'd picked up. Since her back was to the crib, she couldn't actually see Evan. Might not be able to hear him, either, because her heartbeat was crashing in her ears. So she watched the monitor to make sure he wasn't stirring or waking up.

Every few seconds, she peered out, hoping to get a glimpse of Jesse, but he'd obviously moved to one of the windows out of her line of sight. He was no doubt getting updates from the hands and deputy, and even over her own loud heartbeat, she thought she would have heard any shots that might have been fired. Maybe that meant this was a false alarm, someone who'd maybe broken down and had come to her house looking for help.

Of course, that was wishful thinking, but Hanna held on to that hope until she saw Jesse making his way toward her. One look at his face and she knew something was wrong.

"What happened?" she managed to ask.

He had his gun drawn, but he used his left hand to take hold of her shoulder in what was usually a reassuring gesture. Not much would reassure her at this point though.

"It's your mother," Jesse told her. "She's on foot, and she's coming toward the house."

"On foot?" She shook her head. That didn't make sense. If Isabel had broken down, she had a cell phone, and she could have called. At least she would have if her phone battery hadn't died. Or if she didn't have something else planned.

Like getting close enough to attack.

Hanna still couldn't see Isabel doing something like that, but if she was the militia leader and was desperate, she might be willing to do just about anything. Even get her own hands dirty by launching an attack to silence Jesse and her.

"What are you going to do?" she asked Jesse.

"I don't want to pull any of the deputies away from Grayson's operation, and I think we have enough manpower here to deal with whatever she's trying to bring to your doorstep. My plan right now is to allow her to come closer to the house so I can find out why she's here. I won't let her in," he quickly added. "And the ranch hands and deputy will keep watch to make sure she's alone and hasn't brought *friends* with her."

Good. Because Hanna didn't want those so-called friends getting anywhere near the house so they could start shooting.

"Isabel will want to talk to me," Hanna pointed out. "Does she have her phone with her? If so, she might call when she gets closer."

"Can't tell. She might be drunk. Or hurt." He flexed his grip on her shoulder. "I can't see any blood or anything, but she's staggering."

Jesse didn't ask her if she'd ever known Isabel to get falling-down drunk. She hadn't, as far as she knew, but then she only had six months of memories when it came to her mother. However, Isabel could be hurt despite there not being any signs of blood. If she wasn't the leader of the militia, then she could have been attacked by one of them as a ploy to drag them out of hiding.

"I'm not opening the door to her," Jesse said as if reading her mind. "Not turning off the security system either. But the reserve deputy, Norris, is frisking her right now to make sure she isn't armed. If she doesn't have any kind of weapon and wants to talk to you, I can have her brought onto the porch. You'll be able to speak to her through the window."

Hanna had no problems agreeing to any of that. She had to know why the woman was there, but she didn't want that info if it put anyone at risk.

"Keep the baby monitor with you," he instructed, and she followed him toward the front of the house.

He motioned for her to stay to the side so that she wasn't directly in front of the glass. She did, but Hanna was able to look out into the yard and spot her mother and the deputy. Jesse had been right about her staggering. If the deputy hadn't had hold of her arm, Isabel likely would have fallen.

"I think she might have been drugged," the deputy said in a voice loud enough for them to hear.

Drugged. Oh, mercy. Hanna forced herself to stay put, but her worry skyrocketed. At least, it did until she reminded herself once again that this might all be an act. A potentially deadly one.

"Hanna?" her mother called out. "Please help me. Please."

Jesse muttered some profanity that was laced with as much frustration and worry as Hanna was feeling. "I'll call for an ambulance," he told the deputy, and Jesse did that while Deputy Norris led Isabel onto the porch.

When Isabel passed under the overhead light, Hanna could see that her mother did indeed look dazed. Maybe because she was overdosing on something. Maybe having another stroke. But Hanna didn't know if this was something Isabel had done to herself of if someone had given her drugs. If it was the latter, Hanna wanted to know why.

"The ambulance will be here in about ten minutes," Jesse relayed to Hanna and the deputy.

On the porch, Isabel sank down next to the window, leaned her head against the wooden frame and looked up at Jesse. "I need to see Hanna."

"I'm here," Hanna told her, but she didn't go closer. She stayed back in case a sniper was out there, ready to target her the moment she stepped into view. However, she could still see her mother's face through the glass. "What happened to you?"

Isabel shook her head. "I don't know. I was driving, coming out here, and I got so dizzy." Some of her words were slurred. "Uh, I had to stop…and when I got out to try to get some fresh air, I stumbled and fell." She paused again. "I saw the lights to your house and walked toward them."

"Is it possible someone drugged you?" Jesse came out and asked.

Isabel lifted her head, peering directly at him. Her eyes were definitely unfocused, so that part wasn't an act. "I don't know," she repeated.

"They can do a tox screen on her at the hospital," Hanna heard Jesse murmur. "We can find out what she's taken or been given."

"What were you eating or drinking before you came here?" Jesse pressed, shifting his attention back to Isabel.

Isabel responded with another headshake and more slurred, mumbled words. They were obviously going to have to wait for the effect of the drugs to wear off before they got any answers, but Hanna decided to try one more question.

"Why did you need to see me?" she asked.

Isabel groaned and lifted her head. "Because I'm sorry. So sorry."

Hanna sighed since her mother had obviously come here to rehash her guilt over stirring up Arnie so he'd confront Jesse. "We'll talk about that after you're out of the hospital. I'll call Dr. Warner and let him know what's going on."

The doctor might even have some insight about a possible bad side effect from medication Isabel was taking for her recovery from the stroke.

"You were so mad," Isabel went on, as if talking to herself. "That's the worst argument we've ever had. Even worse than the other ones about Jesse."

That got Hanna's attention. "What do you mean? What argument?"

Isabel closed her eyes. "The one about the money." She was definitely getting groggier, and Hanna didn't think it was a good idea for her to sleep. Not until they knew what had caused this.

"Stay awake, Mother," Hanna snapped, hoping that Isabel would respond to the stern tone. She did. Well, in part. She opened her eyes anyway. "What argument did we have about money?" Hanna demanded.

"The money you found in my account," Isabel muttered as if it were something that Hanna was well aware of.

Hanna glanced at Jesse to see if he knew anything about this, but he only shook his head. This was the first either of them was hearing about it.

"Too much money in there, you said," Isabel rambled on. "You saw my bank statement lying on my desk, and you said it had too much."

Hanna definitely didn't recall any of this either. "Why was the money in your account?" she asked.

"A favor. That's all. That's what I tried to tell you. It was just a favor. But you said it looked like money laundering to you."

Sweet heaven. A single deposit wouldn't have caused her to come to a conclusion like that. There must have been a pattern.

"How much was this favor?" Hanna pressed.

"A hundred thousand, added in increments…" Isabel stopped, groaned, but then shook her head as if trying to clear it. "Added in increments of just under ten thousand."

Hanna couldn't be sure, but she thought those amounts wouldn't have been reported to the IRS or some other government agency.

"You said you knew the money couldn't be mine because you'd just had a meeting with my accountant about those bad investments I'd made," Isabel continued.

Again, this was news to Hanna. She hadn't known about the investments, the meeting with the accountant or these mystery funds.

In the distance, Hanna heard the sirens and knew the ambulance would be there soon. Once they took Isabel to the hospital, heaven knew how long it'd be before she got to talk to her again. She wanted to clear all of this up now.

"Who put the money in your account?" Hanna went on.

"A friend," Isabel said, her voice barely audible now, and she closed her eyes again.

"What friend?" Jesse and Hanna demanded in unison.

Isabel didn't even try to answer. She'd lost consciousness. Or worse. The deputy must have thought the worst was possible, too, because he touched his fingers to her neck.

"She's alive," he assured them.

Hanna didn't have time for the breath of relief she wanted

to take. That's because she heard something that chilled her to the bone.

Somewhere out in the darkness, there was a gunshot.

Chapter Fifteen

Jesse automatically motioned for Hanna to step further back. He didn't want to send her running to the nursery just yet because the shot had sounded far away. It was possibly even a night hunter out in the woods, looking for coyotes but considering what had happened to Isabel, that wasn't likely.

Of course, Isabel could have done this to herself, and that's what Jesse kept in mind while he continued to watch out the window. But if Hanna's mom had told the truth about all that money being in her account, then that was something he could confirm once he took a harder look at her financials. The money certainly hadn't been in there recently because Theo had looked at her accounts, but there was no telling how long ago that argument between Hanna and her mother had happened. Since Isabel hadn't been a suspect in Hanna's shooting, Jesse hadn't dug into her assets.

That would change first chance he got.

Deputy Norris dropped down next to Isabel, obviously shielding her with his own body in case any gunfire came their way, but Jesse listened hard and didn't hear anything else. Well, nothing other than the howl of the ambulance as it got closer to the house.

He took out his phone and texted Dispatch to tell them

to have the ambulance hold at the end of the driveway. That way, the EMTs wouldn't be in the line of fire if there were more shots fired. Plus, it would cut down on the risk in case one of the militia thugs had managed to get in the ambulance. Jesse wouldn't put it past them to do something like drug Isabel all so that Hanna and he could be attacked when the EMTs arrived on scene.

"Do you think I came to the ranch that night I was shot to tell you about the argument I had with my mother?" Hanna asked, and the nerves were causing her voice to tremble. Heck, she was trembling, too.

"It's possible," he admitted.

Jesse had questioned himself often as to why she'd come to see him. Yes, she'd had those ultrasound pictures and medical forms with her, but there'd been nothing pressing about them. In fact, he'd later learned that she'd already emailed him the ultrasound photos. He'd also later learned that he could have signed the papers even after she was at the hospital in labor. That had led Jesse to hope that she'd just wanted to see him, to be with the father of her child so they could talk about the upcoming birth. But maybe he had been totally off base.

Instead, it could be connected to Isabel and this money her so-called friend had deposited into her account.

Soon, very soon, he'd also find out exactly who that friend was because it was possible that Isabel would put Arnie, Marlene and even Bull into that friend category. Probably not Agent Shaw, though, unless she'd stayed quiet about knowing the man. That was something else Jesse needed to check.

Because he didn't want to leave Grayson out of the loop, Jesse continued to keep watch and sent him a text.

Isabel showed up here. It appears she's been drugged. We also heard a shot. Not sure if there's an actual threat yet.

He'd just hit Send when Jesse heard Miguel call out. "I spotted someone at the fence near the road."

Maybe this was their shooter, and that was Jesse's cue to take the security up a notch. "It's time for Evan and you to go into the bathroom," Jesse told her.

He looked back at Hanna, trying to silently reassure her that he'd do his best to keep them safe. Jesse wasn't sure he succeeded though. Hanna definitely looked scared out of her mind when she ran toward the nursery.

Hell. He hated that she had to go through this when she'd already been through way too much. Too much that might have been at least partly her own mother's fault. Jesse wasn't sure how Hanna would feel if it turned out he had to arrest Isabel, but if the woman was guilty, she would get what she deserved.

Jesse's phone rang, the sound breaking the silence, and he saw Grayson's name on the screen. He muttered another, "*Hell*," hoping that something hadn't gone wrong at the sheriff's office.

"I'm on the way out to Hanna's," Grayson said the moment Jesse answered. "I'll be there in a few minutes."

"But what about Bull?" It sure didn't seem like a good idea to shortchange the security there at the jail when Bull might be just as much of a target as Hanna and he were. Added to that, they really needed to catch anyone who might try to go after the man.

"It's covered," Grayson assured him. "I asked Mason to come in to take my place. He'll be able to handle anything that comes up."

Jesse didn't doubt the handling part, but this meant yet another family member was in danger.

"Did you hear any other shots being fired?" Grayson asked.

"No, but I've kept the ambulance on hold just in case."

He hoped like the devil that wasn't a fatal mistake for Isabel, but the deputy was keeping a check of her pulse while he continued looking around the yard.

"Isabel might have been talking out of her head," Jesse went on, "but she described a situation that sounded a lot like her involvement in money laundering. I wasn't able to get the name of who hooked her up with that, but it might be connected to Hanna's shooting."

"I can talk to her once she's at the hospital. I'll follow the ambulance there and put her under guard."

Good, because someone might be out to kill her, too. "Let me text the ambulance driver to come on up and get her," Jesse said, getting ready to do that.

But then he heard the crack of gunfire.

It wasn't just one shot this time but three in a row, and he was darn sure it had come from the vicinity of the bottom of the driveway. Right where the ambulance was parked.

"I see the shooter," one of the ranch hands yelled. "Looks like it's a guy on the side of the road with a rifle."

Jesse hissed out a breath because that's exactly where Grayson was heading. "Stay back," Jesse warned him just as he heard the squeal of brakes. "There's an active shooter in the area."

"Yeah," Grayson verified. "He's shooting at me."

That sent his pulse racing so it was thick and throbbing in his head. The SOB was trying to kill Grayson. Or create some kind of distraction. Either way, it wasn't a good situation to have Grayson under fire.

"Do you have any reserves you can call in?" Jesse asked.

"No cops available, but I'll call for some more of the ranch hands. Not sure how long it'll take them to get here, but I'll keep you posted. Just focus on keeping Hanna and Evan safe."

He would. They came first, but he had another problem to deal with.

"I'm going to have to get Isabel inside," Jesse muttered.

It was a risk. Anything he did at this point would be. But he couldn't leave Deputy Norris and her outside where they'd both be easy targets. Of course, the ranch hands were out there, as well, but they could take cover. Norris and Isabel couldn't do that, and with the porch light shining down on them, gunmen wouldn't have any trouble spotting them.

"Watch your back," Grayson advised him, and it appeared he was ready to end the call when Jesse heard him snarl. "Agent Shaw. What the heck is he doing out here?"

"Shaw's there? Is he the shooter?" Jesse couldn't ask fast enough.

"Yeah, he's by the fence across the road from Hanna's." There was the sound of more gunfire. "But he's not the one firing at me."

It didn't mean, though, that Shaw wasn't calling the shots—literally. The gunmen could be thugs acting on his orders.

"The bullets are slamming into the windshield of the cruiser," Grayson added a heart-stopping moment later. "The glass is holding, but I'm not sure for how long. I'm going to try to back up and get to the ranch trail just up the road. I can use it to make my way to Hanna's."

Jesse definitely didn't like the idea of Grayson being on an isolated trail where gunmen could be lying in wait for him, but he didn't want him just sitting there while someone tried to kill him.

"Be careful," Jesse told him, knowing that he wouldn't be able to talk Grayson into just backing off out of the line of fire and waiting.

Part of Jesse didn't want to talk him into it either. Because if Grayson could get to the house, that meant there'd be one extra lawman to make sure these gunmen didn't get anywhere near Hanna and Evan.

Grayson ended the call, but Jesse didn't go to the door. He took a second to try to call Shaw, and it surprised him when the agent answered on the first ring.

"Why the hell are you here?" Jesse demanded.

"I followed Isabel." Shaw hadn't hesitated, but he sounded out of breath. "Don't trust her. I think she's involved with the militia."

For once, Jesse agreed with the agent on both counts. He had no intention of getting into the possibility of money laundering though. Not with Grayson under fire.

"Who's shooting at the cruiser?" Jesse snapped.

"Some guy with a rifle. And, no, I don't know who it is, and it isn't someone working for me. I'm not dirty, and I'm trying to get into position to take out the shooter."

Jesse wished he could be sure of that because it would mean they had extra backup on scene. "Just be careful that no shots come near the house," Jesse warned him.

He didn't wait to hear Shaw's response because time might be running out for Isabel and Deputy Norris, so Jesse ended the call and turned to go to the door.

The sound stopped him.

Not gunfire. But one of the ranch hands yelling. Then, coughing. Seconds later, Jesse saw the white fog sliding across the yard toward the house.

"Tear gas," Norris managed to say though he, too, started coughing. "We need to get inside *now.*"

HANNA'S HEART WAS in her throat, and her muscles tightened with the sound of each and every bullet that was being fired. Sweet heaven, there was a gunfight going on. One that could get Jesse, her mother and everyone helping them killed.

She pressed Evan closer to her, not to soothe him. He was asleep. She was the one who needed soothing, and she wished she knew what was going on. It didn't seem as if the bullets were being fired near the house, so maybe that meant the ranch hands and Deputy Norris were holding off attackers. If so, she prayed they succeeded. Prayed, too, they all got out of this alive.

She thought of her mother, drugged and dazed on the porch, and she added a prayer that Isabel wasn't a major player in all of this. Money laundering was bad enough. So was withholding the truth about what had gone on right before Arnie had shot her. But if Isabel's actions had caused the danger, then Hanna wanted her to pay and pay hard.

Hanna heard one of the ranch hands shouting, and she made out the words. *Tear gas.* Oh, mercy. That caused her heart to skip a beat or two. Because if their attackers had set off tear gas, he or she might have done it so they could get Jesse, Evan and her out of the house.

"It's me," someone said at the door.

Jesse.

The relief washed over her. He was alive, and she hurried out of the bathtub so she could unlock the door for him. He wasn't hurt. That was the first thing she made sure of, but every bit of his expression and body language told her they were in deep trouble.

"How bad is it?" she asked.

"Grayson's on the way," he said, and she knew he was trying to give her the good news first. "Someone set off tear gas canisters at the end of the driveway, and the ranch hands had to scatter."

In other words, they probably wouldn't be able to hold off any gunmen making their way to the house.

"I got your mother and Deputy Norris inside," Jesse continued. "He's watching her to make sure she doesn't try anything."

Anything—as in try to kill them to make sure they stayed silent about her involvement with the militia.

"The house is locked up, and I've reset the security system. No one will get in without us knowing about it. I'm also staying here with Evan and you," he assured her. "The tear gas will clear soon—" He stopped when someone fired a shot.

Not on the road from the sound of it. This was nearby.

Maybe even in the yard.

Hanna tried not to let the fear take over. She couldn't panic because Jesse didn't have time to try to bring her out of a full-scale attack. But her heart was pounding and her breath was already going thin.

Jesse pulled the bathroom door shut and he locked it. "Get back in the tub," he instructed.

Just hearing Jesse's voice helped some even though what he was saying meant the danger was imminent. Still, she used the sound of his voice to start steadying herself. Hanna also kept her attention on Evan's peaceful, sleeping face, which was better than any of the grounding exercises the therapist had taught her. She had to stay in control for the sake of her baby.

There were no windows in the bathroom, and the only illumination came from a cheery turtle night-light plugged into the outlet on the vanity. It was enough light, though, for her to see Jesse. He stayed at the door, no doubt ready to defend them if anyone came through. And he would defend them. Hanna was certain of that. However, she was equally certain that Jesse could die if it came down to it.

As if he sensed what she was thinking, Jesse looked back at her, their gazes connecting. He was trying to reassure her again. But that reassurance vanished when the night-light went out, plunging them into total darkness.

Seconds later, the security alarm went off, the sound blaring and echoing through the house.

Evan jolted and started to cry, though Hanna could barely hear him over the noise. She pulled him to her, tried to soothe him, and once again had to battle her own panic.

Because it was possible the gunmen were in the house.

That was the thought that kept repeating in her head. A thought that was throbbing with her too fast heartbeat and her racing breath. Just when she thought she couldn't take any more, the alarms stopped, and the room went deadly silent. That's when she realized Evan had stopped crying, but he was whimpering as if trying to lull himself back to sleep.

"I had to use the app to turn off the security," Jesse whispered to her. "I have to be able to hear them if they come this way."

She didn't have to ask what he meant by *them*. The gunmen. Maybe even the militia leader. Yes, Jesse would definitely need to know if they were trying to get into the bathroom. But she didn't hear anything like that.

No running footsteps.

No gunfire.

She tried not to assume a worst case scenario: that the ranch hands outside the house had all been killed. But it was possible.

"They got her," a man shouted. He was coughing.

"That was Deputy Norris," Jesse muttered.

So, not one of the gunmen, and Hanna heard those running footsteps she'd been listening for. Steps in the hall coming toward the nursery.

Jesse turned on the flashlight app on his phone and opened the bathroom door. "Someone took Isabel?" he called out.

"Yeah," the deputy verified, causing Hanna's heart to pound even harder. He continued to cough. "Someone broke through the front door and threw in more tear gas. I couldn't see, but whoever it was, bashed me on the head and took her. I'm sorry," he added with a groan. "They took her."

Even though Hanna wasn't sure of her mother's innocence, that still caused her fear to soar. Isabel could be in the hands of killers right now.

"Who took her?" Jesse pressed.

"Couldn't tell. The person had on a gas mask and was wearing bulky clothes."

So it could have been anyone. Including Shaw or Marlene. Or someone one of them had hired to do it.

"How bad are you hurt?" Jesse asked the deputy.

"Uh, I think I'm okay," Norris answered, but he didn't sound okay at all. He was still coughing. "You should stay put. The tear gas is clearing up some, but it's still hard to breathe out here."

Jesse cursed under his breath. "Stay here. I'll let Norris in here and then try to contact the ranch hands."

Hanna nodded and fumbled to get her phone from her jeans' pocket so that she could turn on the flashlight, too. It helped because she could see Evan's face. Could see that he'd fallen back to sleep. That was something at least. It would have skyrocketed her stress if he'd been terrified and sobbing.

Several seconds later, Jesse rushed back into the bathroom, and he had Norris in tow. There was blood on the side of the deputy's head and he did indeed look as dazed as he'd sounded.

"I'm so sorry about your mother," Norris told her.

She nodded and watched as Jesse and the deputy positioned themselves on either side of the bathroom door. They didn't shut and lock it, probably since this way they'd have a clear line of sight of anyone trying to come into the nursery.

Because the room was quiet now, she heard Jesse's phone vibrate, a setting he'd likely used so it wouldn't alert anyone to their position in the house.

"It's Grayson," he told her in a whisper.

Even though Jesse hadn't put the call on speaker, she could still hear Grayson when he spoke. "What's your status?" Grayson asked.

"Not good," Jesse replied. "Someone cut the power and used tear gas to get into the house and take Isabel. The person bashed Norris on the head. I think he's all right," he added, giving the deputy a glance, "and we're holding up in the nursery bathroom."

She wasn't able to hear what Grayson said next, but she thought he cursed.

"What's your status?" Jesse repeated to Grayson.

"I'm threading my way through this trail to Hanna's. So far, no gunmen in sight. When I get to the house, I'll drive straight to the porch and get as close to the door as possible. We can get Hanna and Evan into the cruiser and take them to the ranch. Then, I can look for Isabel."

Hanna wanted all of those things to happen. She didn't want to stay here with Evan. But going outside could be just as dangerous as staying put.

"I'll be there in about five minutes," Grayson said before he ended the call.

Five minutes would no doubt seem like an eternity, but Jesse and Norris continued to stand guard at the door.

"I'll try to get one of the ranch hands to respond," Jesse explained when he pressed in a number.

She heard the rings and, with each one, the sense of dread inside her grew. Finally, though, someone answered.

But it wasn't good news.

"We can't get back to the house," the hand choked out between coughs. "Someone keeps shooting tear gas canisters at us."

Oh, mercy. That had to be so someone could get inside.

"Are you hurt?" Jesse pressed.

"No. Just my eyes and nose stinging like fire from the tear gas. I can't see, Jesse. I can't be sure if somebody's not trying to get in."

More dread washed over her, and it got worse when she heard the voice. Not the ranch hand out in the yard. This had come from inside the house.

"Hanna," the woman shouted.

Isabel.

Hanna jerked in a hard breath. She couldn't be sure, but it sounded as if her mother was in the hall, right outside the nursery.

"Hanna," Isabel repeated, and then added, "Jesse. Please you have to help me."

Chapter Sixteen

Jesse didn't move. He sure as hell didn't go rushing out into the hall to help Isabel, despite her plea.

Because that plea could all be just a ruse to draw him out so Isabel could shoot him.

He didn't know for sure what her motive might be for wanting him dead, but he couldn't take the chance. Not when that would leave Hanna and Evan even more vulnerable than they already were. Later, he'd kick himself for letting things come to this point. But for now, he just kept watch and hoped that a lot of things went right for them. They were going to need some luck to get through this.

"Text Grayson," Jesse whispered to Deputy Norris. "Let him know that Isabel is in the house."

Jesse didn't want to risk taking his attention off the nursery door even for a second to send that message, but he also didn't want Grayson walking in where he could be shot.

"Are you alone, Isabel?" Jesse called out.

With the sound of his voice, Isabel would be able to pinpoint his location, but since she was Hanna's mother, the woman would have almost certainly known where they'd be.

Isabel coughed, maybe from the remnants of the tear gas. Or because she wanted them to believe she was affected by it. It was just as possible that she'd gotten access to a gas mask, given to her by one of the militia goons, and that she'd just now removed the mask so the coughing would make her appeal for help seem more genuine.

"No," Isabel said, her voice barely audible because of the coughing. "I—" She cut off whatever she'd been about to add.

Or had been cut off.

Jesse heard a sound, a sort of swooshing gasp that a person might make if they'd just been punched in the stomach and the breath had been knocked out of them. Again, that could be faked, but the next sounds he heard were the real deal.

Footsteps.

Someone was definitely in the hall.

He hadn't locked the door to the nursery because he'd figured it wouldn't do any good. If the gunmen had gotten that far, they would have just broken it down, and the flying wood might have prevented Jesse from seeing them clearly. This way, he could watch and wait for them to come in, and when they did, he could put an end to their miserable lives.

Jesse didn't relish the idea of shooting anyone, especially didn't want to kill even when the other person was a killer, but he had no intentions of letting them continue to wreak this deadly havoc.

Of course, a gunfight this close to Evan and Hanna could turn out the worst kind of bad. The bathtub gave them some protection. Some. And this was where luck came in. Maybe it would be enough to keep them both out of the path of any bullets that were fired.

"Grayson will come the rest of the way on foot," Norris whispered after he'd gotten a response to his text. "He'll try to sneak into the house and take Isabel and anyone who's with her from behind."

Hell, there were a dozen things that could go wrong with that plan. The gunmen could spot Grayson and shoot him. He might even be hit with friendly fire if the ranch hands mistook him for the militia. Added to that, Agent Shaw was still out there somewhere, and there was no telling what his intentions were. But Jesse reminded himself that Grayson was as smart a lawman as they came. He'd be careful because he knew how high the stakes were.

"I, uh, need you to come out so we can talk," Isabel finally said.

Her voice was strained, but he couldn't tell if it was real or put on.

"Not a chance," Jesse responded. "Are you alone?" he repeated.

The woman didn't make that hard gasp this time, but she also didn't respond to Jesse's question. However, because Jesse was listening carefully, he heard more of those footsteps. Maybe two sets, indicating that someone was indeed with her, but he couldn't be sure.

He glanced back at Hanna and Evan, the light from her phone casting an eerie shadow on her face. He saw the worry. And the fear. But he also saw something else. Her determination to keep their son safe. She shifted in the tub, lying Evan down so she could hover over him.

Shield him with her body.

Putting herself in a position in case she had to fight.

Jesse hated she had to take a risk like that, but it was necessary. They were parents, and their child came first. He hadn't needed a reminder like that to know just how much he loved Evan.

Hanna, too.

Maybe, just maybe he'd get the chance to tell both of them that. But for that to happen, he had to put an end to the threat.

His gaze slashed back to the door when he heard the sound of the knob moving. Possibly Isabel, but it was more likely a gunman. Someone who'd be ready to start firing at first chance.

Jesse turned off his flashlight, slipped his phone back in his pocket, and took aim. Waiting, while every nerve and muscle in his body went on full alert.

"Isabel?" Jesse called out when the door opened just a fraction.

"Yes—" Again, the woman was cut off or merely stopped to make it sound that way. There were a couple of heart-stopping seconds before she finally added, "Don't shoot me."

"Don't give me a reason to shoot you," Jesse countered.

Isabel made a strangled sound, one that might have been terror, and the door opened even wider. Jesse cursed the darkness because his eyes were still adjusting, and he could only see the outline of a person. He wasn't sure if it was Isabel or someone else. But what he didn't spot was a weapon.

"I'm sorry," Isabel said.

Like her coughs and other sounds, it seemed genuine. *Seemed.* "For what?" Jesse demanded. He adjusted his aim as the door fully opened and the woman stepped closer. Not actually into the room though. Isabel stayed in the doorway.

And she wasn't alone.

There was someone standing behind her. And this time when he looked, Jesse did see a weapon.

It was aimed at Isabel's head.

Jesse braced for the gut-slam of adrenaline, and it came.

He did a quick assessment of the situation and realized that even if Isabel was truly in danger, he didn't have a clean shot to take out the person who could be holding her at gunpoint.

A person who could be a man or woman.

Whoever it was, they weren't that much taller than Isabel, which didn't rule out either Shaw or Marlene. Of course, the person could also be stooping down to try to disguise his or her height, and he or she was wearing what appeared to be a gas mask.

"I'm supposed to tell you that you need to come with me," Isabel said, her voice shaking.

She was shaking, too. Jesse could see that now that his eyes had finally adjusted, and he thought she was still feeling the effects of whatever drug she'd taken or been given.

"You and Hanna are supposed to come out," Isabel added when her captor dug the gun harder into the side of her head. She made another sob. "The baby can stay here where he'll be safe."

"Safe," Jesse snapped. "With armed men shooting bullets and tear gas. He woke up crying when the security alarm went off. Terrified and crying." In the grand scheme of things, that probably wouldn't seem like a big deal to some people.

Including a would-be killer.

But Jesse's comment seemed to hit the mark with Isabel. Evan's grandmother. She let out a hoarse sob. She swung as if to punch the person holding her, but that didn't work. Her captor merely tightened the grip around Isabel's neck.

Jesse got the motherlode of flashbacks. To the night Hanna had been shot. It'd been dark then, too, and Arnie had held her in an almost identical pose with the gun to her head. He hadn't had a clear shot then. Hadn't been able to do anything while Arnie had dragged Hanna into the trees and shot her.

Hanna was no doubt hearing all of this, and he prayed she wasn't on the verge of a panic attack. Prayed that they could do enough to get through this. But it had to cut her to the bone to know that her mother was in danger. Or that Isabel was the cause of all of this.

"Grayson's here," Norris whispered, yanking Jesse out of those nightmarish images. "He's in the house."

A different kind of image came. And it played out right in front of him. The image of Grayson being gunned down.

Jesse heard the sound of Grayson's footsteps. Obviously, so did the man or woman holding Isabel.

In a quick move, the person turned and fired a shot. Not in Grayson's direction though.

The shot came directly toward Jesse.

THE SOUND OF the gunshot was deafening. And Hanna's first thought was Jesse. Had he been shot?

She forced herself to look and saw Jesse lurch to the side. For a split second, it seemed as if the worst had happened. But Jesse didn't fall. Deputy Norris did, and Jesse had moved to catch him.

Both of them went to the floor with Jesse pulling the deputy against the wall and away from the door. Even in the darkness, Hanna could see the blood spread across the sleeve of his shirt. He'd been hit in his right arm.

Norris grunted in pain and he clamped his hand over the wound to stop the flow of blood. What he almost certainly wouldn't be able to do was return fire if it came down to that.

And it did.

Someone fired a second shot, and it tore through a chunk of the doorjamb. Muttering some profanity, Jesse shifted, practically shoving Norris behind him, and he took aim at the shooter. He didn't fire. Maybe because he didn't have a clear shot, but the shooter didn't pull the trigger again either.

Hanna figured that wasn't going to last.

Grayson was somewhere in the house, but it was possible he couldn't move closer without getting shot or risking Isabel being killed. Hanna hadn't actually seen her mother, but she'd heard enough of her conversation with Jesse to know that she was being held at gunpoint. Maybe willingly. Maybe not.

"Get in the tub with the baby," Hanna told Norris. "Jesse needs backup."

Jesse was already trying to nix that idea before she finished, but he couldn't actually argue with her because he had to keep his focus on Isabel and the person who'd fired those shots.

Norris was still bleeding, still clearly in a lot of pain, but he made it to the tub and did as she had asked, acting as a human shield for Evan. Hanna took his gun and scrambled to the other side of the door, across from Jesse.

"You shouldn't be here," Jesse snarled. "Do you even remember how to fire a gun?"

She did, though she hadn't known that until that very second. She'd taken shooting lessons after she'd moved to this current house because she'd wanted to be able to scare off coyotes. The stakes were much higher now, and Hanna knew in her gut that she wouldn't miss.

"Hanna," her mother said. It was possible Isabel had gotten a glimpse of her when she'd traded places with Norris.

Hanna made a quick glance around the jamb and saw

her mother. And the person behind her. The person wasn't looking at Jesse or her, though, but rather toward the living room. He or she gave Isabel a hard squeeze before whispering something in her ear.

"Grayson," Isabel called out a moment later, "if you want Jesse and Hanna to live, then you need to leave."

She didn't hear Grayson respond, but Hanna knew he wouldn't leave. But maybe he'd be able to distract Isabel's captor. Or maybe Isabel would drop down. Anything to give one of them a shot.

Deputy Norris's phone was on the floor and the screen lit up with a text. From Grayson. Two words flashed on the screen.

It's Marlene.

Hanna lifted the phone to show to Jesse, and he shook his head in disgust. Hanna felt the disgust, too, but there was also some relief because maybe this meant her mother hadn't actually been capable of killing anyone.

"It's over, Marlene," Jesse called out.

Silence, but Hanna did see the woman stiffen, and when she cursed and Hanna heard her voice, she knew Grayson had been right.

"You've got a choice here, Jesse," Marlene sniped as she yanked off the gas mask she'd been wearing. "I'll leave, and you'll never see or hear from me again. Just let me walk out of here and Hanna and your son stay safe."

Hanna didn't believe that for a second, and she was sure Jesse didn't either. With Marlene's resources, if she escaped, she'd be back eventually. Or send her hired thugs to finish them off.

"Let you walk out of here with a hostage?" Jesse countered. "I don't think so."

Marlene huffed. "I'll let Isabel go, too, just as soon as I'm away from the house. Just as I'm sure you and yours won't gun me down."

"Let her take me," Isabel insisted. She was crying now, and her breath was coming out in short, hiccupping sobs. "That way, she won't be anywhere near Evan or Hanna."

That made up for some of the anger Hanna felt for her mother, but it was an offer that Hanna knew Marlene would take. She couldn't afford not to. Without a hostage, she stood no chance of getting away.

Well, maybe she didn't.

There was probably at least one of her men near the driveway. Either that or Marlene had managed to fire all those shots and set off those gas canisters herself.

"Your militia buddies aren't going to save you," Jesse said while he made a subtle shift in his position. He was still looking for an opening to take a shot. "And we have enough proof to put you away for a long, long time."

"You have no proof," she snapped.

"You were in the trees the night Arnie shot me," Hanna threw out there. Partly a bluff. "You also talked my mother into helping you by depositing dirty money into her account."

Marlene didn't deny any of that, but she was shuffling around, her gaze volleying toward the living room. She was trapped and getting desperate. Hanna doubted she'd just shoot Isabel, but that gun could go off.

"This shouldn't be happening," Marlene yelled. "Why couldn't you just have died when Arnie shot you? Then, I wouldn't have had to worry about what you did or didn't remember, about what you did or didn't see." Marlene wailed and cursed some vile words.

Hanna wanted to ask what it was she could have seen or heard, but Jesse spoke first, and he went with a different angle.

"How long have you known your brother was an ATF agent?" Jesse asked. "One who came back into your life with the sole purpose of bringing down a militia you were running."

"When the hell do you think I found out?" the woman snapped. "It was the night Arnie went off the deep end. The idiot. I tried to calm him down, tried to tell him that I'd deal with it if you arrested him, but he wouldn't hear of it. He had to go out there and mess everything up."

The coldness in the woman's words sickened Hanna. Marlene didn't care one bit that Arnie had nearly killed her and her baby. She only cared about Arnie bringing heat to the militia.

Her militia.

"So, what happened?" Jesse pressed. "You went to the ranch, hoping to intercept Arnie, and you witnessed the shooting. Then, you heard Bull tell Hanna he was a deep cover agent."

"My own brother," Marlene railed, verifying what Jesse had just suggested. "I was shocked, stunned. Horrified. And that's the only reason I didn't kill him then and there. I waited a heartbeat too long, and then you and your cousin arrived on scene. I couldn't kill all of you because I didn't know how many other Rylands and ranch hands were running to the rescue."

"That's why you stayed hidden," Jesse finished for her. "But then you started worrying about what else Bull might have told Hanna."

"Damn right I was worried. I didn't know if Bull had

connected me to the Brotherhood or not. I knew I'd have to keep a watch on Hanna. As long as she didn't remember what happened, she wasn't a threat, but Isabel said your memory was starting to come back."

And there it was.

Finally, the truth.

But it was also what Marlene had obviously hoped to be her parting words to them because she started to back away with Isabel in tow. She muttered something, not to any of them, but into what Hanna thought might be a communicator clipped to her collar.

"I'm on the move," Marlene told whoever was on the other end of the device. "Help me get out of here."

Jesse moved fast, and he took aim. Not at Marlene but at the wall just over her head. He fired, the sound of the gunshot blasting through the house.

On a howl of outrage, Marlene whirled around to aim at Jesse just as another shot slammed into the wall. That one had no doubt come from Grayson. Marlene turned, dragging Isabel tighter against her. Or rather, trying to do that, but Isabel started fighting her.

Hanna got hit with the flashbacks of her own attack, but she didn't give in to them. She just kept the gun ready in case she was the one who got the right shot.

Screaming and cursing, Marlene lost her grip on Isabel, who was struggling hard to get away. The moment Isabel finally managed to drop down to the floor, Hanna was ready to pull the trigger.

But Jesse beat her to it.

He went for the kill shot to the head, probably because he couldn't risk a wounded Marlene getting the chance to return fire. The woman froze, her startled gaze locking with Hanna's for just a split second before the life drained from her eyes. She fell, crumpling into a heap on the floor.

Hanna froze, too, but it was from the relief that was already washing over her. It didn't last though. The fear and worry returned with a vengeance when Grayson rushed into view. He glanced around, helping Isabel to her feet while he all but carried her into the bathroom. It was probably overkill, but he went ahead and frisked Isabel to make sure she wasn't armed.

She wasn't.

Grayson's forehead bunched up when he spotted Norris. "The ambulance is nearby, and I'll give the EMTs the go ahead to come here." He shifted toward Jesse. "You stay here and make sure no one gets in the house. We need to round up every last one of her henchmen. Because they're still out there, and they no doubt have orders to kill."

Chapter Seventeen

Orders to kill.

Jesse had no doubts whatsoever about that, but he hated that the reminder had put a fresh layer of fear all over Hanna's face. Not Evan's though. Jesse didn't know how the baby had managed it, but he'd fallen back asleep despite the hell and chaos going on around him.

"How much backup do you have?" Jesse asked Grayson.

"Enough. Some deputies just arrived, and they've already started looking. The ranch hands, too. Stay here," he repeated. "I'll lock the front doors, and you turn on the security system. Hold on to that a little while longer," Grayson added when he tipped his head to the gun Hanna was holding.

Jesse hated to put that kind of burden on her, but another thing was for certain—she would do what she had to. Despite the trauma she'd been through, no way would Hanna just sit back while they were still in danger.

Grayson hurried out, and once Jesse heard him lock up, he rearmed the security system. Of course, one of the militia thugs could have sneaked in by now, so that's why Jesse stood by the door and kept watch. Hanna did the same across from him.

"I'm so sorry," Isabel muttered in a soft sob, and she kept repeating it.

"Mother, you need to get in the tub with the baby," Hanna told her.

Maybe that was just to get Isabel to focus on something other than her regret, but it seemed to work. The woman paused for just a moment before she swiped at her tears, blinked away some more of them and maneuvered into the small space next to Evan. When she saw the blood on Norris's arm, Isabel even grabbed a towel off the bar and wrapped it around the wound.

Good. That would help Norris, and giving Isabel something to do might keep her from crying. She had a right to start sobbing after nearly being killed, but Jesse preferred she put that guilt on hold.

"My mother will go to jail, won't she?" Hanna asked him in a whisper. "Because of the money laundering."

Jesse didn't lie to her. "It's possible. She might be able to work out some kind of plea deal and get away with parole and community service."

She nodded. "I don't think she has anything to do with the attacks."

"No," Jesse agreed. He was mentally piecing it together, and he could see this all went back to Marlene. Once they'd had a chance to go through all her financials, they might be able to figure out just how long she'd been involved in the tangle of illegal activities.

A tangle that he wished Bull had uncovered before Hanna had been shot.

But Bull and Isabel weren't the only ones at fault here.

"Don't," he heard Hanna say, and she surprised him when she leaned over and brushed a kiss on his mouth. "I know what's going on in your head right now. You're thinking if you'd arrested Arnie sooner, then none of the rest of this would have happened."

"I was thinking it because it's true," he pointed out.

Thanks to the flashlight app on their phones, the room was lit enough now that he had no trouble seeing her fierce expression. "But maybe something worse would have gone down if you had managed to arrest Arnie. Something like his arrest could have triggered Marlene to order hits on all of you. On us," she amended. "And we wouldn't have known to watch out for her."

Jesse knew that was possible, but it was still hard for him to clear his conscience. Hanna must have read his mind on that, as well, because she kissed him again. And this time it had a kick of heat despite everything else that was going on.

Isabel made a soft sound. Not a gasp, but one look at her and it was obvious she'd seen that kiss.

"Not a word from you on this," Hanna warned her. "I'm not going to let your bad blood with Jesse's family bleed onto me again. Understand?"

Jesse expected Isabel to have a say about that. She always had when it came to her daughter being involved with a Ryland, but maybe the night had changed her. Or at least made her see that bad blood could be forgiven.

So could his guilt over not having done more to stop Hanna from being shot.

Jesse figured it wasn't over and done. Ditto for Isabel's dislike of him, but this felt like a start. He would take it.

When Norris groaned, Jesse glanced over at him to see how he was doing. There didn't seem to be any fresh blood on the towel Isabel had used, so that was good news. Maybe it wouldn't be long before the ambulance would be able to get to the house and take both Isabel and him to the hospital. And that prompted Jesse to ask Hanna's mom some questions.

"Did Marlene drug you?" he asked.

Isabel nodded. "She must have put something in my coffee. She came over to talk and claimed she was worried about what was going on with Hanna and these attacks." Some anger flashed through her eyes. "She wasn't worried. She drugged me and then kept telling me how I had to drive out here and demand that Hanna and Evan come back to my estate." She stopped, swallowed hard. "Marlene wanted me to be a distraction so she could get those militia members onto the grounds."

Yeah, that was Jesse's take in it, too. Unfortunately, it had worked, and whoever had fired at Grayson on the road had added to the distraction and prevented Grayson from getting to the house to help them.

"I'm not sure how Marlene managed to cut the power to the house," Jesse muttered, "but it's possible somebody in the militia knew how to do that."

Knew, too, how to get their hands on the tear gas canisters they'd used to scatter the ranch hands. Of course, a group who dealt in illegal weapons and drugs likely wouldn't have had trouble getting supplies like that.

"The CSIs will have to process the house," Hanna said, drawing his attention back to her.

Not that his attention had strayed too far. Along with keeping watch, Jesse made frequent glances at Hanna and Evan to make sure they were okay. They were, but he probably wouldn't be certain of that until he could hold them in his arms. He considered doing that now, but he knew it should wait.

"They will," he agreed. And he hated that her home would be off limits to her for a while. Maybe forever. He didn't know if she'd ever feel safe here after what'd happened tonight.

"Evan and I can go to your place?" Hanna asked.

Isabel opened her mouth, probably to say they could come to her estate, but the look Hanna gave her silenced the woman.

"Of course," Jesse assured her, and while that wasn't a hug, it gave him a whole lot of comfort. Neither Hanna nor Evan had ever stayed the night at his house, and it would be great to have them there.

Not just temporarily, either.

Jesse thought back to those terrifying moments when they had realized they were under attack. The moment when he'd realized just how much he loved her. And he did. That wasn't a false feeling created by the adrenaline. He loved both Evan and her, but he wouldn't lay that all on her now. Best to give her some time to come down from what she had gone through.

"I'm in love with you," Hanna said.

When Jesse heard the words, at first he thought he'd said them, that he had blurted it out, after all. But he looked up and realized Hanna had spoken them.

To him.

"You don't have to do anything about it," she added, making a gesture as if waving that off.

Jesse would have definitely done something if, at that exact moment, his phone hadn't vibrated with a call from Grayson. Talk about bad timing. But in this case, it was warranted because it was good news.

"We got them," Grayson immediately said. "Rounded them all up. I'm at the front door, so I need you to let me in."

Jesse hurried to the front to do just that, but he didn't linger for Grayson to fill him in. He went back to the bathroom. Outside, he heard the ambulance, another good sign.

Grayson came to the bathroom door and looked in at them, obviously checking to make sure everyone was okay. They were, but they probably showed every bit of the fierce battle they'd just fought.

"You're sure you got all of the thugs?" Hanna asked.

Grayson nodded. "Shaw helped. So did the ranch hands once the tear gas had cleared. There were three gunmen. One clammed up, but the other two decided they wanted to confess to any and everything. They independently told us that Marlene had brought three of them with her."

Three. Not an army exactly, but they clearly had managed to do a lot of damage. They could have done more.

"We can wait in here until the EMTs arrive," Grayson went on, "and then I can take you to wherever you need to go in the cruiser."

"The ranch," Jesse and Hanna said at the same time.

Grayson's only reactions were a lifted eyebrow and brief smile, but it was obvious he approved. "It shouldn't take long before I can get you there. Theo and Ava are taking the three thugs to jail now. Obviously, we won't hold them with Bull. We'll be releasing him."

Jesse was okay with that even if he couldn't do the whole forgive-and-forget deal for Bull not being able to stop Arnie from shooting Hanna. But that wasn't a reason for him to stay behind bars. If Bull had been involved in anything illegal, Marlene would have ratted him out since it was obvious she hated her brother for being a deep cover agent.

"So, there's no indications that Shaw was dirty?" Hanna asked Grayson.

"None, and since he jumped right in to help us tonight, I'm inclined to believe he's clean. The ATF will have the final say on that though. I'm sure their internal affairs will pick through everything and make sure both Bull and Shaw haven't bent or flat-out broken the law."

Yeah, that IA investigation would be a given in a situation like this. The ATF would probably also fully take over dismantling the militia, and that was a chore that Jesse knew Grayson would gladly hand over to them.

"Thank you," Isabel said, and she glanced at Grayson, Jesse and then Hanna. "If you hadn't fired those shots, I might not have been able to get away from Marlene. How did you even know it was her?" she added to Grayson.

"I heard her when she whispered something to one of those thugs through her lapel communicator and I recognized her voice."

Jesse, too, had heard those whispers, but he hadn't been close enough to ID Marlene.

"I wonder why Marlene decided to come here and try to do her own dirty work." Hanna threw it out there.

"Maybe because she was fed up with her men failing," Jesse said. "Or maybe she wanted to personally settle this score."

Since Marlene was dead, they might never know. Well, unless she'd shared her plan with the three men they now had in custody.

When the EMTs came rushing into the nursery, Hanna handed Deputy Norris back his gun, and she picked up Evan from the tub. She also pressed a kiss to Isabel's cheek. A gesture that brought tears to the woman's eyes.

"I'll see you soon," Hanna told her mother and she, while cuddling Evan close to her, followed Jesse into the nursery.

"Let me bring the cruiser to the front, and we can go," Grayson explained, heading out to leave Hanna, Evan and him alone.

Jesse took full advantage of that lull to do what he'd been needing to do. He gathered both Evan and Hanna into his arms, and he brushed a kiss on the top of Evan's head. The boy could certainly sleep because he didn't even budge.

Hanna budged though. In a way. She smiled when he kissed her not on her head but on the mouth. Jesse had intended to leave it at just that. Something short and sweet, a little celebration that they'd survived in one piece.

He went to move back, but Hanna took hold of Jesse's chin and pulled him to her. There was nothing short or sweet about the kiss she gave him. It was long, deep and filled with the emotion he could practically taste.

"You said something about being in love with me," he reminded her.

"I am." There was emotion in her voice, and lots and lots of heat.

"Good," Jesse said, "because I'm in love with you, too." That led to another kiss. One with way too much heat considering they were standing in the nursery just a few feet away from EMTs, Isabel and the wounded deputy.

Jesse put the heat on pause, knowing he could fire it right up as soon as he had Hanna at his place.

She looked up at him and ran her thumb over his jaw. "If the trauma of all of this didn't trigger my memories, I might never get them all back."

He studied her for any signs as to how she felt about that. She didn't seem upset. "Are you okay with that?" he asked.

Hanna nodded and gave him another of those dazzling smiles. "Maybe we can make some new memories," she said.

Jesse gave that smile right back to her and pulled Evan and her snugly into his arms. Yes, he was all for making lots and lots of new memories with Hanna and their son.

* * * * *

DISAPPEARANCE IN DREAD HOLLOW

DEBRA WEBB

Chapter One

Valley Lane
Dread Hollow, Tennessee
Sunday, April 30, 7:00 p.m.

"Mama!"

"It's almost done, sweetie. Five more minutes."

Jacob stared out the window. It would be completely dark soon. They didn't get many visitors, but there was a black car parked in front of their house. He had noticed it a few minutes ago when he went to the window to see if he could see the moon. He couldn't remember if the full moon was tonight or tomorrow night, but he wanted to make sure he saw it.

"Mama!" he shouted again. "Come here!"

Jelly Bug raised her head and whined.

"It's okay, girl," Jacob said. He hadn't meant to scare the dog with his hollering.

His dad wasn't home yet. He was usually home by dark. Probably would be soon. He wouldn't miss supper. Mama had said he'd gone to fill up his truck with gas. He always did that on Sundays. Getting ready for the work week, he would say. Except he usually did it earlier in the afternoon.

His mama came to his door. "What is it, son? Supper is done, and your dad just pulled up."

Jacob peered out the window. Saw his dad's truck this time. The black car was still sitting there. The windows were too dark for him to see inside. The windows had that tinted stuff on them. Maybe whoever was inside was coming in with his dad. Could have been waiting for him to get here. Jelly Bug nudged up to Jacob's side. He patted the dog's head and turned his face up to his mom.

"There's a stranger's car out there," Jacob said, feeling like a grown-up since he'd pointed out a possible problem. His parents had taught him to be aware of strangers.

Tired, his mama sighed. She always looked tired. She worked too hard. Still, she walked over to his window. "What car?"

"That one." He pointed beyond the curtain.

"Kris!" his dad shouted from the living room.

Jacob and his mama shared a startled look at the worry in his father's voice.

His dad burst into Jacob's bedroom. He looked scared. Scared real bad. Jacob's heart beat faster like he'd started running when he was just standing still at the window.

Jelly Bug whined, and this time she shivered as if she understood something was wrong.

Jacob's mama backed away from the window. "What? What's going on?"

His dad looked to her for a second then to Jacob. "Hide," he ordered. "Hide in your closet. Behind the clothes."

"Is it them?" his mama cried.

His dad nodded, his eyes so big Jacob thought they looked like the full moon he liked so much.

Jacob's heart pounded now the way it did when he rode his bike up and down the street really fast over and over.

His mama pushed him toward his closet. "Hide," she repeated. "Don't come out for any reason. No matter what you hear." She hugged him. "I love you, Jacob."

"What's—" he tried to ask, but couldn't get the words out. His heart pounded, his legs felt shaky. He was scared. What was happening?

Jelly Bug whined some more and barked softly.

"Stay in there." His dad picked him up and set him behind the clothes in the back corner of his closet. "Don't make a sound and don't come out no matter what. Love you, son."

"What about Jelly Bug?"

"Don't worry about the dog. She'll be fine."

The door shut, but Jacob could still hear his mama making crying sounds. What was going on? Tears rolled down his cheeks. He didn't understand. Why did he have to hide?

He wanted to run after them…to call out.

But they'd told him not to…he had to stay hidden and be quiet.

He held his breath, tried to slow the racing in his chest. Tried to control the sounds trying to escape his mouth. *Be quiet! Be quiet!*

Jacob curled into himself, his knees hugged to his damp face, and rocked gently. The way his mama used to rock him when he was little. Don't make a sound. *Don't make a sound. Not one sound.*

He stilled. Heard his dad's voice. In the living room. He sounded far away, but that was because the door was closed.

Jacob stretched his neck, listened harder.

His dad was yelling now. His mama too, except her voice

was quieter. She was afraid. It sounded like she was begging. Jelly Bug was barking.

Please...please don't hurt my parents.

More voices. Not so loud but deep. Men. Definitely men. Didn't sound like women.

Men from the black car. *Strangers.* People who wanted to hurt his family.

Jelly Bug was barking louder now.

Jacob closed his eyes tightly and prayed.

He prayed and prayed and prayed.

Then the house was quiet.

But he didn't move. His dad had said to stay in the closet no matter what he heard.

The sound of Jelly Bug sniffing at his bedroom door had him daring to ease out of the closet. He crawled over and sat on his knees at his bedroom door for a while, listening, afraid to open it but wanting to let Jelly Bug in. Finally, he held his breath and just did it. He opened the door without making a sound. *Whew!*

Jelly Bug wiggled around him as if trying to tell him something or just glad to see him. He didn't hear or see anything, but he wasn't taking any chances. He quietly closed the door and crawled back to the closet, closed that door too and held Jelly Bug close. She licked his face. He snuggled against her, wishing his parents would walk into his room and tell him to come out, come out, the way they did when they played the hiding game. He liked playing games with his parents. He didn't have any brothers and sisters, but he was okay with that since his parents played with him so much.

He stayed in the closet so long he fell asleep. When he

woke up, his legs and arms hurt from being curled together so tight for so long.

He stretched. Groaned. Jelly Bug did the same.

For a long while, he listened but there was still no sound.

Being really careful, he reached up and opened the closet door. His room was dark now. He crawled out. Too afraid to stand up yet. If he didn't move too fast, no one would see him in the dark. Jelly Bug stayed close.

It didn't sound like anyone was here.

He wanted to call out for his mama, but he kept his mouth closed tight. He wasn't supposed to make a sound.

At his bedroom door, he held still and listened again. The only sound was Jelly Bug's panting.

The whole house was dark. And quiet.

He held his breath as he opened the door, then eased into the hall. Jelly Bug moved with him. Maybe while he was asleep the strangers had left and his parents had gone to bed.

He stood and took a few steps forward. His legs complained as he walked after being curled up so long. He moved quietly, careful not to make a sound on the hardwood floor. He went into his parents' room, but it was too dark to see. He didn't dare turn on the light. Instead he walked to the bed and climbed into it. He moved all around the bed, but it was empty. He checked under the bed and then in their closet to see if they were hiding.

Nope.

Then he walked soundlessly to the bathroom, then the living room and finally the kitchen. No one was in the house. Just him.

Had his parents gone with the strangers?

Maybe there was a job his parents had to do. Since he'd fallen asleep, maybe they decided not to bother him.

The supper sat on the stove. He could smell the beans and ham. His stomach rumbled. He climbed into a chair at the table and waited in the darkness.

When his parents came back, they would all have supper together and go to bed.

Jacob waited. Jelly Bug waited with him.

He waited a very long time. Drifted off to sleep once and almost fell out of the chair. He shook his head. Blinked over and over. He had to stay awake so he'd know when his parents came home.

He sat in the chair so long his butt felt numb.

His stomach growled so much he was sure the neighbors would hear it.

He was starving. His mama wouldn't want him to be hungry. He hoped his parents weren't hungry.

Eventually he couldn't wait any longer. He pushed his chair over to the sink, trying to stay quiet, but it wasn't easy. He got a bowl from the drainer where his mama put the dishes when she washed them. He grabbed a spoon too. Then he pushed his chair to the stove and filled his bowl with the beans and pieces of ham floating in the soup.

Jelly Bug barked and jumped around, so he made a bowl for her too.

He sat down in the chair right there by the stove and ate.

His parents would be home soon. They would be proud of him for taking care of his supper.

When he finished, he put his and Jelly Bug's bowls in the sink and pushed his chair back to the table. He and Jelly Bug went into the living room and sat in the darkness to wait.

His mama and dad would be home any minute now. They had never left him alone.

Except that once…

Chapter Two

Dread Hollow School
School Street
Wednesday, May 3, 2:30 p.m.

Deke Shepherd could no longer deny there was a serious problem with one of his students. As a teacher, it was part of his job to pay attention to the well-being of his students. Part of that included making observations about a child's general appearance and emotional state.

Case in point, last school term he noticed one of his students appeared to be having accident after accident. In October, it was a fracture of the humerus. December brought on a second-degree burn of the right hand. Then it was the mostly hidden bruises and lacerations. There came a point when Deke had to wonder if there was more than clumsiness at play.

Elementary-school students could be accident-prone or, perhaps more accurately, unaware of their limitations. Like trying out power tools or climbing ladders left unattended. Worse, playing with an unsecured handgun or rifle. Tragedy was often buried in good intentions or ill-fated distraction.

Fortunately, Deke's current concern wasn't anything

nearly so heartbreaking—at least on the surface. Jacob Callaway had worn the same clothes to school three days in a row. It was obvious that he hadn't bathed either. Judging by the way he scarfed down his lunch, he likely wasn't getting breakfast at home. Sadly, there were children who were neglected all over the world. But Jacob Callaway wasn't one of them—at least not usually. The child was always clean and well-fed. His homework was always complete and well-done.

Until this week.

Deke had decided this morning there was something going on that needed attention. Sometimes teachers had to put on a social-worker hat. It wasn't always appreciated, but it was at times necessary.

The dismissal bell rang, and the rows of third graders buzzed to life, grabbing backpacks and scrambling to escape the confines of the classroom.

When Jacob hurried to the front of his row and would have followed the throng out the door, Deke said, "Jacob, hold up a minute."

The boy froze. His wide-eyed gaze filled with uncertainty. "Am I in trouble?"

Deke felt instant regret for worrying the kid. "Course not." He produced a grin. "You never get into trouble."

It was true. Jacob was one of the most well-behaved nine-year-olds Deke had had the pleasure of teaching.

Deke propped a hip against his desk, adopting a more relaxed stance in hopes of putting the kid at ease. "Is everything okay at home?"

Jacob's eyes shuttered. "I don't know what you mean."

"Your mom and dad okay? Nobody's sick or anything like that?"

The boy's head wagged side to side in a no.

Deke considered a different avenue. "Have your mom and dad been working a lot of hours lately? Maybe getting home really late and leaving extra early?"

His shoulders went up as if he might shrug, then froze. "I...think...so."

Deke had attempted to call first the boy's mother, then father. The calls had gone straight to voice mail. He had decided a home visit was in order. Something was wrong here, and he wasn't waiting another day to determine the problem.

"Why don't I give you a ride home?" Deke reached for his briefcase. He'd already tucked away the papers he needed to grade and prepared for leaving at the same time as his students.

Jacob's shoulders drooped. "'Kay."

The boy didn't ride a bus. He either walked or one of his parents picked him up. Since he didn't mention the possibility that one or the other would be picking him up, Deke assumed that wasn't going to happen.

He flipped off the classroom light as they exited. The school was a kindergarten through twelfth grade institution. It was small and Deke liked it that way. He'd put in his time at one of the big schools in Chattanooga. The move to this small community had been the best decision of his career. He paused at his truck and opened the door for his passenger. Or maybe it had been more about his personal life than his career. He'd been ready for peace and quiet. Whatever. Three years later, he was still happy with his decision.

Jacob looked up at him. "You sure I'm not in trouble, Mr. D?"

"You have my word, Jacob. You are not in trouble with me," he promised.

The boy climbed into the old Ford. The truck had belonged to Deke's father. It was the one useful thing the old man had left him. When Deke had made the decision to leave the city, he'd left his sports car and his downtown condo to new owners. He was perfectly happy in the old farmhouse he was still renovating and the truck his father had driven for thirty years. Truth was the truck looked better than the farmhouse. His father had been like that, kept everything organized and in tip-top shape. He just hadn't been very good at relationships.

Not that Deke could claim he was much better. At thirty-five, he was a work-in-progress, but he was getting there.

Deke glanced at his passenger as he waited his turn to exit the school parking lot. "You ready for the social studies test tomorrow?"

Jacob glanced at him. "Yes, sir."

"Good." Deke smiled. He'd expected the answer. Jacob was a good student. Until yesterday he'd never failed to turn in his homework. Every kid deserved a pass now and then.

The crossing guard waved him forward, and Deke allowed the truck to roll out onto the street. Dread Hollow was a small community carved out of Lookout Mountain, only miles above the fray in Chattanooga. The area was surrounded by attractions, like the haunted house named after Dread Hollow. But the Hollow remained a small, isolated village deep in the woods, away from the high-end real estate only a few miles away.

Deke slowed for the turn from Main Street onto Hillside Drive. There was a post office, a diner, a small market and a walk-in health clinic. Plus, the school of course. The Hollow wasn't big enough for its own police department, but there was a substation of the sheriff's department. The sheriff's deputy in charge was a regular at career day and anti-drug programs at the school.

He excised the thought of the deputy, his most recent fail at relationships.

Granted that fumble had been his first since moving to the Hollow. He'd avoided relationships for two full years, and then he'd fallen face first. It had ended quickly enough. Too quickly for him. He still had no idea where he'd gone wrong. For once, he'd thought the relationship was going well.

Deke navigated from Hillside Drive to Valley Lane. Jacob lived in the last house on the left. The vehicle he'd seen Jacob's mother driving when she dropped him off at school sat in the driveway. Like the houses on this short lane, the car had seen better days. Deke parked behind it.

Jacob seemed to sink deeper into the seat.

"Looks like your mom is home," Deke commented as he shut off the engine and reached for the door handle.

Jacob didn't respond, just popped his seat belt, opened the door and slid out.

Deke followed him up the drive, past the parked car. He glanced inside. No overnight bag suggesting his mom had been on a trip. No trash indicating extended travel. Nothing out of place.

The steps creaked as they climbed to the narrow porch. Jacob led the way, reaching beneath his shirt for a necklace that held a key. He unlocked the door, glanced back at Deke and then went inside.

The dread on the child's face was unmistakable. Deke's gut tightened. Braced for trouble.

"Mama!" Jacob called out.

A small tan dog, maybe a cross between a dachshund and a cocker spaniel jumped around the boy and yipped.

Deke lingered near the door. Since he hadn't knocked, he decided it was best that he didn't venture inside until he had an adult's permission.

Jacob disappeared into another room, calling for his mother again, then his dad.

The house was dead silent. No smells of recently cooked food though there was an underlying stench suggesting the trash was overdue to be removed. The house was stuffy as if the air conditioning was off. Windows in the living room were closed.

Jacob reappeared. "I guess they're not home yet."

"Why don't we call your mother's workplace and see if she's still there?" Deke suggested.

"She doesn't like for me to call the diner unless it's an emergency." He scrunched up his face. "She might get into trouble."

He stared up at Deke as if the idea of calling his mother's workplace was scarier than the possibility of being home alone—which Deke suspected he may have been all week.

"I'm afraid you can't stay home alone," Deke countered. Tennessee law suggested the age of ten for a child being left home alone. A parent might be able to decide otherwise, but as the kid's teacher, Deke didn't have that leeway.

The kid tossed his backpack on the sofa and shrugged. "I always stay home alone when my parents have to work late. I can take care of myself."

"Let's talk a minute," Deke suggested. He walked to the sofa and sat down.

Jacob shuffled over to a chair and sat down, shoulders slumped once more.

"I noticed you've been wearing that same T-shirt and jeans all week."

Jacob stared down at his clothes but said nothing.

"You didn't have your homework yesterday or today," Deke went on. "That's a little out of character, Jacob. You always have your homework."

"My mom has been working a lot of hours and…" He glanced around as if trying to decide where to go next with his explanation. "My dad is out of town."

This was certainly possible. These days folks did whatever necessary to maintain a decent income.

"Did you see your mother before school this morning?"

Jacob hesitated but then shook his head. "She was already gone."

But why wasn't she home now? Her car was in the driveway. Deke let that go for a moment. "Did you see her last night before you went to bed?"

Again he shook his head. "I was asleep already."

"Then how do you know she was home at all?"

"Course she was home."

"Does she drive to work?" Deke asked.

Jacob nodded. "Sure."

"Her car is in the driveway," Deke pointed out.

The kid chewed at his lip a second or two. "I think she went with my dad today."

"I thought he was out of town." Deke hated making the boy uncomfortable.

Jacob's hands knotted together. "He must have come home today." He scooted to the edge of his seat. "I have to feed Jelly Bug and take her out."

Deke might be reaching here, but he had to do something. He couldn't simply accept the kid's explanations and let it go. "Do you mind if we go to the kitchen? I really need a drink of water."

Jacob twisted his hands tighter, then nodded. "Sure."

He got up and shuffled toward the next room. Deke pushed to his feet and followed. The living room appeared ordinary. Neat. Nothing fancy. The few houses on this street were old, most visibly in need of repairs. The furniture was well worn but clean. Jacob's parents had made the best of what they had.

The kitchen on the other hand was anything but tidy. A jar of peanut butter sat open on the counter. A partial loaf of bread stood along with a half-eaten bag of chips. Crumbs and used utensils were scattered about. There were dirty dishes—cups, glasses, cereal bowls—in the sink.

A pot of beans sat on the stove. Judging by the smell, it had been there a couple of days anyway. Deke's concern moved up several notches.

"You've been making your own dinner?" Deke watched the boy's face. Spotted the deer caught in the headlights look.

Jacob nodded.

"Okay, you need to be completely honest with me here. Where's your mom, Jacob?"

His lower lip trembled. "I don't know."

Deke's gut tightened. "What about your dad?"

The kid's head swung side to side. "I don't know."

Deke crouched down to his eye level. "When did you last see either one of them?"

"Sunday." He shrugged. "Close to dark. The moon was almost out."

"They didn't come home Sunday night?"

"No."

"Did they leave in your dad's truck?"

Another sad shake of his head. "Two men came to the house."

Tension filtered through Deke. "Did you know the men?"

"Mama made me hide in the closet when she saw them outside. I never saw them."

"So, whoever these men were," Deke began, "your mother was afraid of them or something like that?"

He nodded. "She was scared. She told me to stay hidden no matter what I heard, and I did."

Deke braced for more bad news. "What did you hear, Jacob?"

"Shouting." He glanced at the floor. "Bad words."

"You didn't recognize the voices?"

"No. Just my parents begging for them to leave."

"Did they say anything that might tell us why they had come to see your folks?"

"There was a lot of yelling, but I didn't understand what they were saying. I just know they all left. I waited up… until I fell asleep on the couch. But they never came home."

Deke considered how to phrase his next question. He didn't want to make the boy feel any worse than he already did.

"Jacob, why didn't you tell me about this when you came to school on Monday?"

He stared at the floor. "I didn't tell anyone."

"Why didn't you tell anyone?"

"This happened once before." He met Deke's gaze. "Before we moved here. Not the bad men in the black car like the other night. Just the not coming home part. My mama and dad came home really late one night because they had to work. The boss said if they left they'd get fired. I didn't know. I was little, like seven, I think. I just knew they weren't home, and I got worried and went out in the yard looking for them. A neighbor saw me and called the police. When my parents came home it didn't matter, the police wouldn't let me stay with them. It was a whole month before I got to go back home." He stared at his knotted fingers. "I don't want that to happen again. They'll be back. I know they will. It's probably work. Please don't tell, Mr. D."

Deke patted him on the shoulder. "Don't worry. We'll figure this out."

"Just don't call the police," Jacob urged. "Please don't call the police."

As badly as he didn't want to cause the child any further distress, there was no help for it.

"Look," Deke offered, "I have a friend who works at the sheriff's department. We can call her, and she'll help us find your parents. Does that sound like a good plan to you?"

Jacob's gaze narrowed. "Are you sure she's a friend?"

That could possibly be debatable, but Deke was confident she wouldn't let Jacob down. "She's a good friend. She'll do all she can to help you."

"Okay." Tears welled in his eyes. "I'm really getting worried. They've never left like this before."

"Let's take Jelly Bug out and get her fed, and I'll call my friend."

This was one time when Deke wished his instincts had been wrong.

This—whatever this was—was a serious problem.

Chapter Three

"I'm telling you, Deputy Norwood, it's the right thing to do."

Tara Norwood somehow managed to keep a smile in place as she listened to Wilma Hambrick go on and on about the possibility of starting the process of forming a police department in Dread Hollow. For now, the small community was served by a substation of the Hamilton County Sheriff's Department. Until a couple of weeks ago, the arrangement had worked amazingly well.

Wilma Hambrick had other ideas. She had worked long and hard to achieve incorporation for Dread Hollow—a small community which barely met the minimum population of 1500 people required. According to Tara's dad, the woman had started the process just so she could be elected mayor. Having achieved that goal last year, her newest endeavor was to go after a police department. Just another step in the process of giving herself more power, Tara's dad insisted.

Tara didn't see the point. A fully formed city government only cost the locals more in taxes. Hiring a police chief and a couple of deputies would serve the community no better than what they had now. Tara was the sheriff's deputy in charge of the substation. Collin Porch was the only other deputy assigned full time to the substation. He lived in nearby East Ridge. Since Tara lived in Dread Hollow, she was on call 24/7. Thankfully, there wasn't enough crime or trouble of any sort in Dread Hollow to authorize additional personnel, much less an entire department. Tara couldn't remember the last time she'd had to arrest anyone. She spent more of her time finding the occasional escapee from the local assisted-living facility than she did chasing criminals.

Until, she acknowledged silently, two weeks ago when a sudden rash of burglaries started. Most of the stolen goods were basically small time. Televisions. Cell phones and other easily sold goods. No one had been caught, and Tara would have been ready to consider the work that of a group of teenagers playing dare games—except for the handful of witnesses who claimed to have seen two men dressed all in black, including ski masks. Still could be teenagers, but so far no one had ratted them out. Chances were, someone would talk eventually.

"Ms. Hambrick," she said patiently, "it's my firm belief that decisions like this need to be made by the folks who live in Dread Hollow."

"People are talking about these burglaries and your inability to catch the perpetrators," Hambrick warned.

This was true to a degree, but it wasn't as bad as it sounded. A few people had complained.

"You live in Dread Hollow," the woman insisted. "You and your family have been here for five generations. The people listen to Norwoods. If your daddy would talk to the folks and tell them how good this would be, we could make it happen." She smiled broadly, her faded lipstick highlighting only parts of her lips. "And you would be our first chief of police."

And there it was—the real reason Wilma Hambrick was hounding Tara. Her dad's influence. No matter that he was not in the best of health, what he thought still carried weight in this community.

Tara reached deep down for more patience. "Ms. Hambrick, you know my dad doesn't get out much these days."

The fact that he had been diagnosed with second-stage Alzheimer's apparently hadn't given the woman pause. Although he had a lot of good days, there were those that were not so good, and even on his better days there were moments. The steady progression of the disease prevented him from taking care of himself without some degree of assistance.

Frustration and hurt curdled inside Tara. She'd wanted her father to live with her so she could take care of him, but he'd refused. He would not be a burden. Before she had even known the full extent of his condition, he'd made arrangements at Forrest Hills and checked himself in. Tara had been stunned and hurt, more so than she would ever tell her dad. Despite the shock of his decision, she had understood that he meant well.

Forrest Hills was just a few miles up Dread Hollow Road from the home where he and his father and his grandfather as well as his great-grandfather before that had grown up. Theirs was the first farm in the community. Forrest Hills was also the facility that occasionally had a runaway. The rare escape notwithstanding, the place was very nice. It just wasn't where Tara wanted her father.

Hambrick shook her head, her expression arranged into one of sadness. "I so hated to hear about his illness. Your daddy is a fine man. He was the best sheriff Hamilton County ever had, you know. Sheriff Decker is a good man, but he'll never be the kind of lawman your daddy was."

Tara smiled, a real one this time. "Yes, ma'am, I know."

Hambrick leaned forward in her chair. Far enough that her top-heaviness might surely topple her over at any second. "You could speak for your father. When folks see you, they think of him."

"I'll consider your request," Tara said, primarily to get her gone. She stood. "I appreciate you stopping by."

How poor Mr. Hambrick, God rest his soul, had lived with this woman for the better part of his life was beyond comprehension. Her father's words, not Tara's. Any time the Hambricks ever came up in conversation, her dad made that statement. He would say, "It's no wonder he failed to take his heart medication. It was as good a way to go as any." There were rumors that Ms. Hambrick had withheld his medication after his stroke. As annoying as the woman could be, the truth was her husband had been a controlling miser. Even as a kid, Tara had recognized he was mean. Maybe he was the reason the woman pushed her weight around. She had a lot of years of not getting what she wanted to make up for, Tara supposed.

Hambrick hoisted herself out of her chair. "You know my arthritis has been giving me a fit. All those April showers that have lingered into May. With Fred gone, I just don't know how I would protect myself if those thieves stormed into my house."

"I understand, ma'am. Keep your doors locked and the outside lights on. They seem to prefer the easier pickings."

The MO of the burglars hadn't changed so far. If Tara

was lucky, the situation wouldn't escalate before the two were identified and found.

Tara followed the lady to the door and saw her out. She watched until Hambrick had driven away.

There was something else her dad would say about Wilma Hambrick. The woman could talk your ear off.

While her work in Dread Hollow was nothing like the four years Tara had served in Nashville's Metro Police Department, she didn't regret the move one little bit. Her decision to leave Nashville and to take a job with Hamilton County had come after her mother's death five years ago. Though he would never have said as much, her father had needed her. He'd retired early just so he could take care of his beloved wife through her extended illness. After her death, he'd been a little lost.

Tara had helped him through that tough time. Then she'd met someone and suddenly there was a wedding to be planned. As if the stars had abruptly all aligned, the department had decided to open a substation in Dread Hollow and offered Tara the job. No matter that she'd felt confident the work would prove a bit on the boring side, she had hoped to be starting a family right away. Dread Hollow was the perfect place for raising children. Then her father would be too busy with grandkids to be so sad all the time.

But life didn't always work out as planned.

Barely two years later, the marriage had ended. The family never happened, and her father's health had gone into decline.

The cell on her hip vibrated and Tara pushed away the unpleasant memories. If she were lucky another of Sam Brown's llamas hadn't gotten out. A couple weeks ago two of the feisty creatures had decided they liked walking Main

Street. Granted the Hollow didn't have a lot of traffic, but folks got a little upset when the animals traipsed through well-manicured lawns leaving unsightly droppings and foraging on all manner of shrubs and flowering plants. Rounding up the llamas had been no picnic either.

Better escaped llamas than another burglary, she supposed.

"Deputy Norwood," she said in greeting.

The silence on the other end of the line set her senses on alert. There was the occasional call for help after a fall or someone with chest pains. Tara was closer than the fire station, so she typically received the call first.

"Hello," she prompted.

"Tara, it's Deke."

She blinked. Startled. They both lived in Dread Hollow, so not bumping into each other was impossible—hard as she tried to ensure they didn't. They even spoke occasionally in the market or on the street if they happened to cross paths. But they didn't call each other. Ever.

Before she could ask why he had called, he went on. "I'm at the home of one of my students, Jacob Callaway. He lives over on Valley Lane."

"I'm familiar with the Callaways." Tara didn't know them well, but she made it a point to be aware of folks who moved into her jurisdiction. The couple appeared to be about her and Deke's age, midthirties. The father worked at the poultry hatchery in Hixon. The mother worked at the diner on Main. One child, Jacob.

"According to Jacob, his parents have been missing since Sunday."

"Missing?" A frown tugged at Tara's brow. It wasn't unheard of for parents to just take off and leave a child. Sadly, it happened far too often. But not here. And though Tara was only acquainted with the mother, she'd overheard the woman showing off pictures of her son and bragging about his accomplishments at school any time Tara was in the diner. The Callaway woman didn't seem like the type.

"Missing," Deke confirmed. "I noticed Jacob had been wearing the same clothes three days in a row. He insisted everything was okay at home, but when I brought him home today, it was obvious he's been making his own supper. He finally admitted they haven't been home since Sunday." He exhaled a big breath. "Look, he didn't want me to call. Apparently, something similar has happened before, and he's afraid of being separated from his parents again. I promised him that wouldn't happen this time. I told him you would make sure."

She wanted to be angry that he would make such a promise, but she knew Deke. He loved his students. He would make exactly that kind of promise if that was what it took to keep a student safe and happy.

"I'll be right there."

"Thanks, Tara. I appreciate it."

"Yeah." She ended the call and headed for her vehicle. Since there was only one cruiser, she used her Wagoneer.

Collin Porch, the other deputy assigned to Dread Hollow, was out on patrol, so she gave him a quick call to bring him up to speed. The anticipation that instantly filled his voice was a reminder of just how calm life in Dread Hollow generally proved to be. She promised to keep him informed and headed for Valley Lane.

Main Street was home to the post office and the market as well as a handful of small locally owned and operated specialty shops. Martha Jo's Boutique, a children's and ladies' handmade goods shop. Cherry's Candle and Baked Goods. The small Feed and Seed Store, the Dreadfully Good Coffee Shop and Delilah's Diner.

In the fall, the town was full of tourists cruising through on the way to the famous Dread Hollow haunted house. It wasn't actually in their little town, but it was only a couple miles away.

There wasn't an operating gas station along Main Street, but there was a vintage one that was home to a family-owned-and-operated auto repair shop called Franklin's Fix-It. Tara had her 1987 Wagoneer serviced there, mostly because she'd graduated high school with Henry Franklin. Henry had been her best friend. Probably always would be. He knew more of her secrets than anyone—including her ex-husband. She and Henry had been quite the pranksters back in high school.

Most of the residents of the Hollow lived well off Main. There were a couple of renovated condos over some of the shops. At the edge of the newly incorporated town limits, an old elastic manufacturing mill had been turned into four apartments.

Once she was on Valley Lane, Tara spotted Deke's truck at the last house on the left and pulled to the side of the street. There were no curbs or sidewalks. Just a half dozen one-story ranch-style houses that had seen better days. The houses were spaced farther apart than in most subdivisions since construction fizzled out before it was completed.

Deke and Jacob sat on the steps leading up to the narrow porch. Tara climbed out of the Wagoneer and put on her best smile. She wore the same navy uniform as the other Hamilton County deputies with the matching baseball cap style headgear. Black leather shoes and the garden-variety utility belt that held the tools of her trade, including a baton and a service weapon.

Deke stood as she approached. Jacob did the same. If the fear on his face was any gauge of the terror he felt, she just wanted to hug the poor kid. His dark eyes were wide. Dark hair was mussed and in need of a good shampooing. Clothes were obviously in need of a wash.

The image just didn't fit with what she knew of his mother.

But he had a father too, and Tara knew very little about him.

Worry pounded in her veins. She'd been in charge of public safety in this little corner of the world for five years now. So far there had been no murders or grave assaults of any kind. She hoped that blessed record wasn't about to change.

"Hey, Jacob." She crouched down to a squat to give him the height advantage and then extended her hand. "You remember me from the Don't Do Drugs class last fall?"

He nodded. Shook her hand. "You brought that dog to class."

She smiled. "I did. His name is Snoopy. He's still helping my colleagues find the bad stuff."

His hand fell away. "Mr. D said you'd help me find my parents."

Tara glanced up at the teacher hovering next to the boy, suppressed the instant reaction to seeing him then returned her full attention to the kid. "I'll do everything I can. You have my word."

Jacob appeared to relax just a little. "Good. Because I know they wouldn't leave me like this unless something was wrong."

"I think you're right," Tara agreed. "I know your mom

from the diner, and she's always bragging on you. Why don't we go inside and you can tell me what happened?"

"'Kay."

Jacob turned and headed into the house. Tara pushed to her feet. "Any signs of struggle in there?"

Deke shook his head. "None that I saw."

"Let's have another look."

Tara started past him and he touched her arm. She stilled. Rode out the flash of heat that seared through her even at such an innocent connection.

"Thank you for reassuring him. He's really scared."

She moved on without responding. Their shared history had no place in whatever this was.

Inside the house, Tara was greeted by a frisky dog. Once she'd given the animal some love, she glanced around. From what she could see, the place was sparsely furnished and neat. Framed photos of Jacob and his parents hung on the walls. Not studio photographs in high-end designer frames; just the kind snapped with a cell phone, printed at a chain pharmacy and displayed in faux-wood frames bought at a big-box store. Didn't matter. The moments captured told the story. Jacob was a well-loved child by both parents. The father's broad smile and big hugs would be difficult to fake.

But sometimes darkness lurked deep beneath the surface.

She shook off the idea. Too early to form an opinion.

Jacob told her about the two men who showed up at their house on Sunday. He hadn't seen their faces, just heard two distinct voices. The car they had driven was black. Before he'd seen anything more than the car in the driveway, his mom had insisted he hide until the men were gone. Except then his parents were gone too. Not a lot to go on. Two facts were clear: the parents had known the men, and they had been afraid.

Since Jacob hadn't seen the men, she wasn't ready to take the leap that the two could be the pair in black who had been breaking into houses around the Hollow. Small-time criminals often escalated to larger crimes. Part of her hoped that was not the case, but then again, if it wasn't the burglars, then who? She and Collin had concluded the burglars were locals. These perps could be anyone from anywhere…capable of anything.

"How about a tour?" Tara said to Jacob. "I like to begin with a good look around."

Jacob glanced side to side. "This is the living room." He pointed to the television hanging on the wall. "We got that for Christmas."

"Nice gift," Tara commented. It was a low-end model. Not overly expensive. She was looking for clues that the couple was living above their means. A kidnapping event was most often related to money. Either the perps wanted money or were owed money.

Jacob motioned her through a wide, cased opening. "This is the kitchen."

The dog rubbed against him. "Not now, Jelly Bug."

Tara smiled at the dog's name. "She sure does like you."

"She was a present from my mom last year. She said Jelly Bug would keep me company when she was in the hospital."

Tara glanced at Deke. "She's all better now," he told her and gave her a look that said he would explain later.

The kitchen and dining room were one room, slightly larger than the living room. The cabinets formed a peninsula that divided the two spaces. Appliances looked old but clean. Dishes in the sink and sandwich makings were scattered on the peninsula counter. A pot of days-old beans stood on the stove.

Tara checked the fridge. Mostly empty. She frowned. "When does your mom do her shopping?"

"On Mondays. That's when she gets paid."

Only this Monday she hadn't been around to shop and replenish their staples.

Tara turned to Jacob. "So where do you sleep?" She hitched her head toward the stove. "In the oven?"

"No." He laughed. "I have a bedroom."

"Let's see it then."

Jacob led the way back into the living room and into a narrow hall. Deke brought up the rear, keeping his distance. Tara was glad. She couldn't think clearly when he was too close. Confessing as much, even only to herself, was unnerving. Even her ex-husband hadn't been able to shake her up that way.

"This is my room," Jacob announced as they entered the first room on the right.

A Spider-Man comforter half-on and half-off the twin bed confirmed as much. There were somewhat crude drawings of Spider-Man on the wall. As rudimentary as the drawings were, they had definite potential.

"Did you do these?" Tara gestured to the drawings.

He nodded eagerly. "My dad says if I keep practicing, I can draw cartoons when I grow up. I won't have to work so hard like he does."

Another indication of a loving father. He wanted better for his child. "Well, I think your dad is right. These are pretty good."

A wide grin had the boy's eyes sparkling.

She made a show of checking the closet, the dresser drawers and under the bed. Jelly Bug had a bed next to Jacob's. "I don't see anything unusual here," she said. "Where do your parents sleep?"

His smile faded a bit. "This way."

She followed him out of the room. Deke had waited in the hall. She avoided eye contact. He was watching her. She didn't have to look to see that. She could feel his eyes on her. How had a mere six-month relationship so thoroughly and deeply connected her to this man?

The family bathroom was the last door on the right, and then there was the only other bedroom on the left. The bed was made. The drawers in the night tables and dresser were neatly organized. Nothing unexpected in any of them. Tara spotted no surprises at all on her sweep. The closet was the same. The parent's wardrobes were meager. Clearly they spent the bulk of whatever they had for clothing on their son. She checked under the bed. Spotted a box, maybe a shoebox, but decided not to inspect it just now. When Jacob was otherwise occupied, she'd have a look. She didn't really expect to find anything, but if his parents were hiding something perhaps intimate under the bed, she'd rather not discover it in his presence.

She stood and set her hands on her hips. "The room's clear. Why don't we go back to the living room, and you can answer a few questions for me? I'll call my partner and have him come help us look. Does that sound okay?"

Jacob nodded and headed back to the living room. When he was out of sight, she motioned for Deke to join her. When he was close—close enough for her to smell the aftershave he always wore—she explained her first impressions.

"The fact that there's no sign of a struggle and no blood gives me some hope that this might not be as bad as it looks."

The relief that flooded his face was profound. "I hope for Jacob's sake you're right."

"There's a lot we don't know yet, but I intend to keep a hopeful attitude until I have reason not to." That had been her dad's motto, and she'd adopted it when she followed his footsteps into law enforcement. "I'll let you know when I'm worried."

"I appreciate that."

"The mother was ill?"

Deke nodded. "Last year. Breast cancer."

Tara winced. "Bad stuff." She took a breath. "Can you keep Jacob distracted for a minute while I call Collin?"

"Sure."

Deke hesitated as if there was more he wanted to say, then he walked out. When she heard him talking to Jacob, she made the call. Collin would be here in ten minutes. Meanwhile, before she returned to the living room she got on her knees next to the bed and had another look beneath it.

First she pulled a pair of gloves from the pocket on her utility belt and tugged them on, then dragged the box from under the bed. She had been right—a shoebox. The memory of picking through old photos in a shoebox when she was a kid visiting her grandmother made her smile. She removed the lid and peered at the contents. Her jaw dropped, and she sat back on her heels.

Now she was worried.

Chapter Four

Valley Lane, 5:45 p.m.

Tara appreciated Deke keeping Jacob occupied while she brought Deputy Collin Porch up to speed.

"Fifty thousand dollars?" Collin's eyebrows reared up. "I don't think Krissy makes tips like that at the diner."

Krissy Callaway was Jacob's mother.

"And we both know Jeff doesn't make that much at the hatchery." Some small amount over minimum wage she suspected.

"Could have been a gift from a rich uncle," Collin joked, but his face showed no amusement. He shook his head. "Whatever it is, it probably ain't legal. You think this," he nodded to the shoebox sitting on the bed, "is why they're MIA?"

That was the million-dollar—or fifty-thousand-dollar, it seemed—question.

"My first thought would be yes." She considered the neatly banded bundles of cash. Fifty bundles of hundred-dollar bills totaling one thousand per bundle. "If that's the case, why is the money still here? It's not like it was well hidden."

Collin exhaled a big breath. "I'll put out an APB on the father's truck."

Tara nodded. "Call the hatchery and see if Jeff showed up for work this week. I'm guessing not since he didn't come home after. I'll check with Delilah at the diner. See if she's heard from Krissy. Then we can start talking to the neighbors. Maybe we'll get lucky and someone saw something on Sunday."

"If we're really lucky," Collin offered, "one of them has a video doorbell or security camera that might have picked up a license plate."

They'd likely never get that lucky, but it didn't hurt to wish.

"You think this has anything to do with the burglaries?"

"At this point, I'd say no. This is way bigger than a stolen television or a nabbed cell phone."

"I guess it's just our turn for the crazies to come out," Collin suggested. "We did have a full moon on Sunday night."

"Maybe so. I'm calling headquarters and requesting a CSI team." Tara rubbed at the lines of frustration on her forehead. "Maybe we'll get lucky and find some prints that will give us some clue as to who the two men were."

Plus, the cash needed to be entered into evidence. She'd leave that to CSI as well. The sooner the place was gone over and the money was out of here, the better.

When Collin headed outside, she hesitated. At this point there was no denying that Jacob had been abandoned, whatever the circumstances. She had no choice but to make a call to Children's Services and get someone over here to take custody of Jacob. If he'd been through this before, he would know the routine. That said, being aware of the steps wasn't necessarily going to prevent him from being scared.

Her first call was to summon the CSI folks. Children's Services was next.

With the necessary balls rolling, Tara caught up with Deke and Jacob on the back porch. After finding the money, she had decided it might be better not to contaminate what was clearly a crime scene any further. Deke had grabbed a bag of chips and a bottle of water for Jacob and taken him out back. The two were seated at a ramshackle picnic table. Jelly Bug danced around the table as if keeping them entertained or hoping for a dropped chip.

Jacob looked up at her expectantly. "Did you find any clues?"

Not the sort she'd hoped for.

"Nothing that gives us any answers," she evaded. She settled on the bench on Jacob's side of the table. "Look, you know that as a deputy I have to play by certain rules when I'm investigating a case."

The boy stared at her without flinching, but the resignation in his eyes told her he understood what was coming.

"Tara."

She shot a look at Deke. He, of all people, realized she had no choice. And he sure as hell had no right to call her by her first name at a time like this.

"Until we figure out where your parents are and bring them back home," she said to Jacob, ignoring the man now glaring at her, "you need a safe place to stay."

His small face fell from vaguely hopeful to defeat. "I'm big enough to take care of myself. I know how to make my sandwiches and…and tuck myself in at night."

Tara smiled but it hurt to do it. "You are really smart

and very reliable. Mr. D tells me you're a great student, but there are rules. You have rules in school, right? So you understand that when we have rules, we have to follow them."

He nodded, a jerky motion.

"Ms. Carter from Children's Services is coming to pick you up. She'll take you to a home where you'll be safe until your parents are back." The tears that welled in his eyes ripped at Tara's gut. "The really good news is I think you know the home you'll be staying at. Ms. Wright, the nurse at your school, wants you to stay with her family until we sort this out."

He blinked back the tears. "I like Ms. Wright. Her son is in kindergarten. I know him too." The crestfallen expression returned. "But what about Jelly Bug?"

Tara nodded. "Ms. Wright said Jelly Bug can come too. Why don't we pack a bag for you to take on your adventure at Ms. Wright's house?"

"Okay!" Jacob scooted off the bench. "Come on, Jelly Bug, we gotta pack." He and his dog hustled into the house.

Tara prepared to follow him, but Deke waylaid her, his hand on her arm again. Tara rode out the reaction she couldn't seem to quell even after all this time.

"Thanks for making this as easy as it can be."

The sincerity in his eyes tugged at her. How many times had she seen those blue eyes in her dreams? No matter how hard she'd evicted thoughts of him, they just kept coming back anyway. Six damned months was a long time for a pointless yet insistent need to hang on.

"Just doing my job." She turned back to the door, but he held on tighter.

"I'm the last person you want to talk to, I get that." He dropped his hand as if suddenly realizing he shouldn't be touching her. "But I don't see why we can't be friends. Particularly at a time like this."

She shook her head, shifted her gaze away from his. "I don't know what you mean. Of course, we're friends."

Before he could argue with her statement, she hurried after Jacob.

After pajamas and a week's worth of clothes were selected, along with kibble for Jelly Bug, they went outside to meet Ms. Carter. She was young with two kids of her own, and she seemed to really connect with her clients. By the time she loaded Jacob and his dog into her SUV, he was smiling and appeared okay with the situation.

Kids were amazing.

Deep inside, where Tara never allowed anyone else to see, pain twisted. She set her senses to ignore and focused on work. Work never let her down.

Thankfully, the CSI team arrived, preventing too much time alone with Deke.

Being alone with Deke was not safe.

Once she'd filled in the two-person team, she walked to the street where Deke leaned against his truck.

"Thanks for calling me," she said. "We'll take it from here."

He gave a single resolute nod. "That's my cue to go, I guess."

She gestured to the CSI van. "They'll be pulling out the crime-scene tape any time now. Even I won't be allowed back inside until they're finished." The last part might be an overstatement, but she needed him gone. "There's really no reason for you to stay at this point."

He straightened away from the truck. "Well, it was good to see you—the circumstances notwithstanding." He shook his head, laughed softly. "It's funny. As small as the Hollow is, you'd think we'd run into each other more often."

"You're busy," Tara offered. "I'm busy. Time gets away." Not to mention she made it a point to avoid him as much as possible.

"Guess so." He wasn't convinced. She was lying and he knew it.

Guilt pinged her. "If you would, keep a close eye on him at school and let me know if you notice any uncharacteristic behavior."

"You know I will."

She did. "Thanks."

He opened the driver's door but hesitated before getting in so that he could hold her gaze a beat longer. "Maybe one of these days you'll spell it out for me."

She frowned. "Spell what out?" The words were out of her mouth before her brain assimilated what he meant.

"What happened to us." He shrugged. "I thought we were really good together."

For three endless seconds, she couldn't speak. What the hell? Tara Norwood was a cop. She'd made it through the training. She'd dealt with some sick criminals before transferring to the Hollow. As a twelve-year-old, she'd watched her mother bleed to death while trapped by her seat belt in a vehicle hanging upside down on the edge of a cliff. Three and a half years ago, she'd gone through another kind of hell when her marriage fell apart. Now she was holding up under her father's ailing health, understanding that when he was gone she would be alone.

She was damned strong.

Yet this man…a man she'd walked away from six months

and fifteen days ago…had the power to make her want to fall into his arms and cry like a baby.

Damn him.

She braced herself. Kicked aside all those weak emotions. "What did you expect? That we'd move in together? A marriage proposal?" She laughed, couldn't help herself. "That we'd live happily ever after." She shook her head. "I thought I made myself clear. I've been down that road. I didn't like the trip, and I don't intend to ever take it again. Is that clear enough?"

She didn't hang around for his response. Mostly because she couldn't bear the hurt in his eyes.

Hurt she had caused.

Main Street, 7:30 p.m.

THE DINER WAS packed when Tara arrived. She'd checked with Carter, and Jacob and Jelly Bug were safely ensconced at Brenda Wright's house. Then Tara had come to the diner to talk to Jacob's mom's employer. Every table and booth was filled. No problem. She took the only vacant stool at the counter and waited for Delilah to cruise past.

Collin had spoken to the manager and the shift leader at the hatchery. Jeff Callaway had given no indication there was trouble in his life. He'd come to work on Friday, on time like always, and they hadn't seen him since. His cell, as did Krissy's, went straight to voice mail now.

An unanswered cell phone was never a positive sign. Not when a young couple had a kid.

Delilah Merkle skidded to a stop, noticing Tara in the crowd along the counter. "Hey." She made a face. "You look like this isn't about dinner."

During an investigation, Tara never could keep the worry

off her face—especially when a child was involved. "Unfortunately, it's not. You're really busy, but we need to talk."

Without hesitation, Delilah motioned for Tara to follow her. Tara kept pace with her along the length of the counter, then cut through at the end and followed her into the space where the magic happened, weaving through the throng of employees in the kitchen. Delilah opened the door to her office, waited for Tara to come inside and then closed the door.

Delilah was the only person Tara knew whose office was always perfectly organized no matter what was going on.

"What's up? The look on your face has me worried." Delilah plopped into the well-worn chair behind her desk, a testament of how exhausted she most certainly was. "Is your dad okay?"

"My dad's good. No new declines." Tara took a breath and launched into what had to be said. "Krissy Callaway." She hesitated to catch Delilah's reaction prior to sharing the situation.

The long-time diner owner-operator rolled her eyes. "I swear, you'd think I would learn." She threw up her arms. "I hire someone, and they turn out to be great! Always on time. Hardworking. Good with the customers." She shook her head. "I get all happy and certain I have myself a long-term good employee, and what happens? One day they just don't show up. Poof. She really put me in a bind." She gestured to the door behind Tara. "As you can see we're overwhelmed."

There was no easy way to do this. "We have reason to believe she's gone missing under suspicious circumstances."

Delilah's frustration faded. "Missing? Are you serious?"

Tara nodded. "She was last seen on Sunday evening around six o'clock, according to her son."

Delilah leaned forward. "What about her husband? Jeff?"

"He's missing also."

"Oh, my God." Her hands went to her face, cradling her cheeks. "What on earth happened?"

"We don't know yet," Tara admitted. "Had Krissy mentioned any concerns or issues in her personal life? Maybe with her husband or their finances?"

Delilah shook her head with enthusiasm. "They've been doing well. Last year they went through a rough patch financially related to her cancer treatments. Breast cancer," Delilah explained. "But life has been good for them since. She's been as happy as a clam. I haven't heard the first peep about issues."

Tara managed to repress a flinch at the mention of cancer. "No trouble with her husband?"

"No. They are best friends. Have been since high school. He's always doing sweet things for her. He had the sweetest bouquet and box of chocolates delivered here on Valentine's Day."

Tara thought about the money she'd found under their bed. "You're sure there were no money issues?"

Delilah shrugged. "Not that she mentioned. They were even talking about taking Jacob on a big surprise vacation this summer." Delilah narrowed her gaze and nodded. "During her recovery, Krissy said they had filled out all these forms for help from private donors. I'm thinking someone came through in a big way."

"Did she mention any friends of hers or her husband? Maybe out-of-town friends? Someone who visited recently?"

"Not that I know of."

"Was there anyone here at the diner who socialized with

her outside of work? Maybe someone who might have been closer to her?"

Delilah considered the question for a bit. "No one in particular, I don't think. Of course, you're welcome to talk to any of my employees."

"I appreciate that. The sooner we can figure this out, the sooner we can find Krissy and Jeff. Hopefully safe."

"Look." She shot to her feet. "I'll go out there and relieve them one at a time so they can come talk to you. Will that work?"

"That would be great."

"On it." Delilah rushed around the desk and out the door.

That was one of the things that had brought Tara back to the Hollow. People watched out for each other. People cared. She'd wanted to raise her family here.

Except the family hadn't happened.

She pushed the memory away and prepared for the questions she would need to ask.

One by one, she interviewed the six employees at the diner tonight. They all told the same story. Krissy and Jeff Callaway were very happy. They were a great couple. Hard workers. Good people. Loved their son.

On the way home, Tara checked in with Collin. He'd learned basically the same thing at the hatchery. Both the manager and the shift leader spoke highly of Jeff Callaway. His sudden absence was totally unexpected. He'd been a good employee.

Except for the $50K, Tara mused. All that money hidden in a shoebox under the bed set off all sorts of warning bells.

It was nearly ten by the time Tara rolled up to her childhood home. Her headlights flashed over an unexpected vehicle. Truck. *Deke's truck.*

Tara parked and turned off the engine. For a moment, she didn't move to get out. She had no energy left for this. All she wanted right now was a long hot shower and a good night's sleep.

If she didn't get out, he would just come over and knock on her window. She climbed out, shut the door and walked toward him. He waited on her porch steps. How long had he been sitting there?

"It's late," she said. "I'm exhausted."

He stood. "Any news?"

He asked this as if she hadn't just given him two perfectly acceptable reasons to climb into his truck and leave.

"Nothing yet." She walked past him and shoved the key into the door lock and twisted. Reached inside and flipped on the porch light. The last thing she wanted was to be in the dark with Deke Shepherd.

"I checked on Jacob a couple hours ago," he said. "He's doing fine for now."

Tara turned back to him, her back to her open door. She would not—could not—let him inside. "Thanks for letting me know. Like I said, I'm beat."

Go. Just please go.

"Should we be worried about Jacob? Is he safe without police protection?"

"At this time, we can't be sure of anything." She had spoken to Brenda Wright about keeping a really close eye on him. She wasn't to allow him outside without supervision. If there was something going on with the parents that was related to the money, Jacob could become a pawn in the game. "Sheriff Decker will be reviewing the situation and making any necessary decisions early tomorrow. The truth is, until we have more information and some sort of evidence, all we know for sure is that the Callaways abandoned their son. Based on Jacob's statement, there's reason to believe their disappearance was under suspicious circumstances. We'll put their photos on the news and on social media. We'll issue BOLOs. Send the info out far and wide to other jurisdictions and hope someone somewhere has seen them. That's really all we can do at this point."

"How are *you* doing?"

She wanted to tell him again that it was late and she was tired, but she knew Deke. He wasn't going anywhere until she forced the issue or he was satisfied with whatever it was he wanted or needed.

"I'm fine. Tired but fine."

"I'm sorry."

Tara took a mental swipe at the exhaustion in hopes of better analyzing his statement. "Sorry for what?"

"I'm sorry for…" He looked away briefly before setting those piercing blue eyes on hers once more. "I'm sorry I couldn't be or do or say whatever you needed. I'm just sorry."

She couldn't take this. Not right now.

"Deke." She held up her hands in a stop-sign fashion. "We don't need to do this." Not again. Not now. She was too tired. Too weak.

He shook his head. "No. You're wrong. I made a mistake six months ago, and I'm not going to keep pretending I'm okay with it." He laughed, a hollow sound. "No matter that I don't have a clue what I did or failed to do, I want to make it right."

Tara closed her eyes a moment before opening them once more and looking him straight in the eye. "Just say what you have to say and get it over with."

"The one thing I did that I wish I hadn't..." He looked away for a moment. "I shouldn't have let you go. I should have helped you face whatever it is you're running from. I should have done something to fix whatever was wrong."

Good grief. She should just tell him—she wasn't fixable. But she couldn't. Not right now. Maybe not ever.

"Good night, Deke."

She turned her back and escaped into the house. Closed and locked the door and leaned against it, listening to ensure he left.

Deke didn't get it. The thing she was running from was *him*.

Chapter Five

Dread Hollow School
Thursday, May 4, 10:30 a.m.

Deke watched his students through the window in the classroom door. Music was a favorite subject for all fifteen students, especially Jacob. His enthusiasm for music, for school in general, was contagious. He had a way of prompting the same from his classmates.

Brenda Wright had caught Deke at the school mail station first thing this morning to tell him about Jacob's nightmares. He'd awakened at two this morning crying out for help. He'd sobbed and shared the painful dream with her. The bad men who'd taken his parents had come back for him. He'd felt torn between wanting to go with them in hopes of seeing his parents and wanting to run for his life in fear.

No child should suffer that level of anxiety.

But in true Jacob form, he'd appeared all smiles in the classroom. Talking and smiling. Deke had struggled with the urge to hug the kid, but the other students wouldn't have understood. Sharing his story with his classmates was something Jacob hadn't done so far.

Deke watched him now, circling around as the group sang

the alligator song. Jacob got along with everyone. Interacted well with the entire class. He didn't appear to have a specific or best friend. Just played with anyone who wanted to play.

"Deke."

He started at the sound of his name, particularly since it was Tara who'd said it. "Hey." Worry instantly started its incessant nag. Along with the worry was the complete and utter happiness he always felt at seeing her. "You have some news?"

She glanced at the kids beyond the glass, smiling, laughing, circling around as they sang before she finally met his gaze once more. "Is there somewhere we can talk?"

Whatever news she had, it didn't sound good.

"My classroom will be free for another forty-five minutes. The kids go to lunch from here." He hitched his head toward the music room.

"That'll work."

She started in that direction and he followed. Tara had been to his classroom more than once. She knew the way. She'd spent twelve years of her life in this school. Most of her life in this community. He was the newcomer. Three years wasn't that long compared to the better part of a lifetime.

He was glad she knew the way. Gave him an opportunity to just watch. She was definitely the hottest deputy he'd ever met. Long blonde hair that she kept in a sleek ponytail. The memory of removing that tie and watching all that lush hair fall around her shoulders made him smile.

He blinked away the image and thought of how sharp she always looked in her uniform. Never so much as an errant wrinkle. Shoes always shined. The weight of her utility belt alone should have her moving slow. Not Tara. She was as strong and determined as she was beautiful. Nothing slowed her down.

She'd let him catch her. It was the holding on that had eluded him.

She entered his classroom without pause. He did the same, closing the door behind him. When she finally faced him, he said, "This feels bad."

"It's not good," she confessed. "Jeff Callaway's truck was found this morning."

Deke's hopes fell. "Any sign of Jeff or Kristen?" Everyone called Jacob's mom Krissy, but her name was Kristen.

Tara shook her head. "The CSI folks have taken the truck in to see what they can find, but there was no one and nothing of obvious significance inside. The usual papers and stashes of napkins and drinking straws were found in the glove box and console, but nothing else that tells us the story of what the hell is going on."

Definitely not good.

"Collin and I have scoured their social media pages, not that either parent was particularly active. Their cell phones are with them, so we couldn't check those, though we have requested warrants to get a list of calls and text messages made which, you probably know, takes forever. The phones go straight to voice mail, so it's possible the batteries are down or the phones are turned off. So we know pretty much nothing."

The more she said, the more his hope dwindled.

Tara was one of the first people he'd met three years ago. She'd pulled him over for speeding. He hadn't realized he was speeding. Forty wasn't that fast, but the speed limit along Main Street was thirty-five. She'd insisted she'd let his speeding slide twice already. He had been fairly certain that he'd never met a more gorgeous woman. Blonde hair, green eyes and those lips…

"Deke?"

He blinked. "I'm sorry. What?"

"I was asking when the best time for me to talk to Jacob would be," she said, speaking slowly as if he needed extra time to absorb the words.

He did, actually. She'd had that effect on him from the beginning. He always got lost just looking at her.

"After lunch," he said, kicking himself for going down that path. "We have a short study hall before math class. It gives the kids time to settle down after lunch. You could talk to him then." He smiled at the thought. "You'd be surprised how worked up they get during lunch. Maybe it's the music class this semester or just the fact that it's spring and walking outside from the lunchroom back to the classroom has them ready for something more physical than math."

She smiled. "I imagine so. I remember wanting to cut and run for the playground after lunch."

When they were together, he'd found himself in the school library more than once, going through the old year-books to find her. She was beautiful now, and she'd been the cutest little girl with her pigtails and big smiles. He'd wondered if she had been as full of mischief as her expressions suggested. As soon as word got around that they were a couple, some of the older teachers had gone on and on about Tara's escapades back in school. Nothing so bad. Just pranks meant to incite laughter. Never any hurt feelings, just the occasional injured pride. Most times the party with the bruised pride had deserved it. One of her former teachers had referred to Tara and her friend Henry as Robin Hood and a merry bandit for taking down the occasional over-blown ego. Sounded exactly like something Tara would do.

He exiled the memories and focused on the now and his mounting concern for Jacob. "Will you tell Jacob what you've found?"

"I don't see any reason to upset him. I'm hoping he will recall if his father drove his truck home last Friday and if the vehicle was still at the house on Sunday. When I questioned him yesterday, he said the two men came to their house and took his parents with them. In that case, Jeff's truck should have been at home as well—assuming he was there. My impression was that both parents were home when the men arrived."

Deke nodded. "That's the impression I got." But the fact was, Jacob hadn't actually said his father was home. "He did say that when he came out of hiding his parents—meaning both—were gone."

She nodded. "He did, but his mother told him to hide. He didn't mention his father saying anything."

"You think his father wasn't at home? That maybe he'd been gone because he knew those men were coming?" The words left a bad taste in Deke's mouth. What kind of father deserted his family at a time like that?

"I hope that's not the case," Tara said, on the same page with him. "Jeff's coworkers stated that he was a loving father. It's possible the men had already taken him."

Neither scenario was good, but the latter was more palatable. "Did the forensic guys find anything at the house that might tell us who those guys were?" He caught himself. Shook his head. "I'm sure you can't share that information." He shrugged. "It's just Jacob is one of my students and I feel personally involved. With the burglaries, I can't help wondering if there's a connection."

To his surprise, she smiled instead of setting him straight on the rules of sharing on one of her cases. "You are involved. I know how you feel about your students. That's part of what makes you such a good teacher."

"Thanks." He glanced at the clock above the chalkboard. "You want something from the lounge? There's a drink machine and snack machine."

"No thanks." She made a face that said something had just occurred to her. "This is your planning time. Probably your lunch break too. Don't let me keep you from anything. I can come back in half an hour."

"Stay," he insisted, hoping she actually would. "I'll grab two coffees or two ginger ales—as I recall that's your favorite."

She nodded slowly. "A ginger ale would be good."

He backed toward the door, not taking his gaze off her for fear she might disappear. "I will be right back."

"I'll be right here," she assured him as if she understood he wanted—needed—her to still be in his classroom when he got back.

Deke walked quickly from the elementary wing to the admin hall. The principal's office, school nurse and teachers' lounge as well as the lobby and school store were all in that front wing of the school. The U-shaped building contained the middle school wing on the other side. The upper school classrooms were in a separate building across campus. It was a workable setup that had served the community well for half a century. Deke doubted the school would last many more years. The community wasn't growing, and the number of students dwindled each year. The vote to keep the school open two more years had barely passed.

He wasn't looking forward to moving to a larger institution, but the day would come. There was some talk of a private school purchasing the building and continuing classes here, but Deke wasn't sure how many students in the community would be able to afford a private school. The influx of parents, even if only to drop off and pick up their kids, would likely supplement the local economy, but it would also change things. Deke had gotten used to the sleepy little town and knowing life would be calm and quiet most of the time. The recent surge in break-ins notwithstanding.

Things changed. No way to get around the reality that nothing stayed the same.

Like relationships.

The lounge was empty, preventing him from having to explain why Deputy Norwood was here to see him. That was one downside—sort of—to small community living. News traveled at hyper speed. Everyone knew everything about each other. He poked money into the machine and made his first selection. The idea wasn't entirely true. Otherwise Jacob's parents wouldn't be missing without someone knowing something, right?

He added more cash and tapped the necessary image for a second ginger ale. The idea nagged at him. Really, how could the Callaways live in the Hollow—for, what, two and a half years?—and not have anyone close enough to have some clue what was happening with them?

Inspired now, Deke grabbed the two cans and hurried back to his classroom. He hesitated at the door. Tara stood at the bulletin board, studying the items posted there. For the past three weeks, he'd posted a different board every day. Each board a story about a student. These kids would move on to fourth grade together. The school had only one class at each grade level. He wanted the students to better understand each other, so he'd given the assignment to the kids and their parents. Create your story. The students would bring photos of their parents and siblings as well as of themselves. The story boards included their favorite foods and vacation spots, what their parents did at their jobs, what they wanted to do when they grew up and who their heroes were. All fifteen chose a parent or grandparent for a hero. When each story board went up, the other students were asked to provide one nice word each about that student to add to the board. The story boards had been a hit with the students as well as the parents.

The board Tara stared at now was Deke's. The class had insisted that he do one as well. He hadn't expected Tara to be in his classroom or maybe he wouldn't have been so totally honest on one particular point.

He opened the door and walked in. Her gaze, clearly startled, swung toward him as if she'd completely forgotten he would be returning.

"Don't judge me," he said as he extended a can of ginger ale.

"Homemade tacos are your favorite food?" She took the can and popped the top.

He did the same. "You got me hooked on homemade ones. I haven't been able to look at a fast-food taco the same since."

She laughed, almost choked on her drink. She pressed her hand to her lips. "I'm not a great cook."

"But you make great tacos."

The blush that settled high on her cheeks made him smile. "Maybe so," she agreed.

He walked to the board. "Do you like my hero?" He'd posted a photo of her as the person he considered to be a hero. And now she knew.

She nodded, her smile fading. "I'm not a hero, Deke."

He held her gaze, wishing he could see beyond those shimmering green eyes to what she was thinking. "You're the person I use as an example when I talk to the kids about who they can trust if they need help. They all know you. Just another perk of life in a small community."

Tara looked away, downed another swallow of her drink. She cleared her throat and said, "I know at least three women in this little community who would love to get to know you better." She looked directly at him then. "You're a great catch, Deke. You shouldn't be holding yourself back."

He was. Holding himself back. He'd had invitations during the past six months. Enough to be flattered. From really nice women. But he couldn't say yes. He refused to mislead anyone. The last thing he wanted to do was to hurt another person. He'd been down that road. Loving someone who couldn't or wouldn't love him back. He refused to be the reason anyone took that journey. Ever. He wasn't a two-out-of-three kind of guy. Part of him wondered if the reason Tara had pushed him away was that her feelings just hadn't gone as deep as his. But he couldn't see that. He knew what he felt, what he felt in her.

"You know my story better than anyone in the Hollow, Tara. How can you expect me to do anything different than what I'm doing?"

She turned away, walked to the wall of windows that

overlooked the courtyard between the elementary and middle school wings.

"I told you up front I wasn't what you were looking for."

This was true. She hadn't minced words. She had been divorced for just over two years at the time, and she had insisted there would be no going back to that status. She was done. Deke had found the idea foolish. She was two years younger than him. Who gave up on marriage and a family at thirty-two? She was only thirty-three now. She had her whole life ahead of her.

He joined her at the windows. Watched his class march across the courtyard toward the cafeteria. The truth was he wanted children. As much as he adored the students in his class, he wanted a family of his own. It wasn't until he made this admission to Tara that their relationship had changed. She'd pulled back. Three weeks later, they were done—her words.

Deke had gone over those last couple of months a thousand times. He couldn't put his finger on a single other thing that had changed. They shared a love of hiking, of dogs, of life in general. They were happy, or so he'd thought. She had loved him. He knew it when he saw it, experienced it. He'd been in love before and he'd had someone who loved him before. There was no mistaking the feeling. No mistaking the look in your partner's eyes. Tara had loved him.

"You were wrong." He said this without looking at her. She certainly wouldn't look at him now.

She drew in a deep breath. "I have some calls to make. I'll be back in thirty to talk to Jacob."

He watched her walk out without a backward glance... without the slightest hesitation.

She was wrong. He wasn't sure what it would take to make her see just how wrong she was, but he intended to wait.

He had time.

Speaking of time, she waited the full half hour before returning. The kids were back and having quiet study time.

When he saw her at the door, he walked to Jacob's desk and tapped him on the shoulder. Since he'd already given Jacob a heads-up, he was prepared. He left the classroom without anyone else paying any real attention. Deke stepped into the corridor with him.

"Jacob, I'm sorry to bother you at school," Tara said. She kept her attention on the student and didn't spare Deke a glance.

He always ended up pushing too hard.

Apparently, he hadn't learned his lesson yet.

"I don't mind," Jacob said. "I like talking to you."

Deke smiled, grateful Tara had so easily earned the boy's trust. This was a very difficult time for him. He needed people he trusted around him.

Tara smiled and it took Deke's breath. "I'm glad. I have just a couple of questions."

He nodded his understanding.

"When the men came to your house on Sunday, was your father home or was it just you and your mom?"

He shook his head. "My dad had gone to the store. We were out of milk and he needed gas for the work week."

"So it was just you and your mom."

He nodded his agreement. "Wait. At first. Then my dad came home. But everything happened so fast then. Those men were already outside. I guess they saw my dad, and that's when they decided to come in."

"Your mom ushered you into hiding and went to the door."

"My mama and dad both told me to hide. My dad put me in the closet."

"So when your parents left you hidden in your room, what happened then?" She shrugged. "Did you hear your father say anything in particular to the men?"

"I could hear his voice. He was yelling, but I couldn't understand what he was saying." He made a face. "It happened really fast. I mean it felt like forever, but it wasn't long, really. They came in, shouting at my mom. She started shouting too, except her voice wasn't, like, angry." His face fell. "She sounded scared. Like it did that time when I fell out of the tree and broke my collar bone."

Last fall. Deke recalled the incident. Jacob had been out of school for a few days. When he'd returned, the entire class had reveled in hearing the story of how he tried to hang on to a branch after falling part way but lost his grip and hit the ground. His vivid descriptions had enthralled them all.

Tara nodded. "Good. Thank you for clearing that up. One more thing, had your parents mentioned moving?"

Jacob shook his head no. "They did tell me we were going on a special vacation this year. They wouldn't tell me where, but I think I know." He grinned. "I've always wanted to go." He glanced around and lowered his voice. "I think it's in Florida."

Deke hoped like hell that vacation still happened for the kid. It made him sick to think that his life as he knew it might be over.

"Wow," Tara said. "That sounds awesome. I'm sure you'll have a blast. Did your parents ever talk or argue about money?"

She'd asked this question yesterday. Deke had a feeling

she knew or suspected something was up with the family finances.

"Not since last year when Mom was sick." The remembered worry on his face was impossible to miss. "She's all better now and there's no money troubles. She told me just the other day that they would never have to worry about money again."

Tara nodded. "Thank you, Jacob. You're really a big help. I know your parents would be proud."

A big smile slid across his face. "I hope you find them soon."

Tara nodded but didn't make any promises this time.

"Go back to your desk now," Deke told him. When the kid was back in the classroom, he asked, "You think his parents were involved in something that put them in danger?"

She moistened her lips. "Unfortunately, yes. But for now, it's only a hunch."

"Damn." He shook his head. "I don't get how anyone could do something like that when there's a kid involved."

"I can only assume there are things we don't know. Whatever the motive," Tara offered, "it must have felt worth the risk."

Deke got that. There were some things that were worth any risk.

He reached out, couldn't stop himself, and touched her hand. The connection was instant and fierce. Always was. She drew away from his reach just as quickly.

"Thanks for putting up with my interruptions," she said, preparing to escape.

Whenever they saw each other and he attempted any sort of interaction, this is what she did. If not for this case, she would have steered wide and clear of him.

"Whatever you need. I'm happy to help in any way I can."

She flashed a smile that fell sorely short of the ones that so easily stole his breath. "See ya."

She walked away, her steps bordering on a run.

Could he be that wrong about what he'd felt for her?

Maybe it was time he gave real consideration to the idea that she didn't feel and never had felt the way he did.

When she solved this case, she would go back to avoiding him at all costs again. He made up his mind then and there. Until then, he intended to do all in his power to figure out what was and what wasn't real.

Equally important, he intended to figure out how to live with whatever he found.

Chapter Six

Sergeant Darrell Snelling of the Hamilton County Sheriff's Department CSI team had asked to meet Tara at two at the Callaway residence. She checked the time. He would be here soon. She hoped he'd found something significant that would help her find Jacob's parents.

Collin had reinterviewed the neighbors on Valley Drive. No one had seen or heard anything. Most hadn't been home on Sunday evening. Spring brought all sorts of festivals in surrounding communities. On top of that, many churches held evening services on Sunday. None of the neighbors had security cameras, not even the doorbell type. Three more of the father's coworkers had been interviewed, and none could provide any helpful input. Tara had spoken with the mother's coworkers and none were aware of any trouble in the Callaway family.

The best explanation in Tara's opinion was that whatever had prompted the disappearance was new. There hadn't been time to share the details with even the closest of their friends.

Tara had worked a couple of missing persons cases before moving to the Hollow. Both had ended well, but she wouldn't call herself experienced. Or even particularly skilled in the area. To complicate matters further, there was a serious shortage of deputies and officers in Hamilton County, leaving no extra bodies to share.

She and Collin were on their own unless some aspect of the case that had not been ferreted out or had not presented itself as of yet fell under the FBI's jurisdiction. Although she hated to lose control of a case, if the feds could help find Jacob's parents, she was only too happy to hand it over.

A sedan carrying the CSI logo came to a stop nose to nose with Tara's Wagoneer. She was about to find out what they had. She climbed out of her vehicle and met Snelling on the street. The sergeant was a big man. Six-three or six-four. Broad shoulders. Huge hands. His black hair was peppered with gray. Sunglasses shielded his eyes. His neatly pressed shirt and trousers looked right out of the dry cleaner.

"Deputy Norwood." He gave her a nod and extended his hand.

Tara accepted the gesture. "I'm hoping you've found something that will provide some forward momentum for my investigation."

"Let's step inside."

She ducked under the perimeter crime-scene tape and led the way to the front door. Snelling unlocked the door and sliced the tape that marked the house as off-limits to anyone not on the CSI team.

They didn't bother donning gloves or shoe covers since the team had completed its work inside.

"I found a loose floorboard under one of the beds."

He led the way through the house and, to Tara's surprise, into Jacob's room. The twin-size bed had been set aside and the small Spider-Man character rug covering the hardwood floor rolled back.

"There's a compartment built between the floor joists," Snelling explained.

Tara knelt down and inspected the compartment. Two pieces of flooring, measuring about fourteen inches long and four inches wide each, lifted from the top of the compartment. When in place, it was hardly noticeable that they weren't connected to the rest of the flooring. The compartment was somewhat longer and wider than the combined floorboards.

"Was there anything inside?" She got back to her feet, dusted off her hands.

"Twenty-five hundred dollars and a few prints. Based on prints we lifted from toothbrushes and other personal items, we believe they belong to Jeff Callaway."

Damn. "Twenty-five hundred dollars? So maybe this was his hiding place. The couple have a joint checking account but no savings account." This was a reasonable amount of money the couple could have saved from their work.

"Possibly," Snelling agreed. "We didn't find the wife's prints on the money or in and around the hiding place."

"What about the shoebox and the money in it?"

"Again, the husband's, but not the wife's."

Tara felt some amount of relief. Still, just because Jacob's mother hadn't handled the money didn't mean she wasn't involved in however it ended up in the home.

"There's something else."

Tara held her breath, hoped for something useful in finding Krissy and Jeff Callaway. Whatever they had gotten themselves involved in, they obviously needed help and Jacob needed them.

"We recovered a number of other prints from the cash in the shoebox," he went on. "Do you remember hearing about the Treat Foster case?"

"It doesn't ring a bell." Tara silently repeated the name in an attempt to dredge something from her memory bank.

"It's an old case. About thirty years back, I think. Treat Foster stole five hundred thousand dollars from a Chattanooga bank where he served as president. He was never found. He just disappeared with the money. His ex-wife couldn't figure out what happened to him. He just went into the bank one day, took the money and left, never to be seen again. Some said it was because his wife had left him for his former best friend. They had no kids, so walking away from his life was only about his career. Whatever the case, he was never seen or heard from again."

"Unbelievable." All that he'd just told her suddenly bloomed big in her brain. "Are you saying part of the five hundred thousand dollars was in that shoebox under the Callaway's bed?"

He nodded. "The FBI has already reached out. As soon as those prints hit the system, I got a call. Special Agent James Hanson is heading this way. I gave him your name and number."

"Got it, but this is a little out there. The Callaways are my age," she argued, mostly with herself. "They couldn't have been involved with Foster."

Snelling shrugged. "Beats me. I can only tell you the facts."

"What about the secret compartment?" She glanced down at the hole in the floor. "Maybe a former tenant put the money there. Surely there were other prints on the cash or inside the compartment."

"None that came up in the system, but I can tell you the compartment is fairly new." He reached down and picked up one of the two pieces of flooring. "See the cut end."

He was right. She got it. "The cut is recent." Once wood was cut, the new clean edge started to age. It took time for the fresh edge to darken.

He nodded. "The plywood used to make the compartment is new too. You can still smell the cuts made to size the pieces."

Whatever Tara had expected or hoped for, this was not it.

"Anything else I should know before I plow through the reports?"

He shook his head. "The place was clean beyond the cash. That said, we can't release the scene until Agent Hanson has a look. He may be sending his own forensic team."

"Thanks for all your hard work, Sergeant Snelling."

"I wish I'd been able to give you some answers rather than more questions."

"Just makes me have to earn my pay." She smiled. "I had a feeling this case was not going to be easy by any definition of the word."

As they exited the house, Snelling said, "You should talk to your father. He was a brand-new sheriff at the time. He may recall more about the case." Snelling seemed to catch himself. "Oh, hell. I forgot about—"

"No worries," she assured him. "I forget sometimes too. I will ask him though. He seems to be able to remember more about the past than about the present."

Tara sat in her Wagoneer for a bit after Snelling drove away. She should drop by Forrest Hills. Ask her father about the case. It would make him happy to talk about work. He'd spent twenty-five years as sheriff. There was a lot he knew about Hamilton County, particularly Dread Hollow. He should know plenty about the Hollow. He'd grown up here. Was a fourth-generation Norwood in the area.

She started her vehicle and headed in that direction. When her father had entered Forrest Hills, he had been diagnosed as in the second stage of Alzheimer's disease. Nothing Tara had said would change his mind about moving into the facility. They had a special wing for Alzheimer's patients, and when he reached the next stage he would be moving into that wing. For now, he was on the assisted-living side. He had a reasonable level of freedom. But that would change soon enough.

Tara parked and made her way into the posh facility. She had to give her father credit, he had great taste.

She checked in at the front desk or what Forrest Hills called the concierge's counter. The attractive concierge on duty told Tara that her father was in his room. Since the last escape, they'd placed monitor bracelets on all the residents. A system monitored their positions at all times.

Beyond the large windows lining the walls, older folks milled around the beautifully landscaped property. The lounge was full of card players and those tucked away in reading nooks. No doubt it was a classy place. Comfortable and with all sorts of very nice amenities. Lots of other folks her father's age. But it wasn't home, and she wished her father were home.

She knocked at his door. He announced, "Come on in, Tara."

This was another update. Residents were notified when visitors arrived on the property. She opened the door and couldn't help smiling. Her father was hunched over his portable worktable, occupied with the creation of one of his models. He loved vintage sports cars. Since he no longer drove or owned one, he enjoyed working with the models.

"Hey, Dad." She leaned down and gave him a kiss on the cheek. "You feeling okay today?"

Tarrence Norwood set his tools aside and removed his loupe lenses before flashing her a broad smile. "I'm above ground. That's always a good thing, and I feel fine. The real question is can I remember if I took my meds or where I am."

"Well," she settled on the comfy sofa, "can you?"

"I can. Any time I can do that I consider it a good day."

Even at seventy the man was still incredibly handsome. She didn't understand why he'd never married again after her mother's death. Certainly not for lack of opportunity.

"And how is my favorite daughter?"

"I'm good and your only daughter, by the way."

He grinned. "I know that."

"We had a couple go missing over the weekend, and you're never going to believe what popped up in the case."

He stood, stretched his back, swaggered over to the sofa and sat down on the other end. "Don't keep me in suspense, girl. Spit it out."

"In the home of the missing couple, we found a secret compartment in the floor, which in and of itself isn't a big deal. These days, folks like to tuck things away where thieves can't find them."

"Like guns and drugs and such," he offered.

She nodded. "We found twenty-five hundred dollars in there." She shrugged. "No big surprise considering the couple work and maybe they've saved. But we also found fifty thousand dollars in cash in a shoebox under the bed."

"Seems strange the $50K wasn't in the secret compartment."

"Agreed," she said. "Maybe they'd only recently come into possession of it, and there had been no time."

"Sounds to me," he said, "like they were involved in one of the trades."

Tara knew what he meant. "Drugs, guns or human trafficking."

He nodded. "We try to keep our communities free of that kind of activity, but sometimes they slip in. By the way, what's up with all these burglaries lately? All the old-timers around here are talking about it."

"Collin and I are still working on that one," she admitted. "There's no pattern to their targets or their hits."

"Hmm," he grunted. "Sounds like teenagers to me."

"It does. They know their way in and out of the houses. Has to be local. There doesn't seem to be any planning either. They go in, get the first marketable items they see and they're gone. Several of the houses have had far more valuable items in the bedrooms, but they never seem to get past the living room."

Her father shook his head. "Kids, I'm telling you. So what about the money and the missing couple? Any connection to these snatch and runners?"

"Not that we've found. We don't know yet how the couple came into possession of the money, but we do know where the money came from before they had it. Way before, in fact."

His forehead pleated in confusion. "You've lost me."

"The Treat Foster case. The missing half a mil. The fifty thousand was part of that stolen cash."

He perked up, eyes wide. "Are you serious?"

"I am."

"I had just stepped into the sheriff's position when Foster disappeared with that money."

"Snelling told me to talk to you. He remembered the case."

"It was a bizarre mystery, to say the least."

"I'd love to hear whatever you can recall."

He rubbed at his stubbled chin. She'd been surprised the first time she saw him wearing two-day-old stubble. He'd promptly informed her that he'd spent fifty-odd years shaving every morning; now he shaved when he wanted to. She couldn't argue with his reasoning.

"Treat Foster was president of the First Community downtown. He was a deacon at his church. Married more than half his life. Never so much as had a parking ticket. One day he just walked into the bank, packed up $500K and walked out. Wife, friends, coworkers, no one had a clue where he'd gone or why he'd done such a thing."

"Did you know him personally?"

"In passing," he admitted. "He and his family attended the same church as your mother and me, just at different locations. There were times when special events brought us to the same house of God. So yes, we were acquainted."

"Any ideas on how this money ended up in the Hollow?"

He shook his head. "I can't think of a single reason. But if something comes to me, I'll let you know." His frown deepened. "This couple who's gone missing, are they originally from the Hollow?"

"No, they moved here year before last. They came up from Florida."

"Maybe they brought the money with them." He shrugged. "If I had been Foster, I would have headed south. Maybe a little farther than Florida."

"I don't think they brought the money with them." Tara considered what she had learned from their coworkers. "Krissy, the wife, had breast cancer last year. The financial burden was tremendous. They had a really hard time. Those closest to her said things had turned around the past few months. It feels more like a recent windfall."

"I'd say there's your answer. You find out where that windfall came from, and the rest will fall into place."

"The simplest answer is usually the right one," she said, repeating the words of wisdom she'd heard from him a thousand times.

"Exactly." His face formed a hopeful look. "Have you talked to Deke lately? He dropped by for a visit the other day." The frown reappeared. "Might have been on Sunday. I can't recall."

Her father had always been able to hang on to the smallest detail. The idea of losing that ability and so much more had to be killing him.

"Deke visited? That was nice of him."

"He visits every couple of weeks," her father said. "I'm sure I've told you this."

He hadn't, but she held any comment.

"He misses you." Her father's face softened. "You should talk to him, Tara. Work things out."

She shot to her feet. "I should go. I have to meet that FBI guy." She gave her dad a hug. "Thanks, Dad. You call me if you think of anything about Foster's case that might be relevant to my missing couple."

"You got it. Think about what I said," he called after her as she left.

She hated to cut and run this way, but she had no desire to talk about Deke with anyone, not even her father.

As she drove away from Forrest Hills, she couldn't help feeling wistful. Her father was her last living relative. When he was gone, she would be all alone. The thought occurred to her all too often these days. Her mother had been an only child. Her father's only brother had been a casualty of war. Not a single living relative. At least not one that she knew.

The idea immediately summoned Deke's image despite her best efforts.

She dismissed the visual. He was not the answer. There were far more things to consider than just her loneliness. She would not transfer her problem onto someone else just to prevent being alone in the world. It wouldn't be fair.

She wouldn't do that to Deke. He didn't understand her reasoning because she couldn't bring herself to tell him her secret.

If she did, he would only insist that it didn't matter and force the issue of them getting back together. She could not allow that to happen. It wouldn't be right.

When she arrived at the substation, a black sedan sat in the small parking area. Judging by the license plate, most likely the federal agent, Hanson.

She climbed out of her Wagoneer and walked into the office. A man wearing a stylish suit and perfect hair waited. He turned to her, hands on hips.

"Deputy Norwood, I presume."

Deep voice. Classic features. Late thirties, early forties maybe. Clearly he had inherited the cold case.

"Agent Hanson?"

"I see you got word I was coming."

"I did."

"You have some time for me now?"

She resisted the urge to ask if it mattered. He was here.

It wasn't like she was going to say no. "Sure. Come on into my office."

Her office was small, but there was an extra chair for the occasional visitor.

They had just taken their seats when Tara found her manners. "Can I get you a bottle of water or a soft drink?"

"No thanks. I'm good."

"Where would you like to begin?"

"Snelling met me at the crime scene and showed me around. What I really need from you at this point is whatever you can tell me about the missing couple."

"Not that much. They moved to the Hollow year before last. Husband works at the hatchery. Wife works at the local diner. Their son, nine, attends the elementary school. No domestic issues. No criminal connections or record of any sort. There was a medical and financial crisis last year. At this time and considering the financial issues, I'm leaning toward the idea that the family was desperate and made a bad decision and it hasn't gone well from there."

"I'd like a list of the coworkers, family and friends you've interviewed."

"There is no family, other than their son, Jacob. I can ready those lists for you right now if you don't mind waiting."

"That would be perfect."

Tara pulled a notepad toward her. "If you'll share your contact info, it'll be easier to pass along information as it comes in."

"Sure." He reached into an interior pocket and produced a business card.

"Thanks." Tara entered his number into her phone. When they had first started working together Collin laughed at her when she said if her phone didn't tell her to do it, she didn't. But she was dead serious. It was her calendar and her alarm clock, her reminder list and more.

When she'd completed the list, she passed it to the federal agent.

Hanson looked it over, then stood. "I have to get back to the city. I look forward to hearing from you with any additional details."

Tara stood, wishing she had more already. "I'd appreciate anything useful you can share that might help my case as well."

He was at the exit, she'd followed, before he hesitated. "There is one thing you might find interesting, though we were never able to make the connection."

"I'll take anything I can get."

"For an entire year before he disappeared, Foster took one afternoon off each week and made a trip that his wife and employees never understood when they learned about the outings after his death."

"Trip?"

"He drove to your little community, Deputy. Spent a few hours and then went home. No one seems to have any idea why he came here or who he saw—if anyone. However, this is our first solid evidence of his presence here in all this time."

Just her luck.

She had her first missing persons case in the Hollow, and it was connected to a decades-old cold case of another missing person.

And half a million bucks.

Chapter Seven

Lake Trail, 7:45 p.m.

Tara took a deep breath, raised her fist and knocked on the door.

She had struggled with this decision for the better part of an hour. Then she'd done what deep down she knew she had to do.

The door opened and Deke stood there, staring at her as if an alien had landed in his front yard and was now at his door.

"Tara? Is everything all right?"

Of course he would be shocked. She hadn't been here—at his home—in nearly six months. She'd sworn to herself she would never come back. Couldn't. Going back would be a mistake—one she refused to make.

She swallowed back the big lump in her throat—her pride most likely. "Do you have a few minutes? I wanted to ask a favor of you."

He visibly shook himself as if throwing off the shock of her appearance. "Come in. Please."

Bracing herself, she stepped over the threshold. The scent

of something delicious filled her lungs. She cringed. "I'm sorry, I'm interrupting your evening."

He grinned. "No way. I like to cook and you know I always cook too much. You're here, you might as well join me. It'll be ready in about fifteen minutes."

She shook her head so hard it hurt. "No, I couldn't—"

"Tara," he interrupted, "you're here. I'll wager you haven't had dinner. It won't kill you to share a meal with me."

He had no idea.

"If you insist." Surrendering was easier than she'd expected. Probably not a good sign. Maybe the whole alone in the world idea looming over her was getting under her skin.

He closed the door and motioned for her to follow him to the kitchen. She did. Not that she needed a guide. She knew this house inside out. Had spent way more time here than she had at home during their five-month-and-twenty-day relationship.

Why could she not get the dates out of her head? It was like some sort of obsession.

They had now officially been apart longer than they had been together. By a couple of days anyway. Not that she was keeping track or anything. Giving herself grace, she had broken things off on her birthday. It wasn't like she could forget that day.

Perfect explanation. She wasn't obsessing. Not at all.

Deke returned to the stove and busied himself stirring pots. Smelled like his homemade spaghetti sauce.

As if she'd said the words aloud, he flashed her a smile. "It's impossible to cook spaghetti for one person."

She nodded, made an attempt at a smile that felt brittle at best.

"Make yourself at home," he said with a nod toward the table. "Water, wine and beer are in the fridge. What's your pleasure?"

To truly answer that question would not be a smart move.

She shuffled to the counter where the bottle of wine waited and opened it. Water wouldn't make the cut. She selected a glass from the cupboard and poured a hefty serving, then made her way to the table. Downed a long swallow and sat down though she felt vastly uncomfortable, particularly since she was out of uniform.

After her meeting with Agent Hanson, she'd gone home, showered and changed into jeans and a tee. She'd planned to relax and consider where to go with the investigation. That had always been her way—her dad's too. She had even poured a glass of wine and sat with her notepad and pen handy to brainstorm possibilities.

Collin had called and they'd discussed the day's findings. It had been during their conversation that she'd come up with the idea of talking to Deke. It had seemed like a really good idea at that moment. She'd even mentioned it to Collin and he had agreed. Now, sitting in Deke's kitchen watching him at the stove, it felt like a really bad idea.

It would certainly have been easier if she'd still been wearing her uniform. The armor of work attire helped considerably when faced with a too personal situation. She turned her head away from him and stared out the window over the sink. She'd always liked his cottage. The three cottages on Lake Trail were all built of stone with views of the small lake and cloaked by woods. This time of year, the area was particularly gorgeous with all the blooming trees. Dogwoods, redbuds. Lots of lovely whites and pinkish purples. Forsythias splashed yellow around the yards. It was nice.

Like the man.

Her gaze wandered back to Deke, who was busy plating the meal he'd prepared.

She closed her eyes and forced away the deluge of memories of moments exactly like this one. Him cooking dinner and teasing her with taste tests. He really was an amazing cook. An amazing teacher. An amazing man. Amazing lover. She swallowed hard. Fought the urge to watch his movements.

No need to torture yourself. She drank more of her wine instead.

He appeared at the table with two steaming plates. "Here we go."

The plates settled on the table. "You want a refill?" He backed toward the waiting bottle.

"I'll take water this time." Her throat felt incredibly dry.

He grabbed a water for her, poured himself a glass of wine and joined her at the table. She opened her mouth to start her questions, but he held up a hand. "Eat while it's hot."

She focused on her plate and ate. The sauce fired across her taste buds and she had to suppress a moan. God, she missed this.

She swallowed. Almost choked.

Stop. Just stop.

Forcing her mind to other things, she considered the pleasant layout of the cottage. All the cottages were small, two bed, one bath. The living room was good sized, but more floor space had been allotted to the kitchen, which was actually a combination kitchen and dining room. No bar or island, just a big table and chairs in the center. Lots of windows, the casement type that opened out instead of sliding up and down, lending a storybook look and feel.

Deke had bought his cottage fully furnished. The former owner had passed with no remaining family, so the furnishings had been sold with the house. According to the deceased's will, the proceeds would be donated to creating a small library for Dread Hollow. The library was up and running last year. Delilah had owned a small shop just off Main Street that once held a candy store. She'd donated the small space for the library, which left enough money for the reno, the stocking of books and a part-time librarian's salary for a few years.

Folks in Dread Hollow came together that way. The community was nothing like its name, which was based on the legend of hauntings at Ruby Falls. The haunted house named after Dread Hollow was famous, but their community not so much, beyond the big annual Halloween festival.

Her father always said that the Hollow would have withered up and died long ago if not for the haunted house. Tara supposed that was true.

She blinked, recalling something else her father had said. "You visit my father?"

Deke sat his fork aside. "I do."

She hadn't meant for the question to come out like an accusation, but there it was.

"Do you mind?" he asked when she said nothing for a beat or so.

"Sorry. No, of course not. I was just surprised, that's all."

He shrugged, took a swallow of his wine. He was usually a beer drinker. She preferred wine. Was the wine left over from their couple days? Or maybe he was seeing someone else.

Surprise or something like that flared through her. She'd told him to move on numerous times, but she hadn't actually visualized it.

How thoughtless and selfish of her.

How incredibly difficult that would be to watch.

"I was friends with your father before *us*," he reminded her.

The game. Oh yes, she remembered. "The chess games."

How had she forgotten? The two had met once a week to play chess. When Deke moved to the Hollow, he'd asked Delilah if there was anyone who played chess. Tara's father had been looking for what he called a "victim" for ages. Since his old friend, who used to be the principal of the school, had moved to Florida.

"I drop by every other Sunday to play. He seems to really enjoy it."

Her heart squeezed. "That's very nice of you."

"Nice?" He shook his head. "Nice has nothing to do with it. I'm still trying to beat him."

She laughed. "He's very, very good at the game."

"Indeed," Deke agreed. "You may have noticed the secretary desk in the living room of his apartment."

Tara nodded. "It was my mother's favorite piece."

"Inside is the chessboard. When I arrive, he opens the cabinet and slides the board forward. We pull up our chairs and start to play. It's the perfect setup."

She thought of the two wood chairs, also antiques, standing on either side of the large secretary. The apartment wasn't that large, so her father had found a way to organize the small place to suit his interests.

"Where there's a will, there's a way." And her father certainly had a hell of a will.

"You wanted to ask a favor?"

Tara pushed aside all the tender thoughts associated with her father and what used to be and explained the seeming Trent Foster connection to Jacob's missing parents. Even now, after discussing it with Snelling, Hanson and her father, it seemed surreal.

"That's incredible." Deke gave his head a shake as if to dislodge the surprise. "I remember seeing something about the Foster case on some true crime show years ago. How do you plan to proceed with investigating that aspect? Sounds like a shot in the dark at best."

"Since we have no proof of any connection to Foster here in the Hollow, then we dig. Talk to people. Obviously if there was any information to be found online, the FBI would have it. In this case, any connection—if it actually exists—will have to be found the old-fashioned way. Pounding the pavement, so to speak."

"What can I do to help?"

"The Hollow might be small, but it's spread out, and people who lived here thirty years ago and might remember the case could all be gone now."

"Passed away or moved away," he suggested.

"Right. The hope is if we learn about someone who knew him, that a friend or relative of that person is still here. The easiest way to ensure we don't miss any opportunities is to talk to people who are most connected to the community and solicit their help in the search. Like Delilah. Running the diner for so many years, she knows most everyone."

Deke nodded. "You want me to talk to people at the school."

"Yes. Teachers, assistants, bus drivers, anyone and everyone. Foster spent his weekly visits here somewhere, presumably with someone."

Deke considered her request for a moment. "I can do that. On one condition."

Frustration welled instantly. "Deke, this isn't the time—"

"You allow me to be a part," he explained, cutting her off, "of the investigation."

"What does that mean? A part? This is an official investigation. We can't have someone who isn't a member of the department involved. There could be legal issues with information and evidence. There are rules, Deke."

He held up both hands. "I don't mean like that. I'm merely asking you to use me as a sounding board. Allow me to throw out possibilities. You know, brainstorm together."

She understood what he was asking. His goal was for them to spend time together. "Deke, how can I make this any clearer? We are not a couple anymore."

"But," he argued, undeterred, "we are friends."

This was a mistake. She had recognized the error before she made it. But she made it anyway.

"You're right. We are friends. Your help will be greatly appreciated. I would be happy to brainstorm with you." Truth was Collin had a wife and three kids. It was tough to find extra time with him for brainstorming.

"We can start now, if you'd like," he offered.

The excitement in his eyes and in that deep voice of his made her chest ache. "Sure. That would be great."

He stood. "I'll grab a couple of notepads and pens."

She nodded. "I'll clean up in here."

He argued with her about the cleanup, but she won that round. When he offered to help, she ushered him away. She knew this kitchen as well as her own. During their time as a couple, Deke had been the cook and she'd taken cleanup detail. Being the gentleman he was, he had always insisted on helping with the cleanup. The memory of laughing as she washed and he dried echoed in her mind.

This was a mistake, but somehow she couldn't stop herself from barreling forward.

When she finished up in the kitchen, Deke had started a fire. It was unseasonably cool tonight. The stone fireplace, with its ancient beam for a mantle, was particularly lovely with even a small fire blazing. Notepads and pens lay on the coffee table next to the open bottle of red and the vintage stemware they'd found at an antique shop in old-town Chattanooga.

Tara drew in a deep breath and took the dive. He settled on the sofa. In the past, she would have joined him there. Instead, she took the chair on the opposite side of the table. She picked up her wine glass and leaned back in her chair.

"Merrilee Bryant would be a good person to start with," she said of the cafeteria manager. "She's worked at the school for fifty years. I'm certain she knows every single person who has lived in the Hollow during that time."

Tara might be in precarious territory, but she intended to stay on task.

Deke wrote the name down on one of the pads. "How about Geneva Edmonton? She's been around a while too."

"Good idea." Edmonton was the secretary in the principal's office. She'd outlived three principals and four husbands. There was little she didn't know about the Hollow. "She'll be happy to tell her life story to you."

He laughed. "I'm certain she will. Even at seventy-eight, she gets around."

Tara smiled. "I heard she's dating Claude Watson since his wife passed."

Deke shrugged. "There aren't that many eligible bachelors in the Hollow."

"Everyone deserves to be happy," Tara said without thinking. "Who says there's a time limit or a set number of times allowed for that kind of happiness?"

The question was a rhetorical one. A thought foolishly spoken aloud.

Deke said nothing. Focused on the notepad and the two names there.

She was glad he'd decided not to call her on that one. Because her decision wasn't about her happiness. It was about his. He just didn't know it.

"Ralph Baker," he said as he wrote down the name.

"Right," Tara said following his line of thinking. "Mr. Baker teaches that financial literacy class to sophomores. I remember that class. He went really in-depth about banking."

"He's the right age," Deke pointed out. "A lifelong resident of the Hollow."

"And he knows everything about banking," she agreed. "Even if he hadn't known Foster personally, he will remember the case."

"He'll also remember if he ever saw him around town." Deke looked at her hopefully.

"No question."

This was good, she decided. Really good.

"What about Seth Harbinger?" she asked. "He teaches journalism to the juniors. I would imagine he has always kept his finger on the pulse of breaking news. Back when we had a small newspaper, he often contributed."

"He's the right age." Deke added Harbinger to the list.

Tara's mind skipped to Jacob. "Do you know if there is anyone listed as an emergency contact for Jacob besides his parents?"

"I don't remember anyone else, but I can check in the morning."

"If the parents have family even in another state, they may have shared something with them that could help with the investigation." None of the coworkers interviewed recalled distant relatives.

"I can talk to Jacob also," Deke offered, "even if there's no one listed."

Tara had planned to do so, but it would be less stressful coming from Deke. "I would appreciate that. As much as I feel I built trust with Jacob, the less often I can disrupt his life, the better. I'm a reminder that his family is missing and haven't been found yet."

Deke let go a burdened breath. "He had nightmares last night. I talked to him. He feels like he should have helped his parents rather than stayed hidden while the bad men took them."

"No. He did exactly what he should have." Tara shook her head, the news making her feel worse. "I hope you explained to him that his staying safe was the best thing he could have done for his parents."

"I did. I told him if he had been taken, there would have been no one to tell us that his parents needed help. I also explained that his parents would feel better knowing he was safe."

"Good. I can't help being angry at his parents for putting themselves in a position to let something like this happen." She rubbed at her temples. "Don't get me wrong, I understand the way life can weigh on you and make you feel desperate, but they have a child to think of."

"I don't know his father at all really," Deke explained, "but I feel like I know his mother pretty well. I can't see her going there. There has to be another explanation."

"Like Treat Foster," Tara suggested. "Maybe this whole thing is about him."

A thought occurred to her. She mentally toyed with it for a moment before sharing.

"What?" he asked, recognizing she'd had a revelation.

"I've been focusing on the father's coworkers at the hatchery. I think I saw him working in someone's yard last month. You know, landscaping stuff. Maybe he found the money and, considering their desperate times, kept it."

"Oh, that's brilliant."

She smiled, couldn't help herself. Deke had always had a way with compliments. "I think one of the times I saw him, Jacob was with him. Playing in the grass or something. Maybe Jacob would know the homes where he has worked."

"I'll talk to him," Deke offered. "Even if he doesn't recall the addresses, he might recognize the places if we drive him around the Hollow."

"After school tomorrow?" she asked. Every minute they waited lessened the likelihood of finding the couple alive.

"It's a date."

That was the part that worried her.

Chapter Eight

Tara logged off the computer after the department's weekly briefing. During the pandemic shutdown a few years ago, she had started attending via Zoom, as had most substations. After the shutdown was lifted, it was just easier to continue doing the same. Once a month, she attended in person.

Collin rolled his chair toward the door of Tara's office, stopping short of moving on to his own space. "So what are we supposed to do about this Agent Hanson?"

Apparently, the agent had decided to call Collin and check up on Tara's job performance. Really, why hadn't he just asked her?

Tara considered her long-time friend and work partner. "Nothing. We're supposed to be on the same side. Unless he makes an actual accusation, what can we do?"

Collin shook his head, his face arranged into an unpleasant frown. "He really made me feel uncomfortable. It was like he was looking for a way to make it appear as if you don't do your job."

That part really hadn't bothered her so much. Who knows

what motive the guy had. She supposed it was possible he needed to be sure Tara was up to a missing persons case. She had been out here in the sticks, where not much had happened for a while now. Couldn't blame a guy for being concerned about a case that had been hanging over the FBI's head for three decades.

Collin shrugged. "I don't know. When he asked about your dad, that's when I really wanted to punch him. They don't come any finer than Tarrence Norwood."

"Wait." Tara quickly searched her memory of the conversation. "You didn't mention him asking about my father."

He made a face. "I didn't? I guess I was so worked up I left out that part. But he did. I was ticked off and I think he could tell."

Tara pushed up from her desk. "Exactly what did he ask about my father?"

Collin visibly concentrated on the answer before speaking. "He asked if then-Sheriff Norwood ever mentioned the Foster case. I told him I was not aware of him or you or anyone else I know mentioning Treat Foster. That happened a long time ago. Before I was born." He laughed. "He didn't appear amused by that last part."

"Sounds like a reasonable question." The words were bitter on her tongue. The idea of anyone asking a question that in any way alluded to her father's career or personal life, for that matter, being anything other than proper and aboveboard was off-putting.

Collin made a sound of distaste. "I don't like him."

Tara shrugged. "We don't have to like him, my friend, we just have to cooperate and accommodate."

Collin gave her a salute. "I'm off to follow up on that break-in over at the Duggleby cabin."

The Duggleby case was the most recent random strike by their two guys dressed in black. "Did you get a tip?"

"In a manner of speaking," he said, purposely being vague.

She lifted her eyebrows. "Your wife sensed something?"

Tara stifled a grin. Collin's wife, Patricia, once read palms for a living—still did for a few longtime clients. No offense to believers, but Tara didn't put much stock in that stuff. Although, last Christmas Patricia did say she believed the Alcott's missing dog was at the O'Linger's when no one else had—not even with missing posters up all over the Hollow—seen the animal. The Alcotts had been certain the O'Lingers had intended to keep the ridiculously expensive Lowchen. The O'Lingers, on the other hand, insisted they had rescued the dog with no collar on the side of the road miles from the Hollow.

Since the O'Lingers were elderly and spent most of their time at home, Tara figured Patricia had dropped by for an in-home reading and spotted the dog. Whatever the case, the dog was delivered to its rightful owners and the Alcotts chose not to pursue any sort of action.

"I know you don't believe her," Collin said, sounding miffed, "but some of us do."

"Hey." She held up her hands in mock surrender. "I say whatever gets the job done."

He rolled his eyes. "Anyway, she did a reading for Louise Hand and she kept seeing all kinds of colors. It was so distracting she could hardly get through the reading. When she told me the colors—orange and pink—I thought of Duggleby's cabin. Whoever broke into their cabin—"

"Took her pink-and-orange paintings," Tara finished for him. "The ones she claimed cost a mint."

"You got it. Patricia said she kept seeing hands in her vision. Louise Hand's twins have been in trouble at school over and over. Always stealing something from another kid or bullying. As a matter of fact, I talked to a couple of kids who help out with the annual fishing rodeo and they said the rumblings around school point to the Hand boys as being our guys in black."

"Sounds like a decent lead to me." She bit her lip to hold back a smile. But he was right that the Hand boys were a rowdy pair of seniors who were likely to end up in jail if they continued on their current path.

"Yeah," he growled, "I know you're a non-believer. You should try letting her do a reading for you sometime. She would change your mind. I can promise you that."

"I'll tell you what," Tara said as she reached for the keys to her Wagoneer. "Why don't you ask her what happened to Treat Foster. Or to the Callaways. I would love any kind of lead on either of those cases."

Collin sniffed. "I'll ask her."

"Thanks." She did smile then. "I appreciate it."

He called back a see-ya-later as he headed out.

Tara made it to the small lobby and the exit there when Wilma Hambrick waved from the sidewalk.

A groan rumbled in her throat, but she pasted on a smile and opened the door. "Good morning, Ms. Hambrick. How are you this morning?"

Tara knew how she was. Wilma Hambrick was unhappy. She had finished her extensive renovations on her home, burning through her husband's insurance money, and now she needed a new project. She wanted to be mayor and to be mayor she needed a city council and a police department. She needed to turn the Hollow into a city.

Tara scolded herself. In some ways, she felt a level of sympathy for the lady. Perception was very important to the older woman. The idea that the community had watched her penny-pinching life under the rule of her husband's iron fist had made her want to find some important or noteworthy way of saving face. Or proving her value and importance to the community. What better way than to become mayor?

"Oh my, I've been worried to a frazzle about that poor family that's gone missing. Is there any news?"

Tara opted not to invite the lady into her office, or she'd be in for a half hour or more briefing on the latest gossip in the Hollow.

"I'm afraid there's no news at this time," Tara said. "I was just on my way out to pick up the flyers from Ms. Tyler so I could get them posted around town."

With the internet and smartphones, most people relied on alerts from those sources. With the number of retirees in the Hollow who either had no interest in or familiarity with social media, she preferred to also add an old-fashioned method of getting the word out.

"I won't take up much of your time," Hambrick assured her.

Tara reached for patience and said what she had to say. "How can I help you?"

"You see," Hambrick began, "this is exactly why we need a full-service police department. You and Deputy Porch do all you can, but you need more. If we move forward as I'm suggesting, you'll have all the resources you need. This tragedy is a perfect example of why we need to move into the current century around here. This isn't the Hollow of forty years ago."

There was no denying life in the Hollow had changed as

city dwellers moved closer in an attempt to escape the rat race of the metropolis. But really, beyond the occasional vandalism or missing dog, there was little or no crime. The recent break-ins and the missing couple notwithstanding. Wilma Hambrick had lived in the Hollow her entire life. She knew this as well as Tara did.

"I understand where you're coming from, Ms. Hambrick. I assure you we're doing all we can."

"Just remember what I said," she reiterated. "Times are changing and we need to keep up."

"You're right." Tara decided to remind the lady of the most painful part of this case. "You know, Jacob, a nine-year-old child, is the one I'm worried about. His parents are missing and they're the only family he has in the world. He's taking this very hard and he's my top priority."

Hambrick's face softened; her eyes started to shine with new emotion. "You're right, of course. It's very sad."

Tara thanked her for stopping by and followed her out of the station. She locked the door and headed for her Wagoneer. She'd spent two hours this morning reviewing any similar cases in the surrounding area. It seemed unlikely that her missing persons case was related to a serial crime spree, however, it was necessary to check.

It had occurred to her that maybe the small Dread Hollow library would have some information on Treat Foster. Though the library hadn't been open very long, Scarlett Peterson, the librarian, had lived in Dread Hollow for all her fifty-eight years. She would surely remember the Foster case. It was possible the missing Callaways had nothing to do with Foster. At this point, there was no way to conclude how they could come to be in possession of money related to that very old and very cold case.

A short drive along Main and a turn onto Sugar Alley and she was at the library. Inside, Scarlett was busy tucking away returned books. No matter how new or how small, the place had that wondrous smell of books. Tara had loved reading as a kid. Her teenage years had been filled with romance novels. She never seemed to have the time for reading these days. Or maybe it was more about the fact that she no longer put much stock in romance. Who wanted to read about happy endings if there was none to be found in her life?

Self-pity is not a good look.

"Deputy Norwood," Ms. Peterson said with a broad smile. "How nice to have you visit our little library."

"You've done a great job." Tara gave the former sweet shop a long, admiring assessment. It was the perfect replacement for the long-closed candy store. After all, the next best thing to sweets was books.

Peterson laid the book she held on the counter. "Thank you. I'm in heaven."

"I wondered if you might have a few minutes to talk about an old case."

"Oh my, that sounds so very Agatha Christie. Of course." She gestured to one of the seating areas scattered about. "We have the place to ourselves this morning. Let's relax and chat."

They settled into the comfortably upholstered chairs of the nearest seating area. "Now, tell me," Peterson said, "what case are we discussing?"

"Do you recall Treat Foster—the banker who—"

"Disappeared with half a million dollars?" she finished. "Oh yes. It was the biggest news at the time. Why, Mr. Foster was a deacon at his church. No one could believe he would just desert his wife and career that way. They had money. No one could understand why he took that money. God knows he didn't need it." She made a face. "Though, it was thought that his wife had basically cleaned him out by the time she ran off with his best friend."

Tara agreed. "It does seem strange."

"Why not just take the money from his own bank account?" Peterson shook her head. "It made no sense unless he was, indeed, broke."

"Did you know him or ever see him around the Hollow?"

Peterson relaxed into her chair, enjoying the discussion of such a juicy mystery. "I didn't know him per se, but I had met him a few times. Right here in the Hollow."

Tara's senses pricked. "Do you recall the circumstances of those meetings?"

"On the first occasion, it was early May, like now, and I was at the service station—you know, they sold gasoline back then. I had gotten out of the car to get a cola. James Ed always kept those little glass bottles on ice. It was my addiction. Mr. Foster pulled up to the pumps in his shiny automobile and requested a fill up. Before I could step out of the shop, he'd come inside and picked up a bottle of cola as well."

"Did he mention why he had come to the Hollow?" Tara had her doubts, but it didn't hurt to ask.

"No. He only smiled and mentioned what a lovely day it was."

"Was there anything else about the interaction that stayed with you?"

"I've always considered myself a fairly good judge of a person's state of mind. He seemed distracted and impatient.

Perhaps not particularly happy to be here. He paid for his purchases and sped away."

"What about the other times you ran into him?" Seemed like a dead end so far.

"There were two other occasions on which I ran into him under similar circumstances. Once at the diner. I think it was summer. I recall it being quite warm. The other time, at the post office and that was between Thanksgiving and Christmas. The decorations were going up around town."

Coming here to go to the post office seemed like a bit of a drive to mail something. Unless he didn't want it post-marked in his zip code area. "Did you notice if he picked up mail or just dropped something off?"

She concentrated on the question for a moment or two. "You know, I just can't remember. I was going in. Passing through the lobby to the counter when I heard a sound and turned around. He was there. Then he left. Sorry, that's all I remember."

"You never saw him again?"

She nodded, a smile tipping up the corners of her mouth before turning to a perfect O. "Wait. Oh yes, once more. The most memorable time actually. I was visiting a friend over on Lake Trail. In one of those cute little British-style cottages."

The street where Deke lived. "Was he visiting someone there?"

"I can only assume. He was out at the lake fishing. I remember thinking how silly it was to be out there on such a miserably cold day. I believe it was in early February."

They talked a few minutes more about the strange case. When Tara felt confident she'd learned all there was to discover from the librarian, she thanked her and prepared to go.

"You know," Peterson said as she followed Tara to the door, "I wonder if they ever figured out why he took the money from only three accounts?"

Tara frowned. "Really?" She hadn't read anything about that in her research. Of course, she hadn't seen the official case file as of yet.

"I don't know if this was common knowledge," Peterson went on. "It wasn't on the news. I only heard about it because an FBI agent interviewed me. He took a call during our conversation and I heard him say to whoever had phoned him that the money was from three specific accounts, as if he'd wanted to make a statement to those account holders."

Tara would be asking Hanson about that. "Do you recall the agent's name?"

"Samuels. Roland Samuels. I'm sure he's retired or dead by now. He was fifty or so at the time."

"Thank you again, Ms. Peterson. You've been very helpful."

Tara hurried to the street and climbed into her Wagoneer. She put through a call to Hanson and got his voice mail. She left a message asking him to call her. A quick call to Regina McCall, the postmaster, who promised to look into the possibility of Treat Foster having had a post-office box. With those tasks set in motion, Tara drove to Lake Trail.

Deke's cottage was the middle one. Tara pulled into the drive of the first and got out. There was a car in the drive, so hopefully someone would be home. She knocked and waited. No sound inside. Outside was equally quiet. Any time she'd come to Deke's, she'd wondered at how very peaceful the setting was. Calm. Very calm. The view out over the water was so tranquil.

She knocked again, but there was still no sound inside.

She backed out of the drive and headed to the cottage on the other side of Deke's. No vehicle in the drive. Probably no one home here either.

She hadn't quite made it to the stoop when the front door opened. "May I help you?"

The woman who spoke was seventy or so. Petite. Soft silver hair coiled into a bun. She wore an apron and gloves as if she'd been rooting around in her garden or her flower beds.

"Hello," Tara said. "I'm Deputy Norwood and I'd like to ask you a few questions if you have a moment."

"About what?" she asked, her gaze narrowing.

"About how long you've lived on this street and who your neighbors are."

With suspicion still clouding her expression, she relented. "I've lived here for forty years. Next door, I think you know Deke. He's been here about three years."

Ah, so she'd recognized Tara. She nodded. "Yes, ma'am. Did you know the person or persons who lived there before Deke?"

"You can't be this close and not know someone, Deputy. Yes, he was a writer. He lived here for about twenty years before he moved back to France. He was French, you know."

"Before him?"

"That was Gerald Carver. A teacher at East Ridge. He was there when I moved here."

"And in the next cottage?"

"A retired stockbroker from New York," she said. "He told stories about the stock-market crash. The big one in 1929. He retired and moved here. This is where he lived until he passed away twenty-eight years ago. Now there's a former flower child who's seventy and still believes she's a twenty-year-old hippie. She's rarely home, and when she is, she doesn't answer the door. Her name is Selena Merrick. She draws. You might find her in the woods or in a field capturing the view on her sketchpad." She glanced around. "Just so you know, often I smell the odor of pot coming from her back patio. I'm certain she grows it somewhere around here."

"I'll talk to her about that," Tara offered. "One last question. Did you know Treat Foster?"

Surprise flared in the woman's expression, but she quickly concealed it. "No. I don't recognize the name. Is there some reason it should be familiar to me?"

"I was told he used to fish in this lake." Tara gestured to the water glittering beneath the sun only steps from where they stood.

"Whoever told you this was mistaken. Have a good day, Deputy."

"Wait," Tara said, barely catching her before the door closed.

At the lady's expectant expression, Tara asked, "What's your name?"

"Mia Saunders."

"Thank you. I appreciate your time."

The lady nodded and withdrew into her home, closing the door firmly behind her.

It was possible she didn't know Treat Foster, but her reaction to the question didn't quite fit that scenario.

Tara needed to talk to Deke about his neighbor.

Right now, she wished they would get a hit on the alerts that had gone out about the Callaways.

Folks around town were tying up yellow ribbons for the couple. A prayer vigil was planned for this weekend.

The couple had to be somewhere.

Chapter Nine

Dread Hollow School, 3:30 p.m.

Tara was aware this outing could prove a dead end, but anything was better than doing nothing. Deke had spoken to Jacob and the boy confirmed his father had done a number of odd jobs besides working at the hatchery. He mowed lawns. Did a bit of carpentry work. Hauled off tree limbs and other unwanted debris as well as trash too large or too bulky for the weekly county garbage retrieval.

The Callaways had come into contact with the money somehow, and Tara needed to find that source if possible. At this time, it was the only feasible explanation for why the two were missing. Particularly since there had been no ransom demand. The large sum of money represented the single motive so far for the couple either having wronged someone or having performed a task outside the bounds of the law. People went permanently missing or toes up for far less way too often.

She hoped, for Jacob's sake, they were still alive and not guilty of an egregious crime.

Jacob strode alongside Deke. The kid's broad smile and the excitement in his step was a testament to how pleased he was to be helping with the search for his parents. Tara hoped she wouldn't have to let him down. Not all missing persons were found...and when they were, it was not always alive.

For now, she opted to continue looking on the bright side. They hadn't discovered any bodies yet.

Her determination wavered a bit when her mind wandered to more personal issues. Watching Jacob stroll toward her Wagoneer, him walking extra fast to keep up with Deke's longer strides, made her chest ache. Deke looked good with a little boy next to him. He was a great teacher and he would be an awesome father. He deserved that opportunity.

Tara would never be able to give him that.

She closed out that line of thinking. It served no purpose. What was done was done. In time, Deke would find someone new and begin the full life he deserved.

The thought made her chest ache even more fiercely.

"Fool," she muttered.

Pushing the hurt away, she propped a smile into place and said, "Hey, Jacob!"

Deke opened the back door, waited for the boy to climb inside and ensured he was secured safely in his seat.

"Hi, Deputy Tara. We're going on a field trip to find clues about my parents."

Deke laughed. "That's right, buddy. I'm certain Deputy Tara is as excited as we are."

"I am," she assured her passengers. "It's part of my job and I love my job."

Deke settled into the passenger seat next to Tara. "Since Jacob doesn't know the exact addresses," he explained, "I told him we would drive around the neighborhoods and he could watch for houses he remembers."

Deke had told her this was the case and she was good

with that. Collin was back at the station following up on incoming tips. Those didn't always prove reliable, but they had to consider each one. Tara was thankful for any sort of possible lead, especially from the child of the missing couple. He might not understand that things he knew could be important. The more opportunity for comfortable exchange with him, the better the odds he would reveal some tidbit that might make a difference.

"Let's start at the beginning," Tara suggested as she pointed the Wagoneer toward the official town limits. Between that point and East Ridge, there was little in the way of anything beyond woods.

"Does that sound good to you, Jacob?" Deke asked.

The kid was already peering out the window as if he hoped to spot something right away. "Yep! I've got my Spidey binoculars." He held a pair of red-and-blue plastic binoculars sporting the Spider-Man logo. He placed them against his eyes. "I can see everything with these."

She and Deke shared a smile that had a happy warmth spreading through her chest. Tara quickly looked away, focusing on driving.

For several streets, they drove slowly up and then down while Jacob studied each house, with and without his binoculars. The silence between Tara and Deke felt heavier as the time moved at a snail's pace.

"Hey," she said, abruptly remembering his neighbors. "I checked in with your neighbors."

He glanced at her, worked up a grin. "You checking up on me?"

"No." She shook her head, shifting her gaze from his lips and how they moved so easily when he smiled, as if he did a lot of that. And he did. She knew this. His easy smile was one of the things about him that first caught her eye. "Ms. Peterson from the library mentioned having seen him fishing at the lake on Lake Trail when she was visiting a friend. Obviously, you wouldn't know since you didn't live there at the time."

"You talked to Ms. Saunders." Deke shifted a little in his seat and looked at Tara as he spoke.

She kept her gaze focused straight ahead. The less eye contact the better. "I did."

"She's a bit of a conspiracy theorist. The rumor is she has one heck of a stash of goods in her basement in the event that the balloon goes up. Don't feel bad if she was suspicious of you or your reason for knocking on her door; she's suspicious of everyone. She probably thought you were there to learn about her secret stash of guns."

Tara did look at him then. "Should I be worried about her?" Spree shootings were in the news far too often.

Deke shook his head. "I don't think so. She's just an enthusiastic prepper. She's not so tough. She calls me over to get snakes out of her yard."

Tara opted not to mention that just because the lady wouldn't shoot a snake didn't mean she wouldn't shoot a person.

"That one!"

The shout of near hysteria came from the back seat.

Tara eased to the side of the street. "Let's get out here and you show me which house you mean."

They climbed out and gathered on the sidewalk. "Point to the one you remember," Deke said.

"The yellow house over there." Jacob pointed across the street.

"Let's check it out." Tara led the way.

They congregated on the porch of the yellow house and Tara knocked on the door. She imagined that to whoever lived inside, they gave the appearance of a fundraising group or a trio inviting neighbors to church—if not for the uniform she wore.

An older gentleman opened the door. He looked from one to the other, finally landing on Tara since she stood slightly in front of the others. "Can I help you?"

"Yes, sir." She smiled, hoping to put him at ease. Most people's concern rose when they found a deputy at their door. "I'm Deputy Norwood and we're looking for anyone who might have employed Jeff Callaway. Perhaps to cut your grass?"

He nodded, visibly relieved. His hand extended for a shake. "Richard Arrick. And yes, Jeff mowed my lawn all summer last year. He did a great job. I'm hoping he'll be able to take over for me again this year. Once the weather heats up, my heart condition puts the landscaping chores off-limits." His relief faded to concern again. "Wait, I'm not thinking. Has there been news about him and his wife?" He glanced at Jacob and managed a half-hearted smile. "Your dad is a great guy and you're a good helper. I remember you coming with him a few times."

The boy nodded. "Have you seen him? We really need to find him and my mama."

Tara's heart squeezed.

"I haven't," the man said. "But I am keeping an eye out. If I see or hear anything, I'll be sure to let you know."

"Thank you, sir." Deke took Jacob's hand. "Let's go wait in the Jeep, buddy."

Tara had agreed to allow Jacob to be involved to a degree. But when it came to the questioning, he would need to step away.

"Mr. Arrick, it sounds as if you and Mr. Callaway had a good relationship."

"We did. He's a fine young man. I was so sad to hear about his wife's cancer and then very thankful when she got better. Jeff spoke openly about how difficult that time was for them. I was happy to lend whatever support I could. My wife is a breast cancer survivor."

Cancer sucked.

Tara pushed the memories away. "Your dealings with Mr. Callaway were strictly work related?"

"Primarily, yes. He did speak often about his wife, and I offered money to help. At first, he refused to accept it unless I agreed to allow him to repay the gift with work around here. I agreed. He painted the house." He gestured to the yellow siding. "I was most pleased. I paid him five thousand dollars, which was not nearly enough in my opinion, but he would not take more."

Five thousand was a tidy sum, but it wasn't fifty. It could very well explain the twenty-five hundred. "One last question, Mr. Arrick, did you know Treat Foster?"

He made a face as if he didn't understand, then he nodded. "Oh, I see. You're referring to that bank president who stole all that money some—good gracious—twenty-five or thirty years ago."

"Yes, sir."

"I didn't. No. I read about it in the paper, of course. Why do you ask?"

"They're looking into his case again," she said, keeping the potential connection to the Callaways to herself. "Apparently, he used to spend some time in the Hollow before he disappeared. I've been asking everyone if they knew him or if they recall ever having seen him in the area."

"I don't recall ever seeing him in person." His face pinched as if he were working to dig up any potential memory. "I'm sorry I can't help you there. I will keep the Callaways in my prayers." He pointed to the yellow ribbon tied around his mailbox. "And I'm keeping that ribbon on display until they're back home."

Tara thanked him and headed to the Wagoneer. She climbed in and said to her passengers, "Off we go to the next street."

Jacob gave her a resolute nod. "I'm ready."

He seemed to enjoy being able to participate in the investigation. As unorthodox as it seemed, she firmly believed having him participate was a good idea. Not to mention they'd have to ask every resident of the Hollow without Jacob's help. This way they could pinpoint their search in the right areas.

As Tara continued her drive around the Hollow, she considered the no-answer cottage next to Deke's. "What about your other neighbor? No one answered the door when I knocked."

Deke glanced at her. "That's Selena Merrick's house. She's older, an artist, I think, and a little on the eccentric side."

Funny, Tara thought. She'd spent a good deal of time at Deke's place when they were together and she'd never met his neighbors. Made sense now. One was a reclusive prepper, the other was an eccentric self-imposed shut-in.

"I think the one time I conversed beyond hello to Ms. Merrick, she mentioned that she bought the place about twenty years ago, so she likely wouldn't have seen Foster around. As for Ms. Saunders, I can't imagine her being friends with Foster and then pretending she hadn't known him. She would probably have seen him as some elitist who stepped on the toes of the little guy. She would have turned him in herself."

Tara laughed. "I'm sure she would have."

"Or shot him," Deke teased.

"Maybe."

She'd forgotten how much she enjoyed time with Deke. He had a way of making life feel relaxed and easy. He made even the most mundane activity feel relevant. She had missed that…missed him.

No going there. Especially with him so close.

For the next three hours, they drove the streets and roads in and around the Hollow. Collin had called to check in. He had nothing new to report. Tara had the same. Though it had not been a fruitless expedition and Jacob had certainly been gung ho. Four houses that Jacob had recognized had proven to be folks who had employed Jeff Callaway for one task or another. So far, they'd all said the same thing: super nice guy, hard worker, dependable.

How had a super nice, hard-working, reliable guy found himself in trouble?

The next road, Falling Rock Trace, Tara chose was close to the town limits going deeper into the woods and closer to the edge of the mountain. There were only three or four houses along this one.

"That one!" Jacob shouted. "That one!"

Tara slowed to a stop in the road since it was possible to see in both directions and there was zero traffic. "Which one?" She could see two up ahead, and there was the one they'd just passed.

"Behind us. The rock house."

He sounded even more excited than the previous times.

"Let's check it out." She backed up and pulled into the drive. The yard was overgrown. "You're sure about this one, Jacob?"

Whatever his father had done here, it hadn't involved landscaping. At least not lately.

"I am!" he practically shouted. "This was one of his favorites."

Tara and Deke shared an I-don't-know look and got out. Why not check it out?

The driveway was badly cracked concrete. Weeds had sprouted in the crevices. The sidewalk to the front door was the same. Cobwebs and leaves cluttered the small inset area that served as the stoop. The rounded top of the door was crusted with mud dauber nests. If anyone still lived here, they rarely used the front door.

Deke reached in front of her and swiped at the cobwebs.

"Thanks." She knocked on the door; white paint chips drifted to the stone floor.

There was no sound other than the breeze that had kicked up.

"Doesn't look like anyone lives here," Deke said.

Tara turned to their guide. "Jacob, are you sure this is one of the houses where your father worked?"

He nodded eagerly. "There's a big old apple tree around back. Come on, I'll show you."

Tara glanced around the front yard. No vehicle. "Let's check the mailbox first."

"I got it." Deke hustled back to the road and opened the door of the leaning box. He shook his head. "Empty."

"I promise this is right," Jacob urged. "Come on and I'll show you."

Tara crouched down to Jacob's eye level. "There's no one here to talk to and that's what we need. To find people who may have spoken with or seen your parents."

"Please just come around back with me."

Tara gave in. "Okay, let's have a look."

Jacob sprinted ahead as they trudged through the deep grass and weeds.

"I'm guessing this place has been empty for years," Deke said.

Tara agreed. "Keep an eye on Jacob. I want to walk around to the other end of the house and check the electric meter."

"Hold up, buddy," Deke called after Jacob.

Tara picked her way along the back side of the house. There were curtains drawn tight over all the windows. More cobwebs and mud dauber nests. She rounded the far corner and confirmed her conclusion. There was no meter. It had been pulled. No meter, no electricity. No electricity, no lights or heat.

She moved on to the front of the house and gauged the distance to the next two houses on the road. More than half a mile, for sure. If there was anyone home at either of those houses, they could maybe confirm when this house had last been occupied. With that in mind, Tara walked around to the back side of the house again.

Jacob had been right. A large apple tree stood in the center of the yard. He and Deke were walking around the yard where it disappeared into the tree line. The woods along this road were thick and old. Knowing the local terrain, she estimated it wasn't far to the bluff once you entered those woods.

Dusk was creeping in. They should load up, and she would stop by the other two houses before heading back to the Wright home to drop off Jacob. Or maybe she would take both Jacob and Deke back to his vehicle at the school. The latter would prevent her from spending alone time with Deke.

She really should suck it up and be an adult about this thing. They were over and there was no need to constantly be on guard. Just move on and treat Deke like any other citizen of the Hollow. Wouldn't that be nice? If only she could pretend away the feelings that wouldn't let go. The dreams that haunted her sleep. All the little things that reminded her of him and their time together.

The need that tore at her like a beast any time she saw him.

Too bad it seemed like that feat was impossible.

How long would it take, she wondered, to reach that place where she no longer felt such an intense desire…the longing to be with him?

Collin was right, she supposed. She needed to start dating again and that would make the transition easier. Except, she hadn't been able to make herself manage so much as a meal with anyone else.

She was hopeless.

"Jacob, wait!"

Tara's senses alerted. She turned back to see where Jacob and Deke were. Jacob was nowhere to be seen and Deke was rushing into the tree line.

"Jacob!" Tara shouted as she rushed in that direction.

It took a hell of a push, but she managed to catch up with Deke. "Where is he?" she demanded without slowing down.

Deke dodged a group of trees. She did the same.

"He just took off." He glanced at Tara. "We have to catch him before it gets dark."

He didn't have to say the rest: *the cliffs*.

Tara pushed even harder, zigzagged through the trees. Where the hell was the kid going?

Chapter Ten

Jacob ran as fast as he could.

Even though it had been a while since he was here, he remembered the way.

Mr. D and Deputy Tara were calling for him. He felt bad for running like this, but he'd made a promise to his dad.

His dad had showed him this place but made him promise never to tell anyone about it.

Jacob ran harder. He couldn't let them catch up with him. They would make him go back to Ms. Wright's house. He liked Ms. Wright, but he wanted to be with his mama and dad.

They could be waiting for him. He hadn't thought of that until today when Mr. D mentioned driving around to look for the places his dad did work. Jacob realized then that maybe his mama and dad were here waiting for him to come so they could all be together again. Maybe they had escaped the bad men and hidden.

Limbs from the bushes slapped him in the face and dragged at his legs, but he had to keep going. Almost there.

The ground disappeared from under his feet, and he pitched forward.

Jacob bit down hard to stop from crying out, pinching

his tongue. The sting brought tears to his eyes. He hit the leaf-covered ground and rolled a good way before he could stop himself.

He jumped up. Steadied himself. The woods spun round and round. His heart beat against his chest so hard he was sure it would pop out any second like that alien in that movie he watched one night when his parents were working late.

He sucked in more air. Tried to figure out where he was.

Then he saw it. The old dead tree that stood near the cave opening—the mouth, his dad had called it.

He started that way. He heard his friends calling for him. They were going the wrong way.

He felt bad. They were his friends. They were taking care of him and trying to help him.

Jacob stared up at the sky. It was almost dark. He had to hurry.

He picked his way through the bushes and between the trees until he reached the dead one. A big, tall oak that, his dad said, had probably been struck by lightning a long time ago. He said it was probably just a shell now, waiting for the right gust of wind to take it down.

Jacob's heart started pumping hard again as he peered into the cave. The opening was as tall as him and a lot wider. For a grown-up it didn't look that big, but to him it was good sized. It was pretty dark in there and he didn't have a flashlight.

Didn't matter. All he had to do was call out to them, and if they were here, they would come get him. He eased deeper into the cave and called out as loudly as he dared, "Mama! Dad! Are you here?"

There was a sound…dripping. Water dripping. His dad said that was normal in caves. It was a lot cooler in here. He moved slowly, remembering the uneven rocks on the floor. They could be slick.

"Mama! Dad! Are you here?"

Something heavy felt as if it pushed against his chest, but there was nothing there. It was inside. It got heavier and heavier until he could hardly breathe. His eyes burned with the pain of understanding.

They weren't here.

His mama and dad might never come back and he would be all alone forever.

Chapter Eleven

"Do you see him?" Tara pushed through the brush. Her face stung from the limbs slapping at her. Her lungs burned from the hard run.

"I don't see him," Deke said from a dozen yards away. "Jacob!"

How could a nine-year-old boy move that fast?

Tara stalled. Took a couple of gulps of air. She and Deke were no threat to Jacob. He wasn't afraid of them. The only way he would feel this confident running headlong into the woods with it nearly dark was if he knew where he was going.

"Deke!" She headed in his direction. His voice echoed as he called again for Jacob.

Tara caught up with him. He shook his head, took a gasp of air. "Why the hell would he run from us?"

"He's not." Tara pushed the strands of hair that had been pulled free of her ponytail away from her face. "He's running toward something. There has to be an old shack or campsite. Something. He's been there before and feels like he needs to go back."

Deke's gaze collided with hers. "Caves. There are caves in these woods."

He was right. "You keep looking," she suggested. "I'm calling for backup. We can't risk him getting lost out here. There's wildlife in these woods too."

"Mr. D!"

Relief shot through Tara's veins.

Deke took off in the direction of the boy's voice. Tara followed. Thank God. Thank God.

A crashing sound drew them to the left and suddenly Jacob emerged from a line of trees surrounded by shoulder-high shrubs and brush.

He ran to Deke. Slammed into him almost knocking him off his feet. Sobs rocked his slim body.

Deke dropped to his knees and hugged the weeping child. "What happened, buddy?"

Tara moved and crouched down to see his face better. "You okay?"

"I'm sorry I ran from you." He swiped at his eyes with his fists. "I had to go to the cave and see if they were there waiting for me."

"Your parents?" Tara's tension moved to a higher level. "Were you parents supposed to be waiting here for you?"

He shrugged, his face crumpled in a mixture of fear and grief. "I don't know. My dad brought me here a couple of times. He said the cave was a special place. A good hiding place. He said if we ever needed a place to hide until it was safe, this would be the place." He swiped hard at his eyes again, frustrated with the tears and obviously unable to slow them. "I thought they might have gotten away from the bad guys and come here to hide and wait for me."

"Did your dad tell you they would come here and wait for you?"

Jacob stared at the ground. Shook his head. "No. I was just hoping, I guess."

"I'm sorry, buddy," Deke said softly.

"Jacob," Tara said, drawing his gaze to her, "can you show us where the cave is. I have my flashlight. I should probably have a look around."

He nodded and motioned for her to follow him. She and Deke shared another of those worried glances. This kid had been through hell without once showing it, but staying strong was getting to him. Today he'd reached his breaking point. Poor kid.

When they arrived at the mouth of the cave, Tara was surprised at how well concealed it was. The opening was not very large. She took her flashlight from her utility belt and turned to Deke. "Keep him close to you. I'll have a look inside."

"No way. Give me the flashlight. I've been in more caves than you have."

"Deke," she warned.

"No offense, Deputy," he said, holding out his hand, "the facts are the facts. Part of being brave is being smart."

Reluctantly, she handed him the flashlight. Then she reached for Jacob's hand. "We will figure this out, Jacob."

He nodded, but he didn't look at her. It didn't take much imagination to understand that he was losing faith. He was scared and needed his parents.

What the hell had they done?

Fifteen minutes later, Deke exited the cave.

"I was just about to come in after you," she said, thankful to see his face again. Damn it.

"It's not such a wide cave," he told her, "but it's deep. It goes on and on, and there are corridors that go off in different directions. We'll need to be a good deal more prepared if we're going exploring in there. I've been lost once or twice and it's not a good feeling."

"We'll come back tomorrow," she suggested. "Let's get this guy home. I'm sure he's exhausted."

Deke handed her flashlight back to her and took Jacob's hand in his. "Let's go find some pizza and ice cream. I'm starving."

Jacob smiled. "Chocolate ice cream with sprinkles?"

"You got it," Deke promised.

The walk back to the house was longer and more exhausting than the rush into the woods, mostly because it was uphill and adrenaline had robbed her of strength. The good news was Jacob was okay. They hadn't lost him and they'd learned something more about his father. He thought about contingency plans. There had to be a reason. Some people worried about their children's futures and bought life insurance and stocks. Other people worried about the government taking over their lives and prepped for bugging out, like Deke's neighbor. Whatever the case, there was always, always a reason.

When they reached the backyard, Tara studied the dark house lit only by the moon that was out now. How long had the house been abandoned? Who had lived here?

"Jacob, did your dad know the person who lived here?"

"Maybe. He used to bring his riding lawn mower here and cut the grass. He came a bunch of times last year. But he only came once this year. That's when he showed me the cave."

But the grass hadn't been cut. "Did he bring his lawn mower when the two of you came this year?"

"No. We just came in his truck." He shrugged. "I mean we had the trailer and lawn mower, but he didn't use it."

"Did the two of you ever go inside the house?"

Jacob moved his head side to side in a firm no. "We cut the grass or visited the cave."

"Thanks, Jacob, for helping us today," Tara said. "You're really smart. Your mom and dad will be proud when they find out how much you've helped us."

They started toward the front of the house. Tara was ready for a long hot shower. She was sure poor Jacob was ready to crash. Probably the only thing keeping him upright was the promise of pizza and chocolate ice cream with sprinkles.

As they reached the Wagoneer, a vehicle coming from the direction of the other houses farther up the road slowed to a stop. The driver powered his window down.

"Deputy Norwood?"

Tara left Deke and Jacob to climb into the Wagoneer and approached the vehicle stopped on the road.

"Evening, sir," she offered.

He gave a nod of acknowledgment. "Brandon Parton. I live in the first house on the right back that way." He jerked his head in the direction from which he'd come. "Did my wife finally call about the lights we saw a few nights ago? That house has been empty for years, and last week, maybe on a Wednesday, as I was driving by, I saw a flashlight bobbing around in there. I almost stopped to check it out, but I had my granddaughter with me. Then I just plain forgot."

"No one called. I'm glad you didn't stop and go in. It's never safe to approach the scene of a potential crime. Better to call it in."

"Yeah, that's what my wife said too. I didn't really figure she'd called, but she saw the lights that night and said she'd seen them once or twice before and figured it was just some homeless person seeking refuge from that last frosty night. My wife is a bit of a softie. Like me, she knows the place was basically abandoned. Someone might as well take shelter there."

Tara smiled her understanding. "Do you know who owns the house?"

He frowned. "I'm embarrassed to say I don't. When we moved here about fifteen years ago, I was told a woman lived there. Later I heard she'd moved away. I'm not sure anyone really knows."

"The other house down the road, who lives there?"

"Ed Kosh. He lived there for forty years. He passed about six months ago. His house is being renovated for listing on the market."

"Thank you, Mr. Parton. We'll investigate the lights and make sure no one is vandalizing the place."

"Thank you," he said, then he backed up in the road and turned around to go back home.

Tara walked back to her Wagoneer. She opened the door and ducked inside. "That was Mr. Parton, who lives in the next house down the road. He has seen someone with a flashlight in the house, so I'm going to have a quick look before we go."

Jacob had drifted off to sleep in the back seat. Deke glanced at the boy and then looked to her. "I would argue with you going in alone, but I know it would be pointless, so I'll stay here with Jacob and you do what you have to do."

"Thanks."

That was one of the hardest parts of being a woman and a cop. Most men were protective by nature. Having a woman do the protecting was kind of an ego punch. She had to admit, Deke had handled it well when they were a couple.

Tara used her flashlight to guide her since it was fully dark now. She pulled on a pair of gloves and checked the front door. It was locked. Checked the windows since there were several across the front. All the ones in front were either locked or painted shut. She made her way around the south end. Windows were locked. She found the same along the back wall. When she reached the small patio and the back door, she was startled to find that door unlocked. Not damaged or tampered with, just unlocked.

She stepped inside, leaving the door open behind her. "Sheriff's Department," she called out, "is anyone inside the house?"

Her voice echoed through the silence. She roved her flashlight methodically over the space. Kitchen. Very late-seventies decor with harvest-gold appliances and faux-looking wood cabinets.

She made a face. The house smelled like dead flowers. But then she had no idea how long it had been closed up. A few steps across the fake-brick linoleum, and she opened the fridge. There were items inside, but the decomp process had long ago completed and formed hard globs of whatever. Cheese, maybe? She shuddered. A carton of milk that had expired in 1999 sat in the middle of the largest shelf.

The kitchen cabinets were the same, mostly empty. The few canned and dry goods had expired decades ago. An old rotary phone hung on the wall. The curly cord hung to the floor. The kitchen and dining room were one rectangular room. A table and chairs with matching china cabinet, china still inside, filled that end of the room.

The living room was pretty much the same. Vintage furniture. Layers of dust. Old newspapers and magazines on the coffee table. Gold-and-brown shag carpet on the floor. Didn't smell any better in the living room or in the hall as she made her way to the bedrooms. She had decided the smell was sort of like that cave. Musty and dank. She doubted any sunlight made it past the heavy curtains on all the windows.

The first two bedrooms were open. Had the same shag carpet and were furnished in a style consistent with the rest of the house. The bathroom was dusty with those gold-flecked four-inch square tiles covering the walls about half-way up. The gold fixtures were discolored with age.

The final bedroom door was closed. Tara opened the door and instantly understood where the foul odor was coming from. The scene was far different from the rest of the house.

Newspapers stood in waist-high stacks around the perimeter of the room. She shifted the beam of light to the bed. There was a lump under the covers. She followed the form until the glow of her flashlight lit on two dark holes in a skull.

She almost stumbled back. Caught herself and steadied the beam of light. "Damn."

The owner hadn't moved; she or he had died in bed.

Tara moved closer. Tried to determine if the remains belonged to a man or a woman. The hair was longish. Whatever clothing he or she had worn was too far gone to categorize. The color might have been a green, but it was difficult to make a true assessment.

The petrified remains were tucked under the covers. The smell wasn't good but not as bad as she would have expected. She moved closer, almost tripped over the remains of what she presumed to be a dog on the floor. It appeared to have passed while curled up in its bed asleep. She leaned down and spotted the collar. Dog for sure, she decided. *Butch* was engraved on the tag.

Tara shook herself and focused on continuing to review the scene. So far, she saw nothing that marked it as a crime scene, just a sad ending to two lives.

She walked to where the newspapers stood in neat rows. Local papers—back when they were still in circulation.

The headlines on one were circled. *Foster Still Missing.*

No big surprise. The case was big news thirty years ago and for a good number after that. There had been a true-crime show or two about it.

She walked around to the other side of the bed where a small table topped with a lamp stood. She opened the one drawer and surveyed the contents. Handkerchief. Eye glasses. Prescription bottles. She checked the labels. The dates showed the medications had been filled in January thirty years ago. Tara recognized one as being for pain. She did an internet search on the other. Also for pain. Oddly there was no name of the patient or the physician on the bottles. She placed the bottles back in the drawer. Noted a photo lying loose. The photograph was old. Black-and-white. A young girl and boy stood together holding hands. Judging by their clothes, this was something from fifty or more years ago. She turned over the photo to look for anything that might be written on the back. Many of the photographs from her childhood were labeled that way.

Treat and me. The date was listed, but it was the name *Treat* that had Tara startled. The boy might have been twelve or thirteen, the girl maybe ten. She glanced back at the bed, the beam of her flashlight falling on the skull with its leathery skin remains and thin clumps of hair. Was this Treat

Foster's sister or friend? Was she, presumably, the reason he'd come here repeatedly before his disappearing act?

Tara set the photo back in the drawer and called Collin. She gave him the address and asked him to come right away. She wasn't leaving this scene unattended now that she'd discovered it. Then she called Sergeant Snelling. He wasn't going to believe this. She didn't believe it, but she was here, looking at it.

A little voice suggested she call Agent Hanson, but she shut out that voice. She would call him when she had a better handle on what they had. No need to drag him all the way out here and get his hopes up for nothing. The person who had lived in the house may have found these items and kept them.

This was not likely, but Tara was going with it for now.

She walked out the front door, peeled off the gloves and found Deke pacing next to the Wagoneer.

He stopped when he saw her. "You find anything?"

She waited until she was next to him to explain. Voices carried in the dark and she could almost see the neighbor with his head hanging out a window to hear what was going on.

"Jacob still out?" she asked.

"Yeah. Poor kid was exhausted after getting his hopes up like that only to have them dashed."

"There are human remains inside," she told Deke. "So I can't leave until Collin gets here. He should arrive any minute. Sorry to keep you hanging around like this. If you want to take Jacob to the Wrights and then go home, Collin can give me a ride later."

"No thanks. I'm staying with you."

She had known that would be his answer.

"You think the owner just died in there and no one ever noticed?" he asked.

It happened. "Possibly. Some folks don't have any family, and if they don't have friends or people they socialize with, there's no one to check on them." Damned depressing way to go.

"That's sad," he said, his gaze fixed on the house. "No one should die alone."

Unless she went first, Tara would have no family left when her dad passed away. She did have her work, but she could be retired by then. She didn't belong to any social groups or a church. Would she end up that way?

How pathetic was it that she didn't even have a dog to see her out?

"There was a dog," she told him. "Butch. He stayed with her or him."

Deke heaved a heavy breath. "I don't want to go like that. Alone, I mean."

"Who does?" she pointed out, avoiding making her response personal.

He moved closer to her and leaned against the side of the Wagoneer. "Whatever happens in the future, I'll keep tabs on you, Tara. I'll call. Drop by. Whether you want me to or not."

She ignored the warm sensation that accompanied his words. "That might be considered stalking."

"Then Collin can arrest me, but that's what I'm going to do."

No matter that she had pretended dying alone didn't bother her, he understood it did, and he said those words to ensure she knew he would be around, like it or not. That was the kind of guy he was. Caring. Kind.

What was wrong with her?

How had she walked away from this man?

As if she'd stated the words aloud, he said, "I learned my lesson over the past six months. I'm not going to pretend I don't care about you. You're stuck with that, you got it?"

She nodded as she leaned against cool metal next to him. "Got it."

They could be friends.

His arm went around her shoulders and pulled her close. He whispered, his lips so close to her forehead she could feel them move, "I will change your mind if it takes me the rest of my life."

She wanted desperately to turn her face up to his and feel his lips against hers.

Collin pulled up and saved Tara from herself.

Or maybe she couldn't be saved.

The jury was still out on that score.

Chapter Twelve

Falling Rock Trace, 8:30 p.m.

Collin stalled in the doorway of the last bedroom in the house. "Man, oh man. How long you think she's been here?"

Tara considered the room in the better lighting. Collin had brought the portable lighting and generator from his garage. The skeletal remains looked even more eerie in the brighter light.

"About thirty years if the information on those prescription bottles is accurate." Tara had seen a few bodies in her early cop days but never one this far along in the decomposition process. "The clothing and bed linens are still intact for the most part. I'm sure Snelling will be able to tell us more." She checked the time on her cell. "He and his team should be here soon."

"Should we do some more looking around?"

He knew the answer. "We should wait for Snelling. I've already had a closer look than I should have."

"You think she died of natural causes?"

"I'm guessing so. The prescriptions were for pain meds."

"Hell of a way to go." Collin grimaced. "All alone like

this." He shrugged. "Except for the dog. At least she had a companion."

Tara hadn't been able to stop thinking about dying alone since she walked into this room. The thought had her reliving the things Deke had said to her...the way his lips had brushed her temple.

She exiled the thoughts. What was wrong with her? She was standing in the middle of a room with a thirty-year-old corpse and she couldn't keep Deke out of her head. Not good. Maybe she'd had this cushy nothing-ever-happens-in-Dread-Hollow job too long. She'd lost her edge.

As soon as Collin had arrived, she'd had him drive Deke and Jacob back to the school to get his truck. She hadn't been able to think as clearly with Deke here...so close.

She set her mind back to the here and now. No more reminiscing. "We should head back out to meet Snelling."

"The neighbor didn't have a clue?" he asked on the way to the front door.

"He thought the place was empty." Tara considered the nearly knee-deep grass around the house. Why wasn't it deeper? Why weren't the shrubs and hedges up to the roof? At home, the crepe myrtles would take over if they weren't trimmed annually. The boxwoods required far more attention. Jacob said his father had cut the grass here last year. Maybe he'd trimmed all the shrubs too. But they hadn't done any trimming this year. Considering the corpse—presumably the owner—couldn't have hired him, then who?

"The team's here," Collin said from the door.

Tara followed him out to greet Snelling and his team. Tara brought him up to speed on what she'd found inside. She didn't mention the photo for now. Snelling would want to call Hanson before proceeding. Tara's gut said she should hang on to the scene for a bit longer. Jacob had said his father worked at this house, which meant maybe there was a connection between the missing couple and Treat Foster, slim though it might be, or the person who had died in the house.

In Tara's opinion, her missing persons case took priority over a thirty-year-old cold case.

While Snelling's crew carried in more lights and the other equipment they would need, Tara signaled for Collin to join her away from the others. "I need to check out a couple of things. Can you stay here until I get back?"

"Sure thing. Let me know if you need me."

Tara backed out of the drive and headed toward the neighbor's house. She pulled into the neighbor's drive and exited the Wagoneer. Mr. Parton was obviously watching the activity next door since the porch light came on and he was at the front door before she reached it.

"Looks like you've found something amiss over there," he said.

"I'm afraid I can't give you specifics, but the answer is yes. You mentioned the house appeared to be empty since you moved here."

"That's right. Ed, the neighbor who passed recently, said he'd never seen anyone there either. He lived here for nearly twenty-five years."

"Someone was cutting the grass or it would be considerably more overgrown," she said in hopes of prompting information on who had hired Jacob's father.

"Oh, yes, you're right. Ed paid someone to come about once a month to cut the grass and prevent the shrubs from getting out of hand. He thought it devalued his property when a neighboring house was all grown up." He gave a nod. "I suppose it'll be up to me now."

"Mr. Kosh never mentioned who he hired?"

Parton shook his head. "Recently, I noticed a small red truck. An older truck. There was a lawn mower on one of those small black metal trailers behind it. The vehicle was parked on the side of the road in front of the house. I never saw anyone in the yard though. Since Ed passed, I suppose I should have stopped to speak with whoever was driving the truck."

Jeff Callaway drove a small red truck.

"Thank you, Mr. Parton. You've been a great help." She gave him one of her cards. "Please call me if you remember anything else or see anyone not in an official vehicle hanging around the house." She smiled. "My Wagoneer is my official vehicle."

"I'll remember that."

Tara thanked him again and hurried back to her vehicle. She made her way back to what she decided to call the bone house. "Morbid, Tara," she muttered as she parked behind Collin's cruiser.

Bright light simmered behind the curtains, creating a kind of eerie glow outside each window. She pulled on shoe covers and gloves and stepped inside. Between Collin's lights and the ones Snelling's team had brought, the place was lit up like an airport terminal.

Collin was in the kitchen. Tara joined him there. "Anything new?"

"Not that I've been told about." He hitched his head toward the other end of the house. "You know Snelling, he's pretty tight-lipped until he has a good handle on things."

"He'll fill us in when he can. I spoke to the nearest neighbor, Mr. Parton. The other neighbor, a Mr. Kosh, who died recently, had been paying someone to cut the grass and clip the shrubs about once a month during the summer. He felt the overgrown property adversely impacted the value of his."

"I can see how he'd feel that way," Collin agreed. "No one likes a dump next door."

"Mr. Parton says the vehicle he saw at this property most recently was a small red truck with a trailer and lawn mower. That confirms what Jacob told me."

"That gives us a concrete connection between the two cases," Collin pointed out.

"I'm guessing this is where the money came from."

"Based on the photo you found in the bedroom," Collin offered.

"Exactly. If the person who lived here was somehow connected to Foster, this may have been his hiding place."

Collin surveyed the kitchen. "So there could be half a million dollars hidden around here somewhere."

"Maybe. The real question in my mind," Tara said, "is whether whatever Callaway came upon here is the reason he and his wife are missing?"

"We need to know more about the person who lived in this house," Collin offered.

"I'll call Helen over at property records." She checked the time on her cell. "It's late, but maybe she can find the owner's name for us. Then I'm going to see Delilah. She and her family know everyone in this town. I need you to stay here for a while and keep me up to speed on what's happening."

He nodded. "Will do."

Tara had just reached the front door when Agent Hanson opened it.

He glared at her. "You weren't going to call me about this find."

It wasn't a question. It was a flat-out accusation. Snelling had obviously called him.

"I had no reason to believe I should call you, Agent Hanson." This was a lie, but sometimes a little white lie was necessary.

"Sergeant Snelling has found a number of items that connect this scene to the Foster case."

"I also found a connection to the Callaway case."

"I'm not going to war with you over who has jurisdiction. I'm investigating a federal case that involves possibly one or more homicides."

"What you have," Tara argued, "is a thirty-year-old cold case about missing money and remains from a probable death by natural causes. I, on the other hand, have two missing persons right now. I don't think you'll win this war."

"Until I hear otherwise," Hanson warned, "I'm not backing off."

"Suit yourself." Tara turned her back on him and went back to the kitchen. She pulled Collin aside. "The one thing about the Foster case we've learned is that he took money from only three accounts. Do you still have that cousin in the Chattanooga Police Department?"

"Sure do."

"See if she has a contact with the Bureau who can give her the names of those three victims. She may have copies of relevant FBI statements and reports in their case file. Whatever she can find would be immensely useful. If there's a Dread Hollow resident among those three, we need to know."

"On it. I'll go outside and call. She's a night owl like me. She won't mind a call after business hours."

"Thanks, Collin. Let me know what you find out. I'm going to Delilah's house."

Hanson had already disappeared into the bedroom end of the house. Just as well, Tara had nothing else to say to him.

Outside, the breeze had picked up, giving Tara a chill. She settled behind the wheel of her Wagoneer, sent a text to Delilah and headed into town. It was nearly ten and Main Street was rolled up for the night. Delilah lived just a mile down Dread Hollow Road beyond Tara's house. Thankfully, the lights were still on. Tara hadn't received a response to her text and she'd worried her friend had crashed for the night.

Exhaustion had started to claw at Tara by the time she made her way to Delilah's porch. Her cell chirped. Delilah. The message said she should come on in. Tara opened the door and stepped inside the old farmhouse. The house was warm and smelled of something sweet. Delilah's house always smelled like something freshly baked.

"I'm here," Tara called out.

"In my office," Delilah shouted back.

Delilah's house had the same wood floors as hers. Tara was fairly certain her great-great-grandfather and Delilah's grandfather had worked together to build the houses. Neighbors helped each other build back in those days.

The family room was large with the same vaulted ceiling and massive fireplace. Delilah had turned the small downstairs bedroom into an office. Tara was thinking of doing the same; she just hadn't gotten around to it yet.

Delilah was hunched over her desk tallying up the day's receipts. She liked doing things the old-fashioned way. Everything she served in the diner was made from scratch.

"Any news on Krissy and her husband?" Delilah pulled off her glasses and gestured to the chair that sat at one end of her desk.

"We've picked up some additional information here and there, but no hint of who may have taken them." Tara collapsed into the chair, suddenly realizing how very tired she was. "It's the strangest case. We can assume the motive is money, but that doesn't make sense either considering we found a sizeable sum in their home. If the perps were going to take the couple, why not the cash?"

Delilah rubbed the bridge of her nose with her thumb and forefinger. "It just makes no sense. Krissy and her husband would never hurt anyone. They've never been in trouble as far as I know."

Tara shook her head. "I ran checks on both of them. Nothing." She braced her elbow on Delilah's desk and rested her chin in her hand. "We drove Jacob around the Hollow so he could point out places he recalled his father having done odd jobs."

"We? You and Collin?" Her eyes sparkled teasingly. She knew the answer. Word traveled fast around the Hollow.

"Deke and I."

"Are you two talking again?" She held up both hands, fingers crossed.

"Jacob is his student. We're working together for him."

Delilah dropped her hands. "Oh. I see."

Did everyone—including Tara's father—believe she and Deke belonged together?

"It's best if he moves on. I'm not what he needs," Tara reminded her friend.

Delilah's expression turned knowing.

"No," Tara said before she could ask, "I didn't tell him."

Delilah's expression shifted to surprise. "Why?"

"Because he would have said it didn't matter." Was she the only one who recognized what Deke wanted in his future? "He loves kids. Have you not noticed? It would have mattered, but he would have pretended it didn't just to keep me happy. I know him, Dee."

"I feel like I know him fairly well myself and I think you're wrong," her friend argued.

"That's the sort of man he is," Tara maintained. "Honorable. Kind to a fault. He would have insisted it didn't matter and we would have taken that big plunge into wedded bliss that would have lasted a little while. Then he would have grown bitter and started to resent me."

"I think you're underestimating the man."

"Please," Tara countered. "I'm not. I'm simply choosing not to allow him to sacrifice what he wants to fit in with what I can't have."

"People adopt children. Children who need families to love them."

"Moving on," Tara said, unable to talk about it any longer. "There are three houses on Falling Rock Trace, are you familiar with the people who own them?"

Delilah thought about the question for a moment. "Everyone knows Brandon Parton and his wife, Carla. There's Ed Kosh, who died a few months back. His wife died years ago. The other homeowner is barely known at all. Melanie Grant, if I'm recalling correctly. She moved to the Hollow years and years ago. When I was about your age." Delilah laughed. "Mercy, how time flies. Anyway, she kept to herself. Never spoke to anyone on the rare occasions when she ventured into town. She had most things delivered. Pete Bishop, who used to run the market, would make deliveries. He had a reputation as a lady's man, so of course there were rumors. She didn't go to church, which alone, as you well know, made her an outsider. I suppose she eventually moved away. I just remember not seeing her or hearing about her anymore."

A sad story for sure. Deke's words whispered through her again.

"Why do you ask?" Delilah prompted.

"Jeff did some work at the house. Kosh hired him to keep the grass and shrubs trimmed. Jacob seemed to know the place well."

"Ed would do that," Delilah agreed. "I've driven by a couple of times over the years and it always looked deserted to me."

Tara nodded. "We found human remains in one of the bedrooms. I don't know if it's her, but someone died in the home. Nothing is confirmed yet, so what I've just told you is for your ears only."

"Sure. Sure." She frowned. "That's so sad."

"Were there ever any rumors about her and Treat Foster?"

Surprise again flashed across Delilah's face. "Nothing comes immediately to mind, but the time frame of when she was still about works. Do you think there was an affair going on? Maybe that's why he was suspected of coming to the Hollow from time to time."

"I have no idea, but it would be helpful to find out all we can."

"I'll make some quiet inquiries of those old enough to remember the Hollow's recluse. That's what the kinder folks called her. A recluse."

"Any information you can dig up would be helpful."

Delilah studied her face a moment. "I'm going to have

to ply you with coffee or send you home. You look ready to fall out."

Tara pushed to her feet. "I'm off. Thanks for making time for me at this hour."

"You are welcome any time." Delilah showed her to the back door, but hesitated. "Wait, I baked cookies." She walked to the island in the center of the big kitchen and grabbed a tin—the kind Christmas cookies came in. She handed it to Tara. "It's a new recipe. Take it to the office tomorrow and let me know if you like it."

Tara smiled. "Collin will be over the moon."

"I'll call you with anything I learn," Delilah promised.

Tara waved good-night and plodded out to the Wagoneer. The drive home took all of a minute, maybe a minute and a half. The house was dark. Once again, she'd forgotten to leave on a light. But then it wasn't often that she was out this late.

She climbed out of the vehicle and slogged to the side porch. A quick twist of her key and she was in. She debated waiting until morning to shower but felt as if decades of dust and decomposition were layered on her skin.

Rather than pop into the kitchen for a nightcap or food, she left the cookies on the nearest table and went straight upstairs, peeling off her clothes on the way. She'd made it to the bathroom, dropped her uniform on the floor and turned on the shower when her cell rang.

Deke.

"Hey, everything okay?" Her heart instantly beat faster. She told herself it was because he could be calling to report trouble with Jacob, but really it was only because he was calling.

"I hadn't heard from you. You make it home okay?"

"Just now," she said, holding her phone between her cheek and shoulder so she could unfasten her bra. The garment fell away and she sighed with relief.

"You sound tired."

He had no idea. The panties went next. "I was just getting in the shower."

Silence echoed on the other end.

Frowning, she reached for a towel and slung it over the shower curtain rod. "You still there?"

"Sorry the image of you naked and getting in the shower just exploded in my brain."

She wanted to say something emphasizing her shock, but she was too busy navigating the intense heat rushing through her.

"Who said I was naked?"

He laughed, the sound deep and a little rough. "I don't remember you getting in the shower with your clothes on."

She stared at her reflection in the full-length mirror that hung on the wall next to the vintage sink. Her breasts tingled and she suddenly felt damp in places she had no right to as exhausted as she was.

"I remember every inch of your body. Smooth, soft skin. Firm, rounded bottom. And God, your breasts. Sorry. I... I should let you get in the shower."

For a moment, she couldn't speak, her throat had constricted with yearning.

She wanted to tell him she remembered every inch of him as well. Broad shoulders. Narrow waist with those perfect abs. Long, thick legs.

She had to hang up.

"Bye," she muttered and ended the call.

She braced against the sink and wondered how the hell

she could be perched on the brink of an orgasm just hearing his voice.

She ducked into the shower and savored the steaming water while her body betrayed her and her mind refused to exile images of the man she'd loved with all her heart.

Still loved.

She forced the thought away, cried out with anger and physical release at the same time.

Then she slid down the wall of the shower and hugged herself while she cried for everything that would never be.

Chapter Thirteen

A sound woke Jacob.

He listened. It was dark. Not time to get up yet. The house was quiet. Everyone was asleep.

Why'd he wake up?

He reached down to the floor where Jelly Bug lay sleeping. She didn't even lift her head when Jacob rubbed it. She was out too.

Jacob closed his eyes and tried to go back to sleep.

He heard the sound again.

A pecking at the window. He rolled to the other side of the bed and got up. He walked to the window. The sound came again. *Peck. Peck. Peck.*

What if it was his dad? He might have come to get him.

Jacob moved the curtain aside. Someone was outside the window, but it was too dark to see who it was. A hand wearing a glove waved at him.

Jacob pressed his face closer to the window. "Who are you?"

"Your daddy sent me," the voice whispered. "He said to bring you and Jelly Bug to him. Your mom is there too."

"How do I know you're telling the truth?" Jacob was no dummy. He knew all about stranger danger.

One hand used a cell phone to shine light on something dangling from the other hand. A cross necklace.

His dad's necklace. Jacob's heart beat harder. This person really had been sent by his dad. He unlocked the window and pushed it up just a crack.

He felt scared again. What if this was a trick? "You got any other proof?"

The hand showed him a ring. "Your mom sent this."

It was his grandmother's ring. His mom never took it off. But this was an emergency. She knew Jacob would never believe a stranger without proof.

"What do I have to do?" Jacob asked.

"Hand me the dog first."

Jacob hurried around the bed and picked up Jelly Bug. She felt heavy and limp in his arms. What was wrong with this dog? Her head just hung down, but she was still breathing. Jacob moved back to the window, but it wasn't open wide enough. The hand reached in and pushed it upward. Jacob hefted the dog out the window.

"Now you climb out. Your parents are waiting."

Jacob climbed out the window, then closed it.

His mama and dad hadn't left him.

He took the stranger's gloved hand and walked into the night.

Chapter Fourteen

Dread Hollow Road
Saturday, May 6, 7:00 a.m.

Tara placed her weapon into her holster, checked her utility belt. She was set.

She hustled down the stairs, noting that her shoes were in need of a polish. No time now. When this case was wrapped up.

When Jacob's parents were safely back home.

This was day six since the couple went missing. No ransom demand. No nothing. Tara stared at the coffee machine. Six days was too long. They could already be dead. She didn't want to think that way, but her training wouldn't allow her to pretend. As much as she wanted to believe in the power of prayer and hope, she had to be realistic. Jacob was counting on her and she couldn't fail to find the truth. But she also couldn't fail to be straight with him. The truth might not be what he wanted to hear.

If there were no leads or news by the end of the day, she and the kid were going to have to have an unpleasant conversation. She had to prepare him for the reality that this might not end well.

Whatever the reason, his parents had disappeared. If whoever took them didn't want anything in exchange for their safe release, then the abduction was about revenge or punishment for some boundary crossed.

Tara poured coffee into her travel mug and turned off the coffee maker. She grabbed the piece of toast she'd popped in when she started the coffee maker and tucked it between her teeth. She would eat on the way. Almost forgetting, she grabbed the tin of cookies as well. Before going to the office, she intended to check in at the house on Falling Rock Trace. Hanson hadn't given her an update this morning. She had a right to know what was happening in her town.

She opened the door and came face-to-face with Deke. She almost choked on a startled gasp; her teeth pushed through the dry toast and all but the one bite hit the floor.

Deke grimaced. "You call that breakfast?"

She chewed. Swallowed. Downed a swig of too hot coffee. Groaned. "I didn't have anything in the fridge."

Deke held up a bag. "I stopped by the diner. Delilah said you need to eat."

The scent of bacon and eggs on homemade biscuits teased her senses. She grabbed the bag. "Thanks. I really have to go."

"Five minutes," he argued, his hands up like a crossing guard's. "You can sit down and eat. Five minutes."

Big breath. "You're right. Okay." She did an about-face and took a seat at her table. "There's more coffee in the carafe." He knew his way around her kitchen. No need to give him directions.

The way he'd taken her to the edge last night with nothing but that deep voice and sweet words flashed in her mind, heated her cheeks. She tore into the bag. Found two loaded biscuits. She placed one on the other side of the table, at the seat farthest from her. Then she unwrapped her sandwich and took a bite. Her eyes closed and she savored the taste of Delilah's amazing ability to create an explosion in the taste buds. The woman should have her own cooking show.

"I hope you managed some sleep last night."

"Slept like a rock." Which was a miracle considering she'd found human and pet remains. She'd made no major headway on her case. Not to mention this case had caused her to allow Deke way too close.

"I couldn't sleep." He bit into his biscuit.

She felt guilty for not considering how worried he was about Jacob. The boy was his student. He was close to the kid.

"This is hard for you. You've spent a lot of time with Jacob. Your students are like extended family." He'd said as much when they were together.

He reached for his coffee. "I wish I could protect them all. Teachers see lots of good things. The joy of watching the children bloom academically and socially. But we also see the bad. The abuse. The painful medical issues. And times like this when they lose a person or people they love and depend upon."

"It's a tough job," she agreed. "Every bit as tough as being a cop. You protect and serve just as we do." She smiled. "Your weapon is the power of knowledge."

"You know how to make a guy feel special." He finished off his biscuit.

That smile. His eyes. They were too familiar. Too able to slip deep inside her and make her want things she shouldn't want.

"Thanks for the breakfast, but I really have to go."

Their cells sounded off simultaneously. Her call was from Collin.

"Hey," Deke said in greeting to his caller.

Tara moved away from the table. "What's up? I'm heading in now."

"Ms. Wright just called the station," Collin said in a rush.

"When?" Deke said, his voice taut.

Tara tried focusing on her call, but the pallor that had slid over Deke's face had her needing to hear his conversation.

"Jacob is missing," Collin said.

"What?" Tara's attention zeroed in on his voice. "Missing?"

"I'm on my way," Deke said. His call ended.

"When Ms. Wright went to wake him, his bed was empty. She thinks he's been gone for a bit because the sheets were cold."

"Heading there now," Tara said, "meet me." She ended the call and met Deke's gaze. "I'll drive."

They rushed out of the house. Loaded up and roared out of her driveway.

"What did Ms. Wright tell you?" Tara knew without asking that she would have called Deke right after calling the police.

He repeated the same thing Collin had told Tara in his call.

"Why would he run away?" Deke shifted, turning his body toward her. "Would the people who took his parents come back for him after six days?"

"I don't know." Tara wished she could provide a different answer, but she couldn't say what she didn't know. "Going to the cave may have triggered fears we didn't recognize."

"Surely he wouldn't try to get back to the cave." Deke

stared out the window. His face told her he felt sick at the idea of Jacob out there somewhere in trouble.

"For now," Tara said gently, "we'll have a close look at the Wright home to ensure she didn't overlook anything. We'll go from there."

The steps she would need to take whizzed through her head. Amber Alert. Damn.

Jacob, where are you?

Five endless minutes later, they arrived at the Wright residence. Collin was there already. He and Ms. Wright were in the front yard talking.

Tara and Deke exited her vehicle and joined them.

Wright swiped at her eyes. "I can't believe he would run away on his own. He's been so sweet and respectful all week."

"What time did you put him to bed?" Tara asked.

"As soon as Deke brought him back. Since they'd stopped for pizza and ice cream, I ushered him into the bath and then we tucked him into bed. It was maybe ten or ten fifteen. I checked in on him before I went to bed, and he was fast asleep. We all crashed pretty early." She shook her head. "I can't believe Ben and I slept through whatever happened. We're usually hyper aware of every little sound."

Ben Wright was her husband. Whoever had broken in had been particularly quiet not to wake anyone in the household, not even the dogs.

"What about Jelly Bug?" Deke asked.

"The dog is gone too," Wright explained.

Tara turned to Collin. "I'll have a look in the room. Start talking to neighbors. See if anyone saw or heard anything."

"On it."

Collin headed next door and Tara turned back to Wright.

"Can you or your husband help with talking to neighbors until we can assemble a search party?"

"Ben will stay here. I need to be the one helping." Tears welled in her eyes once more. "I feel like this is my fault."

Tara gave her a quick hug. "This is not your fault. Now, let's find him." She shifted to Deke. "Come with me."

They entered the house. The Wright child was on the sofa next to his dad. They both looked worried.

"I need to have a look in the room where Jacob was sleeping."

Mr. Wright nodded. "First door on the left."

Tara followed the hall to the row of bedrooms. Two on the front side of the house. A third on the back side as well as the family bathroom.

The covers were turned down on the bed. Since no pj's lay on the floor or on the bed, Tara assumed he'd left with those on. "We need a description of what he was wearing."

A gentle whisper of air moved the window curtain. Tara looked up to the ceiling, no ceiling fan, and then down to the floor near the window for a central heating and air register. The register was on the floor right under the window. She moved close enough to check for air movement. Nothing. She moved aside the curtain.

The window was open just a crack. The screen had been removed.

"He went out the window."

Deke moved closer to her.

"Don't touch the window." She turned away from the obvious exit point. "I need to secure this room."

The next few minutes were a whir of activity. Collin returned to the house to lift prints from the window and the screen that had been placed on the ground outside the house.

He would seal off the room for now. Tara issued an Amber Alert for Jacob, then said a quick prayer.

Within the hour they had dozens of volunteers gathered for starting a search. Tara left Collin in charge of coordinating the volunteers. She needed to check Jacob's house and the cave on Falling Rock Trace. Granted, she couldn't imagine how he would have gotten there. That said, after his reaction yesterday, it was necessary to rule out the location.

Wright had confirmed that Jacob had been wearing Spider-Man pajamas. Her son's bicycle was still at the house, so if he hadn't left the house with someone, he'd left on foot. If that was the case, Tara hoped he would come to his senses and knock on a door for help.

Tara slid behind the wheel of her Wagoneer, and Deke climbed into the passenger seat. They drove first to Jacob's house. Checked inside. Checked the yard. Nothing. It took only a few minutes more to check with the neighbors. No one had seen Jacob.

From there they headed to Falling Rock Trace.

"Someone took him," Deke said after several minutes of silence. "Jacob is too smart to take off like this."

Since it hadn't rained in days, there were no footprints anywhere in the Wright's backyard. Not that she'd expected to find any in that lush lawn. So far, none of the close neighbors had exterior video cameras of any sort.

"I'm with you on that," Tara said. "It's possible the perps came back for Jacob for leverage if the parents aren't co-operating."

"It took them six days to reach that point?" Deke said, incredulous.

"It doesn't make sense," Tara agreed. "I'm tossing out scenarios. Your job is to find the flaw in the reasoning."

"I can do that."

She glanced at him. Grateful he was calming down a bit. "I'm certain you can."

"What else you got?"

"Is it possible Jacob hasn't told us everything from Sunday night or from before his parents went missing?" The idea had nudged Tara, but the boy seemed sincere. Still, he was a kid. Kids lacked the reasoning skills that maturity would bring. If his father or mother asked him to keep a secret, he likely would. Like the one about the cave.

"My gut says he isn't keeping anything from us," Deke said. "But you're right. He may feel like he's protecting his parents. Although I can't imagine his mother doing such a thing, they could have stolen money from some drug lord and he's afraid to tell you they committed a crime."

"That's what worries me." Tara gripped the steering wheel tighter. "If he ran away this morning or last night, then my guess is he's hiding something."

"If someone took him…" Deke began, his words trailing off.

"Then he's in trouble because there's only one reason for a bad guy to come after a kid when he already has the adults."

"Leverage."

"Yes."

The silence that followed was thick with worry.

Official vehicles sat in the grass and along the road at the bone house. She spotted Hanson's vehicle right away. As they walked toward the house, suited techs came out carrying evidence boxes.

"I guess Hanson hit a gold mine." She hadn't seen anything particularly relevant other than the photo. Then again, she hadn't searched the closets and drawers. Or the attic. For all she knew, there could have been loads of evidence in the crawlspace. None of that mattered to her just now. Finding Jacob was her only priority.

At the door, she selected shoe covers and gloves from the box left on the porch. Deke did the same. They wandered in, found Hanson in the kitchen. He didn't look particularly happy to see them.

Before Hanson could chastise her for entering his crime scene with a civilian, she said, "Jacob Callaway went missing sometime during the night. We need to have a look around outside and in the woods to make sure he didn't come here."

"I'm sorry to hear that. Feel free to search anywhere on the property except in here. The house is off-limits."

"Thanks."

She had nothing else to share with him and he clearly didn't intend to share anything with her. Deke followed her back into the yard.

"I don't like that guy."

"Nobody does."

They headed for the tree line. Thankfully, this time they weren't lunging through the brush and darting around trees.

Tara's cell phone sounded off. She desperately hoped it was Collin with good news. Her father's face flashed on the screen. Disappointment speared her. Guilt followed. She loved her dad. It just wasn't a good time. "Hey, Dad."

She flashed a smile at Deke as her steps slowed.

"I just saw the news about human remains being found. What's going on?"

"I don't know a lot," she said. "The first of those three houses on Falling Rock Trace. Small brick rancher. We were in the area searching for anyone who had hired Jeff Callaway for odd jobs like landscaping."

"I know the area. Let's see…" He hummed a moment while he dredged the memory that failed him all too often. "Kosh—Ed and his wife, and the newer folks, Partons, I think. The other house was a woman. Something…"

Tara didn't give him the answer. Doing so would only frustrate him. Instead, she waited. Kept moving forward, avoiding trees and the thicker areas of brush.

"Grant. You know, like the sunglasses back when I was a younger man."

Tara smiled, thankful he'd managed. "We haven't confirmed, but we believe her name was Melanie Grant. Not my case though. Our friendly FBI agent swooped in and took over the scene. He believes it's connected to the old Treat Foster case."

"I always hated when that happened." He exhaled a big breath. "Tell Deke we're still on for tomorrow's game. You should come. We can all have lunch together."

"I'll tell him." She hesitated. Hated to do what she had to do next. "Look, Dad, I hate to cut the call short, but Jacob Callaway has disappeared on us. He either ran away or someone took him. Deke and I as well as dozens of volunteers are out looking for him now."

"Good Lord. Let me know when you find him. You got this, sweetie. Love you."

"Love you too." Tara put her phone away, wished she could stop the disease stealing her father away.

"He's doing well, considering," Deke said, reading her mind.

She nodded, fought the burn of tears. Damn it.

"I was wondering," he said, when she didn't say more, "you think it's strange Jelly Bug is missing too?"

"Not at all. The dog would likely have barked if Jacob had gone out that window leaving her there. He—meaning the perp—wouldn't have wanted to risk waking the Wrights."

"Could be a woman," Deke offered. "A woman would have an easier time manipulating Jacob."

"Another good point." She shot him a smile. "If you ever decide to give up teaching, you'd make a great cop."

He laughed. "I'll stick with what I love."

She parted a thicket and eased through. "Smart move," she agreed.

They reached the cave opening and Deke insisted on going inside first.

"Keep in mind," she said as she gingerly moved across the rocks, "I'm the one with the gun."

He paused. "Good point." Then he grinned. "Stay behind me."

Always the chivalrous one. In this case, maybe to a fault.

The cave was just as damp and dank as before. No sign of Jacob or Jelly Bug.

To cover all bases, they decided to call his name repeatedly as they made their way back to the house. Even if Jacob wouldn't answer, Jelly Bug would probably bark.

Tara called his name until she felt hoarse. Deke echoed her every call. No response. No barking.

Hanson was waiting outside when they reached the tree line. "No luck?"

Tara shook her head. "It was a longshot that we'd find him here, but we had to be sure. I'd appreciate it if you'd keep an eye out for the boy and let me know if you see or hear anything that might help our search for him and his parents."

"Sure thing."

Somehow his assurance didn't give her much comfort.

When they were back on the road, Deke asked, "Where to now?"

"I'll check in with Collin. We'll fill in wherever we're needed."

"Can we swing by my house?"

"Of course." She divided her attention between him and the road. "You think he'd go looking for you?"

"It's worth a shot. I mean, I didn't check around the yard or garage when I left this morning."

"I keep thinking there was something I should have said to him last night," Tara offered, "to reassure him. Maybe this wouldn't have happened."

"If someone gave him a ride, and we know that's what happened, nothing you failed to say is why he's missing."

Deke was right. She knew this, but she felt sick anyway.

Silence simmered for a minute.

"Is there something I didn't say or do that made you go?"

How could he bring that up now?

"Deke."

"Just tell me so I can stop making a fool out of myself." He stared at her profile, making the moment even more uncomfortable. "What did I do?"

"It wasn't and isn't you," she said, frustrated. "It's me."

"Come on. That's a cop-out. There has to be a reason that involves both of us. It can't be just you."

"I'm sorry to disappoint you, but you're wrong. It's me. Only me. You're an amazing man, Deke. Good looking, great personality. Dedicated to your work. It's not you. You can take your pick of the available women anywhere, and whatever happens, the problem will never be you."

She braked to a stop and shifted into Park.

"You do still have feelings for me."

She closed her eyes and reached for patience. "Deke."

"Tell me I'm wrong." He stared at her, his gaze searing right through her skin. "I need to hear something real… something good right now."

She released her seat belt and turned to him. She understood. The feeling of helplessness was overwhelming. "I have feelings for you. I want to be your friend, but we can't go there because you are stuck in this other place that we can't be anymore."

He tugged his seat belt loose. "Double talk. Just say it. You have feelings for me. The same feelings I have for you. You just refuse to admit it."

Tara got out. She wasn't dealing with that right now.

"I rest my case," he said, following her.

Without saying a word, they checked the garage and the shed. Walked down to the lake and had a look around. Called his name.

No Jacob. No Jelly Bug.

Collin called. He had nothing either.

Tara's gut was in knots. Where the hell were these people? What the hell had they done?

"We should rendezvous with Collin. Figure out the strategy from here."

Deke said nothing. Climbed into the passenger side of her vehicle. She settled behind the wheel and started the engine.

No one vanished into thin air.

She suddenly had this awful feeling that the answer was right in front of her.

The simplest answer was usually the right one.
All she had to do was clear away all the clutter and static.
And find Jacob.

Chapter Fifteen

1:00 p.m.

Deke had started to sweat. Not from the heat, and it was un-seasonally warm for early May, but because they'd found nothing on Jacob.

No reports of anyone having seen him. No breadcrumbs to suggest where he'd gone. Not one damned thing.

He felt sick. How had he spent five days a week this en-tire school term in the classroom with Jacob and not rec-ognized something was going on with his family? Last fall when his mother was so sick, Deke had visited the family. He'd rallied the parents of other students in the class to help the family with meals. More than a few had made signifi-cant donations.

But everything had appeared to turn around by early this year. By February his mom was working again. Jacob was back to wearing his characteristic big smiles. Deke had spent some time last night mulling over what he knew of Jeff and Krissy Callaway. Good people. Earnest people. He couldn't see either one of them getting involved with criminals.

Except desperation and fear changed the best of folks.

"Let's load up and head to the school." Tara's voice dragged him from the gut-wrenching thoughts.

"Is it normal not to get any hits on an alert?" All the television crime shows always showed an abundance of information coming in when the police asked for help from the community. They'd gotten nothing on Jacob this morning. It was past noon, and they'd found the same. Nothing.

"This is a small community. We're not going to get a lot of false leads in an area this small where everyone knows everyone else. Eventually the bizarre ones and even plenty of sincere ones that turn out to be not connected to Jacob will trickle in from the larger communities."

Deke paused at the front end of her Wagoneer. "You think this is going to turn into the latter?"

The uncertainty on her face gave him the answer before she spoke. "I hope not."

They drove to the school without talking. Deke wasn't sure he could open his mouth again without being sick. Not something he cared to do in Tara's presence. She had always seen him as strong and tough. With a kid missing, he wasn't feeling nearly strong or tough enough.

She pulled into the parking lot at the gym. Dozens of other cars were already there. This much support from the community buoyed his hopes. They made their way to the gym and as he'd expected judging by the number of vehicles in the lot, the crowd was pretty big. The smell of hamburgers and French fries had his stomach rumbling.

"Look," Tara said, pointing up ahead, "Delilah's got her crew from the diner serving food."

This was just one of the reasons Deke loved the Hollow. For a place associated with hauntings and eerie goings-on, the people were amazing, good and kind.

He and Tara queued up in the line for food. It was a necessary break. The search could go on the rest of the day... or for the next several days. Staying hydrated and energized for activity was important. Jacob was depending on them to find him and his folks.

Once they were seated on the bleachers, Collin joined them, and he and Tara went over where they were with the search and incoming tips.

"Patricia called me," Collin said before taking a draw from his drink.

Deke had met Collin's wife. Nice lady. A little on the odd side.

Tara said, "The kids okay?"

"They are. She says wherever Jacob and his parents are, it's dark."

Tara frowned. "Like in a cave?"

Deke immediately thought of the cave on Falling Rock Trace.

Collin shrugged. "Dunno. She just said it's dark. They're okay, but it's dark and they're scared."

"Thank her for the info," Tara said. "If you hear anything else from her, let me know. Right now, I'll take any tips I can get."

Collin nodded at Deke. "She's the real thing."

Deke gave a nod. Like Tara, he didn't care where the tips came from, he just wanted them to keep coming.

From the moment Tara issued the alert, the Sheriff's Department quickly sent out the information and readied a staff to take incoming calls and information, all of which would be forwarded to Tara and Collin in the field. More deputies had arrived to help. Hamilton County Sheriff's Department uniforms were sprinkled throughout the crowd in the gym.

Deke forced himself to take a bite of his burger. It tasted good, like everything else Delilah prepared, but it was difficult to enjoy the food. He ate for fuel.

Tara picked at her fries. Nibbled at her burger. Finally, she set her paper plate aside and turned to Deke. "It's time for the briefing. This won't take long and then we're back out there in the search."

He nodded, forced another bite.

Tara and Collin moved to a higher level on the bleachers and called the crowd to attention. Taking turns as if they'd practiced for this moment, they explained the lack of leads, which very well could indicate Jacob was still close, adding another layer of urgency to the local search. If he was close, he might not be for long. Tara encouraged the volunteers to finish up with the break and grab a new assignment at the table by the door. Tom Collier, a retired local deputy and avid researcher of Dread Hollow history, had volunteered to map out grid areas for the searchers. With his wife at his side, they would be handing out assignments to groups of ten.

It still amazed Deke how they'd pulled this together so quickly. He was immensely grateful.

When the briefing was finished, he and Tara followed the crowd to the table at the exit. Collier had laid out the remaining areas of the Hollow into ten manageable sections. He used a larger map to indicate each section. Smaller maps would be given to the groups.

The groups already working together split off, the group leaders coming forward one by one to accept assignments.

The group Deke and Tara joined had Scarlett Peterson from the library as their leader. Tara and Collin might have to break away at any moment, so they didn't take leader roles in any of the groups. Smart move in Deke's opinion.

With surprising speed, the groups filtered out of the gym. Deke walked alongside Tara, still marveling at how quickly all these steps had been set in motion.

Tara paused at the driver's-side door of the Wagoneer and took a call. "Hey, Dad, what's going on?"

Deke waited on the opposite side of the hood before getting in. If her father was calling, he'd either heard something or thought of something helpful.

Deke was game for either.

"We'll be right there," Tara assured. She tucked her phone away. "Dad says he has some information he wants to show us. He believes it's relevant to what's going on with Jacob and his family."

"We heading to Forrest Hills?"

"Yeah. He says he has it all laid out for us."

"Let's go."

Hope pushed into Deke's chest. It was the first he'd experienced all morning.

Tara navigated out of the parking lot and onto Main Street. "Let's be prepared for the possibility this may be a theory the less-reliable part of his brain has created."

Deke understood. Her father was fine—or so it seemed—but sometimes he went off on a tangent that made no sense whatsoever.

"There's a lot of memories about the Hollow stored in that man's head," Deke said. "If we're lucky, he's tapped into something no one else has thought of or has reason to know."

From the stories Tara had told Deke, Tarrence Norwood had handled people and situations a little differently than most sheriffs. He used his own judgement at times rather than following the letter of the law. Deke could see him doing that. He was a good man, a fair man and sometimes the law left no room for mercy.

"He's very fond of you," she said as she made the turn onto Dread Hollow Road that would take them to Forrest Hills.

She didn't look at him when she made the statement.

Was she afraid of what he'd see in her eyes? Though she fought the idea, he was well aware she still wanted him on some level. He intended to fuel that want every chance he got.

"I'm fond of him." Deke grinned to himself. Another first for the day. "I'm fond of you too." He thought of their conversation late last night. "I apologize for going too far with my call. I guess I got a little excited."

A little? Hell, he'd lost all control. He wouldn't tell her what he'd had to do when that call ended. It was either take matters in his own hands or snap.

She cleared her throat. "Apology accepted."

He watched her. Studied the way she moistened her lips and blinked a couple of times as if recalling something she didn't really want to remember.

"You didn't get excited?"

She turned into the parking area of Forrest Hills. "I have no idea what you're talking about."

"You were breathing pretty fast. Getting a little heated maybe."

She shoved into Park and glared at him, her cheeks red with something like indignation. "That was frustration you heard. And the only heat I felt was anger at your inappropriate remarks."

Now she was mad.

"Sorry. I couldn't help myself."

"I'm glad one of us was having fun."

She was out and marching toward the entrance before he could remove his seat belt. There he went again, shoving his whole foot into his mouth. In this case, he was mostly latching onto a distraction to prevent losing his mind.

He hustled to catch up with her. "You're right. I was being a jerk."

"You were. That call was way out of line."

"I meant just now," he said. "I don't regret the call, just the pushing boundaries part."

She paused at the door, stared up at him. "Just remember, payback can be a bitch."

She opened the door and stormed inside.

Stunned, he watched. The door closed in front of him, snapping him out of his trance. He rushed after her.

When they'd signed in at the desk and walked on, he asked, for her ears only, "What does that mean?"

She kept moving, making the turns in the corridor that would lead to her father's apartment. "You'll see."

He wasn't sure whether to be excited or worried.

She knocked on the door and it opened. Her dad waved them inside. "Wait until you see what I've figured out."

He had cleared his model-assembling tools from the table and spread pages on it. His laptop sat in the middle, the screen open to an online article.

"What's all this?" Tara asked.

"You told me on the phone about the house on Falling Rock Trace. The one you think is owned by Melanie Grant. You think the remains you discovered are hers."

Deke surveyed the pages as they spoke. Most were about Treat Foster.

"We haven't confirmed it yet," Tara reminded him, "but yes, that's where I'm leaning."

"You're probably right. Grant would be about eighty by now. Anyway, after you called, I couldn't stop thinking about her and that house."

Tara shared a glance with Deke, then asked her father, "Are you feeling okay, Dad?"

He waved her off. "I'm fine. Fine. Better than fine. Listen to me."

"Okay," Tara agreed.

"Long time ago, when I was just a deputy, I don't recall the exact year, but before I became sheriff…"

Deke watched him closely, noted the struggle with getting his words out that he'd never noticed before. Maybe it was only because the man was agitated, excited, whatever. But the idea of him struggling sent an ache through Deke.

"When I was just a kid," Tara offered.

He nodded. "You'd just had that princess birthday party."

There it was, the year. The princess birthday party had been when Tara was two. Deke smiled. "She was a cute kid."

Her father's face softened. He relaxed. "She was." He blinked. "Anyway, I got a call from dispatch to go out to Falling Rock Trace. The house turned out to be the one where the recluse lived. That's what folks around here called her." He shrugged. "Some were unkind about her. She was a little strange. She rarely came into town, but when she did, she was often dressed in her housecoat and barefoot. Sometimes she'd wear nothing but a slip—the kind your mother wore under her dresses."

"She may have had a mental illness," Tara suggested.

Her father nodded. "She did. At the time, there were rumors she'd been in Moccasin Bend, but she wasn't listed as having been a patient. Maybe she had an alias. I can't say about that."

He reached for the laptop, pointed to the screen. "If you do a search on her name, nothing about her comes up. There are lots of Melanie Grants but not that Melanie Grant. I remember she didn't have a record. No family. It was like she was completely alone in this world."

At every pause, Tara waited patiently. Deke had to hold himself back from saying *and...?*

"So I went to her house that night. She'd called in about an intruder. When I arrived on the scene, there was no one there except her. She was wearing a dirty nightgown and her hair was a mess, like she hadn't combed it in weeks. She was very upset. Crying. I didn't smell any alcohol on her breath. I concluded that she was having an episode. I calmed her down and ushered her back into the house." He shook his head. "It was piled high with stuff. Like one of those people...hoarders. It was truly sad."

"You didn't find any signs of anyone having been there?" Tara asked.

He shook his head. "I checked every window, inside and out. I walked all around the yard, checked the tree line. Couldn't find a thing. Finally, she seemed satisfied that no one was about. She wanted tea." He laughed, a sad sound. "Of all things, the woman wanted me to make her tea. I rummaged through her cabinets and found an old box of the peppermint stuff. Little bags. Finding a clean cup was the hard part. Anyway, I made her tea—without the requested honey because she didn't have any. While she drank it, she told me she hadn't always been like that. I asked what she meant and she gestured to her dirty gown and the mess around her house."

He fell silent again. Deke and Tara shared a glance as they waited.

"She said her father abused her horribly. Her mother died when she was a kid and her father was a demon, for sure. She ran away from home when she was seventeen. Then every man she thought might love her only used her and tossed her away. By the time she was twenty, she found herself pregnant with no place to go. She tried her best to take care of the child, a girl named Gillian, but by the time the little girl was in school, it was no longer possible to hide her lack of ability, financially and otherwise, to care for the child. Social Services took her and she never saw the child again."

Deke knew that kind of story all too well and he hated it. "I'm sure she appreciated you listening to her story."

Mr. Norwood nodded. "She said she'd never told anyone before. From there, her life only got worse. It wasn't until she was forty and nearly starved to death that she found her brother. He'd run away the same time she did."

Beside Deke, Tara's breath caught. "Treat Foster."

Her father nodded. "He bought her that house on Falling Rock Trace. Course, I didn't have a clue who he was. She just called him T, like the letter, anyway. But now I know."

"How'd you figure it out?" Deke asked.

He lifted his hand and tapped a finger next to his eye. "The sunglasses."

Deke had no clue what he meant.

"When her brother ran away, he changed his name. Started a whole new life."

"His last name was originally Grant," Tara said knowingly. "He changed it to Foster. Foster Grant, the sunglasses you said were so popular when you were a kid."

Her father nodded. "The one and only. Anyway, when I asked how to contact him, she closed up like a turtle in its shell. I'm guessing he didn't want his past associated with his present. He was on his way up in the banking world."

"Thank you so much, Dad," Tara offered. "This helps tremendously. Jeff Callaway, Jacob's father, did work at the Grant home. If Treat Foster left some of the money he took with his sister, that would explain how Callaway came to have it."

"That's not the end of the story," her father said, his eyes gleaming.

"There's more?" Tara prompted.

He nodded. "She told me that night all those years ago that her brother helped her to find her daughter. Grant just wanted to make sure she was okay. And she was. The girl was living in Nashville at the time. Gillian Randall, her foster family had adopted her. She had gone to college and become an accountant. Grant's eyes just lit up when she talked about her, even though her daughter had asked her not to come back. Grant didn't hold that against her. She understood. She was just so thankful that her daughter had married a well-to-do young man by the name of James Hanson. He worked for the Tennessee Bureau of Investigations."

"Wait." Tara looked taken aback. "Hanson? James Hanson?"

"You got it. I just looked up James and Gillian Hanson. They have one child, a boy—well, a man now. He's an FBI agent assigned to the Chattanooga office."

Deke rallied from the shock. "The FBI guy! He has to know. He's at her house now." It wasn't likely the man was involved in the abductions. "He has to know the remains in that house probably belong to his biological grandmother."

"And," Tara said, her tone just shy of outrage, "he must be aware that Treat Foster is his biological uncle."

"Why the hell would he keep this from you when the Foster case connects to your missing persons case?" Deke asked.

"I'm sure he doesn't want to reveal his connection to Foster." She hugged her dad. "Thanks, this is incredibly helpful. I gotta go."

Deke gave her dad a nod and followed Tara into the corridor. "Are you planning to confront Hanson?"

"Damn straight, I am. He's guilty of a number of crimes already, obstruction in an ongoing investigation for one." She pushed through the exit doors and into the sun. "We have a nine-year-old boy missing. What the hell is Hanson thinking?"

Deke figured they were about to find out.

Chapter Sixteen

Falling Rock Trace, 3:00 p.m.

Tara felt furious. She took a curve faster than she'd intended. Her grip tightened on the wheel.

"You might want to slow down just a little," Deke pointed out.

She shot him a glare.

A skidding stop in front of the Grant house startled even her. When the rocking stopped, Deke dropped his hands from the dash, where he'd braced himself.

"We made it." He wrenched his door open, muttered under his breath, "Miraculously."

Tara ignored his jab and climbed out. She stalked toward the house, ignoring the new crime-scene tape and the white-clad techs coming in and out.

"May I help you, ma'am?"

She stopped just short of barreling into a well-polished suit—another fed no doubt.

"Deputy Sheriff Tara Norwood. I'm looking for Agent Hanson," she managed to demand. Her throat was tight with fury.

"I'm afraid he's not here, ma'am."

Beyond the agent, she could see just far enough inside to recognize they were taking the house apart, one wall at a time, down to the studs.

"Find anything yet?" she asked. She was aware Deke had joined her. He hovered right behind her, probably glaring at the guy.

"I'm afraid I'm not at liberty to say." The fed glanced at Deke.

"Where is Hanson?" she demanded. That she didn't shout was a sheer miracle.

"He needed some privacy for holding a teleconference. One of the other deputies went with him to let him into the substation."

A new blast of fury roared through her. "Thank you."

Deke had the good sense to step away just in time for her to stamp back to her vehicle. He pulled up the rear, climbing in as she started the engine.

"Maybe I should drive," he offered.

She didn't respond, just cut him a look that dared him to say it again.

When you knew a man the way she knew Deke Shepherd, you had earned the privilege not to mince words.

Drawing in a couple of calming breaths, she drove more judiciously to the substation. When she confronted Hanson, she needed to be calm and rational. It wouldn't be easy considering she had three missing persons, one being a child. She didn't have time for games.

"Thank you," Deke said when they parked.

She pulled in another breath. "Sorry. I was upset."

He bit back a grin. "I noticed."

Tara couldn't get out quickly enough. The door was locked; she unlocked it and stepped inside. Just because

Hanson was a federal agent didn't mean he was allowed to bend the rules in Dread Hollow.

She heard his voice and followed it to the small conference room, which was really just another office. He spotted her and ended his call.

He closed up the notebook he'd been using and stood. "I hope you don't mind me using your conference room."

"Would it matter?"

His hands went into his pockets. "I suppose not." He glanced at Deke, who leaned in the doorway, arms crossed over his chest.

Deke looked angry as well. She was glad. She hoped he made Hanson uncomfortable.

"What's up?" Hanson had the audacity to ask.

Tara laughed, a very unpleasant sound. "You do realize I have two missing adults and as of this morning a missing child." This was not a question. He would have to be hiding in a cave somewhere with no cell service not to know. Bastard.

"Any progress on finding them? The Bureau can help if you're ready to go that route."

Wasn't he just the picture of helpfulness?

"Have you told your superiors about your personal connection to this case?"

He frowned but it didn't go deep. "Which case? Your case? I'm afraid I don't know what you mean."

"Lying never looks good on a lawman, Mr. FBI agent. There's only one case. *The* case that involves my missing persons and the legendary Treat Foster. The remains of the woman in the house was your maternal grandmother. She was the sister of Treat Foster. She is why there were rumors and all sorts of reports of people having seen him in this area before and even a few after his unexpected departure from his life."

Hanson dropped back into the chair he'd vacated upon her arrival. "How'd you figure it out?"

She pulled out a chair at the table and sat. "Are you seriously asking me that? What difference does it make? I know and I need to understand if and how any aspect of your grandmother's case is related to my missing persons."

Hanson glanced at Deke, who remained in the doorway.

"You can say whatever it is you have to say in front of him," Tara said. "He already knows anyway."

"I never met her, obviously," he said. "I didn't know about her until my mother's sixtieth birthday a couple of years ago. I planned to surprise her one afternoon, and I found her crying, staring at a photograph of a woman and a child. My mother explained that the child was her when she was eight. It was the last photo she had of her real mother."

"Did she not know her mother was in Dread Hollow?" Tara hated that she felt sympathy for him. Then again, maybe it was for his mother and grandmother.

"She did. She said her mother came to see her once, when I was just a toddler, thirty-two years ago."

It was difficult to imagine Hanson as a toddler. But everyone was a toddler at one time, even FBI agents.

"Her mother had heard about me and wanted to see her grandchild. She hoped to make amends with my mother, but Mother was having none of that. That day, when I found her crying, she admitted that she wished she had. But at the time all she saw was a haggard old woman who hadn't taken care of her who looked like a prison escapee. So she sent her away. Told her to never come back."

"You weren't curious about her?" Curiosity had often gotten Tara into trouble, but she could never help herself.

"A little at first, but my mother begged me never to contact her. She really didn't want me to know about her childhood. It was really awful. Abuse. Starvation. You name it. I couldn't go against her wishes. I couldn't hurt her that way."

Wow. The guy had a heart after all.

"If it means anything," Tara offered, "I would have done the same."

He gave her a nod. "I had no idea there was any sort of connection to the Treat Foster case. What agent wouldn't want to solve that one? It's a legendary black spot on the local field office's record."

"How did you find out?"

"When you found the money. The name and case popped up. I noted that it was in Dread Hollow, the place where Melanie Grant lived. Knowing how small the town was, I couldn't help wondering if she had known him. She had moved here just before he disappeared, I learned, and there were reports he'd been seen here. I mentioned it to my mother, and she said she couldn't be sure, but she thought he and her mother were somehow related. She'd heard her mother mention someone named Treat, but she never imagined they were siblings."

"But you figured it out after you came down here and took over my case."

He nodded. "I asked for the assignment to check up on where the money came from, and when you discovered her house and the remains, I started digging. My mother never knew exactly where she lived or even if she was still alive. She only knew she lived in this area."

"Did you find anything that relates to the Callaways?" Tara needed a break on this case. Damn it.

"We found prints where Jeff Calloway had been in the house, at least as far as the bedroom door. I think he probably saw the remains and got the hell out. I can't say for sure. If the money was in her house, it's all that was there. We haven't found anything else. I did find a man's shirt that I'm thinking may have been Treat Foster's. There's no way to know for sure. She had files and notes about the purchase of the house and the furnishings. However they reconnected, it was before he took the money and walked away. I'm assuming he used his personal funds to buy the house."

"Based on the prescription bottles I saw, she was ill around the time Foster made his big exit." It was so strange that the dates and drug names were on the bottles but not the physician's or the patient's. Sounded fishy to Tara.

"It appears that way. My medical examiner has given me a preliminary time of death and it works with that timeline. He may have stayed with her while she was dying. Again, I'm speculating. As far as the money he took, it was from only three accounts. I have found letters written to the men who owned those accounts. It seemed each one—at different times in her life—carried on an affair with Grant and left her heartbroken. In her letters, it sounded as if the men were particularly abusive. Based on what she suffered at the hands of her own father, I can see how she would be particularly damaged by what happened."

"You think she told Foster while he was caring for her and he took his revenge on the three?" An interesting way to do so.

"Again, the timing works. He would have learned this information about six months before he took the money.

Just before that, his wife had left him for his best friend. He may have had a crisis of some sort and sought out the only family he had. At least that's what my training as a profiler tells me."

"Bottom line," Tara concluded, "Melanie Grant and Treat Foster couldn't have given the money to Jeff Callaway."

"You're assuming," Hanson suggested, "that Foster is dead. We've found no other remains."

Deke moved into the room and sat down next to Tara as she asked, "Are you saying he could still be alive?"

"It's not impossible," Hanson said. "He would be in his eighties. Then again, he may have taken whatever portion of the money was left after Grant died and moved to the Cayman Islands or some other faraway place where we have no extradition treaty."

"Have you checked the caves?" This from Deke.

"Caves?" Hanson shook his head. "I don't know what you mean?"

"In the woods behind the Grant house," Deke explained, "there are caves. Deep caves with lots of twists and turns."

The idea of just how deep those caves could be struck Tara. "What if…" She turned to Deke, considered a moment before speaking the thought aloud in front of Hanson. What the hell? At this point, they needed to work together. "What if the Callaways are hiding deep in that cave somewhere? Or they were restrained there by the thugs who took them. If Jacob was taken to his parents, he would be there too."

Deke's face lit with the idea. "They may be waiting out the feds to see if they find more of the money." He glanced at Hanson. "No offense."

Hanson held up his hands. "None taken. But about these caves, we need to see them. Can you take me there?"

"We can." Tara stood. "You want to ride with us?"

Hanson grabbed his keys. "I'll follow you to the house."

"Sounds good."

Outside, Tara said, "Heads up." She pitched her keys to Deke. "How about you drive?"

He caught the keys. "I was only kidding before."

"I need to make some calls. You should drive."

They climbed in and headed for Falling Rock Trace.

First, Tara called Collin to brief him and find out if there was any news. There wasn't, of course. He would have called if any of the search teams had found anything. Next, she checked in with the department about the incoming calls she'd noticed. She received text alerts letting her know calls were coming in. Unfortunately, none panned out enough to even be pitched to Tara or Collin.

By the time she put her cell away, they had arrived at the Grant home. They climbed out and met Hanson in the driveway.

"Lead the way," he said.

Tara looked him up and down. "You sure you want to go into the woods in that suit?"

He laughed. "It's my uniform. Why not?"

Tara shrugged. "I can understand that."

Deke led the way. Five minutes of picking through brush and saplings and around trees and they were at the cave.

"This is the one," Tara told Hanson, "Jacob's father showed him when they came here for him to cut the grass."

"One of the neighbors," Hanson said, "a guy named Parton, said the other neighbor had kept the property cleaned up to avoid living on the same road with an eyesore."

"Right." Tara nodded. "I spoke to him as well. Based on

what you've told me, I assume Callaway found the money and used it for his wife's medical expenses."

"Except for the $50K you found under the bed," Hanson pointed out.

Tara shrugged. "Except for that." She wasn't ready to label Callaway a bad guy. One who had made a grave error, she had decided.

"The Callaways are good people," Deke said, a warning in his voice. "If he took the money, it was out of desperation."

Hanson shrugged. "Maybe so, but robbery is robbery."

Deke looked ready to fight the guy, but instead he took Tara's flashlight and entered the cave. Tara stayed close behind him. Hanson brought up the rear.

The cave wasn't very wide at first. But after a few yards, it made a turn that widened to a fairly large size. The journey had been at a downhill trajectory, which made the ceiling higher and higher. The deeper they went, the higher the ceiling.

As they reached the end of the corridor, another rock corridor, this one quite narrow, ventured off to the left.

Since Hanson had brought his own flashlight, they were able to get a better look around the larger area. There were definite signs someone had camped here, though not recently.

"We should check out the other corridor," Tara said.

Again, Deke took the lead. It was necessary to move forward single file. At some points, even slipping through sideways put Tara's nose too close to the rock in front of her. This was why she wasn't a spelunker.

No one talked. There was a feeling that there wasn't enough air. Claustrophobia, Tara suspected.

When they moved into a larger stone room, Tara sagged with relief. This one too was a dead end, it seemed. Not as large as the first one but maybe twelve by twelve. The idea that nature had formed all these spaces was awe-inspiring.

Hanson and Deke slowly roved their lights over the walls. The ceiling was lower here. Just a foot or so above their heads. The air seemed thick and smelled like dirt.

"Here we go," Deke announced. He backed up his light and roamed the beam over what appeared to be clothing.

They all moved closer. There were canned goods. The pop-top kind. Boxes of crackers and cookies. The print on the boxes was barely readable. A few feet away from the food stockpile was evidence of a campfire.

"Have a look at this," Hanson said, his voice oddly dull.

Tara and Deke moved closer to his position.

His light had settled on a decaying quilt and a human skull.

Hanson passed his light to Tara and pulled on a pair of gloves. He drew back the quilt, which basically fell apart as he did, and surveyed the remains. A full skeleton. The clothes were in the same condition as the quilt, falling apart. Around the right wrist bones was a gold watch.

Hanson leaned closer. "Rolex."

"They have serial numbers," Tara pointed out.

"You're right," Hanson said as he pulled the watch free from the bones. He studied the watch before placing it into his jacket pocket. "One of Foster's colleagues at the bank said he bought himself a Rolex after his wife left him. I'd lay odds on this being it."

"I think you'd win that one," Deke said.

They searched the area for a while longer. Discovered more of the long-time missing money in a plastic bag. The money was in a shoebox tucked into the bag. Fifty thousand dollars. On the opposite side of what Tara couldn't help thinking of as a stone crypt, there were two more shoeboxes filled with cash.

"I believe," Tara said, "your case is solved, Agent Hanson."

He nodded. "I think you're right."

But none of this explained where Jacob Callaway and his parents were and what kind of trouble they'd gotten themselves into.

Chapter Seventeen

Dread Hollow Road, 9:00 p.m.

The search had been called off for the day, but Tara wasn't finished yet. She did, however, have to change shoes. She sat on her bedside. She held her breath as she pulled off first one shoe and then the other. She rolled off the sock on her left foot and winced at the blisters there.

She groaned. "You really screwed up today," she grumbled. She should have worn her sneakers for the search. Wearing her uniform hadn't been necessary and yet she had. "Ugh." And she'd thought Hanson was a fool for wearing his suit into the cave.

The other sock came off next. Her right foot had fared slightly better. She stood and hobbled across the hall to the upstairs bathroom.

"You okay up there?"

She closed her eyes and groaned again. "Yes. Go home, Deke. I'm going to take a shower and head back out."

She walked past the claw-foot tub she'd loved swimming in as a little kid. Her mom would laugh and clap her hands as Tara splashed around in the big old tub.

Another memory…one from the day her mother had died

tried to intrude. Tara attempted to push it away, but failed. Her mother had been ill for a very long time and her father had taken care of her as well as any nurse. Nothing, not the call of his career or anything else, could have torn him away from her as long as she was still breathing. Tara had tried time and again to give him breaks but he refused to leave her. That day—the day she died—her mother had somehow emerged from the haze of pain medications long enough to smile and thank him for never allowing her to feel alone. That moment had made her father's sacrifice worth it. Had made Tara understand the meaning of true love.

Grabbing a towel as she passed the tiny closet, she made her way to the corner shower nook that was added when she was a teenager. She turned on the water. It would take a while to heat up, but she wasn't complaining. Other than the half bath downstairs, this was it. Folks hadn't clamored for three or more bathrooms when this house was built. Her father had grown up here as had her grandfather and great-grandfather and so on. Sadly, Tara would likely be the last of the Norwoods to live in this house. She was the last in her family. She closed her eyes and forced away those thoughts.

"Hey."

Her eyes flew open, and Deke stood in the doorway.

"I thought you went home!" she snapped. God, she was tired. Her feet were killing her. She was exhausted and her body complained that she needed to eat. The few bites of burger and fries she'd downed had been hours ago.

She hoped Jacob wasn't out there somewhere hungry. She closed her eyes and leaned against the nearest wall. Day six was ending, and they had nothing, N.O.T.H.I.N.G., on the missing family.

"Take your shower," Deke ordered. "I'll pull together something to eat. Then you're going to bed."

"Seriously?" She shook her head. "I do not intend to go to bed. I have calls to follow up on and I'm taking a drive around town. Past the school. Maybe out to Falling Rock Trace."

"Everyone," Deke said, daring to enter the room, "has gone home. Like you. Like me." He slapped his chest. "They are all exhausted. It's better to get some sleep and start fresh in the morning."

"The volunteers and you," she sent him a pointed look, "are not the deputy sheriff in charge of this community. I don't get to stop yet."

"Tara, I get that." He sank down onto the closed toilet lid. "But you shouldn't go back out tonight. You stay here and take care of the other stuff you have to do, and I'll take a drive around town, past the school and all that."

"Go," she ordered. "I can't do this right now."

She turned her back on him and started unbuttoning her shirt. To her surprise, he left the room, closing the door behind him. She striped off the uniform, slid her panties and bra off and stepped into the shower. The hot water beat against her skin instantly relaxing her muscles. She sagged against the wall.

She and Deke had spent way too much time together the past few days. She needed some time and space away from him before she did something totally reckless. Having sex with Deke would be awesome, no question. She hadn't been with anyone else since they ended their relationship.

Since you ended it.

If last night was any indication, she was badly in need of a round between the sheets. But she couldn't. It would be a mistake. The past six months had been far too difficult to take that kind of huge step backward.

She rubbed the soap over her skin, rinsed and took her time shaving, something she hadn't done in a week or more. Then she washed her hair. She stood beneath the water for a long while, enjoying the heat and steam. She needed it to cleanse her of all the troubling thoughts. She needed to relax.

But the haunting thoughts wouldn't go away.

Was Jacob okay?

What the hell had his parents gotten into? Had someone else learned about the money and wanted Callaway to take him or them to it?

What would she do if Deke came back tonight?

Don't think about it. He was off-limits. He'd promised to go.

Tara took her time, dried her hair and her body. She slathered lotion over her skin and then blew her hair dry. She sat on the toilet lid and attended to her blisters, adding salve to all and bandages to the worst ones. She checked her face in the mirror and decided she needed moisturizer there too.

Washed, dried and lotioned, she went to her room in search of a pair of comfy pj's. She dragged on clean underwear and the pink cotton pajamas she'd worn thin over the years. Next up was a thick pair of socks to pad her sore feet. Now to find her cell and respond to the dozens of text messages and several calls.

As she made her way along the upstairs hall, the smell of something amazing drifted up the stairs. Deke was supposed to leave, wasn't he?

What had he said? He'd drive around town while she took care of the things she needed to do? Right?

Whatever he'd said, someone was down there cooking

and she would bet her beloved vintage Wagoneer that it was him.

Damn it.

She made her way down the stairs. Followed the smell of something delicious into her kitchen.

Deke closed the microwave and turned to place a serving bowl onto the table.

"What're you doing?" Hands on hips, she walked into the room.

"Heating up the food Delilah sent over."

Had Delilah been here? "I thought you were doing that drive around for me."

"I did. I drove down Main Street, past the library and the diner and around the school. I drove out to Jacob's house, got out and looked around. Then I drove out to Falling Rock Trace. I didn't see any sign of Jacob or his folks. When I headed back this way, Delilah called and said she had stew for us and that I should pick it up."

"Stew? For us?" It was a conspiracy. Tara was certain. Between her father and now Delilah, they were determined to throw Tara and Deke back together.

He stared at her patiently. "Sit. Eat. You'll feel better then."

She wanted to tell him that she wasn't going to sit and she wasn't going to eat, but she no longer had the wherewithal to fight that battle.

He ladled up a bowl of beef stew with root vegetables. It looked as good as it smelled. Delilah knew how Tara loved carrots and potatoes and parsnips.

She ate. Delilah would be hurt if she didn't eat. The fuel would help her brain function better. She needed to think clearly. To focus.

Deke filled his own bowl. Before sitting down, he went to the fridge and looked inside. He held up a carton of milk and a can of beer.

She gestured to the beer. He put the milk back and grabbed a second beer. One he settled on the table in front of her, the other in front of his own bowl, then he sat down and started to eat.

Talk wasn't an option. At least not for Tara. She was too exhausted. Too overwhelmed to participate in even the simplest discourse. She wanted to eat and then to collapse into unconsciousness for a few hours. Setting her alarm for five in the morning would ensure she was up and ready to go by daylight.

When Tara could hold no more, she finished off her beer and carried her bowl to the sink. Deke passed his bowl to her and covered the leftover stew before stashing it in the fridge. It was a dance they'd shared many times before. Sometimes in this house. Sometimes in his cottage.

When she'd washed the dishes—this old farmhouse did not have a dishwasher—she turned to the man and tackled what she hoped would be the final hurdle of the evening. It had to be done. She couldn't deal with the tension any longer.

She leaned against the counter. "We can have sex if that's what you want?"

She'd decided to go the direct route.

The startled look on his face said she'd won the first round.

"What? That's not why I'm here."

"You don't want to have sex with me?" she demanded, laying on the pressure.

"Hell yes, I want to have sex with you." The fingers of

one hand plowed through his hair, his gaze searching for some place to light on that didn't include looking at her.

"I've told you over and over that we can't go back to what we had, but we can have this—sex—if that's what you want. Friends with benefits, I guess."

He shook his head. "No. That's not what I want."

Her eyebrows flew upward. "Are you sure?"

"Tara, stop." Hands on hips now, he stared at her, his face a study in concern. "What're you doing?"

"I'm offering options. A long-term relationship is out, but there's always sex."

"You know that's not how I want it to be."

She stepped away from the sink, placed her hands on his chest and pushed them up and around his neck, enjoying the feel of hard muscle beneath his shirt. God, how she'd missed the feel of him.

"Kiss me," she ordered.

He reached for her hands to pull them away. "This is not going to work."

She tiptoed, brushed her lips against his. Felt his sharp intake of breath. "Isn't it?" she whispered.

His hands closed around her forearms. "Tara, I don't—"

She pressed her lips against his, cutting off his words. He held perfectly still for longer than she'd expected, but that didn't stop her. She pressed her body against his. Deepened the kiss. Traced her tongue over his lips.

He lost it then. His arms went around her and pulled her firmly against him. His body was hard and so damned warm. Hers melted into his. She lost herself to the feel of him. The scent of him.

A smart woman would stop this charade.

But she couldn't.

She hoped he would. Needed him to.

He lifted her onto the counter. Her legs spread instinctively, and he leaned into her. The layers of clothing separating them felt too confining. They needed to come off. She tried to pull her mouth from his, but she couldn't bear the loss. His lips slid away from hers, working down her throat. Her nipples peaked in anticipation of his mouth closing over them.

Her hands roved over his back. Against his neck and into his hair.

She warned herself again to stop. To pull away.

No way. No way.

He stilled. His forehead against her breastbone, his arms around her waist.

She did the same, her fingers buried in his hair. Her cheek against his head.

Their frantic breathing was the only sound in the room.

"Tara, I can't do this." He lifted his face to hers. "I want you more than you can know. But not like this. I want *all* of you."

The jolt of his words had her feeling ashamed that she'd started this and allowed it to go so far.

"You should go home. Please."

"I will. You have my word. I just need the truth. I need to know why. What did I do wrong?"

Delilah's voice…her father's voice echoed inside her.

"I allowed you too close," she confessed. "I made a mistake."

The haze of need still in his eyes and clouding his face, he said, "What does that mean?"

She leaned against the cabinets behind her and surrendered to the inevitable. "I told you my ex and I divorced over irreconcilable differences."

He moistened his lips. Nodded.

"The irreconcilable part was my round with cancer."

"What?"

"It was only a year after I moved back here to accept the position at the Sheriff's Department substation. I wanted the position to take advantage of the slower lifestyle and—at least until now—the lack of crime. We'd been married for a year, and I couldn't wait to start a family. But the cancer came first."

The pain in his eyes was like looking into a mirror and seeing what she felt. But he couldn't possibly feel this… emptiness.

"Tell me about the cancer," he said softly.

"I'd rather not go into the dirty details, but the bottom line is they had to take everything out. Uterus. Ovaries. There's nothing left." Her eyes burned with the emotion threatening. She forced it back. Would not cry. She'd had three years to get used to the idea of being barren. There was no excuse for tears at this point.

"You can't have a child." He stared directly into her eyes. "That's your issue?"

The urge to punch him was palpable. "Yeah. That's my issue. My ex wasn't interested in the new damaged me. So if you want all of me, that's what you get: No children."

She'd heard all the suggestions about surrogates and adoption and that just wasn't how she'd seen building her home. Besides it wasn't only her decision. The person with whom she'd spend the rest of her life would need to be in on the decision. So she'd bowed out. Opted not to bother.

Until this man crashed into her life. She'd been so alone.

He'd been so sweet, so handsome, so damned perfect. She had foolishly fallen in love with him. Then reality had kicked her in the face and she'd had to pull out.

"There are other options."

She laughed. Couldn't help herself. "That's what people say when they're not in this position." She looked him square in the eyes now. "It sounds so easy right now, but what if those other options don't work out? Create other problems? You see, if we dive into this, you're not the one who doesn't have any other choices."

Some realization she couldn't fathom appeared to dawn on him.

"I get it. You're afraid in time I'll change my mind and leave you the way the other fool did."

Her heart thumped then sank. He'd hit the nail directly on the head. "He did and so will you. So would anyone who loves children as much as you do. This feeling of 'my barrenness doesn't matter' you're experiencing right now might not last. You can't be certain that you'll be satisfied with the other option. I don't want you to wish you'd made a different choice."

He nodded. "For the record, I'm no fool. But you're right." His hands dropped to the counter on either side of her thighs. "I do love children, but the fact is none of them are mine legally or biologically. More important, I love you. I'd love nothing more than to make babies with you. But if I have to choose between having babies and you, I choose *you*."

Her heart stumbled and she had to struggle to get a breath.

"You say that now," she argued, those damned tears charging onto her lashes, "but I'm left with the fallout when down the road you change your mind."

"I won't change my mind, Tara. If we decide we want the

pitter-patter of little feet in our house, we'll adopt. There are lots of babies and kids out there who need a family to love them."

If only he'd stop saying all the right things.

Somewhere in the house, her cell sounded off. They both looked in the direction of the chime.

"I have to get that." She was already scooting from the counter.

Deke picked her up by the waist and stood her on the floor. She took off. She'd left the damned thing in the bathroom. She rushed up the stairs, her legs rubbery after making out with Deke, her heart torn after their talk.

She snatched up the phone just as it rang a final time before going to voice mail. "Deputy Norwood."

"Tara, it's me."

Brenda Wright.

"Is everything okay? Have you heard from Jacob?"

"No. No. But something has been bothering me all afternoon."

Tara sat down on the rolled top edge of the claw-foot tub. "Tell me what's going on."

"Last evening before Deke brought Jacob back, I had a visitor."

"Who?"

Deke was at the door now and Tara put the phone on speaker.

"Wilma Hambrick came by and raved on and on about how sad she was for poor Jacob. She'd been thinking about him all week. She brought over this lovely canister full of cookies for him. Peanut butter cookies. She said they were his favorite. I have no idea why she thought this. Jacob said he doesn't like peanut butter cookies, but we all love them. It was just odd. When Jacob came home that night, he passed on the cookies. Told me they were his least favorite. But we all ate at least one. I ate two. Even Jelly Bug had a cookie."

Tara wanted to say the effort was very nice of Wilma, but she suspected the other shoe was about to drop. "Go on," she urged.

"Today, after the lunch break, I was assigned to the search area that included her house. When I knocked on her door, she acted funny. She didn't even ask about Jacob, she just rushed me away with some excuse about her not feeling well. It was, I don't know, very strange. I told myself that maybe my appearance at her door was bad timing. Maybe she had a migraine. When I have one, I can't bear the light or to talk. But it has nagged at me since, and I just couldn't go to sleep without telling you."

All the times Hambrick had visited Tara and waxed on about how badly they needed a "real" police department fired in her brain like bullets. At this point, a lot of other folks were saying the same thing…but for different reasons. Three people were missing. Half a dozen or so burglaries had occurred in the past two weeks.

All of it adding to Hambrick's narrative.

How badly did the woman want to make this happen?

"Do you have any of those cookies left over?" Tara was up and moving past Deke and toward her bedroom, gesturing for him to follow. She handed the phone to him, and while Wright talked, Tara grabbed a sweatshirt from her closet, a pair of jeans and her sneakers.

"I think there's a few left over. The canister is still on the counter in the kitchen. When I told Ben how this had been bothering me, he even suggested that maybe she put something in the cookies. We all slept through whatever happened with Jacob. I don't know. It was just wrong some-how." She sounded flustered. "Am I being too much? I feel like it's my fault he's missing. Maybe I'm reaching. Look-ing for someone else to take the blame."

"I'll look into it. Just put that canister up where no one can touch it. I'll need to pick it up."

"Oh, Lord, what're you going to do? If you go to Wilma, she'll think I'm a nutcase."

"Don't worry about it. She'll never know you called. Now, put the canister up and stay calm. I'll get back to you."

Deke ended the call while Tara ripped off her pajama top and dragged on the sweatshirt. "We're going to pay Wilma Hambrick a visit." She shimmied out of the pajama bottom and into her jeans.

"Why would she do something like this?" He handed Tara her phone.

She led the way out of the room and down the stairs. "Maybe she didn't, but we're going to find out. The thing that gives me pause is that the woman is obsessed with get-ting a full-fledged police department for the Hollow. She wants desperately to be mayor. Who knows how far she'd go?"

Her cell sounded off again. *Collin*. "Hey," she said, on her way to the backdoor. "I was just about to call you."

"Well, we had another burglary," he said. "Deputy Wil-helm spotted the perpetrators fleeing the scene on his way back home."

Wilhelm was one of the deputies who had been sent to the Hollow to help. "Did they get away?" She walked out, waited for Deke to follow and locked the door.

"They did not. He got them and guess what? It is the Hand boys. Wilhelm is holding them at the office right now.

They're handcuffed and stowed in the conference room. He said he'd hang around until one of us could get there."

"Tell Wilhelm to stay. We're going to need him," she warned Collin. "Meet me at the station."

"Already headed that way."

"Thanks. See you in three." She ended the call and passed along the news to Deke.

"Louise Hand is going to be pissed," he said, climbing into the passenger side of the Wagoneer.

"Louise will have to wait," Tara warned as she slid behind the wheel. "Hambrick comes first. At this point, we can't be sure just how far she intends to go." There was an off chance this theory was just that, a theory. But Tara didn't think so. The woman's pushiness and insistence had all come crashing in on Tara with Wright's call.

"She is one to obsess." Deke fastened his seat belt. "I remember that Christmas parade year before last. She was in charge and wanted the elementary kids to have a big part. She drove me up the wall."

Tara started the engine. "Whatever she's done, I just hope everyone is okay."

"Wasn't there some rumor about how her husband died?"

"Yeah." Tara backed from the carport. "That's what scares the hell out of me."

Chapter Eighteen

Dread Hollow Sheriff's Substation, 10:30 p.m.

By the time Tara and Deke arrived at the station, the twins were ready to spill their guts.

Tara and Collin sat in the conference room with the two black-haired, brown-eyed eighteen-year-olds who had been caught red-handed with a stolen laptop and cell phone from yet another Hollow residence. Their mother, Louise, sat next to her boys, quietly fuming.

"She hired us to shake things up," Edgar said. He glanced at his brother. "Wouldn't you say that's what she wanted?"

Elton nodded. "She said petty crimes. Just enough small-time trouble to make people start complaining about the lack of police support in the Hollow."

The longer Tara listened the angrier she grew. "You're stating," Tara reiterated, "that Wilma Hambrick hired you to cause trouble. To steal from people's homes."

"First," Louise spoke up sharply, "before my boys say another word, you said their cooperation would make this go a lot easier for them. Let's not forget that."

Tara nodded. "You have my word." She looked to the boys then and motioned for them to go on.

Edgar nodded. "She said we'd end up in juvie since we just turned eighteen and had no criminal record. No big deal. She paid us five hundred bucks each for every hit."

Tara almost laughed. "What else did you do for her—besides the break-ins?"

The two stared at each other before Edgar said, "We'd like a lawyer now."

"Mom," Elton whined.

Louise's eyes rounded. "Oh God, what have you not told me?"

Tara held up her hands. "Call your lawyer. We can continue this later."

Tara walked out. Collin did the same.

"What now?" he asked once they were clear of the conference room door.

"Let them sweat," she said. The two would get no sympathy from her. "We have three missing people to find and I think it's safe to say we know where to start looking."

Hydrangea Place, 11:30 p.m.

WILMA HAMBRICK LIVED in a perfect little cottage on a tiny cul-de-sac with only one other house just off Main Street. Previously, she and her deceased husband, Gordon, had lived on a small farm just outside the Hollow. Wilma made no secret that she loved the little cottage on Hydrangea Place. When her husband had his stroke and became disabled, she begged him to allow her to sell the farm and move to the little cottage that had come up for sale. Gordon had refused. Although his body no longer served him as it once had, his mind remained unexpectedly sharp.

Not long after the cottage went up for sale, Gordon died of a heart attack. No one was surprised. In time, there had been rumors that Wilma stopped giving him his heart medication. Since the man was dead and buried, no one ever pursued the idea. Some even suggested they didn't blame poor Wilma. Gordon had been as mean as hell. Even his grown children had stayed away for the most part.

"You think she really killed her husband?" Deke asked.

Sitting in the dark with Deke was making Tara antsy after what went down in her kitchen. With the call from Wright and the news about the twins, everything else had gone on the back burner—until now, alone in the dark.

Focus. This was the first solid lead they'd gotten and Tara was praying it would pay off. Before she and Collin had gotten out of the substation, Louise Hand had called them back. The three had decided not to wait for the lawyer after all. Based on the statements made by the twins, Hambrick was guilty, for sure. She had ordered the boys to nab the Callaways, but they had refused. Considering her offer to pay them a lot more money, they figured she had found someone else for the job.

There was always the chance she had decided against the plot and had nothing to do with their disappearances. In the end, the break-ins and the missing Callaways might not be connected.

Tara hoped like hell they were and that Hambrick had the three stashed safely somewhere.

Tara and Deke had come in his truck. She had been concerned that Wilma would look out the window and spot her trademark Wagoneer. Collin was parked at the corner of Main and Hydrangea. He would head this way on Tara's signal.

"Maybe," Tara said in answer to Deke's question about

Hambrick's husband. "Dad said if she did, he got what he deserved."

"If your dad said that," Deke noted, "her husband must have been a really bad man."

"I don't remember him, but I'm with you. If my dad said it, it's probably so."

Tara considered something else her dad had told her. "Dad said she sold the farm and bought this cottage. Then she took his insurance money and turned it into the showplace she wanted. She bought herself an expensive car and a whole new wardrobe. She travels all the time. Evidently there's plenty more since she paid the twins to promote her desire to be mayor."

"The longer I think about this," Deke said, "the more convinced I am that she might not be playing with a full deck. If that's the case and Jacob and his parents are in there being held hostage, I just hope they're okay."

"Maybe she only kills bad husbands." Tara wasn't sure she believed the woman had deprived her husband of his medicine, but if the Callaways were actually being held somewhere and she was the reason, she would feel differently.

The bedroom light—the last one on in the house—went out. Time to move. Tara wanted to catch the woman off guard.

"I'm going to the back door," she said. She turned to face him, though seeing his eyes in the dark was not happening. "Do not get out of this vehicle unless I say so. Having a civilian in an op could create serious consequences for me. Got it?"

He exhaled a big breath. "Got it."

"I mean it, Deke, do not get out of this truck."

"Okay, okay. I won't get out until you say so." He hesitated. "Unless I hear gunfire or see flames. Something extreme like that."

That was likely as good as his answer was going to get. Tara got out and moved quickly through the darkness. She'd dressed in her black sweats and pulled on a black beanie and tucked her blond hair into it. Her sneakers were black, so she was mostly concealed. They had parked a good distance from her house. The other house was dark too. Collin said the Bedwells were on a fourteen-day cruise and had asked him to drive by now and then. With them gone, Tara didn't have to worry about their big dog. He would likely be with a friend or at a kennel.

Tara made it to the yard. Wilma's gardens, as she called them, front and back, were like botanical parks. Massive blooming shrubs. All manner of blooming vines. The numerous layers of plants and shrubs created a perfect shield. Tara slipped around back and had a look around as best she could with only the moonlight for guidance. Based on the inactive real estate listing still online, the house had two bedrooms and a basement. Like a lot of older homes, the basement had an exterior entrance. Tara hoped Wilma hadn't closed it off.

If she'd added something in the cookies to put the Wrights to sleep, she could be drugging the Callaways to keep them pliable.

Tara couldn't help feeling as if she were on a movie set. The very idea of what the woman may have done…of what was happening at this very moment…was surreal. Tara had almost called her dad on the drive over. How could Wilma Hambrick have done this right under Tara's nose? While the whole community went on with life?

Things like this didn't happen in Dread Hollow.

Even the Treat Foster story wasn't as bizarre as this one.

In light of the possible alternatives, Tara really hoped the Callaways were safely tucked in this basement. That scenario was far better than the others.

At the bottom of the steps that led down to the basement entrance, Tara surveyed the door. She tested the knob. It was locked of course. There was no window in the door, so seeing inside was a no go.

She tried the knob again.

Damn it.

When she would have turned around, she felt the subtle change in the air around her.

Someone was behind her. Up one or two steps.

When she would have whipped around ready to fight, the creeper whispered, "Tara, it's me."

Deke.

She turned around, resisted the urge to punch him. "What the hell?" she whispered back.

He moved closer. Her body reacted. She wanted to punch herself for her inability to control the reaction.

"I can open it."

She grabbed him by the ears and pulled his head down to hers and muttered, "Why did you get out of the truck?"

"I thought about what you said about the basement entrance. I figured if it was locked, you'd be in a pickle."

A pickle? Really.

She wanted to stay mad but couldn't. "Well, you were right. I'm in a pickle."

"Lucky for you, I know how to get out of pickles when locked doors are involved."

She frowned. He grinned. She felt the movement against

her hands. She dropped her hands and stepped aside. "Have at it."

She had no idea how meek and mild Deke Shepherd would know one single thing about picking locks, but she was more than happy for the assist.

He reached into his pocket and removed something, then both hands hovered around the doorknob. Ten seconds later, he opened the door a crack.

She put a hand up when he would have gone in. He leaned closer to her face and she whispered. "Stay behind me."

Usually a warrant would be necessary to enter someone's property, but there was a little exception called exigent circumstances whenever there was imminent danger to life or property. Like now. Hopefully.

Tara slipped into the basement. Deke stayed so close she could feel his breath on her neck. The inky darkness seemed to close in around them. The partially open door allowed a sliver of moonlight to slice across the floor. Concrete.

She stood still and listened for a full minute. No sounds upstairs. She slipped her cell from the pocket of her sweatpants. Holding her breath, she switched on the flashlight app.

The room was small. The steps going up were only a few feet to the right. Shelves covered the available walls. All were lined with boxes and other stuff. She moved left along the opposite wall until she found another door. She gestured for Deke to do his magic with the lock.

Deke considered the lock. He shrugged, then whispered, "It's a deadbolt. A new one added to allow the door to be locked from this side. I can try, but…" He shrugged again.

Damn you, Wilma Hambrick.

Deke went to work on the lock. Tara kept an eye on the

door at the top of the steps on the other side of the room. The more she thought about Wilma pulling this off, the angrier she grew.

The seconds ticked off like hours. She glanced at Deke again and he finally shook his head.

Damn. The key had to be upstairs.

At this point, a good lawyer might say she had exceeded the limitations of exigent circumstances and maybe she had. For all they knew, Hambrick could be keeping her best recipes locked away in this room. It couldn't be very large.

What Tara needed was proof.

She got down on her hands and knees, put her face close to the concrete. There was a space beneath the door of about an inch. She edged close to that space and shined her light inside. She couldn't see a thing.

Taking a breath, she whispered, "Jacob! You in there?"

Deke didn't say anything or move. He probably thought she'd lost her mind.

"Jacob!" she whispered a little louder.

Time to try something else. She propped her phone up against the door so that the camera was aimed into the space below the door and toward whatever was beyond it. She tapped the screen, and the flash flickered and held in the darkness. When the flash died, she pulled up the newly captured image.

Her breath caught in her throat.

Inside the room, seated on the floor and leaning against one another were Jacob and his parents. Tape secured their mouths and they were bound together. The dog, Jelly Bug, was curled up next to Jacob. All eyes were closed. No movement.

Heart racing, Tara scrambled to her feet and showed the image to Deke.

"Are they alive?" he whispered.

"They must be, or there wouldn't be a reason to secure their mouths."

"Son of a bitch!"

Tara put her hand over his mouth and called Collin. Whispering, she ordered him to come to the front door and go with the plan they'd come up with as a backup. He would warn Wilma of a fire at the neighbor's house. There was no fire obviously, but Wilma, startled in the middle of the night like this, would be out of sorts long enough for Collin to get her out of the house.

"Are you saying they're in her basement?" Collin echoed.

"I just said that." Tara gave herself a mental shake. What was up with the guy?

"Ha! Patricia was right. She said they were being held in a dark place."

Tara wanted to say something snarky, but damn, he was right. "Get ready to move," she murmured, keeping her voice as quiet as possible.

Tara shoved the phone into her pocket and retrieved her backup piece, a thirty-eight, from her ankle holster. She pulled Deke's face down to hers. "Stay right here at this door. Do you hear me? Do not move under any circumstances."

He nodded.

Tara started to pull away, but he stopped her, kissed her hard on the lips. "Tell me you love me," he murmured.

"I love you." Tears welled in her eyes. Why had she pretended not to all this time?

She pulled away from his touch and moved quickly and

quietly up the stairs, praying none of the wooden steps would squeak. She made it to the top without a sound. At the door, she carefully tested the knob.

Unlocked.

She left the door cracked and waited.

The pounding came a minute later.

"Ms. Hambrick! It's Deputy Porch. There's a fire next door." He pounded again. Long and hard. "Ms. Hambrick, wake up! There's a fire next door!"

Tara heard the woman stumbling about. Lights came on. Tara eased back into the darkness.

"What?" Hambrick called out.

"It's Deputy Porch. There's a fire next door. You need to get out of the house. The fire department is en route."

Muttering under her breath, Hambrick flipped the locks on her door. She opened it. "What's on fire?"

"Wilma Hambrick," he said, "you are under arrest for the abduction of the Callaway family."

Tara moved then. Slipping silently through the kitchen and into the dining room that adjoined the living room. Hambrick's back was to her.

"Collin Porch, are you inebriated?" Hambrick demanded. "How dare you come to my house in the middle of the night making such accusations!"

"Put your hands up, Ms. Hambrick." Tara was behind her before she could turn around. Unlike Collin, she had her weapon in hand.

Hambrick turned around, stumbled back, bumping into Collin.

"Where's the key to the room in the basement?"

Her hands in the air, Hambrick said, "Under my pillow."

"Cuff her and call for an ambulance," Tara told Collin.

She rushed to the bedroom and found the key under the pillow. Running now, Tara hurried down the steps and to the door where Deke waited.

She passed the key to him and he opened the door.

Tara went to the Callaways and checked the carotid pulse for each member of the family. "They're alive."

Thank God. Thank God.

By the time Deke and Tara had the three freed, they were trying to rouse, but whatever drug Hambrick had given them kept them groggy. Tara was grateful when the ambulance arrived and took them to the hospital in East Ridge. Thankfully, they took the dog too.

Hambrick had provided the drug she used to sedate them at night.

Tara and Deke followed the ambulance. Collin would transport Hambrick to holding at County. Deputy Wilhelm was already en route with the twins.

East Ridge Hospital
Sunday, May 7, 2:30 a.m.

THE CALLAWAY FAMILY had been thoroughly examined and were deemed to be unharmed beyond the ligature marks from their bindings. Because of the drug, the doctor felt it best to keep the family the rest of the night for observation. He'd also given the go-ahead for the father to be interviewed. Deke was spending time with Jacob and his mom. Another deputy had taken Jelly Bug to a local vet clinic.

Tara had called Agent Hanson so he could be involved in the interview. She had decided he wasn't such a bad guy after all. Everyone had a history and everyone had a motive for their actions. Herself included.

Tara pulled a chair up next to Callaway's bedside. She

was too tired at this point to continue standing. Her blisters were stinging. Hanson stood at the foot of the bed.

Callaway's rights had been explained to him and he had waived his right to an attorney.

"Mr. Callaway," Tara began, "you'll need to write up an official statement once you're out of the hospital, but for now, we'd like to ask a few questions to clarify certain aspects of the case."

"Whatever you need." The man stared at his hands. "I'm embarrassed at what I've allowed my family to be a part of."

"We understand how you came to be at the property on Falling Rock Trace. Witnesses have stated that you were hired to do lawn service."

He nodded. "That's right. I cut the grass and any overgrown shrubs once a month from May until October last year."

"How did you find the cave?" Tara asked next.

"My wife was very sick last summer and fall. She had breast cancer. This one day, I was supposed to go to the house to work, and I took the dog with me. Jelly Bug was just a pup then and I hated to leave her. You know how puppies are. My wife was far too ill to deal with that. I thought it was a big yard, no problem, right? I figured it would be fine. And all went well until I was finished and loading up the mower. I think the dog maybe saw a rabbit or something and took off into the woods."

"You went after the dog," Tara suggested.

He nodded. "When I found her, she was barking into the cave. She was afraid to go inside, but I guess the rabbit or whatever didn't mind."

"What made you go into the cave?"

He shrugged. "Plain old curiosity. I used to love caving

with my father when I was a kid. I went back to my truck, put Jelly Bug in the cab and got my flashlight. Once I went into the cave, the farther I dared go, the more interesting the place was. I'd never found a cave like that one."

"Did you find anything in the cave?" This from Hanson.

Callaway nodded. "Yes, sir. I came upon what looked like a campsite. Someone had lived there a long time ago, but he was long dead." He made a face. "I didn't touch him. But I did look through his stuff. That's when I found the money."

"How much of the money did you take?" Tara asked.

"The first time, I took forty thousand. Exactly the amount we needed to pay my wife's medical bills. It was wrong, I know, but it felt like a godsend."

"But then you went back recently," Hanson pointed out.

Callaway nodded. "The cancer is back. We haven't told Jacob yet, but she starts treatments again next week. The doctor warned us the treatment would be more this time, so I took fifty. I'm not sorry I did," he admitted. "I'm just sorry I couldn't take care of my family on my own."

"How did you end up in Wilma Hambrick's basement?" Hambrick was refusing to talk. She'd lawyered up. The twins stood by their assertion they'd turned down the job.

"She knew about our medical bills and came to see me after I got off work at the hatchery one day a couple weeks ago. She asked me if I would like to earn ten thousand dollars. I said yeah, sure. She said she needed my family to pretend to be abducted. She wants a real police department and she thought if she showed you how difficult it was to take care of a real crime, you'd help her make that happen."

"What did you say to her proposition?"

"At first I said yes." He shrugged. "I thought the extra money would be a good cushion if the fifty wasn't enough."

"Why didn't you just go back to the cave for more money?" Tara asked.

"Because she said if I didn't do what she asked, she would start rumors about me and my wife. We'd lose our jobs and maybe our son. I know how much influence she has around here. I was afraid to say no."

Tara thought about that for a moment. "Jacob said you and your wife were surprised when those men showed up to take you. Why is that?"

"Krissy didn't want to do it. She didn't care what Wilma threatened to do. She said Delilah would never believe anything Wilma said. So I called Ms. Hambrick up and told her we weren't doing it. She said it was too late. The men she'd hired to play the kidnappers were coming. I tried to get home in time to take Krissy and Jacob and run, but I was too late."

Damn. Obviously Wilma Hambrick had gone over the edge.

"Why did she take Jacob from the Wright home?"

"She said she heard how upset he was and she couldn't bear the idea of him being without us any longer. She made us tell her the kinds of cookies Jacob wouldn't eat. It was surreal. She's lost it. She drugged the Wrights and told Jacob she could bring him to us."

"I'm sorry this happened to you and your family," Tara said. "And I'm even more sorry your wife's cancer is back."

He nodded, his face telling the story of the sadness he felt.

"I just have one more question, Mr. Callaway," Hanson said.

Callaway met the other man's gaze. "Yes?"

"Why didn't you take it all? The money in the cave, I mean."

Callaway looked away. "I'm just a regular guy. I work hard. I love my family. But I'm no thief. And I'm damned sure not greedy."

Tara stood. "Thank you, Mr. Callaway. We'll need your help as well as your family's to ensure Ms. Hambrick doesn't get away with what she's done."

"We'll cooperate fully." He glanced at the agent then back to Tara. "What about the money? I can pay it back. It'll take me the rest of my life, but I'm willing to do it. And just so you know, my family had nothing to do with what I did. I acted alone."

The fact that the man wanted to protect his family was further proof of how much he loved them.

"Considering the money is tied to a robbery more than thirty years old," Hanson said, "the statute of limitations has expired on the federal level as well as the state level. Found money has its own rules. You turn it over to the police and wait. If no one claims it, it's returned to you."

Tara smiled, her respect for the agent growing.

"What're you saying?" Callaway asked, his expression hopeful.

"I'm saying you didn't break any laws. The fifty thousand has been placed in police custody. If no one claims it, it will be returned to you."

"Won't the bank claim it?"

Hanson shook his head. "That bank closed years ago. The account holders were covered by the bank's insurance."

"But I didn't turn over the other money. The first time."

Hanson glanced at Tara and shrugged. "Do you know anything about other money? Besides what we found in the cave? We have no idea how much Foster spent of the money he stole."

Tara shrugged as well. "You're right. There's no way to know." She turned to Callaway. "What money?"

Callaway's mouth trembled and his voice broke as he managed a thank-you.

Hanson gave him a nod and left the room.

"Take care of yourself and your family, Mr. Callaway. Jacob is a great kid."

Tara left the room. Hanson waited in the corridor for her.

He thrust out his hand. "It was a pleasure working with you, Deputy Norwood."

Tara shook his hand. "I like you better than I wanted to," she admitted.

He laughed. "I get that a lot."

"You did a good thing in there."

"The guy did me a favor. I just solved a thirty-year-old cold case. I may get a promotion." He gave Tara a salute and walked away.

Tara found Deke stepping out of Jacob and his mom's room. He turned and smiled at her. "Hey. Everything go okay?"

"Callaway won't face any charges," she told him, knowing he needed to hear that news.

"That's great."

"Hambrick won't get off so easy." Tara intended to see to that.

"She shouldn't," Deke agreed.

They walked quietly through the hospital and on to the parking area where she'd left her Wagoneer.

"What now?" he asked.

"Now," Tara said, "I'm taking you home and then I'm going home. We both have a lot to think about."

"True. Don't forget lunch with your dad tomorrow."

"Today, technically."

"Today," Deke agreed.

Tara climbed behind the wheel; Deke slid into the passenger seat. She pointed her Wagoneer in the direction of home.

The past six days had clarified a lot of things.

Tomorrow she intended to see if those changes were going to be part of their futures. But first, they both needed sleep and time apart to think.

Except it was already tomorrow and her mind was made up.

"I changed my mind," she announced.

Deke turned to her. "About what?"

"I'm taking you home with me, Deke Shepherd, and this time I'm never letting you go."

He smiled. Reached for her hand. "Good, because I'm planning on marrying you, Tara Norwood. The sooner, the better."

At the next light, they kissed. "Good," she said, repeating his word, "because I want my dad to walk me down the aisle."

* * * * *

COMING SOON!

We really hope you enjoyed reading this book. If you're looking for more romance be sure to head to the shops when new books are available on

Thursday 6th July

MILLS & BOON

LET'S TALK
Romance

For exclusive extracts, competitions and special offers, find us online:

f MillsandBoon

🐦 @MillsandBoon

📷 @MillsandBoonUK

♪ @MillsandBoonUK

Get in touch on 01413 063 232

MILLS & BOON

THE HEART OF ROMANCE

A ROMANCE FOR EVERY READER

MODERN
Prepare to be swept off your feet by sophisticated, sexy and seductive heroes, in some of the world's most glamourous and romantic locations, where power and passion collide.

HISTORICAL
Escape with historical heroes from time gone by. Whether your passion is for wicked Regency Rakes, muscled Vikings or rugged Highlanders, awaken the romance of the past.

MEDICAL
Set your pulse racing with dedicated, delectable doctors in the high-pressure world of medicine, where emotions run high and passion, comfort and love are the best medicine.

True Love
Celebrate true love with tender stories of heartfelt romance, from the rush of falling in love to the joy a new baby can bring, and a focus on the emotional heart of a relationship.

Desire
Indulge in secrets and scandal, intense drama and sizzling hot action with heroes who have it all: wealth, status, good looks…everything but the right woman.

HEROES
The excitement of a gripping thriller, with intense romance at its heart. Resourceful, true-to-life women and strong, fearless men face danger and desire - a killer combination!

To see which titles are coming soon, please visit

millsandboon.co.uk/nextmonth